FORBIDDEN MATES:

COMPLETE SERIES

AMELIA SHAW

CONTENTS

HEIRS OF THE WOLF

BABIES OF THE WOLF

PROPHECY OF THE WOLF

BOOK ONE

CHAPTER I
ALIYA

There was only one thing worse than realizing you were alone in this world, and that was knowing that fact would never change. I was the last of my line. The final princess of my kingdom.

But was it really a kingdom without people? Without staff, without villagers?

I got up from my plush seat in the library and wandered over to the window that looked out over our once vibrant town. If I closed my eyes and focused really hard, I could still see my people out there in the streets. Mothers carrying their babies as they walked along the cobblestone streets. Market stall vendors bartering their wares.

They'd all died when the plague came. First, the old and sick had left us. But then the healthy and young too. Then my parents. My strong, healthy, beloved king and queen.

I'd waited for my own death to arrive as everyone I loved crumpled around me.

They'd all died of that terrible sickness.

Everyone but me.

The brush of a fluffy tail against my leg had me looking down, happiness filling my heart. "Everyone except you, my dear one."

I picked up my closest friend, my only companion. Willow, my cat. She cuddled into my arms, nestling in and purring loudly.

"But you'll leave me too one day, won't you?" I asked aloud, scratching her head and pressing my cheek to hers. The idea of losing Willow also made my heart fill with dread.

Then the thought struck me... *Did she really have to die also?*

My jaw dropped open in shock as the question resonated inside my head. *Well, did she?*

None of my parents' money nor their power had saved them. I'd been told we'd been Wielders, once upon a time. Magic users that could tap into the ether and channel it into the world. But once we had succeeded in vanquishing our enemies of the past—the black wolves— my forefathers had let their magic fall into obscurity.

By the time my parents were born, magic was a thing of the past. No one had practiced or taught the knowledge of the Wielders for a hundred years. I had no skills, no powers. Though my father had always said that my intuition skills were strong, and I'd always been taught to follow the nudge of what my mother called "the spirits". My guides.

My gaze slid to the top of the bookshelves, where dust gathered on the ancient leather spines untouched for so long. I wasn't even sure they were written in a language I'd be able to understand.

I couldn't study magic, could I? Learn those things that had been left behind by my ancestors? If I could extend Willow's life, or change my future in some way, wouldn't it be worth the effort and trouble?

And if I didn't succeed and failed miserably, what had I lost? Nothing but time. The only thing I had in abundance.

The words were out of my mouth before I'd decided to say them. "What else have I got to do?"

I kissed the top of my cat's head and put her down on the red carpet beneath our feet. She stretched, arching her back, then jumped up onto the seat I'd just vacated, circled the area and curled up onto a pillow.

I put a hand on my hip and mock-glared at her. "Don't suppose you want to climb to the top shelf and grab those books for me?"

The cat closed her eyes and made a contented snuff as she fell asleep.

"Great. Okay. No help there. Okay... I can do this."

I walked across to the ladder that extended to the top of the twenty-foot-tall bookshelf and tugged it across the railings until it was lined up with the stack of books my intuition was pulling me toward.

I grabbed hold of the ladder railing and shook my head, calling myself all types of a fool. If I fell, there was no one around to help me. I'd lie crippled on the floor and die even slower than the plague would've taken me.

"You won't fall. Just get up there." I shook myself and started climbing.

When I was younger, I would have scaled this ladder in moments, then ridden it down like a slide. But my fears had increased with each passing day that I'd been alone. And there were too many to count now.

"Who are you kidding?" I told myself, having a two-way conversation with my thoughts. Another silly habit I'd picked up. "You know exactly how many days it's been. Four hundred and twenty-two."

I lifted my legs slowly, climbing higher and higher. My heart banged in my chest as an unreasonable amount of fear pulsed through me.

I got right to the top and didn't look down. I took some steadying breaths and stared at the dusty shelves of books. Huge books, in fact. I'd never seen such thick, leather-bound tomes before, or at least had never looked up at these to notice their size.

I had no way of truly knowing if any of their pages held the history or secrets of wielding magic. But I'd scour through every single one until I found out. It wasn't like I had anything better to do.

I reached out, letting my intuition guide me.

At first, I went to grab one with gold writing on the spine, but at the last minute, I grabbed the book next to it. That one was slightly thinner and had no writing on the spine at all.

I pulled it out, then gripped it hard.

Now it was time to get down. "Shit. I didn't think this through properly."

I didn't want to throw the book down to the floor. It was old and probably wouldn't survive the fall. But neither would I. How the hell was I going to get down in one piece now?

Feeling defeated, I went to put the book back on the shelf, but my intuition began to sing. I couldn't push it back in. Everything in me tingled and told me to take the book. Hold it. Read it.

Don't put it back.

"Okay, okay," I hissed at the voice in my head.

So how the hell was I going to get down with it?

I decided to try descending one-handed, clutching the book tightly to my chest with my left hand. That idea worked surprisingly well, and after a short minute or two of shaky, hesitant steps, I had my feet back on solid ground.

"Oh, thank God." My knees wobbled, and happily, with no one around to witness my ridiculousness, I sank onto the plush carpet at my feet. "Whoa, that was intense."

I knew that talking to myself was strange and probably a sign that I was losing my mind. But with not a single human for company for over a year, I'd go insane without some noise to break the incessant silence. On the bright side, I hadn't begun imagining that Willow talked back, and I took that as a good sign.

I crossed my legs and pulled the book closer to me, studying the front cover. There was no image, only large cursive letters embossed with gold paint.

"Wow. That's so pretty."

My voice was a little high and chirpy today, which was a welcome change. After my parents died last year, I'd sunk into a pit of despair that I never thought I'd climb from. If I hadn't needed to get out of bed to feed Willow, I wasn't sure I would have eaten myself.

It had taken a lot of conscious energy to stay alive and awake. I'd had to maintain the vegetable garden after going through most of the food stores, and though I had yet to attempt slaughtering one of the chickens in the royal coop, I kept them fed and watered and collected their eggs every day.

It would have been so easy to just let myself go. Not get up to eat or drink water. Hope and pray for the moment I could join my family in death.

Why I'd survived the plague, I still didn't know. Before they died, the elders had said I was blessed. Immune. Strong.

Special.

Alone in a huge castle filled with nothing but memories and empty rooms wasn't what I considered blessed.

I shook myself, pushing away all the horrible feelings that threatened to drag me down. "Let's see what we've got here."

I began to read the book in front of me. The first few pages seemed to be mostly about the history of Varinya, our once great kingdom. About the black wolves, our enemy. How they'd torn through the woods and attacked our home, again and again for generations.

I'd heard those tales since I was a small child. My bedtime stories hadn't been of princesses falling in love, but instead of kings and queens beating the black wolves back from the borders of Varinya.

Quite literally. My great-grandparents had been warriors. They'd been magical and powerful and had hunted the wolves to extinction. It seemed so strange to me that after all their efforts and sacrifice, the greatest threat had come from an organism that was so much smaller.

I sighed as I picked the book up and walked over to a corner couch. I shook the dust off a pillow and flopped down onto the cushions. Time to get reading.

After the preface on the history, the book turned into a magical guide. Each page revealed a new spell, ranging from trivial and mundane tasks to complicated and deadly spells.

The details and instructions were written in the modern tongue, but the incantations were in the old language. Some words were complete gibberish to me, while others glowed and sang to me in a strange way. Almost like reading music, if notes jumped off the page.

Could I actually attempt one of these? Even if I could work out the pronunciation of the ancient words, did I have it in me to perform this sort of magic?

Some of the spells also involved complex arm and hand choreography, like movements to a dance. Others required specific ingredients, most of which I'd never even heard of.

If I was going to try any of them, it needed to be something simple and basic, just to test if I had any magical aptitude at all. No sense in memorizing dance moves if I turned out to be a dud.

I flipped through page after page, searching for a spell I'd be brave enough to tackle while also pawing over those that were much more difficult and wondrous.

So many possibilities in this precious book. Spells for healing, spells for harming. Spells to help you remember or make you forget. Spells for bringing luck and spells for cursing. Sleeping spells, elemental spells, combat spells. There were so many!

At last, I found one that not only seemed fairly simple but would also help me with a current predicament—if it worked.

Filled with a mixture of excitement, curiosity, and foolishness, I hopped off the couch and took the book through the castle and out the kitchen exit to the garden. The damp earth felt nice on my bare feet, and I didn't care that I'd track in clumped dirt when I went back inside.

I made my way through the various vegetable plots until I reached the rather pitiful looking tomato plants. Despite my best efforts, the thick bushes wouldn't bear fruit. I had trimmed them and watered them carefully all spring, but the stalks would just fill out with more leaves.

Considering that tomatoes were a major component to most Varinyan recipes I knew, they were a vital food source to me. Sure, I could survive on potatoes, carrots and leafy greens, but tomatoes offered such rich flavor, and I really craved that small comfort.

I knelt beside the garden bed and looked down at the open book in my lap. The spell was called *Fruit of the Earth*, intended to tap into the magic in plants to help them thrive and bring forth fruit. It was a simple incantation.

Aste brennum vuarte.

I had no idea what the actual words meant, but I didn't think that mattered.

"Okay, here goes nothing," I said.

I looked at my tomato plants and concentrated on that place inside me where I felt the tug of intuition. Then I spoke the words aloud.

"Aste brennum vuarte."

I waited, holding my breath and staring at the plants, but nothing happened.

Sighing in disappointment, I hung my head and looked down at the page. Something tugged inside me, guiding my gaze to the instructions.

"Ugh! Idiot," I mumbled.

I was supposed to be touching the plant while I spoke. I took a long breath and flung out my fingers before putting both hands on the base of the stalk in front of me, then repeated the words, concentrating again.

A soothing yet exhilarating warmth pooled in my belly, then trickled up my chest, across my shoulders, and down my arms. I could see the faintest golden glow radiating from my hands as the warmth transferred into the stalk.

When the warmth left me, I felt oddly cold and drained. But I ignored those sensations as I stared open-mouthed at the ends of the branches, which all at once sprouted little yellow flowers, then green bulbs. To my amazement, right in front of my eyes, the bulbs grew and turned from green to vibrant red as they became plump, juicy tomatoes.

Holy shit! I actually did it! I can wield!

So many possibilities were now open to me. I could change my life for the better, could ensure that Willow and I stayed healthy and lived long lives.

Maybe I could even find a spell to help me locate survivors, if there were any. Maybe I wouldn't have to be alone for the rest of my life!

I reached up and wrapped my hand around a fat tomato, then plucked it off the stem. It felt so delightfully firm. Bringing it to my lips, I took a big bite.

Oh, sweet heavens! I couldn't remember the last time I'd tasted something so delicious. I devoured the whole thing, letting the juices run down either side of my mouth and soak into the fabric of my thin slip.

I was a Wielder, and I was going to study every inch of this book, memorize every word, and make my ancestors proud.

CHAPTER 2

ALIYA

By the time the sun had risen high in the sky, I'd gone a little overboard with the tomatoes, gorging on them until my belly was full and my slip was covered in tomato juice stains.

I had gone from plant to plant, invoking the incantation so that each one was covered in large tomatoes. Then, for good measure, I went to all the other plants, and the garden was now so full of thriving vegetables that I could hardly walk between them.

I knew there was no way I'd be able to eat them all before rot set in, and that perhaps my use of magic was a bit wasteful, but I didn't care. I was too excited that I could wield to stop at rational thoughts today.

But as I rose to my feet and tried to walk inside for a basket to collect my bounty, my limbs quaked and my head spun. I felt as if I'd gone without food for days despite having eaten so many tomatoes that my slim belly swelled.

This was obviously the consequence of expending too much magic too quickly. That's what my intuition told me, at least. I couldn't just go around wielding carelessly. There had to be a purpose to my magic.

That was a lesson I wouldn't soon forget.

After taking a moment to compose myself, I slowly made my way inside and took a basket off the counter. For now, I would focus on tomatoes. They'd be the first target for bugs and birds. Tomorrow, I'd preserve them into jars of sauces and chunks. I didn't have the strength tonight.

It took longer than I'd expected to pluck and collect them all, but finally I put the overflowing bucket on the counter and stumbled to the den, where Willow was already curled up in the corner of my favorite couch.

All I wanted to do was collapse onto the cushions and relax, but a chill was creeping into the castle that would soon have me quaking. I needed heat, first and foremost. I went to the large, beautiful carved fireplace and flicked the switch that operated the firing mechanism.

The hearth burst into glorious orange flames, and I lingered there for a moment, soaking up the heat before shuffling to the couch and plopping down beside Willow.

That electricity still worked in Varinya had been my salvation. It ran on its own, collected by fields of solar panels as well as windmills. I wouldn't have survived these long, lonely months without heat in the winter and air conditioning in the summer, let alone a working refrigerator and stove. Starting a fire by hand was a skill I was never taught as a princess. But then again, I'd also picked up many skills uncommon for a princess.

Chopping wood, gardening, cooking, cleaning—though, I really didn't do a whole lot of that. The extent of my cleaning was washing dishes and clothes, and even there I tended to let things pile up, or wear the same dirty dress for days, maybe even weeks.

Why wouldn't I? I had no one to impress. Although Willow would avoid me if I wore something for too long.

As she prowled closer and curled up on my lap, I realized that must not currently be the case, even if my slip was soaked in tomato juice.

I petted her head, the purr that rumbled from her body comforting me.

"We're going to be okay," I said. "I can wield. Isn't that amazing? Hopefully, we won't be alone for much longer."

She didn't acknowledge me, just continued to purr as I scratched behind her ear.

Bang, bang, bang!

The unapologetic slamming made me jump and scream. Willow bolted off my lap with a disgruntled hiss.

With every hair on the back of my neck standing on end, I slowly turned around and looked across the expansive ballroom floor beyond the den to the large entrance doors.

I had to be hallucinating due to fatigue. There was no way someone had knocked on that door, right? I hadn't seen or heard a single person in over a year. It was probably just the wind.

Or maybe... I'd finally lost it.

Bang, bang, bang!

I startled again, this time rushing towards the sound.

"Hello?" a desperate male voice called through the thick wood. "If there's anyone in there, please help us."

Us? There was more than one person out there? How? Who?

"Please!" the voice pleaded again, spurring me into action.

I scurried through the ballroom, reaching for the door handle and then hesitating. If I opened this door and there was no one there, I would know I'd finally gone mad. That would be the beginning of the end.

But if there was...

Before I could spiral into a vortex of hope and horror, I turned the bolt and pulled open the door—and my eyes widened in shock.

Standing on the doorstep were two men bathed in sunlight. One was unconscious and being supported by an arm over the shoulders of the other. Both were injured and bleeding in several places. And both were completely naked.

I just stood there, staring like a moron, for several seconds too long.

The conscious man tilted his head at me and blinked in confusion. "C-can you please help us?" he hedged, talking to me like I was crazy.

And maybe I was. Maybe this was some solitude-induced hallucination, but I doubted that my mind could fabricate such a convoluted image. If I was going to imagine two naked men, they certainly wouldn't be injured and banging on my door in the middle of the night.

I snapped out of my stupor and decided to just play along until I knew if this was real or not. After all, if there really were two wounded men in my castle, shouldn't I help them?

"Er, yeah, sorry, come in," I stammered, stepping aside so he could carry his fallen friend inside.

I quickly closed the door behind them and ran to offer support beneath the unconscious man's other arm. He felt real. And warm. And muscular!

"Over there," I huffed through the effort of carrying him, gesturing toward the couch.

Together, we carried his friend to my favorite couch and hefted him onto it. In the light of the fire, I could see that this man's body was covered in deep scratches, the most prominent one a gouge in his abdomen, which was oozing deep crimson blood.

My hands shook as they fluttered frantically over the wound. I had helped the staff with the sick in the castle, had tended to the plague blisters and festering sores as my parents lay dying, but this injury was so much more urgent and fatal. I was completely out of my depth.

I tore a strip of fabric from the bottom of my slip, bundled it up, and pressed it to the oozing cut.

"Hold this firmly against the wound," I instructed the other man, who was kneeling beside me. "I need to get some supplies."

With a fervent nod, his hand replaced mine over the cloth. In the brief exchange, the contact of his skin on mine sent a strange zing through me, almost like a shock of static electricity, but warmer, and almost...comforting.

I shook myself from the abrupt surprise of everything that was happening and ran to the kitchen, rifling through drawers and cabinets to collect the necessary items into an empty basket. Then I filled a bucket with clean water and dropped a clean rag into it before carrying everything hastily back into the den.

I dropped to my knees beside my strange visitors and got to work, cleaning the wound with the rag and bucket.

"What happened?" I asked, my voice shaky.

"We were on our way to...Rodak," he sputtered, his eyes darting from side to side. "A group of cusith attacked us in the forest. Can you save him?"

Cusith? What the hell was that?

"I don't know," I said. "This wound is deep, and without better resources, I can't tell if any vital organs have been damaged."

His admittedly handsome face puckered in sorrow, forcing memories of my dying parents to the surface. The desperation I'd felt knowing I couldn't do anything to save them.

"But I'm going to do the best I can," I reassured him. "Hand me that needle and thread."

He nodded and passed me the spool and hook-shaped needle.

With trembling fingers, I accepted them and began to sew the wound closed. Pulling the gaping flesh together was an arduous chore, but the man helped by pinching his friend's abdomen while I worked, and I managed to seal the wound tightly. My sewing was sloppy at best, but at least the bleeding had slowed.

I taped a patch of gauze over the sewed gash, then went about tending to the other, smaller cuts across his body. The passed-out man had a muscular build, looking formidable even in this state. And naked as he was, every sculpted inch of him was fully exposed to my wandering gaze as I strived to patch him up. He looked like a warrior, his thick raven hair caked with dirt and blood.

What could have possibly defeated such a man as this?

When that was finally done, I turned to his conscious companion, getting a good look at him for the first time. He had a similar build, though slightly leaner. Where his friend had black hair and a chiseled face that leant itself to a cruel beauty, this man's hair was a soft brown, his features less harsh, pretty in a gentle way.

I peeled my gaze from his face and scanned his body for wounds, which turned out to be plentiful but less critical.

"Okay, let's get you tended to now," I said.

He rose and let me guide him to a nearby armchair, where I poured over each cut, cleaning and bandaging them.

"Thank you," he said as I applied the last bandage to his upper arm. "After finding the village empty, I really didn't think I'd find anyone here."

"Yeah, I'm... uh... I'm the last one," I said, my voice tight. But I didn't want to talk about that. "What did you say attacked you?"

He cocked his head at me, frowning. "A cusith." He said the word as if I should know what that was.

I shook my head.

"You really don't know what a cusith is?" he asked with a note of astonishment.

Again, I shook my head.

His eyebrows flared. "Wow. That means they haven't ventured this far yet. You're lucky."

I cleared my throat. "What *is* it?"

He sighed, grunting as he shifted on in the chair. "The only way I can describe it is a shadow-beast, a hellish demon. They were thought to have been eradicated centuries ago, but in recent months, they've come out of hiding and began terrorizing inhabited areas. We didn't expect to encounter them in your neighboring forest."

I wracked my mind for any mention of such a creature in Varinya's history, but the black wolves were the only threat I'd ever heard of.

"Do you think this...*cusith* is resurfacing because the black wolves are gone?" I asked.

Something flickered in his green eyes when his gaze slid to mine, seeming to assess me for a moment. "I don't know."

I pursed my lips and looked down, my gaze falling on his fully nude lap. I snapped my head to the side and shot to my feet.

"I'll get you some clothes," I blurted out, my cheeks burning as I refused to look at him.

Skittering upstairs to my father's old room, I hoped to find some garments that would fit my guests. I hadn't been in my parents' old bedroom in months, and the moonlight pouring through the windows caught the thick dust that hung in the air, forming cloudy blocks throughout the space.

Echoes of my father's voice sounded in my head, treasured memories flashing behind my eyelids. I bitterly pushed them away and began to dig through his clothing chest. I found two pairs of trousers and two button-down white shirts that might suit the men downstairs. Then I fled the room before grief could capture me in its snare.

They were exactly where I'd left them. I went to the conscious man and handed him the clothes first while struggling to avert my gaze from his raw, masculine form.

"These should fit you," I said as he accepted them.

I turned away as he put them on, setting the clothes for his friend on the arm of the couch and covering him with a blanket.

"I'm Aliya," I offered, my back to him.

"Tannin," he replied. "And his name is Jax."

Tannin and Jax. The first people I'd seen or spoken to in four-hundred-and-twenty-two days.

Tannin came up beside me, fully clothed now, and looked mournfully down at Jax. "Do you think he'll pull through?"

I hesitated before answering. "I did the best I could. Only time will tell." I turned to look at him. "You're both welcome to stay as long as you need to. You know, while you heal."

A grateful albeit forced smile spread across his lips. "Thank you. For everything."

That brief absence of pain on his face made my heart flutter and my breath catch. He was so much more handsome when he smiled.

"Would you like some lunch? Water?" I asked excitedly, wanting to see more of that smile.

"Yes, that would be very kind," he said.

I carried the bucket and blood-soaked rags to the kitchen, and as I prepared a makeshift meal for him, hope began to sing in my chest.

For the first time in over a year, I had company. For the first time in so long that it hurt, I wasn't alone.

I just hoped and prayed that they weren't some manic hallucination, and that when I came back from the kitchen, they wouldn't be gone.

CHAPTER 3
TANNIN

This wasn't how it was supposed to go down. Our orders were to make it here without issue and assess the status of Varinya. It should have been easy, simple.

Now I was sitting in an empty castle, covered in scratches and bites, staring at my best friend on a dusty couch and unsure if he'd survive.

The cusith had come out of nowhere, manifesting like wraiths from the shadows of the trees and bushes in the forest around us, descending upon us like rabid hyenas. At least when they weren't mutating and bending at impossible angles.

Our scouts had reported no signs of them before our journey, and it was alarming to know they'd spread so far. How long before they reached Varinya? How long before they destroyed everything?

I squeezed my eyes shut, pausing in chewing the stale bread I'd been given. I couldn't think like that. We weren't going to let them win. That was the whole reason for coming here. Well, one of them, anyway. Taking back our rightful place inside the kingdom would give us the power we needed to stand against the cusith, not only for our pack, but for all people.

But if Jax didn't wake up... Only the Alpha had the power of moon song. If he didn't make it through this tragedy, our pack wouldn't know it was safe to come, and this journey—his sacrifice—would all be for nothing.

I glanced at the girl curled up on the armchair across from me. Aliya. She was staring at me with a sort of awe, like I was fascinating to behold. Her honey-brown hair was messy and tangled around her heart-shaped face, and her torn slip that did little to hide the curves of her body and perked nipples beneath was stained and tattered.

How long had she been alone here? What happened to this once flourishing kingdom?

"What happened here?" I asked, setting my bread back onto the plate in my lap.

She folded her legs against her chest and wrapped her arms around them, hugging herself into a ball and casting her sad gaze to the floor.

"There was a plague. Little by little, everyone died. Everyone but me. They said I was immune." She shrugged and let out a nervous giggle. "It's lonely at the end of the world."

When I offered her a sympathetic frown, her attempt at amusement fell like a dead fly, and she returned to staring at me.

"H—" I paused for a moment, debating on the most delicate way to phrase the question. "How long ago did that happen?"

She shrugged and chewed on her bottom lip. "A little over a year ago."

My throat tightened. She'd been alone in this castle for over a year? I couldn't imagine such a tragedy. Watching as everyone you loved died around you and being left in isolation to fend for yourself. As a wolf, that was the most terrifying prospect of all. The pack was everything.

"I'm so sorry," I said. And I was. Though it was to our benefit that the plague had left the kingdom barren and ready to welcome our return, I truly felt sympathy for this kind girl.

"Why didn't you just leave?" I asked. "You could've wandered to a neighboring kingdom and sought help, sought a new place for yourself." I liked to believe that our pack would've helped her.

She shook her head fervently. "I could never leave Varinya. My subjects may all be dead, but I still have a duty as princess. Varinya is my home. This castle is where I belong."

I struggled to keep my eyes from widening. Princess? She was the last living descendant of the royal line who'd slaughtered countless members of my pack?

It was my sworn oath to destroy her.

And yet, she'd saved us. She'd welcomed us into her home and patched us up. I sat here now, dressed and fed, thanks to her. She'd shown me nothing but kindness. She was innocent. I could see that. But I didn't think the rest of my pack would see it that way, especially not Jax.

If he woke up at all...

Perhaps I could get her out before they came, convince her to move on. It was the least I could do in return for her kindness.

I cleared my throat. "I can understand your sense of duty, but that doesn't mean you have to be alone for the rest of your life. You owe it to your people to continue your line. You could marry a prince of another kingdom, forge an alliance."

The muscles of my chest squeezed around my ribcage, an irrational sense of rage flaring inside me at the thought of her marrying anyone else.

Where the hell did that come from?

She chewed on her lips again, her pretty face crinkling with conflict. "I have no way to send word anywhere to arrange any such alliance, and making the journey on my own would mean certain death, especially after seeing the wounds the two of you endured."

She had a point there. An image of her being torn to pieces by a cusith flashed in my mind, forcing a powerful protective urge to ignite inside me.

What was this? These feelings came out of nowhere. She was nothing to me.

Unless...

"Besides, even if I did make it to the next kingdom, who would believe I was a princess?" she said with a self-deprecating laugh. "I mean, look at me."

I did, and she was right. In her current state, she was a far cry from a princess. But she was still beautiful, in a wild, feral way that drew me in. She looked like a forest nymph, like a goddess of the hunt.

"Without the proper appearance and going through the official channels, I can't prove my pedigree without carting heaps of lineage books." She shook her head. "It's just not possible. Varinya is the safest place for me."

Not for much longer.

When the rest of my pack showed up and discovered who she was, she would never be safe again. They'd lock her up as a prisoner of war or publicly execute her for the crimes committed by her forebearers. And every fiber of my being sizzled in rejection of either outcome.

I didn't like these foreign and compelling emotions I felt toward her, and I feared what it meant. Suspicion whispered in the back of my mind, but I denied it, shoving it deep down. It couldn't be. She wasn't one of us. She was our enemy.

She unbent her legs and scooted to perch on the edge of her armchair. "You must be tired after what you went through. Would you like me to make up a room for you?"

I shook my head and looked at Jax. "No. I should stay with him. I want to be close when he wakes up."

"Okay." She rose. "I'll get a pillow and blankets then, so you can at least be comfortable."

She skittered away up the stairs before I could reply. She was too sweet for what was coming for her.

I pushed my reluctance aside and focused my attention on Jax. He had to pull through this. He wasn't just my Alpha, he was my oldest and dearest friend. We'd grown up together, gone through every first, every hardship, every battle together.

When we were pups, I was the runt of the pack, and therefore the subject of ridicule and hazing by our peers. And though he was the Alpha's son, he stood up for me. He defended me when a pack of pups ganged up on me and declared me untouchable.

Without his intervention, I wouldn't have grown to be one of the most formidable of the black wolves. I was his second-in-command, his beta, and I would do anything for him. I loved him like the brother I never had. Seeing him like this, battered and barely hanging onto life, shredded me up inside.

Aliya came back into the den with a bundle of pillows and blankets piled in her arms, and rather than handing them to me, she went about setting up a sleeping space on the floor beside the couch Jax was on.

"Oh, you don't have to do that," I said. "I'll be fine in the chair."

"Nonsense," she said as she aired out the comforter and draped it over the sheet and pillow. "You need some sleep after your journey, and this way, you can be right next to your friend if he needs you."

My heart squeezed again at her compassion. We were strangers to her, intruders in her kingdom, and yet she went out of her way to care for us. Little did she know our true intentions, and guilt over that fact gnawed at my gut like maggots on a festering sore.

I didn't deserve her kindness. None of us did, least of all, Jax.

"Well, I'm going to have a rest too. So I'll see you later?" she said awkwardly when she was finished, then nodded at me once before sweeping from the room.

Leaving me alone to wrestle with my troubled thoughts over what I must do.

CHAPTER 4
ALIYA

I didn't fall asleep during my afternoon rest. The excitement and gratitude at having *actual people* in the castle with me after so long was overwhelming and had anxious energy coursing through my body.

I wasn't alone. I wasn't alone!

I was so happy over that fact that joyous tears trailed from my eyes and soaked into the pillow beneath my head.

And then there was the obvious perk that they were so handsome. I couldn't stop the images that circled inside my mind. Their impressive naked bodies kept popping into my restless brain, though honestly, I didn't really want to stop.

I'd never seen a man without clothes before, at least not one that wasn't an artistic statue or in a painting. After months of solitude and despair, I'd become convinced I never would. And though they'd come bloody and injured, I couldn't help but fantasize about them naked in good health.

What if I could convince them to stay?

I rejected the foolish thought as soon as it came. They were obviously headed somewhere. They had lives, goals, probably families. Why on earth would they stay here with me, in this dusty, deserted castle? I was no longer a pampered princess, but a raggedy vagabond wench. I was no prize anymore.

But that didn't stop me from falling into frenzied, passionate dreams when sleep finally did find me, leaving me aching and frustrated when I woke.

As soon as the sun began dropping behind the mountains, it cast glowing rays through my window. It was time to get up. I threw off my blankets and got dressed—much more presentably this time. It had been months since I'd worn a proper dress, and getting the ties fastened behind my back was a cramp-inducing chore that took far longer than necessary.

When I got it as tight as I could, I went through the herculean task of brushing the knots out of my long hair, deciding to leave it down because I couldn't stand another second of not seeing them and making sure they were real.

I flew down the stairs with hasty feet, nearly tripping over the skirt of my dress. When I found Tannin still there, kneeling by Jax's side, a huge wave of relief washed over me.

At least until I saw the lines of dread etched into his handsome face when he turned at my entrance.

"He's feverish," Tannin said, his voice heavy. "I think his wound is infected."

I rushed to his side to examine Jax. Indeed, his pallor had turned a sickly yellow, and his forehead and chest were covered in a film of sweat. I peeled back the bandage on his abdomen and gasped at the blooming redness that surrounded the sutures and the yellowish puss that oozed between them. It reminded me all too much of the sores on my parents' bodies.

"You're right," I said through a tight throat. "It is infected. Badly."

"Do you have any medicine?" Tannin beseeched desperately. "Anything to combat the infection?"

I swallowed thickly. "No. All the medicine stores were depleted before the end of the plague. I'm so sorry."

"No!" he bellowed, making me flinch. "No, he can't die! There must be something we can do. Please, don't let him die."

My brows puckered at the heartache on his face and in his voice. I wanted to help them, I really did. But there was nothing—

My breath hitched as an idea sprang to my mind.

"There might be something I can do," I hedged cautiously. "B-but it might not work."

"Yes, please!" he begged. "Anything. Just try!"

"Okay," I agreed.

I ran to the kitchen counter where I had left the book of spells last night after my obsessive garden adventure and began to hastily flip through it. I remembered seeing a few spells for healing. At the time I'd thought that if only I'd had access to this during the plague, I might've been able to save some of those who were lost. I could've saved my parents.

There were different healing spells. One for illness, one for broken bones, one for reviving from a coma...

"Ha! Found it!" Spell for healing a flesh wound. This one didn't require any ingredients like some of the others, only the complete focus of the Wielder and the intention to heal.

I clutched it against my chest and made to dart back out, but something made me pause. My intuition told me to keep the book safe, even from my guests. So, I lowered the open book in my arms and read the short incantation over and over, committing it to memory, then closed the book and stashed it in a cabinet.

I returned to the den, repeating the incantation in my mind. When I knelt beside Jax once more, I removed his bandage completely and put both hands over the stitched gash.

"What are you doing?" Tannin blurted out in fretful confusion.

"Just be quiet," I told him, closing my eyes. "I need to concentrate."

When he didn't make another sound, I set my intention and spoke the incantation out loud.

"Vulte riay kai altum."

Just as yesterday in the garden, a comforting warmth blossomed in my belly, rose up my chest and spilled down my arms, flowing into the angrily hot flesh beneath my palms. I could feel the magic working through me like I was merely the conduit, stitching back together the separated flesh.

Then the sensation grew cool, like pool water on a hot summer's day, sucking the heat of infection from Jax's skin. And then the flow stopped altogether.

I opened my eyes and looked down as I pulled my hands away, and though I knew what I'd find, it still shocked and thrilled me to see the gash gone, the thread I'd used to sew it laying loosely on top of his belly.

"Holy shit!" Tannin breathed. "Did you just use magic?"

"Yeah, I—"

Jax suddenly bolted upright with a hoarse gasp, the surprise of it making me stumble backward and fall on my butt.

"What the—" His head turned wildly as he took in his surroundings, then his eyes fell on me, and outrage flared his nostrils. "Who the fuck are you? What are you doing to me?"

I was too shocked to reply, to say anything in defense for myself.

"Hey, brother," Tannin said, putting a hand firmly on Jax's shoulder. "This is Aliya, and she happens to have just saved your life. She saved us both. You could show her some respect."

Jax continued to glare at me with hateful suspicion, and I felt small and foolish.

"What happened?" he barked at Tannin.

"We were attacked by a pack of cusith in the forest," Tannin explained in a much calmer tone than I would've been capable of.

"Yes, I remember that," he snapped. "But how did we get *here*?"

"You got badly injured in the fight," Tannin continued with a patience reminiscent of pacifying an unruly child. "I carried you here, to Varinya. The village was completely empty, and I banged on the castle door, expecting to find nothing and no one, but this nice young woman here let us in and tended to our wounds. She healed you."

Jax eyed him warily, then slid his slitted gaze back to me, assessing me. He jutted his chin out. "Where is everyone? The villagers, the castle guards, the staff?"

I licked my dry lips, struggling to find my voice. "Gone."

"Gone?" he snapped. "What do you mean, gone?"

"Th-they all died. There was a plague. I-I'm the only one who survived."

His expression softened slightly as he mulled that information over, his tense posture loosening. "The king and queen?"

I nodded mutely.

He huffed a sigh. "Well, I'm sorry. What a terrible tragedy." He glanced briefly at Tannin, then back at me. "Who were you, you know, before the plague?"

In the corner of my eye, I saw Tannin tense, making me hesitate in my response. "I... I was—am—the princess of Varinya."

Hostility returned to light Jax's eyes. "The princess?"

Tannin's grip tightened on his shoulder. "Yes. Aliya is the princess. And she was kind enough to offer us shelter and assistance when we needed it most. We owe her a great debt."

"Debt, my a—"

"Jax!" Tannin cautioned loudly, cutting him off.

Jax's mouth pressed tightly closed, his jaw clenching. After a long breath, he said through gritted teeth, "Thank you for offering us your assistance, *Princess*." He said my title like it was a filthy word.

I didn't know how to react. It had been so long since I'd spoken to anyone, but even then, I wasn't accustomed to being addressed so harshly, so rudely. I could only assume they had very humble backgrounds, that this Jax especially had poor manners, and maybe that wasn't his fault. It wasn't every day the common man had an audience with royalty, and it was my duty to act my station and show grace.

Blushing at his once again exposed nudity, I reached for the other set of clothes I'd fetched last night. "Here. These were my father's. They should fit you."

He snatched them from my hands, then began to climb into them without a speck of shame for my presence, but I turned my head anyway.

It was difficult not to peek. Despite his brusque and hostile demeanor, he was gorgeous, and the dreams that had plagued me all night only fueled my temptation. It wasn't every day that a *princess* got to see such raw, carnal beauty, and I was pretty much at the end of my rope as it was.

How long would it be before I got to see a naked man again, if ever?

But by the time my resilience failed, and I turned my head, he was already buttoning up his shirt. I internally kicked myself for not visually gorging on the whole ordeal while I'd had the chance, especially since he hadn't seemed to care if I saw him naked or not.

Damn my stupid, inane sense of propriety!

Once he was done with his shirt, they both looked at me with some expectation I didn't immediately understand.

Oh. They want privacy.

I took a step back. "I'll give you two some time and go make up rooms for you."

"Thank you, Aliya," Tannin said with a warm smile. "That would be nice."

Jax didn't reciprocate his friend's attitude, only looking down his nose at me without a word.

I nodded once, then made my way to the west wing to decide on suitable rooms for them. Everything everywhere in this castle aside from the few places I frequented was covered in dust, and it would take quite some effort and time to make them guest ready.

But I was determined to win them over, especially the stony, untrusting Jax. Tonight, I'd make them a wonderful dinner. His miraculous recovery was a cause for celebration after all, and I had to do everything in my power to make them want to stay for as long as possible.

I knew it was selfish, but I couldn't bear the idea of going back to being alone again. I'd survived the first time I'd been abandoned, but now... I wasn't sure I'd survive it a second time.

CHAPTER 5
JAX

A storm of conflicting victory and outrage seethed beneath my skin as I glared at my beta—my oldest friend. The kingdom was empty, the castle unguarded and basically welcoming our return with open arms. The epic battle I'd anticipated and planned for was now unnecessary, and there were no obstacles before us.

But the princess, the last of our enemies, still lived.

"Why didn't you just kill her?" I growled at Tannin.

He didn't cow at my harsh question. Unlike the rest of my pack, he never shrank in the face of my anger, and I found that both admirable and annoying. Especially right now, when I demanded accountability for this egregious error in judgment.

Instead, he cut me with a deadpan frown. "You really expected me to kill the only person in a hundred miles who could help you when you were knocking on death's door?"

I huffed, my nostrils flaring, but I couldn't exactly argue with that.

"Plus, I didn't find out she was the princess until after she cleaned and sealed the wound in your side," he continued, gesturing to my right abdomen. "She's dressed up this morning, but last night she wore rags."

I lifted my shirt and looked down to inspect myself. "There's nothing there. Not even a scar."

"That's because she used magic to heal you when fever set in,"

Tannin said, his eyes widening meaningfully. "You were almost dead. Literally."

My pulse spiked, furious heat exploding in my chest. "She's a Wielder?! A Wielder and the princess, and you still let her live!"

He shushed me loudly, holding up both hands. "Keep your voice down," he hissed. "She saved your life—both our lives! Like it or not, we owe her a life debt. Only a mongrel bites the hand that feeds it, and we are not mongrels."

I didn't like his chiding tone, but he was right. The laws of our pack were ironclad, and as the Alpha, it was my solemn duty to uphold them flawlessly. We couldn't kill her after she'd saved our lives, no matter who or what she was. And that posed a unique problem.

"What do you propose we do with her then?" I asked behind gritted teeth, folding my arms obstinately over my chest.

He sighed, a hint of resignation in his eyes. "We continue as planned. When the moon rises tonight, you can call the pack and invite them to come. When they do, we take the princess as a prisoner."

A strange reluctance darkened his tone when he said the last part, and I narrowed my eyes on him in suspicion.

"You don't seem very pleased with that outcome," I said accusingly.

This time, he did shirk, but only slightly. "She has been nothing but kind to me—to us—since the moment she opened that door. She's an innocent, and if she weren't the princess, this wouldn't even be a problem."

Righteous anger cracked inside me like a whip. "Innocent? She's the descendant of the very monarchs who betrayed and slaughtered our people, who banished us from this kingdom and forced us into the wastelands. And if she knew what we were, do you really think she wouldn't use that magic of hers to do the same?"

He frowned and looked down at the carpet. "I don't know."

The tension in my shoulders loosened as I looked at him, my anger cooling. Tannin always was a more compassionate wolf than most, and I admired that about him, but now wasn't the time for it.

I walked up to him and put a comforting but firm hand on his shoulder. "I understand your moral struggle, brother. But we must consider what's best for the pack before all else. Justice will prevail, one way or another. The right path will make itself known."

He nodded.

"In the meantime, I think I'll explore the castle, get myself acquainted with our new home." I patted his back and strolled toward the stairs.

Despite the layers of dust that coated every surface, this palace was even more beautiful than the stories I grew up on suggested.

White marble floors with gold veins. The walls were smooth cream-colored plaster with embossed coffers and crown molding along the vaulted ceiling and bordering the archways between rooms. And the grand staircase to the upper level was truly stunning, with rails of thick, polished cherry wood, and each step was layered in the same marble as the floor.

Every inch of this place had been lovingly crafted with expert craftsmanship for the highest of royalty, and as I walked up the stairs, for the first time in my life, I felt like I was home.

For too long, my people had been living in shabby huts in the farthest reaches of the northern forest, scrounging for food and living like humble savages. No more. Never again.

After I made my moon song tonight, it would only be a matter of days before the pack came in droves to live in the luxury that had been stolen from them all those generations ago. Soon, the streets of Varinya would be filled with frolicking pups, and I could hardly wait.

I took my time venturing through the castle and inspecting each room, making mental notes of which of my highest-ranking pack members might reside in which bedroom. There were so many.

Honestly, my entire pack could live in the castle comfortably, but it would be wrong to let the surrounding homes go unoccupied, and I had to leave room for the ranking families to grow.

Plus, there were also guestrooms to consider. Once we established ourselves as the new kingdom, there would be trade opportunities with neighboring kingdoms, and we'd need places for those dignitaries to stay.

In the upper levels, where the royal chambers were situated, I found the girl in one of them, hastily making the massive canopy king bed. I leaned against the doorframe, watching her.

I couldn't deny that she was beautiful. The tight purple dress she wore flattered her body perfectly, sinching around her thin waste and giving way to the wide curves of her hips below and pushing up her supple breasts above.

If she had only been a villager, or a handmaid perhaps, we could have offered her asylum, maybe even wed her to one of my generals.

Or I could take her for myself.

Potent desire flared inside me at the thought, even as I recoiled in disgust. She was the blood of my enemy, no more worthy of sharing my bed than the lowest omega. Why would such a loathsome notion even occur to me?

And why did the idea of her in the arms of another man fill me with murderous rage?

She turned and startled at the sight of me. "Oh! Sorry, you scared me."

I fought a smug smirk. *I should scare you, Princess.*

She stepped away from the bed and clasped her hands at her waist. "I hope this room will be okay for you."

"Yes, it'll do nicely," I replied. *For now.*

She smiled nervously, biting her lip, and I found it difficult not to stare at her mouth as she did.

"I prepared the room next door as well. I'll let you two decide which one you'd each like."

"Thank you for your hospitality," I said, pushing away from the doorframe and slipping my hands into the pockets of my slacks as I approached her. "It sounds like I owe you a debt."

"Oh, no, not at all," she said, shaking her head. "I did what anyone would. You don't owe me anything."

If only that were true.

"Tannin tells me you used magic to heal me," I said conversationally. "I'm very grateful. You must be exceptionally talented at wielding, indeed."

She blushed, her sweet scent teasing my nose and pulling me closer to her. "Well, I don't know about that. I've only recently begun to study the old ways. I didn't even know I could heal before trying the spell on you."

My brows twitched with interest, and I nodded. So, she wasn't taught. Her referral to the "old ways" suggested wielding had become a lost art. She might not be that big of a threat, after all.

"Well, er... I should go," she said abruptly, walking past me.

"Go where?" I asked, turning to watch her.

"To make dinner," she said, pausing at the door. "I thought you two might enjoy a nice meal." Then she ducked out.

She was an odd girl, that was for sure. She didn't seem to know how to hold a conversation, and she stared for longer than was comfortable. Tannin had said she'd been alone here for over a year. I supposed that would make anyone a little eccentric. Maybe we could use that to our advantage.

Following her from a distance as she descended to the ground floor, I watched as she went out the kitchen door to the garden. I wanted to study her, gain an understanding of the foe I was dealing with.

Surprisingly, the garden was lush and plentiful. She'd tended to it alone all this time. An unlikely skill for pampered royalty. It showed resilience, and I both respected and resented that. It meant she might put up a fight when we took the kingdom as our own.

If only she'd starved before now. And yet, that thought stabbed at my gut like the talon of the cusith who'd nearly killed me. Why was this princess, this odd girl, my mortal enemy, affecting me in this way? I should want her dead, but the prospect pained me in a way I didn't understand.

I followed her around the back of the castle to a fenced-in yard where the clucks of chickens sounded. She opened the gate and slipped inside.

The next ten minutes were an entertaining show of her chasing annoyed hens around and failing to catch a single one. It was both amusing and pathetic. So much for resilience. She clearly hadn't done this before, which suggested to me that she hadn't eaten meat in over a year. No wonder she was so thin and frail.

When I couldn't stand watching her ineptitude any longer, I shoved into the yard to show her how it was done. I snatched a fat hen with ease, clutched its wriggling body against my chest, and snapped its neck in front of her.

She winced at the terrible cracking sound, then looked mournfully at the dead bird bundled limply in my arms.

"Th-thank you," she said in a small voice.

I took the bird by its loose neck and extended it to her. "You're welcome," I said, not bothering to hide my irritation.

She accepted it with hesitant hands and cradled it like an infant. So gentle. And so foolish.

"I don't suppose you need me to pluck and gut it, too?" I ask gratingly.

The first sign of anger pinched her features as she glared at me, and she straightened her posture indignantly. "No, I can manage."

Then she strode past me with her head held high, and I snickered at her display of attitude. I rather enjoyed getting under skin. I trailed behind her, intent on watching her struggle with the task of cleaning the bird, which should prove highly amusing.

I smelled the odor of putrid decay before I heard the snap of a twig in the nearby trees. I whipped my head in that direction to see the ash-gray beast emerge from the shadows.

And its glowing red eyes were set on the girl.

"Princess!" I shouted, and she spun around angrily to glare at me.

My shout spurred the cusith into action, and it leapt, charging right for her with poised claws and gnashing teeth.

Instinct took over, and I sprinted for her as fast as I could in my human form, intercepting the beast seconds before it could tear her to pieces. She screamed as I caught its paws at the wrists, then shoved it forcefully backward.

I whipped around frantically searching in that brief reprieve for anything useful, spotting a shovel leaning against the castle wall. I grabbed it by the handle and brandished it like a sword, bashing the metal end at the side of the cusith's face as it lunged at me.

It fell to the ground, rocked, and I swung at it violently over and over until finally stabbing the blade into its neck and severing the head from its body.

I stood, chest heaving and heart racing as I studied the trees for any sign of more. But there was no sound, no smell other than the reek emanating from this feral corpse.

"Wha—what the hell is that thing?" the princess squeaked from where she pressed herself against the wall, her face pale as a sheet.

"It's a cusith," I panted, staring down at the heinous monster. "It seems to have been alone, but where there's one... Go inside. I'll burn it so its scent doesn't attract the others."

She nodded shakily but pulled herself together enough to grab the dead chicken, then ran for the kitchen door.

Why had I saved her? Fuck! That had been my chance! I should've just let it kill her and be done with this.

"Consider our debt paid," I muttered at her absence.

She'd saved my life, and now I had saved hers. We were even. At least there was that.

But this didn't bode well for any of us. The cusiths in the forest were one thing, but seeing one so close to the castle... They were getting bolder, venturing farther. I would not let them threaten the safety of my pack, not when we were so close to reclaiming our home.

The princess was the least of our worries, and now that our debt was settled, there was nothing standing in the way of eliminating her.

Nothing except for the little fact that I had clearly mate-bonded to her. Everything I did pointed to it. I was ridiculously drawn to her and wanted to fuck her, even now. I'd reacted to protect her from danger without even thinking about the fact that I was meant to kill her or at least let her die.

No... it was clear to me now. I wanted her. And I would protect her until my dying breath.

Fuck.

CHAPTER 6

ALIYA

I couldn't stop seeing that hideous beast in my mind while I was preparing food for our dinner. Not even gutting the chicken was able to distract me.

All my life, I'd heard stories of the black wolves, our enemy from generations past. They were said to be ferocious yet beautiful creatures. But that...*thing* was far from beautiful. It was more like something out of my worst nightmare.

Its skin had been a sickly bluish gray, like the rotting flesh of those who'd died during the plague. The color of their corpses before we'd burned them. Its back was humped and arched unnaturally, with strange spikes down its spine. Its limbs were spindly and knobby, ending in razor-sharp claws. And that face... a shiver coursed over my spine at the memory of drooling fangs and red eyes.

A cusith. Jax and Tannin knew what they were and had obviously fought them before, but I'd never even heard of them. Where did they come from?

And the way Jax had slain it so easily, so swiftly... I sighed with a mix of gratitude and awe. His combat skill and strength had been incredible to witness, and I was so grateful to him for saving my life. He may be a smartass and kind of a jerk, but he'd defended me when he didn't have to, and I adored him for that.

What would I have done if he hadn't been there, if these men hadn't come at all? That thing would have eaten me alive. Now, more than ever, I had to convince them to stay. I needed them, but I also wanted them more than I could explain.

Even when Jax had been rude to me in the hen yard, I'd felt drawn to him, compelled to win him over and get closer. I ached to touch them both, burned to do even more than just that. No potential suitor, or any man for that matter, had affected me like this in the past.

Was it only because they were the first people I'd seen in fourteen months? Was it because they were both so heartbreakingly gorgeous, and I'd first seen them in all their brutal naked glory?

Remembering their exposed bodies made my core throb and my thighs clench as I took the chicken out of the oven, nearly dropping it in the process. I was being ridiculous. I had to control myself or I'd scare them off.

I carried the roasted chicken, vegetables, and apple pie to the dining room, then went about setting plates and silverware to make everything look perfect. The table in here was long, meant for the times when we hosted many people, but I focused everything around the three chairs at one end.

Willow had popped her head in at one point but had quickly assessed the situation and vanished again. I made sure her bowls were filled with food and water so she could come and go as she pleased.

It was a little strange that she was so stressed about our guests, but they were strangers after all. And she was probably as shocked to see other humans as I was.

When I had everything set and as perfect as it could be, I found the men huddled in quiet discussion in the den by the fire. They stopped their conversation at my entrance and looked at me expectantly.

I cleared my throat. "Dinner is served in the dining room. I prepared roasted chicken, vegetables, and apple pie for three of us."

Jax arched a brow, but Tannin smiled.

"Sounds delicious," he said, then rose from the couch, slapping Jax's arm with the back of his hand to encourage him to follow.

I ushered them to the dining room and took the seat at the head of the table, patting the spots on either side of me for them to sit.

Jax rolled his eyes as he sat to my right with obvious reluctance, and

Tannin politely settled into the chair on my left, beaming at the meal before him.

"This looks and smells very good," Tannin said as he reached for the large knife beside the chicken and began to slice off one of the legs. "You are so kind to do this for us."

To my surprise, he set the leg on my plate instead of his, and my heart melted.

"You should have seen her trying to catch the chicken," Jax said with a laugh, pulling off the other leg with his bare hands. "She'd still be chasing them around the yard if I hadn't swooped in and caught one for her." He took a big bite out of it as he scooped a giant helping of vegetables onto his plate.

I clenched my jaw at his derision, struggling to remain silent and just take it. It really helped that he was so fucking handsome. Maybe if I just looked at his face, I could ignore his words and attitude.

"Forgive my friend," Tannin said, shooting a warning glance at Jax as he carved himself a piece of the breast. "He's not used to being in the presence of royalty."

"Ha!" Jax barked a laugh with a mouthful of food.

I picked up my knife and fork and cut a small bite from the chicken leg. "That's alright. I'm not used to being in anyone's presence, so who am I to judge. I'm just glad to have company."

Tannin offered me a sad half-smile before focusing on his food, and an uncomfortable silence fell over us.

For a seemingly endless few minutes, no one said anything, and the quiet was unbearable. I didn't know what to say or how to start a conversation. So many times I opened my mouth then closed it again, thinking better of what I was going to voice.

"Oh, for God's sake, will you just spit it out already?" Jax complained. "You look like a floundering fish, and it's getting really annoying."

Embarrassment burned in my chest and up my neck. I bit my lip, feeling foolish.

"And stop biting your lip like that," Jax muttered under his breath.

Tannin glared at him before turning to me with an apologetic frown. "Ignore him. I know it must be difficult to converse after so long in silence, but you can talk to *me* about whatever you want."

He put his hand softly on my arm, and a warm tingle saturated my skin at his touch, making me gasp. The way he blinked at our point of contact told me he felt it too. But he didn't remove his hand right away, instead letting it linger for several seconds then slowly pulling away, lightly dragging his fingertips across my skin in a way that made me ache.

I looked up into his soft green eyes, and he held my gaze for a moment. I wanted to disappear into them, and I found myself leaning closer until Jax loudly, rudely cleared his throat.

I rested back against my chair and chose one of the many questions racing around my mind. "When you came here, you said you were heading to Rodak. That's the outpost town in the west, isn't it? Why were you going there?"

Tannin took a bite and nodded while chewing. "We're from a very small village in the north. Life became unbearable there, so I guess you could say we were on a sort of pilgrimage, looking for something better."

My heart jumped up into my throat with excitement. They had nowhere to go. They wanted a new home. This could be their new home!

I swallowed against the eager tightness in my throat. "Well, as you can see, there's a lot of room here. You're welcome to stay as long as you want."

Tannin's responding smile seemed bittersweet, and I wondered if I offended him somehow. Was I being too eager? Did I sound desperate?

"I think that sounds like a fantastic idea," Jax said suddenly. "Especially if meals like this are going to be a common thing. You may not be good at catching chickens, but you're fairly decent at cooking them."

I smiled, deciding to take that as a compliment. Mama always said the way to a man's heart was through his stomach.

"Well, if you like the chicken, then you'll love the pie." I got out of my seat and stepped around Jax to get to the dessert, which was just past his plate.

He scooted his chair out to give me better access to it, and the gesture surprised me. Maybe he wasn't a complete asshole after all.

I cut into the pie and set slices onto each of their plates.

"Thank you," Tannin said, licking his lips as he eyed the caramelized apples spilling from beneath the crust.

I giggled at his response, then tripped on my skirt as I made to return to my seat and fell awkwardly into Jax's lap.

"Whoa!" His arms closed around me, his hands firmly gripping the sides of my waist.

Just as with Tannin, Jax's touch sent a hot shiver through me. I looked at his face over my shoulder, finding concern in those icy blue eyes as well as heat.

Smoldering heat that threatened to incinerate me from the inside out. "Are you okay?" he asked, his fingertips pressing into me.

I nodded dazedly, distracted by the telltale bulge nudging at the bottom of my thigh. I knew enough about the bedroom to understand what that was and what it meant, and a thrill throbbed between my legs.

"Mm-hmm... just tripped," I muttered. "Not used to wearing dresses anymore."

I pressed my buttocks into his lap, and the quietest yet sharpest gasp escaped his lips. I wanted so badly to kiss them.

Suddenly, he lifted me off him and set me back on my feet beside him.

"Try not to be so clumsy, please," he scolded, looking pointedly away from me, scooting back into the table with blatant irritation.

But his jagged edges didn't cut me because I knew the truth, which he was reluctant to admit. He wanted me every bit as much as I wanted him.

I glanced at Tannin as I made my way back to my chair, and the two of them were glaring at each other in a different way than before. In challenge.

Was Tannin jealous? Did he want me too? That would be crazy.

The sinful, frenzied dreams that had haunted me all night came back to me, shooting sharp desire through my center, and I closed my eyes against its potency. The idea of having one of them was almost too much to bear. But both of them... was that even possible?

"No, that would be crazy," I muttered to myself.

"What?" Jax asked, looking quizzically at me with one eyebrow raised.

"Oh, nothing," I blurted, internally kicking myself. "I, uh... talk to myself sometimes."

Dammit! Why did I say that? I'm just making it worse!

Jax made a derisive snort, and I sagged into my chair. Attraction or not, I'd be lucky if they even wanted to stay at this point.

Suddenly, Jax pushed away from the table and stood. "I need some air," he grunted, then stomped out of the room.

I deflated even more, as much as my tight corset would let me.

"I'm sorry about him," Tannin said. "I know he can be an asshole sometimes, but he's a good guy under all the bravado and ego. I'll go talk to him. Thank you so much for the food."

He gave me one last smile, then stood up and left too.

No. No, no, no. They couldn't leave. I had to do something. I could not go back to being alone in this castle. I would die first. And truthfully, I would die without them if more of those cusiths came.

CHAPTER 7

ALIYA

After cleaning the table from dinner, I wandered around the castle in search of them. I didn't really know what I was going to say, but I hoped the right words would come to me in the moment.

They weren't in the den or anywhere outside, so I ventured up to the royal chambers where I had set up rooms for them. I could hear muffled voices carrying down the wide hallway as soon as I emerged from the staircase.

They were in the room in which Jax had found me this morning.

Okay, I can do this. Offer them whatever they want. Food, riches, even my body if that's what it takes to make them stay.

Though, at this point, that wouldn't be much of a sacrifice. I didn't understand this intense desire for both men, but I was more than willing to give in to it.

I walked up to the door and lifted my hand to knock, but something stopped me before my knuckles could touch the wood. I paused there, curious at this strange hesitation.

"I saw the way you touched her at dinner," Jax's voice said angrily on the other side. "You can't fool me, *brother*!"

"You're one to talk," Tannin countered. "Your hands were all over her when she fell in your lap, and you were looking at her like you wanted to bend her over the table!"

My breath hitched. They were talking about me. My intuition told me to listen in, and though I felt slightly guilty for eavesdropping, I was also burning with curiosity. So I hunched down and peeked one eye into the keyhole.

Tannin was leaning against the bed post, his arms folded, and Jax was pacing across the floor, moving in and out of my limited scope of sight.

"Ugh! I didn't want to say anything, but I've bonded to her," Jax said.

Bonded? I'd only heard that term in reference to...

"You what?" Tannin growled.

"I know," Jax shot at him. "I tried to deny it, and I'm trying very hard to fight it. We don't get to choose who the mate bond connects with, okay?"

"That's not possible," Tannin said, shaking his head.

"Why? Because she's a Wielder? Or because she's the Varinyan princess? Trust me, I'm aware of the irony."

Tannin pushed away from the bed post. "No, because *I've* bonded to her. She's mine."

Jax immediately stopped his pacing and stared at Tannin. "No, you didn't," he seethed.

"Yes, I did," Tannin asserted. "I felt the stirrings of it last night, before you even knew she existed."

Jax shook his head, tapping his foot. "That's not possible. Two men can't bond to the same woman."

"I know, and yet here we are," Tannin said. "So, what do we do about this?"

Jax shrugged arrogantly. "Well, as Alpha, I have right of first choice."

"Bullshit!" Tannin barked, stomping up to within inches of him. "That right doesn't apply when a mate bond is present."

"But if you're saying that we're both meant to be with her, then we have to settle this." Jax argued, puffing up his chest. "And the way to settle the dispute of who gets to claim her is to defer to hierarchy. I'm the Alpha, you're my beta, and you *will* relinquish her to me."

Alpha? Beta?

"The fuck I will!" Tannin rebuked. "I saw her first. And she likes me better anyway. You've done nothing but treat her like shit since you woke up!"

I nodded and frowned in agreement as I hovered above the door-knob, spying. Tannin had a point there.

"You're only nice to her because you want to fuck her and can't control yourself," Jax snarled. "I'm the one who saved her life from that cusith, so I should be the one who gets to have her."

"You would have killed that cusith whether she'd been there or not, so don't pull that chivalry bullshit with me," Tannin said. "I have just as much right to claim her as you do, and you know it."

"Then I guess there's only one way to settle this." Without warning, Jax swung a punch at the side of Tannin's face.

I gasped and pressed my hands over my mouth.

Tannin spat blood off to the side. "Bring it on, asshole." Then he lunged at Jax, tackling him to the floor and out of sight.

I moved my head all around the space in front of the keyhole, trying to get a better angle to see them, but they were too far away.

They were fighting over me. Two drop-dead gorgeous men were fighting over me and beating the shit out of each other from the sounds of the bangs, grunts, and slaps.

I couldn't remember ever being this excited about anything in my whole life, and I was desperate to see this play out. Who would win? Not that their stupid fight would prove anything, because I was a fucking princess and not some voiceless trinket. I would choose my suitor, and silly as it may sound, I didn't know who I'd pick, given the chance.

Tannin was sweet and gentle, and Jax could be snide and callous. But he'd risked his life to protect me, and I'd caught small glimpses of his caring heart.

What if I didn't have to choose? I could stop this fight right now and tell them I wanted both of them. Oh gods, I wanted to do that so bad!

I lifted my hand toward the knob, but a loud crash from inside made me jump back. What the hell were they doing in there?

I leaned closer, peering through the keyhole again. Tannin was in sight, taking off his shirt and pants. My insides tightened at the sight of his naked body, and I didn't even care why he was stripping for a fight.

But then thick black fur sprouted all over his body, which grew and stretched and mutated, and in the next instant, he was no longer my handsome, kind Tannin, but a massive black wolf.

Another wolf shot out from the side and swiped a clawed paw at him. Jax.

In horrified disbelief, I stumbled backward until my back smacked into the wall.

Black wolves. My men were black wolves!

As quietly as I could, I ran down the hall and into my room, softly closing the door behind me and sliding my back down until I slumped on the floor.

They'd been lying to me from the very moment I met them. They were black wolves, the ancient enemy of my kingdom. That's why they'd been talking about Alphas and betas and mate bonds, but I'd been too lust-driven and desperate to think rationally.

Mate bonds. They said they'd mated to me. And even now with my pulse racing and my body trembling in fear over what I'd just seen, I couldn't deny the powerful yearning I felt for each.

What was I going to do? They were the enemy of the kingdom I now ruled alone. It was my duty to my ancestors to kick them out. But I'd already invited them to stay, and with this whole mate bond business, there was no way they'd leave willingly.

A shadow caught in the corner of my eye, and I snapped my head in that direction.

"Willow," I sighed in relief after she came into the moonlight spilling through my window. "It's just you."

She curled up on my lap, and I busied my anxious hands with petting her.

I really didn't want them to go, even with this revelation. I couldn't bear the thought of returning to the solitude I'd been wallowing in before they stumbled into my life.

But I was the last of the Varinyan line. Allying with them went against everything my ancestors fought and died for. Letting them stay would be like spitting on my parents' graves.

There was only one right choice. I had to protect my castle from its enemies, even if that meant shattering what was left of my battered heart.

CHAPTER 8
TANNIN

Rage. Primal, animalistic rage consumed me as I fought against my Alpha. But right now, he wasn't my Alpha, he wasn't my life-long best friend... he was my nemesis.

I leapt onto his back, digging my claws into his sides as I bit the back of his neck as hard as I could. He yelped and rolled, slamming me hard against the floor, but I refused to let go. I refused to lose.

But he was bigger than me, his weight crushing down on me as he continued to roll and pinned me between his back and the floor. He bucked his powerful body, slamming me over and over, until I finally lost my grip on his sides.

Then, faster than I could react, he spun around to face me and drove his mouth into my neck, clamping down. His teeth sank into my skin, squeezing my windpipe. I knew he could crush my bones with those powerful jaws, but he was holding back. This bite was a warning.

"Why... are we... fighting... over her?" I grunted with what little voice I could strain out. "You don't... even want her. She's... your enemy."

His bite tightened, completely cutting off my airway, and for a moment, I really thought he was going to kill me.

But then he released his jaws and pulled back just enough to snarl down at me. I sucked in air, gasping and coughing as he kept me pinned beneath him. Slowly, his upper lip lowered over his fangs, his features relaxing.

"You're right," he growled, pushing himself off me and shifting back to his human form to stand over me. "This temptress is clouding our judgment, turning us against each other, and making us forget why we're here. We can't allow that."

I shifted back too, still wheezing and gasping to catch my breath. I rolled onto my side and tried to push myself up. Jax offered me a hand, and I reluctantly took it and let him pull me up to my feet.

"Our duty is first and foremost to our pack," he said, keeping my hand in his even after I stood. "And to each other. I don't want to fight you, brother."

His words humbled me, cooling the flame of jealous rage that had been broiling within me. Now human and rational again, I remembered how much I loved him.

"I don't want to fight you, either," I admitted shamefully. "I'm sorry for challenging you."

He chuckled as he stepped back into his pants. "I'm sorry for nearly killing you. Aliya must have more magic than we thought."

He would have had every right to kill me under pack law. I challenged him and lost. Challenging the Alpha was not something any wolf took lightly, and I never should have done it.

But this mate bond—or Aliya's magic—had me losing my mind, descending into possessive jealousy and a determination to claim and protect my mate. It made me foolish and impulsive, two things neither of us could afford to be as pack leaders.

I sank onto the end of the bed and ran a hand through my hair. "What are we going to do about this? About her?"

He pushed his arms through the sleeves of his shirt and started to button it up. "I think there's only one thing we *can* do."

I cocked my head at him curiously.

"We have to remove her as a temptation," he said with a shrug.

My heart squeezed in panic, and my mouth went dry. "What?"

"That girl is a threat to everything we've been fighting for our whole lives," he said. "We've already seen how easily she turns us against each other, and we're best friends."

I shook my head, my chest filling with desperation. "But she didn't do that. We did that to ourselves."

"No, the mate bond did it to us," he countered. "And as long as that bond exists, we can't think or operate rationally. So, the only logical conclusion is to sever it."

I stared at him in astonishment, but he refused to meet my gaze.

"You can't even say the word, can you?" I accused.

He didn't answer me.

"How do you expect to *remove her* if you can't even say the word out loud?" I pushed, hoping to dissuade him from this horrible, ruinous thought.

Finally, he did look at me, his expression stony. "That's why you're going to do it."

All blood drained from my face. "What?" I breathed.

"As your Alpha, I'm ordering you to kill that girl," he said, authority ringing in his voice and reverberating through my bones.

I shook my head, shrinking away from him. "No. No, I can't do that."

He loomed over me menacingly, his eyes narrowing to dangerous slits. "Are you refusing an order from your Alpha?"

The pull of his power tightened like a leash around my neck, compelling me to submit. Fighting the command caused me physical pain, but the idea of killing the one person I was fated to protect hurt far worse.

He sat on the bed beside me and put his hand on mine, surprising me with his gentleness. "I know it hurts. I feel it too. But it will only hurt until it's over. When she's dead, this affliction will leave both of us."

A wolfish whimper peeled up my throat. "But she's innocent. She hasn't done anything wrong."

He gave my hand a comforting squeeze. "I know that. But her existence is a threat to our pack. As long as she lives, the bond will continue to turn us against them and each other. One human life isn't worth the loss of so many others. We have to think of the greater good."

I nodded sadly in agreement.

He was right. The future prosperity of our pack was more important than the life of one outsider. More important than the pain I knew her loss would cause me. She was my mate, and Fate only offered the bond once. I wouldn't get another. But every wolf had sacrifices to make for the pack. This was mine.

"Okay," I said. "I'll do it tomorrow. I need a little time to prepare myself."

I looked into his eyes pleadingly, and he smiled sadly and nodded.

"Tomorrow then."

Relief washed over me, and he patted my back as he stood.

"The moon is up," he said. "I'll go outside and make my moon song. The pack will rejoice at the good news."

He went to the door and left the room, leaving me alone with my despair. I didn't want to be alone. The silence only made the cries in my head louder, and I couldn't stand it.

I shot off the bed and jogged after him, catching up to him at the stairs. Neither of us said anything as we made our way through the castle, and although I hated the quiet, I didn't want to talk. His presence was the only comfort I could draw on, and it would have to be enough.

We went out through the kitchen door to the garden, and the bright moon above cast its glorious silver light on us, soothing my soul ever so slightly. I let myself savor it as I followed Jax past the garden to the base of the tree line, where he stopped and closed his eyes as he turned his face up toward the moon.

He took in a deep breath, his chest expanding with it, then let out a mighty, melodious howl. The moonlight absorbed the hauntingly beautiful sound, pulling it up into the sky and sending it out into the night.

The message rang in my mind, as I knew it would soon ring in the minds of my pack.

Varinya is abandoned. The castle is empty, just waiting for our occupation and dominion. Come and thrive.

As the message faded, a sort of peace settled over me. Our pack was coming. We'd finally have everything we'd prayed for over so many generations. This was all a good and wonderful thing for everyone.

I just had to cut my heart out first.

CHAPTER 9

ALIYA

After finding out what Jax and Tannin were, I grabbed the magic book from its hiding place in the kitchen and fled to my bedroom.

There, I went through the entire spell book but didn't find anything that I thought might help me. So in the middle of the night, I went into the library, thinking that if there had been one book of spells, there had to be a lot more. Magic had been a big part of our history, and it was foolish to think it would all be condensed into one small book.

I slowly scanned each level of shelves, letting my intuition guide me, pulling out every book that gave me even the slightest tug. By the time I'd checked the entire collection of books, I'd amassed a pile of fifteen.

I'd spent yesterday going through every last one. That first book I'd found really was just the tip of the iceberg. I found so many spells that they started to blur together in my mind.

But which one would be the right one for my situation?

The combative spells would be an obvious solution, but I didn't want to hurt them. Just the thought of harm coming to either Tannin or Jax made my insides knot painfully, and my heart felt as though it were hollowing out.

No, I couldn't hurt them. That was out of the question. It was hard enough contemplating getting them to leave and imagining never seeing them again.

There was a forget ee spell and a compulsion spell, but both of those required foreign items I didn't have access to. Those would have been the easiest if they were possible. I could erase myself from their minds and order them to leave. Then at least they wouldn't have to suffer the loss that I would endure alone.

Willow found me through the night and curled up in my lap, giving my heart solace for the difficult times ahead.

Finally, just before the sun came up, I found the right spell. A protection ward. It involved wrapping a braid of sage with a gold chain and burning the end, then going around the perimeter of the place needing protection and reciting an incantation while waving the smoke along the walls.

The ward would cause an invisible barrier that could only be crossed by those invited by the master of the house—or in this case, castle.

So, my plan was to cast the ward most of the way around the castle, then lure Tannin and Jax into the forest and run back to finish the ward.

But it would take time. The castle was huge, and by myself, it would take me hours to circumnavigate the whole thing while waving smoke and chanting. And I had to do that without being seen by either of them or raising suspicion.

That would be tricky, especially now knowing their mate bonds drew them to me.

The other difficult part would be gaining their trust enough that they would follow me into the forest. They craved me, but that didn't necessarily mean they trusted me.

I'd have to seduce them—which I honestly was excited about—but I'd have to do it without getting seduced in return. And as badly as I wanted them, I wasn't entirely sure I could manage not to fall for them.

"But I have to," I told myself.

Willow meowed in agreement from her coil in my lap.

"Thanks, Willow," I said, scratching her head. "I need all the encouragement I can get."

I looked at the window, where the golden morning light was spilling in. "Well, I'd better get started."

I lifted her off my lap and climbed to my feet, my joints stiff and achy from sitting cross-legged on the hard floor for so long. I stretched until my body felt loose once more, then went up the stairs toward my room. I needed to look my best for my plan to work.

When I got to the top floor, I hesitantly peered around the corner down the hallway. Their doors were closed, and the hall was quiet. Hopefully, they hadn't woken up yet, and I could get a head start.

I tiptoed past their rooms and into mine, then had a quick but hot shower. Then I scoured my wardrobe for the sexiest dress I could find. I decided on a sleeveless, slinky red and purple dress with a heart neckline that made my boobs look incredible and a hi-low ruffled skirt that showed off my upper thighs.

Then I brushed out my now clean hair and styled it in a simple up-down do that much of my neck was exposed. Mama always told me that my long neck was one of my most flattering qualities.

I could only imagine what she'd think of what I was doing now.

I pushed my sorrow deep down and grabbed a gold necklace chain from my jewelry box, then went down to the garden to gather the sage I needed. Making a braid out of the stiff strands was harder than I thought, but I eventually managed to force the sage into place and tied it with the gold chain.

When I was done, the sun had risen a quarter way into the sky. It was mid-morning now. I wondered how long I had before Tannin or Jax woke up and came looking for me.

There was no more time to waste.

I started just beside the main entrance doors of the castle.

"Flamare," I said, focusing on the far end of the sage braid.

The fire spell worked like the flip of a switch, the end of the braid igniting with a burst of flames. A big one. I really needed to work more on my intention. I was lucky the whole stick didn't incinerate and burn me in the process.

I blew it out, needing only the smoke from the sage.

"Parum nir alte tunak." I invoked the spell, concentrating on my desire to protect my castle, and waved the smoking sage up and down in front of me.

Then I moved two steps to the right and repeated the words. On and on I went, slowly making my way around the castle, two steps at a time.

I hadn't anticipated how exhausting it would be. This was powerful magic and wielding it like this for hours on end drained me. By the time I'd made it a dozen yards or so, dizziness gripped me, and I stumbled forward, bracing myself against the wall until it passed.

"I think that's enough for now," I told myself, resting my forehead against the cool stone. Then I pushed the end of the braid into the wall, dragging it slightly to stop the smoking.

I needed water, food, and to sit for a while. But I needed some way to mark my place, so I'd know where to continue when I was ready to start again. Angling my foot, I dug the heel of my boot into the ground, carving out a line that I'd be able to recognize.

"Aliya, there you are."

I gasped at the unexpected voice and shoved the sage braid into the pocket of my skirt before turning to face Tannin as he approached.

Out here, in the light of day, he looked so handsome. The sun's rays caught in his brown hair, making it look lighter and softer, and brought a rosy tint to his boyish cheeks.

"What are you doing all the way over here?" he asked, his charming smile on full display as his eyes dragged down my body.

"Oh, I just wanted some air," I said as casually as I could. "I like to walk around the castle sometimes, especially this time of year."

His gaze caught on my chest, where my breasts were pushed up and heaved over the thin fabric that barely covered them. From the look on his face, I'd made the right choice.

"That's—er—you look...beautiful," he stammered, his stupefaction making him even more adorable.

I clasped my hands behind my back to push my chest further forward and fluttered my lashes coquettishly. "Thank you."

His throat bobbed, and he finally managed to rip his gaze from my chest to look me in the eye. "Uh, would you like some company while you stroll?"

I gave him a coy smile. "I would like that very much."

I took a step toward him, and my head began to spin again. My body crumpled forward in a moment of dizziness, and Tannin caught me.

"Hey, are you okay?" he asked, concern lacing his voice as he held me firmly against him.

His hands on my arms sent fire dancing over my skin, and his chest beneath my palms was so hard, so strong. I wanted to bury myself in his embrace and never emerge again.

I looked up at him, our faces only inches apart. "Yeah, I think I might have had too much sun. I feel a little…"

My eyelids fluttered, and my head drooped against his chest as my knees buckled.

"Okay, let's get you inside," he said, squeezing my arms to keep me up.

He slid one arm around my back, scooping it around my waist, and braced my upper arm with his other hand, then slowly ushered me toward the kitchen entrance.

"Can you walk?" he asked softly.

"I think so," I murmured. "I'm sorry. I don't know what's come over me."

Other than the fact that I wielded a lot of draining magic as part of a convoluted scheme to exorcise you from the castle…

"That's okay. We'll get you some water."

He escorted me through the garden and into the kitchen, then guided me to a stool at the island and helped me climb onto it.

"There. You just sit." He rushed to the faucet and filled a glass with water, then brought it back to me.

I reached for the glass, and our fingers brushed each other in the exchange, sending a shiver through my torso.

"Thank you," I said, teasingly curling my fingertips over his hand before lifting the glass to my lips.

As soon as the cool water touched my tongue, my thirst became overwhelming, and I guzzled down the whole thing, accidentally spilling some down the sides of my mouth. The tiny streams dripped down my chin and splashed onto the tops of my breasts.

"Oh, dammit," I muttered.

"Here, I got it!" Tannin rushed forward with a washcloth in hand and began patting the droplets.

And he didn't stop even when it was clear that the rag had soaked them up. He just kept staring, transfixed by my flesh, and as for me… I could hardly breathe through my gnawing anticipation.

I leaned forward, daring him to touch me, to give in to his obvious desire. *Please, touch me…*

He pulled away and stepped back. "Are you hungry?"

I nodded my head, trying not to show my disappointment.

"Okay, I'll fix something for us," he said, then went about searching through the cabinets.

This was going to be harder than I thought.

CHAPTER 10

TANNIN

Why did she have to wear that fucking dress? Her perfect tits were practically falling out of it, and her skirt was so short I could... I could reach right under it and pet her warm, wet—

Fuck, I wasn't sure how much longer I could control myself!

Focus, Tannin. Remember your task.

I promised my Alpha that I would kill her today. Why hadn't I done it outside? She'd nearly fainted, and she was clearly in a weakened state. It would've been so easy to slit her throat with the knife I had tucked into my pants behind my back. Or push the blade into her gut.

Those mental images flooded ice through my veins, and bile rose in my throat. I couldn't do that. How could I? Even if I wasn't fighting a painful hard-on at the sight of her, that would still be nearly impossible.

I cut a ripe tomato into slices for sandwiches, keeping my back to Aliya and focusing on what I needed to do. I just had to stop looking at her. Stop getting distracted by how torturously sexy she looked and rip the band-aid off.

I wouldn't feel this way anymore after it was done. I'd be free of these impulsive feelings.

Just kill her. Just do it!

"Do you want some help?" she asked, making me freeze completely.

I could hear the ruffles of her skirt rustle as she slid off the stool and the air moved with her steps as she came up behind me. I held my breath against the sweet assault of her scent.

Her arm brushed against mine as she joined me at the counter. She reached in front of me and took another knife from the block, then grabbed a head of lettuce from the basket and began chopping it.

Slowly, I returned to slicing the tomato, lifting the knife handle and pushing it down in precise, careful movements.

It would be so easy. I could make it quick. Stabbing her would be a merciful death. Then she could move on to the afterlife and be with her parents again. I'd be doing her a favor, really. It was better than what the pack would insist on when they got here.

But every time I tried to force myself to take action, my body refused to move. My hand only tightened around the handle, my chops coming down harder and harder, and—

"Fuck!" I hissed in pain, realizing too late that I'd brought the blade down right over the tip of my thumb. Blood mixed in with the juice from the tomato on the cutting board.

"Tannin! Are you okay?" Aliya cried.

She frantically reached for a clean washcloth, then took my hand in her free one and wrapped the rag around my thumb.

Stupid. I was so stupid. I was making a fucking mess of this whole thing.

"Hold on, let me get you a bandage," she said. "Keep pressure on it."

I nodded, squeezing the rag in my hand, and she ran behind me to rifle through a cabinet. After a moment, she came back and took my hand in both of hers.

"Okay, let me see it."

She pulled away the washcloth and carefully inspected my thumb. I'd cut a layer of skin clean off. But I couldn't feel the sting anymore. The touch of her soft hands on mine and the gentle caress of her fingertips as she cleaned the cut were the only thing I could feel.

She pushed out her bottom lip fretfully as she worked, and I couldn't tear my eyes away from her mouth. My lips burned to press against hers. What would she taste like? Would she gasp if I pulled her into my arms and claimed her mouth right now? Would she open those pink lips to welcome my eager tongue?

"There, that's better," she said, and I dazedly realized that she'd wrapped a bandage around my thumb.

She held my hand in hers, and I didn't pull it away, unable to willingly remove myself from her touch. In this moment I was her puppet, and I had no desire to cut the strings.

Keeping my eyes captured in her gaze, she brought my hand up to her face and planted the softest, sweetest kiss over the bandage on my thumb.

Mesmerized. She had me completely and utterly under her spell.

I slowly loosened my hand from hers, keeping my thumb against her lips as I cupped my palm lightly around her jaw. Though I couldn't feel the softness of her skin through the bandage, I traced my thumb along the petal of her bottom lip.

So beautiful. So sweet.

She parted her lips, an invitation to give me better access for whatever I wanted—and there were so many, many things I wanted to do to her. But I stayed very still, desperately grasping the last bit of restraint I still had.

She puckered her lips and kissed my thumb again and again, nuzzling her cheek into my palm. The crippling need throbbing in my cock was almost irresistible.

She was irresistible.

I slid my hand around the back of her head and pulled her to me, crushing my lips against hers. Fire. My whole body was on fire!

With a soft whimper, she opened her mouth, and I greedily deepened the kiss, exploring her mouth with my tongue. She tasted even better than I imagined. Like warm honey. Like bliss.

Her hands roamed down my chest, over the brim of my pants, then cupped gently over the bulge of my stiff cock.

I groaned at the need her touch elicited and pushed away from her, forcing myself to take a few steps back.

Her face cracked with worry, her kiss-swollen lips pouting again. "I'm so sorry! Did I hurt you?"

"No, I—"

I couldn't do this. I *wouldn't* do this. She was my mate, and harming a single hair on her beautiful head went against everything I was and everything I wanted to be.

"I have to go," I blurted out, then spun on my heel and rushed out of the kitchen, making a beeline for the stairs.

Not stopping, I didn't slow down until reaching Jax's room on the top floor. I pushed open the door without announcement or apology.

Jax was sitting in the armchair by the window, book in hand. He shifted in surprise at my outburst. "What the hell?"

"I'm not doing it," I declared.

He closed his book, set it on the windowsill and stood, glaring at me. "What do you mean, you're not doing it?"

He stalked closer, looking every bit the Alpha he was, but I refused to back down. I would not be intimidated, not about this.

"I won't kill her," I said.

"Won't or can't?" he asked, accusation in his tone.

"Both," I professed with confidence. "She's my mate, and the sweetest girl alive. I won't harm her in any way, no matter what you do to me."

He stopped a foot in front of me, grilling me with his furious gaze.

"You want her dead? Do it yourself." I went on. "I won't stop you. Take her from me if you must. But know that if you do, I will never forgive you."

His glare intensified, his upper lip twitching. I didn't care. Let him kill me for my insubordination. I was done with this. And if I had to be done with him too, then so be it.

But he didn't do anything but continue to sneer at me. So, I turned my back on him and stomped out of the room, slamming the door behind me.

I went into my own room next door and bolted the lock. Whatever he was going to do, I wanted no part of it. I didn't want him to kill her. I strongly believed he wouldn't be able to, just like me.

But this was his choice to make. He had to learn this lesson on his own. And if he failed, if he committed the ultimate crime, I was done with him.

CHAPTER 11
ALIYA

A tidal wave of conflicting, confusing emotions crashed over me after Tannin ran off.

Our kiss was amazing! Not that I had much to compare it to. I'd never been kissed before, other than chaste pecks on the cheek or forehead from my parents. They'd died before arranging my marriage to a neighboring prince, and I'd been protected from the men in the kingdom even before then.

But I couldn't imagine anything better!

His lips were so soft, his mouth hot and demanding. And when he pushed his tongue between my lips—I didn't even know one *could* kiss like that! Incredible! My lips still tingled from the delightfully rough treatment, and I unconsciously lifted my hand and ran my fingertip lightly over my bottom lip.

But he'd run off so quickly afterward. Perhaps he didn't feel the same way? Maybe I was a bad kisser. What if my breath offended him?

I cupped my hand in front of my mouth and exhaled into it, then sniffed. Nope. That wasn't it. At least, I didn't detect a foul odor. If anything, my breath smelled kind of sweet.

Maybe I went too far by reaching for the bulge between his legs? That was when he stopped everything. He'd seemed shocked or possibly scared, maybe. I didn't know.

I hadn't meant to do it. In the heat of our kissing, my body had acted on instinct. My hand had a mind of its own, seeming to know what to do when I consciously didn't. And, oh, the thrill that spiked inside me when I pressed my palm against the proof of his desire!

But he'd shoved me away. Clearly, he didn't feel the same excitement and longing I felt for him. He stumbled away from me like I might hurt him, then ran off without a word of explanation.

And now I felt rejected, naïve, and filled with self-doubt and confusion. I used to think of myself as beautiful. The castle staff and villagers in the streets would comment on my beauty often.

"Your hair glistens like warm honey."

"Your eyes shine like sun-kissed amber."

"Your skin is as smooth as alabaster and as creamy as milk."

Perhaps they only said those things because I was their princess, and they felt they had to flatter me. Maybe in reality I was average, plain, undesirable.

With a heavy heart, I finished making the sandwiches Tannin had started. Though my appetite had thoroughly vanished, I still felt weak and lightheaded, and I knew I had to eat something to regain my strength and energy.

I carried my lunch to the island counter and forced myself to eat it while my thoughts churned over and over. I didn't really know how to be intentionally alluring. Attention had never been something I was deprived of, not before the plague.

It didn't make sense that it was only about beauty. There were women in the village who weren't particularly pretty that had still commanded the attention of men and had arranged fine marriages for themselves with men above their stations.

Those women were intelligent, confident, bold. They knew what they wanted, and they took it. It seemed that men respected that quality in women. Confidence.

I was going about this all wrong. I'd been playing the sweet, naïve princess—which, okay, I was—but that hadn't gotten me anywhere. It was time I stepped into the role I was born for—the bold, unwavering queen. It was time I took the things I wanted.

And, really, how hard could it be? They said they were both mate-bonded to me. I didn't know much about that, but I knew what *I* felt.

This powerful, insatiable urge to be with both men. To touch them, to kiss them, to melt into them. They had to feel the same, or they wouldn't have fought over me.

Hmmm… maybe that was why Tannin had pushed away from me—he'd lost the fight. He wanted me, but he felt like he had to step aside because of some weird black wolf politics.

And if he lost, that could only mean Jax won.

And Jax was the Alpha. Tannin would side with whatever Jax said. I didn't have to seduce both, just Jax.

I swooned at that notion, squeezing my thighs together.

With that in mind, I quickly ate the rest of my sandwich and guzzled down another glass of water. With my belly full, I felt much better, and I was ready to wield my feminine power.

I swept upstairs to prepare myself. I had to make myself irresistible, make it impossible for him to refuse what I was offering. And this dress, as flattering as it was to my body, wasn't going to cut it.

Quickly rinsing off in the bath again, I then rubbed sweet smelling oils over my skin and teased it through my hair. Then I went through the dowry chest my mother had presented me with on my eighteenth birthday when she and Papa were beginning the process of finding me a suitable husband.

Hard to believe that was three years ago, just before the plague set in. I still remembered so vividly the day she had shown me everything that was inside. That was the occasion I first felt like a woman, and it had been such a special moment between us.

But right now, I wasn't interested in the gold bars and extravagant jewelry, nor the immaculate wedding dress and sparkly satin high-heeled slippers.

I only cared about the sexy lace negligee. It had been made for my future wedding night, but seeing as I was likely never getting married, and this was the sexiest item of clothing I had, it was perfect for what I had in mind.

Carefully, I hooked my fingers through the thin straps and pulled it from the chest, admiring it as I held it aloft.

It was pale, baby pink, and so thin I could see right through it. Scalloping lined the plunging neckline, midsection and the hem of the flowy skirt. It was so beautiful, the color complimenting my peachy skin.

But could I really wear this? Every inch of my body would be on full display, leaving little to the imagination. Blush heated my skin all over, and I once again felt foolish. What was I doing?

Nevertheless, I lifted it over my head and pulled it down, gingerly slipping my arms through the straps.

If it looks ridiculous, I'll just take it off. It probably will. The other dress will be fine. No big deal.

I looked down at myself, smoothing the soft material over my torso. It felt like I wasn't wearing anything at all, and that only made my skin burn hotter.

Holding my breath, I turned around and faced my full-length mirror.

And I just stared at myself for a long moment.

I didn't look silly or ridiculous. Not even close. I looked stunning. I looked like my mother. Strong. Beautiful. Commanding.

The timid, frightened girl I'd become since her death was nowhere in sight, and I could hardly recognize the woman looking back at me in my reflection.

There was no way Jax wouldn't become putty in my hands when he saw me. And once I had him wrapped around my delicate little finger, I'd lure him and his beta out into the forest and banish them from my castle—and my heart—forever.

The woman in the mirror frowned sadly as my heart squeezed.

"It has to be done," I told myself. "They are the ancient enemies of my kingdom, and I owe it to everyone who died to remove their presence. I can't let my selfish desires tarnish the history of Varinya."

I forced my features smooth, straightened my shoulders and held my head high. Then I turned around and headed for the door.

The hall was empty, and both their doors were closed. I couldn't even be sure Jax was in his room. What if he was out wandering the castle and this was all for nothing? I really should've planned this better.

But something told me he was beyond that door. Not just my intuition, but something deeper. Was it our mate bond? Did I even have one of them, since I wasn't a wolf?

If I closed my eyes, I could feel a tug pulling me in that direction, like an invisible rope connecting us. I could sense Tannin too, in the other room. It was a magical realization. And one that gave me pause.

Maybe I shouldn't do this.

"No, I have to," I whispered.

But not only that. I *wanted* to. This might be my only chance to know true intimacy. And even if it was for deceitful purposes, I desperately wanted to experience that intimacy with Jax. I needed to know him that way, just once, before I let him go forever.

So I padded across the hall and stopped in front of his door. I took a vitalizing breath, lifted my hand, and tapped my knuckles softly against the door.

Now was the moment of truth. And I was both heart-poundingly excited and utterly terrified.

CHAPTER 12

JAX

I didn't know who was more deserving of my rage—Tannin for expressly disobeying my direct order, or the princess for tempting us both and placing this massive wedge between us.

Fucking cowardly Tannin. I should have known he wouldn't be strong enough to do the job with his endless compassion and gentle heart. It made him weak. He was supposed to be my brother, my second-in-command, and yet he'd turned his back on me for that conniving royal brat.

I should never have delegated the task to him in the first place. I was the Alpha. Eliminating threats was *my* job. I should have taken the responsibility of killing her myself.

Yet, as I sat in my armchair, stewing and chewing on my dark thoughts, I couldn't convince my body to move.

Why hadn't I just killed her before? Or let the cusith destroy her. Last night after I made my moon song would have been the perfect opportunity, while she was asleep and unable to use her feminine wiles to disarm me.

Why wasn't I getting off my ass and doing it right now? At least an hour had passed since Tannin had stormed in here and berated me, and all I had done was brood impotently.

I didn't want to kill her. The thought of it seized my muscles and joints, making it difficult to breathe. But it was just the mate bond doing that to me. I knew nothing about the girl to whom Fate had cruelly decided to shackle me. The only thing I knew for sure was that she was the Varinyan heir, and I should hate her for that.

But I didn't. Not in any measurable way I could use to fuel my muscles into action.

Was I weak like Tannin? Was I too beguiled by the mate bond to do what I knew must be done?

Furious tension ripped through my seemingly frozen muscles. No. I was *not* weak. I was the fucking Alpha, and I was going to take care of this once and for all.

Right now.

With great effort, I shoved myself off the chair and strode for the door. I would not stop until I found the princess, then I'd grip her by the neck with both hands and choke the life out of her before she even knew what was happening. Then she wouldn't be my problem anymore.

Just as my hand reached the doorknob, a soft tapping came from the other side, and I hesitated.

Perhaps it was Tannin coming to apologize for his incompetence and beg for my forgiveness?

A smug sense of satisfaction swept over me, loosening my shoulders. But then it disappeared just as suddenly. Maybe instead he'd come to plead with me to spare the girl's life like the sniveling pup he was.

Either way, I would be the magnanimous leader he needed and set him straight. The princess had to die. End of discussion. And he *would* come to heel.

I turned the knob and pulled the door open, ready for whatever Tannin had to say.

But it wasn't Tannin.

The princess was standing in the hall, draped in a lace negligee so sheer that I could see every torturously sensuous inch of her through it. My blood flash-boiled with desire as my mouth hung open, my dick instantly hard beneath my slacks.

"Can I come in?" she purred, flaring a perfectly arched eyebrow as those amber eyes locked me in their snare.

Too stunned to speak, I mutely took a step to the side to welcome her inside. She sashayed past me, and I was helpless not to visually devour her perky ass that swayed from side to side as she made her way to the center of the room.

My mouth ran dry. I closed the door, facing the wooden panels for a few seconds as I struggled to regain my wits and resolve. Then, with bated breath and thundering pulse, I turned the dead bolt.

Whatever happened next, I didn't want any interruptions from Tannin.

This was perfect. I didn't have to hunt her down. She'd practically delivered herself to me on a silver platter. And now trapped in my room with only me, there was nothing and no one to stop me from killing her.

But she was so goddamned sexy, and every molecule in my body burned to destroy her in an entirely different way—to pin her sweet little body against the wall, plunge my cock between those creamy thighs, and fuck her while she screamed my name in ecstasy again and again!

No. I was stronger than that. She would not dissuade me from my duty.

She dies now.

Solidifying my purpose, I turned on her with a predatory gaze, then stalked toward her.

"What do you think you're doing, little princess?" I growled low in my throat as I came to loom over her.

She looked up at me with those innocent yet yearning eyes and ran her tongue over her lips, this time in a very intentional, seductive way that had primal need stabbing into me.

"I'm making things easy for both of us," she purred, stepping even closer and putting her hands softly on my chest. "I know you want me just as badly as I want you."

I swallowed dryly, keeping my face fixed in a disdainful expression. "And what makes you think such a silly thing?"

"Because you look at me like you want to devour me," she said, running her hand down my body and past the waistband of my pants. Then she pressed against the ridge of my stiff cock, making me grunt. "And because of this."

She rubbed her hand up and down the length of me, and a lustful haze filled my head, dissolving the motivation I fought to hold onto.

Grab her neck. Snap it and be done with it!

She lifted onto her toes, her face so painfully close to mine that I couldn't help but inhale her sweet scent with each tight breath.

"Take me, Jax," she cooed, brushing her lips teasingly against mine.

I fucking lost it.

With hungry, clawed fingers, I clutched her hips and crushed her against me, conquering her mouth with mine. Her lips parted, inviting my eager tongue in to rake against hers. She tasted just as sweet as she smelled, and her mouth was so delightfully hot and pliant, giving into my dominion over her.

I wondered if her other lips would taste as sweet, and I gripped her ass to press her pelvis over my starving cock. Even through the two thin layers of fabric, I could feel the moist heat of her pussy teasing my shaft, and it was all I could do to stop myself from yanking my dick out and thrusting it into her.

No. I can't succumb to her temptation. Kill her. Now!

With a snarl, I backed her up to the wall and gripped her neck, pinning her there like the helpless prey she was.

"Yes," she whimpered, nipping at my bottom lip. "Please."

She thought I was playing with her?

Did she really not understand the mortal danger she was in? How easily I could snap her pretty little neck?

But instead of tightening my hand around her throat, I shoved my tongue into her mouth until I couldn't think straight. She was the most intoxicating creature, and the taste of her, the smell of her... it was all too incredible to resist.

My other hand lifted the lacy negligee and roamed between her legs, which she spread wide to welcome my touch. And oh, the sweet, warm wetness that greeted my fingertips as I slid them over the slick, delicate folds!

I found her clit with my fingertips, swollen and juicy. I ran my fingers over the tiny bud again and again, luxuriating in the sounds of her pleasure. Her soft gasps and whimpers were a serenade to my greedy soul, encouraging me to push her even further.

I strummed her pussy like it was an exquisite instrument that I was born to play. Finally, when I couldn't take it any longer, I plunged my index finger inside her entrance, eliciting a sharp gasp from her lips. Greedily, I swallowed the sound.

Fuck, she was so wet, so tight. And she was mine. Mine!

I dragged my finger in and out, pumping my palm against her clit as I made her squeal louder and faster. She was getting close to ecstasy, her pussy tightening around my finger, which seemed to know exactly where and how to touch her. And fuck, I wanted—no, *needed*—to bring her to ruin under my mercy.

Just a little bit more, my sweet little princess...

"Come for me," I demanded into her mouth.

And like a good little girl, she obeyed immediately. She moaned into my feverish kisses as her pussy squeezed and contracted around my finger, her juices dripping over my knuckles. I continued to pulse the heel of my hand against her clit, coaxing out every last ounce of pleasure from her body until her quaking finally stopped.

Then I withdrew my finger and brought it up to my mouth, sucking it between my lips. Gods, her juices were even sweeter than her mouth!

Before I could question my intentions, I dropped to my knees, forced her legs apart, and lapped my tongue against her pussy. Her fingers tangled into my hair as I ate her, her thighs trembling around my shoulders like they were the only thing holding her up.

Finally, I rose back to my feet, standing over her, paralyzed with indecision.

I was far from done with her. I wanted to ruin her in every possible way. And the pleading way she looked up at me, she was begging me for all of it. I suddenly realized she wasn't at my mercy. I was at hers.

Damn it.

I brought my face close to hers once more, and she leaned forward, eager for more kisses.

"Get out," I snarled dangerously.

She flinched, blinking at me in confusion. "W-what?" she squeaked.

"Are you deaf?" I barked. "I said, get out!"

She shrunk inwardly like I'd hit her, then slid out from between me and the wall and rushed out the door, covering the front of her body like she was ashamed of herself.

The door slammed closed, followed by another muffled slam across the hall, and all I could do was stand there, facing the wall, wrestling to collect myself.

I couldn't do it. I couldn't kill her. I'd had her right in my grasp, and I'd failed.

But more importantly, I didn't *want* to kill her. Tannin was right. Harming a mate went against every instinct we had. In fact, the very opposite was true. I wanted to protect her, cherish her, worship her.

I'd gone about this the wrong way.

Our pack would be here in a few days, and they'd be out for blood. How was I supposed to do right by my pack and protect the woman I was completely, irrevocably in love with at the same time?

CHAPTER 13

ALIYA

I couldn't stop my body from trembling even after I locked myself in my room and curled up into a ball in my bed.

I'd never been so confused in my whole life. The things Jax had done to me... I hadn't even known it was possible to feel such overwhelming pleasure. I could still feel his lips... his tongue pressing against mine, his fingers sliding inside me and driving me wild with lust.

And then his mouth between my legs... Holy shit! It was the closest thing to heaven I'd ever experienced.

It must not have been the same for him, because he'd gone from touching and kissing me to shouting at me to leave. He'd seemed so angry. Had I done something wrong?

No. I couldn't have. I hadn't even had the chance to do anything. I'd just stood there and taken what he'd given me. He had been the leader in everything we'd shared, and dammit, it felt so good!

So why then did he completely reject me afterwards like that? Like I was somehow to blame for his actions and feelings.

This bond between us was potent and bewildering, but maybe not as strong as I thought it was. Not if both men could reject me so easily. I was a fucking princess, dammit!

Maybe I was giving the supposed 'mate bond too much value. And if they could resist the pull of it, then so could I. If they could completely dismiss it and ignore the throb of attraction, I should too.

And if they weren't going to give in and let me seduce them, so be it. I didn't need to gain their trust to get them to leave. I could just claim some threat outside the castle, play the helpless damsel, and ask them to get rid of it. If I said there was a cusith out there, I was confident Jax would demand he and Tannin take care of it.

Willow hopped up onto the bed and tucked herself against me on the comforter. Even though my body continued to shake, her purring soon began to send soothing vibrations through me. Running my hand over her back, I savored the comfort of her presence.

Hot tears filled my eyes, and I dashed them away, feeling stupid. For a moment, while Jax was working his magic between my legs, I'd lost myself to how right it felt to be with him. I'd actually entertained surrendering to this bond and just being with him. With both of them.

I'd foolishly believed that maybe it could work, that we would be happy living together and nurturing this mate bond.

But they weren't human, and I had to stop forgetting that. They were every bit the bloodthirsty, primitive, brutish dogs they turned into. They couldn't be trusted to be civilized and decent. They couldn't be trusted with my heart or my body.

And they certainly couldn't be trusted to remain in the castle. I was convinced that they had to get out now. I didn't need them. Being alone was far better than being toyed with and jerked around by their hot-and-cold bullshit.

"Besides, I'm not alone," I whispered, continuing to pet Willow. "I have you. That'll have to be enough for me."

She meowed softly in agreement.

I'd spent long enough licking my wounded pride. I was the princess of Varinya, and it was time I started acting like it.

With renewed purpose and determination, I whipped off the covers and got out of bed. I pulled off the ridiculous negligee and threw it angrily in front of the idle fireplace, too disgusted with it to ever want to lay eyes on it again. Tonight, when I'd finished what I needed to do, I'd burn it.

But for now, there was work to be done.

I got into a pair of warm leggings, a plain shirt and a pair of work boots, perfect for moving about freely outside. Then I pulled my hair into a ponytail and left my room, creeping down the hall until I reached the stairs and descending them quickly.

The sun was hanging a quarter above the western horizon when I went out the kitchen door. I still had plenty of time to work before nightfall, and I was dead set on completing the ward before the day was over.

Making my way around the castle, I found the spot I'd kicked into the ground, then lit the sage braid and continued where I left off this morning.

Though I knew my time was limited, I went slowly, taking breaks to snack on nuts and drink water to keep my strength. I didn't have the luxury of draining myself like I'd done this morning. I had to be smarter than that. I couldn't afford to faint out here and the wolves to find me with my tell-tale sage braid. They couldn't know what I was up to, not until it was too late for them to do anything about it.

My arms ached and my brow was slick with sweat, but I trudged on regardless of the exhaustion.

Little by little, I made my way around the castle, finally finishing the ward up to the other side of the front doors just as the sun grazed the mountaintops in the west. All that was left to seal the ward was the few feet that spanned the castle entrance, and I'd be able to do that with one wave of the sage smoke and one recitation of the spell.

Hopefully, that would be simple enough to do before they caught up to me. It had to be.

It occurred to me then, as I stood in front of the large carved doors, that I might need to use some kind of force to keep them at bay and give myself enough time to get back inside to safety.

They were black wolves, after all, far stronger and faster than me in their shifted form. Compared to them, I was little more than an easily crushed rodent. It would be foolish of me to go into this endeavor without any kind of defense at my disposal.

Luckily, I had several books from which to learn combative spells.

I stashed the sage braid under a large rock next to the entrance of the castle, then brushed myself off and went back to the kitchen door. I was relieved to see that neither Tannin nor Jax had emerged from their rooms, so spending some time in the library studying the books would go unnoticed.

Fuck them.

One of the books I'd set aside to read was filled with the spells I needed. Originally, I'd dismissed it as unnecessary. Even now, as filled with resentment and heartache as I was, I didn't like the idea of hurting them. But I was prepared to do whatever was necessary, now that my other plan had failed.

The elemental spells were the most interesting. I already knew I could conjure fire, as I'd done while lighting the sage. There were spells for conjuring and forming fireballs to project at an enemy, but they came with a ton of warnings. If the Wielder wasn't careful, they could burn themselves badly, and I wasn't foolhardy enough to test that.

The spells for unearthing roots or summoning vines to hurt or bind an enemy looked fascinating, and they'd be perfect for trapping the wolves in the forest, but they were far too advanced for me to attempt at this early stage. Lots of hand movements and incantations, and they took a taxing amount of energy and focus, more so than even the protection ward.

No, that wouldn't work. Whatever I chose needed to be quick and relatively simple.

That left air spells. Wielding air looked easy enough. One had to imagine the wind as an extension of one's own limbs and focus on their breathing to make it work properly. The spell would take a lot of energy, but if I timed it right, I was confident it would do the trick.

But I had to test it first. I couldn't go into this fight blindly, and gods forbid whatever I tried backfired on me in the moment I needed it most.

I looked towards the window. There was a bit of daylight still clinging to the sky though the sun had set behind the mountains.

Tucking the book under my arm, I rushed outside into the garden.

The scarecrow that hung on a stake in the fence was in poor shape. Most of the straw had spilled out of the armpits, and its makeshift head was slumped forward, hiding the face that was meant to frighten off the birds. But he'd make a fine target for practice regardless.

I set the book down on the garden bed and opened it to the page for this spell. The incantation was only one word, and memorizing it wasn't the problem. No, the difficulty came in aligning my breathing with my movements and connecting my will with the wind itself.

I closed my eyes and focused on the air around me, paying attention to how it moved and what it felt like. I lifted my arm, willing the air to move with me, and my heart leapt with excitement as a gust of wind brushed upward at the underside of my arm.

Holy shit, that was incredible!

Don't get too excited. Don't lose focus.

Centering myself, I concentrated on that connection once more. Then I took a breath and wafted my arm across my body as I exhaled. The wind stirred around me, blowing across me to the left and sweeping loose strands of hair in front of my face.

Okay, so I could summon the wind and make it move. But could I use it defensively?

I glanced down at the diagram on the page again, then set my sights on the scarecrow. As I sucked in a long breath, I pulled my hands, palms-out, to my chest. Then, blowing it out with force, I thrust my hands outward, aiming at the scarecrow.

A powerful blast of air released from my palms and slammed into the scarecrow, making it explode in a flurry of straw, dirt and shredded clothing. With a gasp, I shielded my face with my arm and ducked, then peered under my arm at the now splintered, useless wooden post.

"Whoa," I breathed, gawking at the destruction that one simple move had caused.

I hadn't meant to destroy the scarecrow. But then again, I didn't really know what I'd intended. How would that attack affect Tannin or Jax? My stomach twisted at the mental image of their bodies exploding into chunks of guts and blood, and I hastily shoved that thought from my mind.

I didn't want to hurt them, and I certainly didn't want what happened to the scarecrow to happen to them. But that thing was made of straw and sun-bleached fabric. Surely, wind couldn't cause that much damage to a human—or black wolf.

But I wasn't willing to take that chance. I had to practice more. I had to learn how to control this magic so that it only did as much harm as I desired.

As much as I hated both of my mates at the moment, I couldn't stand the thought of killing either of them. I only needed them gone, and it was worth every moment of training to make sure I did just that and nothing more.

CHAPTER 14

JAX

It took longer than I was proud of to collect myself enough to go to Tannin's room.

Nothing I did worked to alleviate the arousal that haunted me after the princess left. I tried meditating and clearing my head, then when that failed, I imagined all sorts of off-putting things. But with her smell still clinging to my fingers and her taste still filling my mouth, it was pointless.

So, I gave in to my crippling need and stroked my cock furiously until the demand subsided, letting myself imagine all the ways I wanted to ruin and worship her sexy little body. Even after coming the first time, my damn erection wouldn't go away, so I did it all over again.

This girl was so deep under my skin that I was certain I'd never be the same again. And I didn't want to be. I wanted to be her monster that pinned her to the wall and made her scream. But after the way I'd treated her... I'd made so many mistakes, I wasn't sure I could fix things now.

With her or Tannin.

But I had to try.

I cleaned myself up in the adjoining bathroom, scrubbing her scent from my body until I could finally breathe. Then I ventured to Tannin's door like a pup with my tail between my legs. I knocked twice, then waited.

Nothing.

I knocked again. "Tannin? We need to talk."

Silence for a moment.

"I have nothing to say to you," his voice finally said on the other side of the door.

"Perhaps not, but I have plenty to say to you," I said, swallowing the lump in my throat as surely as my pride. "Including that you were right."

There was shuffling inside, the sound of feet padding toward the door. "And just what was I right about?" he asked just on the other side of the thick wood.

"Everything," I conceded with a sigh. "You were right about everything."

The deadbolt clicked, and the knob turned, the door opening to reveal Tannin standing with one hand braced against the doorframe and the other on his hip. A resentful yet intrigued expression hung on his features.

"Come in," he said with a reluctant tone.

I strode into the room and sat on the edge of his bed while he closed the door and walked toward me, arms folded obstinately over his chest.

"Forgive me, brother," I began, humbling myself before him. "I was a fool before."

"Tell me something I don't know," he said with a roll of his eyes.

His tone grated at me, but I let it slide.

"I thought eliminating her was what was best, for us and our pack," I went on. "But I couldn't do it either. And I've realized now that I'm not supposed to be able to do it. She's my mate—our mate—and it's our job to protect her."

He arched an eyebrow at me. "What happened?" His nostrils flared and his shoulders bunched with hostility. "Did you hurt her?"

"Calm yourself," I soothed, holding up my hands in reassurance. "No, I didn't hurt her. I couldn't."

"Then what happened?" he demanded.

I pursed my lips, not wanting to tell him what had transpired between the princess and me. Mostly because I knew it would wound him. And after all I had done already today, I didn't want to cause him further pain.

He stormed toward me, clenching his fists at his sides. "What did you do?"

Dammit.

"I couldn't help myself, okay?" I barked defensively. "She threw herself at me wearing practically nothing, and the mate bond took over."

Murder blazed in his eyes like green fire. "You fucked her?"

"No," I hedged, averting my guilty gaze. "Just some kissing and petting."

"You bastard!" he yelled, then his fist slammed against the side of my face, the force of it making me slip off the bed to the floor.

"I know, okay!" I shouted, holding my hands up again, both to disarm him and to shield against another blow. "You have every right to hate me. But I want to fix it."

He snarled at me, shaking his head as he began to pace in front of the bed. "After all the shit you gave me for giving in to her, and you went so much farther than I let myself go."

I sighed, the weight of my shame pressing down on me. "Tell me how to fix it, Tannin."

He shook his head again. "Look, I'm glad you came to your senses and realized we're not meant to harm Aliya, but I don't know how we move forward. I can't stand the thought of you touching her."

Jealousy coiled inside my gut. "And I can't stand the thought of *you* touching her. So where do we go from here? We obviously can't abandon her."

Tannin paced for several long seconds, then slowed to a stop. "What if... What if we worked out how to share her?" he suggested.

"What?" I balked.

"We're both mated to her," he said. "That had to have happened for a reason. And it's not entirely unheard of for wolves to have more than one partner."

"Yeah, but for *male* wolves to have more than one *female* partner," I corrected, my upper lip twitching in disgust. "Not the other way around. And those unions don't happen when there's a mate bond involved. Mating to more than one person doesn't happen."

"Well, it has," Tannin countered. "And seeing as how we can't kill her or each other, the only reasonable option left is to come to some sort of agreement where we both get to have her."

My insides were burning and clenching with possessive rage. Male wolves didn't *share* women. That wasn't how we operated. Especially not an Alpha like me. And that thought alone made me want to rip his throat out with my teeth.

Tannin perched on the bed next to where I still sat on the floor. "Look, I know it's not ideal, but mate bonds are the most sacred thing in our world. I don't think it's a coincidence that we, the leaders of the black wolf pack, both mated to the princess of Varinya. Fate has some sort of grand plan. We'd be foolish to stray from it."

I didn't like any of the words coming out of his mouth, but I couldn't deny the truth that resonated in my soul.

"You really think we can share her? Without killing each other?" I asked, a growl rumbling in my chest.

"You're my best friend," he said. "The two of us have been closer than brothers our whole lives. I think if any two wolves can share a woman, it's us."

I sighed through the low growl that wouldn't stop rattling my throat. He did have a point. "How are we going to make it work? There have to be ground rules."

He nodded, rubbing his chin thoughtfully. "Well, I think we have to agree that neither of us is intimate with her alone."

"You're suggesting we lie with her at the same time?" I asked.

"Can you think of a better arrangement? Would you want me touching her beyond your reach?"

I snarled. "No."

"Then there you have it," he said. "But none of that means anything without her consent. We've both treated her like shit. I think we need to tell her the truth. All of it. And leave the decision up to her."

My heart fell. Would she even want me after the way I'd acted today? I'd fingered her until she came apart so perfectly, then I'd snapped at her to leave. She'd looked so hurt. Would she be willing to give me a second chance? Could I live with it if she chose to only be with Tannin and reject me?

Well, if she did, it would be my own fault. Then I would do everything I could to win back her favor and prove myself a mate she could depend on.

"How do you think she will take it?" I asked in a reserved, doubtful tone. "I mean, the black wolves are the enemy of her kingdom. Do you think she would disregard that because her kingdom fell?"

"I don't know," he said. "But she has such a kind heart. I think once she sees the depth of our devotion to her, she'll come around."

I nodded, still doubtful. "Okay, but let's hold off on telling her about the pack coming soon. At least until we know what to do about them."

"Any thoughts on that yet?" he asked.

I shook my head, and it felt heavy on my shoulders. "No."

"I don't feel good about lying to her," Tannin lamented.

I hopped back onto the bed and put a hand on his back. "It's for her own protection. Until we figure out how to handle the relations between her and the pack, it's best for her not to know about them. For now, we just need to make amends with her and prove ourselves to her. If this is fate, then the rest will reveal itself in due time."

He nodded. "Okay. I can live with that." Then he turned and smiled at me. "Thank you."

I frowned. "For what?"

"For not killing her," he said. "For being the Alpha I always thought you were."

My heart squeezed. I really did love Tannin like a brother. We'd been through so much together, and the thought that I'd almost lost both him and Aliya because of my arrogance and pride brought me great shame. I'd never let that happen again.

"I'll do my best to live up to your expectations," I said sincerely. "And hers. From now on, I'm going to do right by her. Both of you."

He hugged me, and though we'd shared brief embraces in the past after battle, this one felt different. I didn't truly know if I could share the princess without some adjustment, but if I had to share a mate with anyone, I was glad it was Tannin.

I just hoped it wasn't too late for either of us. Our fate hung in Aliya's hands now. And I didn't like our chances.

CHAPTER 15

ALIYA

By the time I finally came back inside, I was exhausted and covered in sweat. The sun had fully set, and night was creeping up the eastern sky. I had managed to hone my targeting and narrow my impact, causing only as much damage as I wanted.

I'd practiced first on shrubs and trees in the forest, then on birds I spotted in the branches. I only killed the first one, then afterward I'd learned to soften my blows to merely knock them off their perches.

I felt bad for the dead dove. She hadn't deserved to die for my training, and I'd felt compelled to honor her sacrifice. So I picked up her body when I was done and brought her with me inside. I could add her to dinner. Though, at this point, I didn't care if Jax and Tannin ate or not.

To my surprise, both of them were busily working in the kitchen when I walked in. Tannin was chopping vegetables, and Jax was stirring something in a big pot on the stove.

They both paused their work when I entered and turned to smile at me.

"There she is," Tannin greeted, and the charm on his handsome face made my insides melt against my will. "Where did you wander off to?"

"Er…"

I was lost for words. Not only because I hadn't planned an alibi, but also because the scene playing out before me was so beyond my expectations that it left me dumbfounded.

"I was just practicing my skill with a slingshot," I lied on the spot, then held up the dead dove by its feet. "Figured we'd need other sources of meat than just the chickens."

"Oh, good," Jax said, coming to me and taking the dove from my hand. "I can add it to the stew. But, Aliya, you really shouldn't be outside alone. It's dangerous out there."

The look on his face was so sincere and devoid of his typical snark that all I could do was stare at him. And did he just say my name? He usually only referred to me as *Princess*.

"Uh, okay," I stammered. Who were these guys?

Jax took the bird to the counter and began plucking the feathers. "Tannin and I thought we'd make *you* dinner tonight. You know... to show our appreciation for everything you've done for us."

My eyes widened, my bewilderment growing to the point of stupefaction. What the hell was going on here? Was I dreaming?

"So, why don't you go take a nice bath or something and just relax until dinner is ready?" Tannin suggested.

"O-okay..." I mumbled in a daze, then walked like a zombie out of the kitchen.

Was this actually happening? Tannin had always been the nicer of the two, but after he'd run out on me this morning, I'd expected him to continue to avoid me. And Jax? He was never nice. Even when he was giving me unbridled pleasure, he was kind of an asshole about it, and especially after.

What had caused this sudden turn in them? Maybe I'd misjudged them... Or maybe they were up to something.

I wasn't about to let my guard down just because their attitudes had suddenly changed. I wasn't that easy or that foolish. Not anymore. I was the princess of Varinya, and no matter what tricks they pulled, I was still going to banish them from my castle.

However, since the responsibility of preparing food was off my shoulders—for the first time in over a year—I was going to do what Tannin suggested and relax. I was bone-deep exhausted after all the magical energy I'd expended today. And a long, hot bath sounded lovely!

As soon as I got up to my room, I filled the tub with the hottest water I could stand. Then I stripped out of my dirty clothes and slowly sank into it, goosebumps of pleasure covering my skin as the heat saturated into my sore muscles.

Ahhh. Heavenly.

I must have dozed off because a knock on my door made me snap to awareness, my jumpy movements sending water spilling over the edges of the tub.

"Aliya? Dinner is ready," Tannin called through the door. "Take your time."

Damn, how long had I been asleep? Long enough for my fingers to be pruney and the water to be tepid, obviously.

I got out, dried myself off, and put on a simple yet elegant dress befitting a princess. Nothing too flattering or ostentatious. I was done trying to impress those men, and I wanted to be comfortable in my own home.

When I entered the dining room, I was shocked by how artfully the table had been set. Bowls of stew were placed in front of the three chairs at the end of the table, and a dish of roasted vegetables sat in the center, surrounded by candlesticks that lent a cozy orange glow to the room.

Jax and Tannin were standing behind the table, apparently waiting patiently for me.

Tannin pulled out my chair as I approached, then tucked it in after I sat. Then they both took their seats on either side of me, looking at me with some emotion I couldn't decipher. Whatever it was though, made my insides feel warm and gooey.

I looked away, unwilling to let their gazes affect me, and focused instead on the food in front of me.

"This looks really good," I said, my tone somewhat reserved. "Thank you."

And it smelled good, too.

I lifted the spoon from the bowl, careful not to let any of the stew spill, and blew on it to cool it. I could feel their eyes on me the whole time, but I kept my eyes fixed on liquid and chunks in the end of my spoon.

Tentatively, I touched the broth to my lips, then put the spoon in my mouth when the heat wasn't too much.

"Mmm," I hummed in delight. It was so hearty and savory, and the meat and vegetables were the perfect texture. I hadn't tasted stew this good since before the kitchen staff fell ill.

"Do you like it?" Jax asked, watching me as I swallowed.

I nodded, my enjoyment of the flavors lowering my defenses. "Yes, it's really delicious."

He smiled a beautiful smile. "I'm glad. It's an old family recipe, but I haven't cooked in ages, so I'm relieved it has your approval."

Then they began eating as well, and we fell into an oddly comfortable silence.

Maybe it was their new demeanors, or the comfort-food feel of the stew, or perhaps the cozy glow of the candles, but a deep sense of contentment settled into my bones. Last night, when I'd made them dinner and we sat together like this, I'd been too full of excited energy to enjoy their presence.

How ironic that I only appreciated their company when I knew they'd soon be gone.

No. I couldn't begin to question myself. Couldn't allow doubt to get in. Not now when this was so close to being over. When they were gone, I would stop wanting them so badly. Out of sight, out of mind.

"Aliya," Tannin said, breaking the peaceful silence. "Jax and I have something to confess to you."

And just like that, my comfort vanished like the flame of a candle being snuffed out. In its place, a heart-skipping curiosity bloomed in my chest.

I wiped my lips with my napkin, then set my hands in my lap. "Alright," I said, hiding my intrigue.

The two of them exchanged glances, making my interest spike further.

"Well, first off, we both owe you an apology for the way we've behaved toward you," Jax began, his expression endearingly awkward and vulnerable. "Me, especially. I have been inexcusably cruel and dismissive of you, and I'm truly sorry."

He reached over and put his hand gently on my arm. The sensuous heat of his touch mingled with the sincerity of his words had my walls crumbling.

"The truth is, Tannin and I have mate bonded to you," he confessed.

It took me a moment to remember that I wasn't supposed to know that. I scrunched my brow at him, feigning confusion. "Mate bonded?"

Tannin put his hand on my other arm, making me burn even hotter, and I turned to face him.

"We are both black wolves," he said like it hurt to speak the words.

I gasped, a sincere reaction to hearing him say it out loud.

"We're so sorry for keeping it from you," Tannin added hastily, as if afraid I'd freak out. "Things were so frantic when we first arrived, and Jax was dying, and then you healed him. There just hasn't been a good chance to tell you the truth. And with you being the princess of a kingdom that has hated us for centuries, we were afraid how you'd take it."

I didn't know what to say. I knew all this already, but the fact that they were telling me, even though they feared my reaction and rightly so... I was utterly speechless.

"It's not a good excuse, by any means," Jax said, "but the reason we've been so strange with you is because of the mate bond. The last thing either of us expected was to be mated to the princess of our ancient hunters. We tried to fight the feeling, to spare all three of us from unwanted complications... but we can't fight it anymore."

My heart began to pound, and my core throbbed with a shocked thrill. Did Jax really just say what I thought I'd just heard? Jax? The man who'd made me feel so incredible earlier today, before pulling the rug out from under me.

He leaned closer, and I could feel the heat of his breath on my face. "I'm not strong enough to resist you any longer. And I know you feel it too. That's why you came to my room today. Tell me I'm wrong."

Memories of those sultry lips and his skilled fingers flashed inside my mind. I squirmed in my seat.

"No, you're not wrong," I confessed breathily. "I feel insatiably drawn to both of you..." I bashfully glanced at Tannin, and the heat in his eyes only intensified the growing need inside me.

"Good," Jax said, closing his eyes briefly in relief. Then he squeezed his hand on my arm. "Can you forgive us for the way we treated you? For keeping the truth of what we are to you?"

My chest tightened with heavy sadness.

"I don't know," I said honestly. "Black wolves are the ancient enemies my forefathers died to protect us from. I don't know how I can overlook that."

"The same way we can overlook the fact that you're the heir of the kingdom that slaughtered our ancestors," Jax said, an edge growing in his voice. "It wasn't easy, least of all for me. But this bond links us in a way that's unbreakable. And now that I've found you, it doesn't matter to me who or what you are."

I swallowed, my insides so tight with desire, I could barely think straight.

"I know it's a lot to take in," Tannin said. "Finding out that we're wolves must be overwhelming, and I'm sure this bond has been making you feel crazy and confused."

I nodded. "Yes, it has."

"For two wolves to mate to the same woman has never been heard of among our people," Tannin continued. "We can't explain how or why it happened, and it's a struggle for Jax and me to know how to handle it, so we decided to leave the choice up to you."

My breath hitched. Surely, they didn't want me to choose between them.

Jax's thumb began to rub lightly over my arm. "Our proposal is that the three of us indulge this bond as nature intended. Together."

"Together?" Blood rose to the surface of my skin everywhere, making me feel hot and a little lightheaded.

They wanted... me and both of them? At the same time? Okay, now I knew I was dreaming. This couldn't be real!

"Only if you want to," Tannin reassured me softly. "We'll both understand if you can't see past our differences or forgive us for our actions. Neither of us is going to force you to do anything you don't want to do. What happens between us, if anything, is completely up to you."

My hormones were racing rapidly now, making every inch of me burn for them. It was all I could do not to throw myself at either one of them right this instant.

Thankfully, I was able to hold onto the last remaining thread of my rational functions.

"I-I need some time to think about this," I said slowly.

Longing pinched Jax's features, but he nodded. "Of course." He withdrew his hand, and the absence of his warm touch made me feel strangely destitute—like I never wanted him to not touch me ever again.

"Take your time. We'll respect whatever you decide." Tannin did the same, and though my heart screamed for his touch to be restored, I was grateful for the chance to clear my head.

I rose and made a beeline for my room. This was all too much.

This day had been a cruel emotional whirlwind. So much flirting and teasing, so much rejection followed by amazing kisses and touches. And now they were laying themselves before me with open arms, offering the greatest temptation I'd ever known!

Wicked, powerful Jax, and sweet, gentle Tannin, both touching me together, kissing me together, teaching my body all the ways to feel pleasure together. It was a dream come true. And my insides ached painfully, blissfully, to experience every sinful thing they had to offer.

But I'd spent the entire day plotting their banishment. And they were still my enemies. Did their confession really change anything? I still didn't know if I could trust them. My way forward wasn't certain, and I hated that.

I had a big decision to make, and my whole future depended on me making the right one.

CHAPTER 16

ALIYA

My heart was fluttering like an excited bird in a cage as I roamed the castle in search of Jax and Tannin. After several hours of laborious back-and-forth deliberating, I had made my decision, and to say I was nervous about declaring it was the biggest understatement of my life.

I found them in the den. Tannin was sitting on the couch, hunched forward with his hands clasped between his thighs as one knee bounced anxiously. The concern on his handsome face was almost precious. My vulnerable, gentle Tannin.

Jax stood next to the crackling fireplace, leaning beside it with his hand braced on the top of the hearth, his serious expression fixed on the dancing flames. The light cast on his features made him look even more predatory. Beautiful and deadly, that's what he was. Like a black widow. Like a siren.

When I walked towards them, they both straightened their postures and turned to me with expectant yet apprehensive gazes. Even though a tremor quaked through my limbs, commanding the attention of such powerful creatures like them gave me the confidence I desperately needed. I was the one with the power in this moment, and I had to wield it wisely.

"This wasn't an easy choice to make," I prefaced, my voice ringing in the silence. "Though my kingdom is all but gone, I am still its princess, and you are black wolves. My whole life, I was raised to fear and hate your kind, as I'm sure you were mine."

I paused, letting that resonate with them for a moment. Their features sagged with despair, and seeing it made my heart ache.

"That being said, I can't deny the powerful hold this bond has over my body and my heart," I continued. "I have been alone for so long, and the fact that the first two men I've encountered in sixteen months were mated to me must mean something. I feel like I'd be doing myself a disservice by denying the opportunity to explore this connection we share."

Their features lifted with hope, and I fought the urge to smile in relief.

"I'm willing to try," I said. "But, after everything that's happened, how do I know I can trust you?"

Tannin shot to his feet and rushed toward me, taking my hands in his. "You *can* trust us, Aliya. We are fated by the stars to honor and protect you, to cherish you. And we will do whatever it takes to reassure you it's true."

His words touched me, warming my insides and soothing the anxious tension in my muscles. Tannin, I believed. He was the sincere one, the kind one.

But Jax was a different animal entirely. Mysterious, elusive, tricky.

He walked toward me with slow, measured steps, as if approaching a forest fawn he feared he might spook. Then he stopped inches from me, lifted his hand to my face, and oh, so gently brushed his knuckles down the side of my cheek, sending electricity sizzling over my flesh and making my eyelids flutter.

"I know we haven't given you much reason to trust us," he said softly. "But give us the chance to prove our devotion to you. I promise you won't be disappointed."

The dark promise in his sensuous tone sent a thrill stabbing through me, and I wanted so badly to surrender myself to it—to him.

But I fought it, holding my ground for at least a bit longer.

"Devotion?" I asked. "Only yesterday, you were mocking me like I was an ignorant child. And just today, you shouted orders for me to leave your presence. How am I to believe this sudden *devotion* won't be washed away by the tide of your next mood swing?"

He nodded, pulling his lips between his teeth in an acceptance of guilt. "I can't apologize enough for my earlier behavior. But I only acted that way because I was fighting a losing battle with this all-consuming hold you have over me. I'm done fighting. I surrender to you, my mate, my queen. I am yours, if you'll have me."

To hear Jax, this powerful, brutal Alpha, say those words to me…I couldn't describe the way that made me feel. Strong and weak at the same time, vanity and humility all mixed into a potent cocktail of devastating desire and undying affection.

I was gone.

I nodded, letting myself nuzzle into the knuckles he still held against my cheek. He opened his hand and gently cupped my jaw.

I licked my lips, trying to force a breath into my lungs. "So, um… what do we do now?"

A wicked smile spread across Jax's beautiful lips, and he curled his fingertips teasingly under my chin. "Now, we show you just how much we adore you."

Before I knew what was happening, Jax picked me up and hoisted me over his shoulder, carrying me across the den and up the stairs. His free hand spread over my ass as we ascended, kneading my flesh, his fingers dipping so close to my center that I couldn't help but squirm in anticipation.

Tannin followed behind us, holding my gaze the whole time with both feral need and tender love. I didn't care where they were taking me, I only knew I couldn't wait to get there.

Once in the hall on the top floor, I heard a door open behind me, and Jax carried me into a room. Tannin closed the door as Jax set me down on my feet. I only distantly realized we were in Jax's room as both stared at me like wolves about to pounce on unsuspecting prey.

Jax reached out to run his hand up the back of my head, gently raking his fingers over my scalp.

"We'll go slow," he said in a deep, gravelly voice that had my core clenching. "If there's anything you don't like, tell us. We only exist to please you."

I nodded dazedly, and then they descended on me.

With his hand behind my head, Jax pulled my face toward his and pressed his lips to mine. Tannin came up beside me, his hands gripping my hips as he nibbled and sucked on my neck.

Jax's kisses were slower now than this afternoon, but no less rough and demanding. His tongue invaded my mouth like a conquering warrior, and I welcomed his dominion.

At the same time as Tannin's teasing kisses were on my neck and earlobe. Both their hands were everywhere—my breasts, my waist, my ass. They had me in a dizzying thrall from which I never wanted to surface.

With one last nip at my bottom lip, Jax turned my face toward Tannin, offering my mouth to his gentle yet hungry kisses. Jax went to work unfastening the laces of the back of my dress, kissing my shoulder as the falling gown exposed more flesh. The fabric dropped and pooled around my ankles, leaving me standing in only my scant underwear.

They took turns claiming my mouth as they each removed their articles of clothing. It was a struggle not to get lost in the maelstrom of pleasure that their demanding lips and tongues.

It didn't matter that I had seen them both naked before. That was a whole lifetime ago, and in a completely different context. Before they were mine to touch, to kiss, to lick.

Seeing them now, they were gods. Their bodies were chiseled perfection. Hardened muscles under smooth, suntanned skin. And the proof of their desire for me, the stiff appendages standing at attention between their legs—I couldn't take my eyes off them even as they continued to block my view with their feverish kisses.

Together, they guided me to bed, and I clumsily fell onto the foot of the mattress as they kissed and caressed me.

Jax slid his hand between my legs, cupping the flesh of my thigh, then dragging his hand down to my knee and pulling it outward. Obediently, I spread my legs wider, desperate for whatever he intended.

With my legs open, my center fully exposed, they both drew back enough to stare at my pink folds, the heat of their gazes making my cheeks heat furiously.

Jax leaned close to Tannin, speaking softly into his ear while his eyes burned into mine. "Taste her, brother. She's delicious."

Like a starved man, Tannin dropped to his knees before me and brought his face to my center. I watched his every move, barely breathing. Finally, he stuck out his tongue and gently flicked my clit with the tip.

I sucked in a sharp gasp at the incredible sensation, and he took that as his invitation to proceed, closing his mouth over my flesh and devouring me like a delicacy. I arched onto the mattress, throwing my head back as his tongue roamed and swirled and licked. I was now a slave to the incredible pleasure.

Jax claimed my mouth once more, then kissed down my neck and over my collarbone. He stopped at my breast, sucking my nipple into his mouth and flicking it with his tongue. I gasped loudly at the double assault, my nipples tingling with pleasure.

All the while, Jax was stroking his rigid cock with one hand, and the sight made my mouth water.

Tentatively, I reached out and lightly touched the rounded tip. His cock was so warm and soft yet hard.

Amazing.

Jax hissed, and I instinctively retracted my hand, afraid that I'd hurt him somehow.

But he pushed his pelvis closer, then took my hand and guided it back to his cock, silently instructing me with his fingers to close my hand around the shaft.

This shot the most potent excitement through me, intensifying the magic Tannin's mouth was working between my legs. His cock was so hard, yet so smooth. I never would have thought that such a thing could be pretty, but his was beautiful.

Curiously, with my hand still closed around the shaft, I began to stroke it like I saw him do, flicking a glance at his face to gauge his reaction to see if I was doing it right. His eyelids fluttered closed, a long, low breath escaping his lips.

I wanted to make him feel good. No, I *needed* to.

I tightened my grip slightly, running my hand up and down a little faster, and he grunted in pleasure. Staring at it transfixed, my mouth ached to taste it. Such a thought would have been absurd to me a few days ago, but their mouths felt incredible between my legs. Would Jax enjoy my mouth on his cock?

Too enticed to resist anymore, I leaned forward and gently ran the tip of my tongue over the tip.

"Oh, fuck," he hissed, looking down at me with heavy-lidded eyes, then gave an eager nod.

Yes!

I opened my mouth over his dick and wrapped my lips around it, not expecting the sharp thrill that pulsed inside me at having his cock spreading my lips. Holy gods! Just as I did with my hands, I moved my mouth up and down his shaft, pressing my tongue over his tip as I took it deeper.

His sharp gasps and deep groans encouraged me. I tightened my lips and groaned myself as he began to thrust forward and back, sliding his cock between my lips over and over.

Abruptly, he pulled free, and Tannin's mouth left my center. For a split second, confusion and self-doubt gripped me. Were they going to abandon me again after we'd shared so much?

But they didn't leave me. Instead, together my mates flipped me onto my stomach over the corner of the bed, Tannin taking position at my backside and Jax standing in front of me with his hard length pointed right at my face.

Something nudged between my legs, rubbing over my moist entrance and teasing me into desperation.

"Do you want Tannin to fuck you, Princess?" Jax asked darkly.

"Yes, yes!" I whimpered. If that's what was going to make this incredible ache go away, it was exactly what I wanted.

Jax nodded to Tannin behind me, and slowly, Tannin pressed his cock into me. Inch by slow inch, he penetrated my body, stretching and filling me until he was buried fully inside.

The sensation was mind-blowing in the extreme, but almost too much. I felt so full and achy in a new sort of way, and prayed they knew how to make it better.

Then Tannin gradually pulled out then thrust back in, forcing a groan from my lips as his dick hit my pleasure center deep in my core. He repeated this over and over, falling into a torturous rhythm that I never wanted to end.

Jax rubbed his shaft in front of me, then guided it to my mouth.

"Suck my cock, beautiful," he commanded in a low growl.

I eagerly parted my lips, and he shoved his dick into my mouth, the thrusting of his hips mimicking the same pace as Tannin's behind me. Together, they were conquering my body in every way imaginable and it was incredible.

It was too much and yet not enough. I could hardly stand the pleasure they were giving me, but I never wanted it to stop.

The sounds of their groans amplified my own pleasure, knowing they were drawing as much ecstasy from my body as they were delivering to mine. If it weren't for Jax's cock filling my mouth, my moans would surely drown out theirs.

"She's moaning on my dick," Jax panted, tangling his fingers into my hair. "Fuck her harder. I want to feel her screams."

Tannin obeyed his Alpha, thrusting into me harder and faster until I was indeed screaming as Jax had foretold. Pleasure erupted in my core and radiated outward, making me convulse and cry out.

"Oh, gods!" Jax hissed, suddenly yanking his cock from my mouth. He gripped it hard and furiously stroked it as creamy white liquid shot from the tip onto the floor.

His body shuddered in front of me, strained grunts bursting from him until he stopped his frenzied squeezing.

Seconds later, Tannin followed us into bliss, slamming into me one last time and letting out a long, loud moan. His hot seed spilled inside me, his pleasure drawing out the last of my own pulses.

He pulled out of me, then they dragged me up to the head of the bed and snuggled in on either side of me. Our heavy panting formed a chorus as their hands continued to roam my body like a playground.

These men were my mates, my saviors, my monsters. And as sleep crept over me, I knew they would be the ruin of me.

The last princess of Varinya. Mated to two black wolves. Oh, the irony of it all...

CHAPTER 17

TANNIN

The sun was just cresting over the mountains, its soft golden light catching in the locks of Aliya's hair that were strewn messily across the pillow beneath her head.

She was so beautiful.

I'd been awake for at least an hour, and I couldn't get enough of staring at her face as she slept, memorizing every line, angle and curve.

Last night had been wild. The memory of the three of us together was a struggle for me to get straight in my head. Not because it had been awkward or weird, but because it had felt so *right*.

Before our escapade in this room, seeing Jax touch her was a strain on me, and the very idea of her sucking his dick would have driven me to chop it off.

But the two of us working together to claim her changed everything, and watching her suck him while I took her from behind was the most incredible thing I'd ever experienced. I would never forget the muffled sound of her filled mouth as my thrusts made her come.

Jax and I naturally fell into a rhythm with her, neither one of us competing over her but rather teaming up to please her. I didn't even mind that he'd taken the lead, that our pack mentality had trickled into this unique romantic union. He was my Alpha, and I had to admit, at

119

least to myself, that I kind of enjoyed him telling me what to do with her.

Especially since he'd let me be the first to claim her pussy. Plus, I think she liked his dominance, too.

Just thinking about sex with Aliya made my erect cock twitch. I was so tempted to crawl beneath the covers and wake her up with my tongue between her legs once more, but I couldn't bring myself to disturb the peace of her slumber. And, if I were being honest, I couldn't keep my fears of the pack's arrival from creeping into my mind and making me sick with dread.

What was going to happen when they got here? How were we going to protect her?

Jax rolled over on Aliya's other side to face me, his eyes open as if he'd been awake for a while, as well.

"Hey," he whispered.

"Hey," I whispered back.

He held my gaze for a moment, and he seemed just as conflicted as I felt. "Can't sleep?"

"I can't stop worrying about what's coming," I confessed.

He gingerly propped his head on his bent arm on the pillow, careful not to unsettle Aliya. I rolled onto my side and did the same. Aliya stirred slightly, so we waited silently for a few heartbeats to make sure she was still asleep before continuing.

"Now that we have officially claimed her as our mate, the pack will have to concede to our union," he whispered, though he couldn't hide his doubt from me.

"She's not a black wolf," I countered. "Our laws won't apply to her."

"Anyone who mates with a black wolf becomes a member of the pack by default," he stated, as if quoting some ancient text I'd never seen.

"Even the Varinyan princess?" I asked. "You know as well as I do that they'll want her head on a pike."

His jaw ticked. "I am their Alpha. My word is law, and they will recognize her as a member of the pack if I command it so."

I raised a dubious eyebrow at him. "Are you certain of that?"

"Let anyone who disagrees challenge my role," he said. "I will destroy them."

I sighed at his tedious ego. "One or two, perhaps. But more than that will be outraged by her continued existence. You really think you can fend off the entire pack?"

His gaze fell on her face, and his features softened. "I will do whatever it takes to keep her safe."

I chewed on my bottom lip, debating whether to ask the question on my mind. "What if that means siding against the pack?"

"It won't come to that," he snapped in a harsh whisper.

"But what if it does?" I insisted.

His jaw clenched again as he looked protectively down at her. "Like I said, I will do what I must for her."

I nodded, and we both stared at her for a long moment.

"We should tell her the truth," I whispered. "I don't like lying to her. Not after what we shared."

He exhaled slowly through his nose. "I know. We will tell her, but not yet. I just want to savor this bliss for a little while longer."

I didn't say anything to that. I knew how he felt. A big part of me wished we could stay here like this forever, just the three of us in this castle. I wished he hadn't called the pack, then they'd never show up.

But the reality was that they were on their way, and they'd be here any day now. And as much as I wanted to enjoy this carefree fairytale version of our threesome, the guilt over keeping the whole truth from her was eating me up inside.

"I'm telling her tonight," I whispered.

His eyes whipped at me angrily, but I wasn't backing down on this.

"We'll have one last day of peace and fun, but that's it," I declared. "She needs time to prepare for their arrival. We all do, as a team. Letting her go unaware any longer isn't fair to her."

He simmered over that for a moment, then gave a stifled scoff. "Fine. I guess you're right. I hate it when that happens."

I couldn't help but smirk at that. It always made me proud when I was able to change Jax's mind and make him see reason, as rare of an occasion as that was. I believed the princess softened his stubbornness, but only a little.

"In that case, shall we wake her up?" He flared his eyebrows, licking his lips suggestively.

"You read my mind," I murmured.

He grinned, then before I could make a move in that direction, he dove under the covers and situated himself between her legs.

Asshole.

She sucked in a breath, arching her back against the sheets, letting me know that he had begun his feast of her pussy. Her thick lashes parted, her amber eyes locking on my face as she roused.

"Good morning, gorgeous," I purred, caressing the side of her face with my fingertips.

"G—mor—ugh!" she panted.

I snickered, then lowered myself over her to greet her lips with a soft kiss. She opened her mouth, her tongue flicking out in a silent demand for deeper affection as her hand wound around the back of my head and pulled me in closer.

It appeared I had two Alphas now, and I was more than willing to obey her commands.

I swallowed her moans as I kissed her, tracing teasing lines over her tits and belly while Jax ate her out. I whipped the covers back, needing to see what he was doing to her.

His face was buried between her creamy thighs, which clenched around the sides of his head as she writhed in pleasure. And when she came, she squealed tightly into my mouth, followed by a series of sweet whimpers.

Jax lapped at her until her tremors waned, then slid off the foot of the bed, pulled her down by the ankles, and flipped her around like she weighed nothing.

"Bend your knees for me, baby girl," Jax instructed.

She curled her legs beneath her, and Jax helped her spread them, propping up her ass just high enough for his pelvis to reach.

"Good," he growled, then he guided his cock to her entrance and pushed inside, making her arch again and thrust those perfect tits toward me. "Now, let's show Tannin how good that little mouth of yours feels."

Her eyes opened dazedly, falling on me as she bit her bottom lip. I slid down the mattress, positioning myself in front of her.

"Only if you want to," I said, though I was aching to have her in whatever way she'd let me.

"I do," she panted, then lowered herself over my cock, stretched her lips, taking me inside her mouth.

Fuck, that felt incredible! *She* was incredible.

Her mouth was so warm, so wet, and so gentle. Her tongue slid up and down my shaft, her eyes closing like I tasted delicious to her. I couldn't stop watching her enjoy me.

Jax's thrusts increased, pounding into her rougher than I had last night, and that only seemed to invigorate her sucking.

I couldn't take it much longer. She felt too damn good. And with Jax making her moan, the vibrations in her sweet mouth were pushing me close to the edge far too fast.

"I'm gonna come," I hissed and reached down to withdraw my cock.

But her hand whipped out and grabbed my wrist, her eyes fixing on mine with a knowing warning, and she took me in deeper.

Holy shit!

I came hard, groaning loudly as every muscle in my body clenched in failed restraint. Her eyes widened in surprise as my cum spilled into her mouth, but she only paused for a moment before continuing to bob her head.

"Good girl," Jax growled, slapping a hand against her ass before buckling over her and finding his own release with a vicious howl.

I felt her mouth tighten as she swallowed, then released my spent cock with a choked gasp.

Pleasure was still wavering through me, my cock still twitching from what she'd done, but I bent forward and cupped her face in my hand.

"You didn't have to do that," I panted.

She wiped her mouth as Jax pulled out of her. "I know. But I wanted to try it."

My heart warmed as I leaned in to plant a soft kiss on her forehead.

"That's our girl," Jax praised before going into the bathroom and returning with a small towel. He gently cleaned her with it before wiping himself down too.

She blushed, looking both so innocent and so insanely seductive.

She was perfect.

"How would you like us to wake you up like that every morning?" Jax asked.

Aliya giggled as she sat with her legs curled to the side. "I don't think I could handle that."

Jax barked a laugh. "We'll see about that, beautiful." He winked, and her blush darkened.

He pulled on a pair of pants, then slapped my shoulder. "Get dressed. We're going to make our mate a breakfast fit for a queen."

I reluctantly rolled out of bed and found my pants from last night. What I really wanted to do was stay in bed with her all day, even if all we did was kiss and talk. I wanted to know everything about her before we lost the opportunity.

But Jax was right. She deserved to have us fawn over her for one last day. Before we told her the truth about the wolves, and possibly ruined what could have been... forever.

CHAPTER 18
ALIYA

The room was quiet in the wake of my men's exit, but the thoughts roaring in my head were so loud they would've drowned out anything else regardless.

I didn't want to hear them. I wanted some time and space to think. Or maybe to not think at all.

After the intensity of last night, I certainly hadn't expected them to wake me up with more carnal play. My body was sore in an admittedly delightful way, making it easy to curl up beneath the sheets and surrender to the comfort they offered.

I wanted to stay in this bed all day. It smelled like them.

I smelled like them.

And I was a traitor for loving that smell. I was a traitor for going along with their fun this morning. And I was a traitor for feeling anything for them but hatred.

They hadn't known I'd been awake during their whispered conversation. I hadn't even been sure I was truly awake, that it wasn't part of some dream, until Jax's tongue ran up between my thighs.

Then, I'd known it was all true. That they'd been lying to me this whole time. I'd believed them about everything they'd said. I'd trusted them... but it was all for nothing.

Their pack would arrive soon, and according to Tannin, they'd want to put me to death.

I bit my lip. Tannin's lies hit harder than anything else. He'd been so sweet, so wonderful the whole time I'd known him. How could he hide something so important from me?

I hated myself for going along with what they'd done to me this morning, for not putting a stop to their seduction and making some excuse to make them leave. I told myself at the time that I needed to act normally, that if I didn't play along, they'd get suspicious, and I'd lose their trust.

But the truth was, everything they did to me felt so good. I couldn't bring myself to deny them even though I knew who and what they truly were, and what they'd been planning all along.

Now I felt dirty and ashamed. I was a disgrace to my people. I'd given myself to a pair of wolves who were only using me. I'd been so blinded by my immature, bullshit fantasies of love and fate, I hadn't been able to see what was right in front of me.

Why hadn't I questioned if they had a pack? Jax had said he was the Alpha, and I had foolishly assumed that was just part of the dynamic between the two of them. I was so stupid for not realizing he was *the leader* of the entire black wolf pack.

I put my hands over my face, wishing I could rub my idiocy away. *Stupid girl.*

Their pack was coming, here to Varinya, and I could only assume it was for the purpose of conquering it for themselves. I'd had a plan to get Jax and Tannin off the property, but what was I going to do about an invasion?

I sat up in bed as a sad thought slithered through my mind, silencing all the others.

Was Varinya even worth protecting anymore? There was no one left to even call my home a kingdom. The villagers, the castle staff, and my parents were all dead and gone.

Maybe I should just leave. I could pack up my necessities while my *mates* were making breakfast and sneak out before they knew I was gone. I'd throw a few outfits in a bag, grab Willow, and slip out through the main doors.

The main problem however, was that I wouldn't be able to get any food for my journey. Jax and Tannin were in the kitchen, and they'd see me if I tried to rifle through the garden. How long would I last without food?

Where would I even go? Ashala, the neighboring kingdom, was three days' travel from here, probably more with my limited knowledge of the terrain and poor navigation skills. If I was cautious and constantly alert, I stood a small chance of defending myself against predators with my magic. Though I didn't like my odds against a cusith, let alone more than one of them.

And if I managed to reach Ashala, what would I do? They wouldn't believe I was who I claimed to be, not without proof. I didn't know what I could snatch before being caught to show them as evidence of my pedigree. And even if I could, they might not care. What good was a princess without a people to rule?

I was little more than a useless woman now. Especially to an outsider.

If I was able to escape and arrive anywhere safely, I'd have to completely start over. And the world wasn't kind to lone, nameless women, especially those with any manner of beauty.

The door opened, and Tannin peered inside. Dammit, why did he have to be so handsome? A wolf in sheep's clothing, indeed.

"Breakfast is ready, Your Highness," he said with a flirtatious wink.

I forced my lips to spread into a small smile. "Okay. Thank you. I'll be right down."

He puckered his lips and made a smooching sound before ducking back out into the hall.

With wobbly legs, I climbed off the bed and crossed the hall to my room. I didn't feel like wearing a dress today, but I had to act like everything was normal. If I wore anything that hinted at function over fashion, they might get suspicious. So, I put on a simple summer dress with little frill—one that would be easy to run in if needed.

Then I brushed out my hair, leaving it down, and took my time joining them downstairs.

Just like last night, the dining room table was set with care. In the center was a big tray of scrambled eggs, bread, and various jams from the pantry.

Jax pulled out my chair for me before returning to his seat to my right, brushing his hand lightly down my arm as he did so. I hated how good it felt to be touched by him. How it made my insides feel like molten lava.

"Did you sleep well?" he asked as he spooned a large helping of eggs onto my plate.

"Yes," I said, picking up my fork. The eggs smelled delicious, but my appetite was non-existent.

"Are you alright?" Tannin asked, his brows pinching in concern.

"Uh, yes, why?" I asked awkwardly.

"You just seem...a little reserved today," he said. "Did we hurt you?"

Yes. More deeply than you'll ever know.

"No," I lied with a sugary smile. "I'm just tired, and honestly a bit sore from...you know..." The memories heated my cheeks, and I hated myself even more.

Tannin pouted sweetly and nodded. "I'm sorry. If it was too much for you, we can slow things down."

Jax reached over and put his hand on my arm, rubbing his thumb back and forth. "Your comfort and peace of mind are our top priority. Whatever you need or want from us, just say it."

I want you to leave, call off your pack, and never come back.

But even as the words shot through my thoughts, I couldn't speak them aloud. I knew they were a lie. I didn't want them to leave me. They'd lied to me, manipulated me, and used me, but I still craved them like a woman lost in the desert craved water.

The look in his eyes was so sincere. I wanted to believe him.

I nodded and tucked my hair behind my ear. "Yeah, I think maybe slowing things down a bit would be good. At least for now. It's kind of a lot to process." I gave a nervous giggle.

"Of course," Jax said. "You're our mate, and it's our job to keep you happy and safe."

"Do you really mean that?" I blurted out before I could stop myself.

A serious expression fell over his face. "With all my heart." After holding my gaze meaningfully for a long moment, he patted my arm and removed his hand.

They were both still staring at me like I was a sheet of broken glass about to shatter, so I poked my fork into a clump of egg and put it in my mouth. That seemed to satisfy them, and they began eating as well.

I wanted so badly to trust what they were saying to me now. They had said they would protect me from their pack, who obviously all wanted me dead. Jax was their Alpha, their leader. If he vouched for me, would they accept me? Would our mate bond be enough for them to spare me?

But even if that did happen, I wouldn't be the princess of Varinya anymore. No matter what, I'd lose my kingdom. I didn't want to be part of their black wolf pack. Surrendering to them would be the ultimate betrayal of everything my bloodline stood for.

I wasn't sure I could relinquish my possibly meaningless title just to survive among primitive monsters who hated me. And even if they did pretend to accept me, they might still slaughter me in my sleep while Tannin and Jax had their backs turned.

No, there was only one right course of action. Only one way to preserve the sanctity of my kingdom's legacy.

I had to proceed with my original plan, and that was to coax Jax and Tannin outside the castle walls, then leave them there to greet their pack on arrival.

How were my supposed mates going to explain to their people that Varinya was now off limits? Once my magical boundary went up, there was no way they were ever getting back inside.

CHAPTER 19

JAX

Aliya's silence at breakfast concerned me. She was usually lively and chipper, but as she sat beside me at the table, she ate quietly, like a timid mouse.

Perhaps I'd been too rough with her this morning. She'd shown so much enthusiasm last night, such a willingness to learn and explore new sexual avenues. It had shocked and thrilled me when she'd started sucking my cock without any prompting from me. And fuck, it felt so damn good!

I'd let that excitement run away with me. She'd been a virgin before last night, still so innocent and fragile. I should've respected that she'd need some time to adjust before having sex again, but instead, I'd propped up her tight little ass and fucked her with wild abandon.

At the time, she'd sounded and acted like she'd enjoyed it as much as I did.

Had she only done that to please us? Was she just playing along because she felt beholden to us in some way? Or was she too shy to speak up about what she really needed? We were two strong and powerful men having our way with her, and perhaps some part of her felt helpless against us.

I'd been selfish. I'd been negligent of her needs. Would I ever stop fucking things up when it came to her? I needed to show her that she was the one in control of this unconventional relationship, and that sex wasn't a requirement for our affection.

When everyone had finished eating, an idea came to me as Tannin and I cleared the table, and I rushed to set it into motion.

"Tannin, can you handle washing the dishes on your own?" I asked as I set the last plate in the sink.

He turned to me with a frown. "Why?"

"I have an idea that I think will make Aliya happy," I said. "Finish up in here and then join us in the ballroom."

"But—"

I dashed out the archway before he could respond. I didn't want his pessimism to dissuade me from what I had in mind.

I opened the door beside the kitchen and skipped down the flight of dusty, cobweb-covered stairs. The air down in the basement was musty, made thicker by the cold temperature that rose goosebumps on my arms.

But it was perfect for chilling and preserving the hundreds of wine bottles kept in the honeycomb-style shelves lining every wall of the modest space.

I'd discovered the wine cellar two days ago during my exploration of the castle. From the dust coating every surface of this room, it appeared that no one had been down here in a very long time.

I wondered if Aliya even knew about it. If she had, she probably would've indulged during her solitude. Being alone for so long would be intolerable sober. For a wolf, it wouldn't be tolerable at all.

Wolves were pack animals. We needed each other, not only for our survival but also for our sanity. A wolf who was banished was doomed to death. On the off chance they survived the crippling isolation, they wouldn't be themselves anymore. Instead, they'd become something feral and inhuman.

I'd wondered if that was how the cusith emerged. If they were some ancient species of shifter that had been civilized once upon a time, but after being individually cut off from their packs, they'd been forced to band together once they'd mutated into whatever they were now.

I shook my head of the thoughts and began to survey the various bottles on the nearest wall. What would Aliya like?

Wine was a rarity for our pack, something we only acquired through infrequent trades. Some members brewed a sort of mead from honey and berries, but it was far too sweet for my liking. I preferred dry red wine. It was bold and hearty, like an Alpha.

But that didn't seem like it would suit the princess. She was sweet and gentle, and she deserved a drink to match.

I plucked champagne from the middle shelf and inspected the bottle. The date on the bottle was twenty years previous, and the cork was wrapped in elegant gold foil. Yes, this would do nicely. A bubbly, pink drink for my bubbly, pink girl.

I turned for the stairs, then paused. Who was I kidding? One bottle was *not* going to be enough for the three of us. I grabbed a second bottle, then jogged back up the steps.

Tannin was just rinsing off the last plate when I returned to the kitchen, and I reached over him for the cabinet where the glasses were kept.

"What are you doing?" he groused, stepping aside and drying his hands on a towel.

I pulled three champagne flutes from the cabinet. "I think we should have a little soiree today. A grand ball of our own to celebrate our union. You know, before you blow the whole thing up with your confession."

He cut me a deadpan glare.

"I know, I know. It's the right thing to do," I said. "Doesn't mean I have to be happy about it. I just want to show Aliya a nice time before it's too late."

He sighed and nodded. "Okay. It's not the worst idea you've ever had."

I snorted. "There's a Victrola and some records in the study. Set them up in the ballroom. I'll fetch our mate."

With a roll of his eyes, he strode for the study beneath the grand staircase, and I went off in search of Aliya.

After checking dozens of places throughout the castle, I finally found her in the library. The relief that crashed over me at the sight of her curled up on a couch beneath the window was palpable. Some part of me had feared she was hiding from us. From me.

I had to remember to be gentle with her. To show her the man I could be for her.

I tapped the knuckle of my index finger against the door frame, and her face shot from the book she was reading up at me. She quickly closed her book and set it aside.

"I'm surprised to find you in here," I hedged as I stepped into the room.

"I like to read in here," she said, lowering her feet to dangle off the edge of the couch. "Before you two came, I used to sleep in here for days at a time. I guess the words on the pages made me feel less alone."

Pity tightened the muscles in my throat as I came to sit beside her. "I can't imagine what it must have been like for you to be alone for so long. And after losing everyone you cared about. I'm truly sorry that happened to you."

She offered a sad smile, then shrugged. "Well, I'm not alone anymore. Now I have you and Tannin."

My heart softened, and I took her hand gently in mine. "Yes, and we will never leave your side. Unless, of course, you want us to. I know I can be a bit of an asshole, and that my past actions have given you a bad impression of me. But I want you to know that I—we—don't have any expectations of you. I don't ever want to do anything that you don't want. I only want to make you happy, whatever that means."

She nodded, and though her smile remained, there was still some unspoken sadness in her eyes.

"To that point, I have a surprise for you," I said.

She cocked her head at me with intrigue, and my smile widened in anticipation.

I stood, still loosely holding her hand. "Come with me."

She narrowed her eyes curiously but rose from the couch and let me usher her out of the library. She was quiet as I led her through the halls, and I hoped my surprise would be something she'd enjoy. I was determined to give her a fun day before our brittle utopia crumbled into oblivion.

Tannin was setting a record onto the Victrola as we entered, and when he saw us, he placed the needle on the edge of the black disk and flipped the switch on its base. Music began to play softly, a symphony of string instruments whose title I didn't know, but I still appreciated its elegant beauty.

Aliya sighed wistfully, putting her free hand to her chest. "This was my mother's favorite song."

I smiled at the nostalgic look on her face. "I thought we might have ourselves a little ball. We've gone about this courting thing all wrong, and a princess should at least have the chance to be swept off her feet by her two dashing suitors."

"Oh," she said, surprise dancing across her features.

"And what's a ball without wine?"

I placed a brief kiss on her hand, then released it and strode over to the buffet table against the wall where I'd set the champagne bottles and three glasses.

I tore the gold foil off one, then popped the cork, catching it in my palm as a flurry of foam gushed from the spout and spilled over my hand. I hastily poured the bubbly, rose gold liquid into the glasses, then wiped my hand on the tablecloth before bringing the glasses to Aliya as Tannin joined us.

I handed one to each of them, then raised my glass in the space between us. "To a bright new beginning and to our cherished princess."

Tannin clinked his glass against mine, and Aliya timidly followed suit.

"I've never had champagne before," she said, sniffing the glass. "Is it like wine?"

"It's even better," I said. "Try it. I think you'll like it."

She tentatively brought the glass to her lips and took a sip. Her eyes widened, and she took a bigger drink. "That's delicious!"

I beamed in delight, then took a large gulp of my own glass before setting it back on the table.

I returned to her with a dramatic bow, holding out my right hand. "May I have the first dance, Princess?"

She blushed as she accepted my hand, and I led her out to the center of expansive floor, then scooped my hand behind her waist and began to twirl her around. In truth, I had no idea how to dance in any proper, royal way she might be accustomed to. Our dances were less formal, less structured, but I took her lead, easily anticipating the steps she expected until I had the basics mastered.

The song ended, and Tannin approached, tapping her shoulder.

"May I cut in?" he asked, flashing his most charming smile.

Aliya smiled at him, her whole face lighting up. I graciously handed her off to him, stepping back to watch them dance.

After the first several songs and more glasses of champagne, formality went out the window. Happily, Aliya seemed to be finally having fun. We took turns twirling her around and sharing with her our dances, which she picked up quickly, lending a delicate poise to the movements that the women of our pack never had.

Her jubilant laughter filled the ballroom, and I couldn't get enough of watching her let loose and embrace her wild side. She was radiant, her honey hair whipping around her as she spun round and round.

I wanted to preserve this moment forever. Just the three of us, alone in the castle.

It might be the last time to ever experience such peace.

CHAPTER 20

TANNIN

Watching Aliya writhe and bounce to the music in Jax's arms was just amazing. I couldn't remember the last time I'd ever been so happy. I had my doubts about Jax's ball idea, but it turned out to be one of the best experiences I ever had.

We fit, the three of us. We could easily carve out our own private version of heaven right here in this castle, with nothing and no one but each other.

If only we could have enjoyed these moments sooner. I wished I'd stood up to Jax when we realized we were mated to her and stopped him from calling the pack, but it was too late now. That conversation would be the greatest regret of my life. And soon our frolicking freedom would end.

Jax and Aliya joined me at the buffet table after their dance finished, breathy and laughing. Jax grinned as he threw back the last glass of champagne.

"Should we get another?" he asked, holding up the empty bottle.

Aliya put her hand to her head. "No, I think I've had enough. In fact, I might need to sit down."

"Yes, I think we could all use a break." I went to Aliya's side and extended my bent elbow in a gesture of gentlemanly assistance.

She slipped her arm through mine, and I escorted her to the den, where we all collapsed onto the couch. Me on the left, Jax on the right, and Aliya in the middle. That was our perfect pattern.

With her arm still around mine, she rested her head on my shoulder. "That was fun. It's been so long since this place has had a proper ball."

Jax barked a laugh. "I don't know if you could call it proper, being just the three of us, but I couldn't imagine better company."

She giggled. "It's certainly better than me dancing with Willow to the ghost of music past in my head."

The orange tabby let out a disgruntled meow from her place on the armchair as if she disagreed with that statement.

"I know, Willow," Aliya replied. "You are an excellent dancer."

Jax and I exchanged a glance and snickered.

I'd grown used to Aliya's conversations with her cat and with herself. They both charmed and saddened me. I hated the thought of her alone all that time. For that reason, I was glad we'd come to Varinya, even if our motives had been malicious at the time.

The light outside the castle was growing dimmer, and my clock was ticking. I'd made a promise to Jax and myself that I would tell her the truth before the day was over. But as we sat there in the cozy silence, I couldn't bring myself to say the words.

She deserves to know.

I opened my mouth, but it seemed to have a mind of its own. "What was it like before the plague?"

Her features lightened, her eyes sparking with remembered joy. "Oh, it was wonderful. The castle was so full of life, and the village never seemed to sleep. I was lucky in those days to get a moment of privacy, between my maids running around, my tutors lecturing me, and my mother fussing over me. I never thought I'd miss it so much."

"What was your mother like?" Jax asked, surprising me with his interest.

Aliya pouted sweetly, her brows pinching together. "She was amazing. She was everything I wished I could be—intelligent, confident, commanding. Whenever she entered a room, everyone would go so silent you could hear a pin drop. But she was also kind and nurturing. Several days a month, she would work at the orphanage and nursing home. She never seemed to have a shortage of patience, something I always envied."

I placed a kiss on her forehead. "She sounds a lot like you."

She snorted. "Hardly. I'd be happy to become half the woman she was."

"What about your father?" Jax asked. "Was he a good king?"

She shifted beside me, sitting up. "I believe so. I didn't see him as much as my mother. He was always busy working. But everyone loved him, and our kingdom thrived. If that's not a sign of a good king, then I don't know what is."

"I wish I could have met him," I said before I could think better of it.

If he had been alive when we got here, one of us would have killed him before we ever realized we were mated to his daughter.

I swallowed against the lump of guilt that formed in my throat. How ignorant and intolerant our prejudices had made us. We were so driven by hatred for past grievances that we weren't able to judge a person by their character, and there was no greater crime than killing an innocent person.

I stole a glance at Jax, and the serious look on his face told me he might be thinking the same thing.

"Actually," Aliya said, releasing my arm. "Would you like to meet him?"

Jax and I both turned our heads at her in confusion.

"There's something I'd like to show you both." She slid off the couch and stood to face us. "Come on."

Jax and I rose and followed her out of the den, curiosity simmering in my chest. What could she possibly mean by "meet him"? Was her mind so far gone that she believed him to be alive somewhere? *Was* he alive somewhere, trapped in some form of diseased coma?

The list of possibilities was endless, so we said nothing as we followed her through the castle's front doors and across the courtyard toward the village. Night was falling around us, casting an eerie aura on the empty storefronts and dark houses lining the main road.

Beneath the serenade of chirping crickets, I could almost hear the ghosts of those who once lived here, the echoes of laughing children, the whispers of pedestrians long gone. Though there wasn't a soul in sight, I could feel a thousand pairs of eyes on me, making the hairs on the back of my neck stand on end.

They were watching us, judging us... condemning us.

"Aliya, where are we going?" I asked as we neared the end of the main road.

"When people first started dying from the plague, we would bury them in the valley just outside the village," she explained, pointing to the treeless plain that opened beyond the last row of houses. "We didn't know at first how horribly contagious the disease was, and it was always our custom to bury the dead."

We passed the final house, and I could see a grid of modest stones and wooden posts revealing themselves among the tall grass and wildflowers.

"It wasn't until the bodies started piling up that we began burning them instead," she continued, leading us into the overgrown cemetery that seemed all but forgotten. "It got to a point that we'd light funeral pyres every night. So many lives went un-memorialized."

Our steps pushed through the grass, and I took great care not to trip over any of the markers. Though Varinya had long been our enemy, I took no pleasure in knowing all its people were dead. We wouldn't have killed them if we'd found it well-populated. Only the royals and those who opposed us.

Aliya would've been one of them, of course, so that didn't make me feel much better.

"When my parents died, I didn't want that to happen to them," she said. "They were some of the last to go and seeing as I was apparently immune to the disease, I insisted they had proper burials."

We came to the end of the graveyard, where two large piles of stones stood above the rest. The tops were draped in woven garlands of dried flowers.

"They deserved to be laid to rest with the people they loved so dearly," she said, stopping in front of them and bowing her head at each.

"You buried them yourself?" Jax asked, his tone breathy with astonishment.

She nodded. "It took me two days to dig the holes deep enough, and another day to drag them here and fill in the dirt."

I shook my head. "You poor, sweet girl."

She wiped a tear from under her eye, the liquid glistening on the back of her hand in the moonlight. "I just couldn't stand the thought of burning them. And I wanted to have a place where I could visit them.

Every few weeks, I fashion new flower garlands and bring them out here to replace the dead ones."

Jax stepped forward and knelt in front of them. "Your Royal Highnesses, it's an honor to meet you at last. I only wish it could have been under different circumstances."

I followed his lead, kneeling beside him in front of the graves of the monarchs we'd come here to kill. The guilt was overwhelming, crushing me like the memorial stones that marked their final resting place.

"You may be gone," I said. "But your legacy lives on in your daughter. She's an incredible person, and I think you'd be proud of the woman she's become."

"I know you can't answer, but we'd like to formally ask for your daughter's hand," Jax said, and my throat constricted painfully. "Against all odds, we've mated to her. Fate works in mysterious ways… But we promise you that we will love, cherish and honor her until our dying breath. We will do our best to live up to the expectations you would have had for her husband."

I smiled tightly, because I felt those words with just as much conviction with which he spoke them. I couldn't put it off anymore. I had to tell her the truth.

I rose to my feet, squeezing my eyes against the refusal that pursed my lips. "Aliya, there's something we have to tell you."

I turned around and opened my eyes.

"Aliya?"

She was nowhere in sight.

Jax sprang up at my concerned tone, then began whipping his head in all directions in search of her. "Where is she?" he snarled, his blue eyes glowing in the darkness.

"I don't know. She was just here. Aliya!" I called out.

In the distance, racing footsteps sounded against the cobblestones. She was running back to the castle. She was running away from us.

I moved to sprint after her, but Jax's hand shot out in front of my chest.

"Wait, do you smell that?" he asked, his ears perking as he scanned the night around us.

I sniffed the air, the foul, rotting odor teasing my senses. Oh, gods. "Cusith," I breathed.

With one mind, the two of us leapt forward, shifting in midair and shredding out of our clothes. My claws kicked up clumps of earth behind me as I raced for the castle at top speed, Jax's larger wolf form gaining as he charged beside me.

I didn't know why Aliya had left us there or what she was planning, but I didn't care. There were cusith here, and she was in grave danger. I only hoped we could get to them before they found her.

CHAPTER 21

ALIYA

My pulse was pounding in my head even louder than the stomping of my feet beneath me. I ran faster than I'd ever run in my life, back toward the castle entrance. My legs ached, and my lungs burned, but neither could compare to the agony shredding my heart.

The day with Jax and Tannin had been so lovely, and I would cherish it forever. So many times as we danced and laughed, I questioned whether or not to go through with my plan. I had all but decided not to when Jax started asking about my parents. Those questions had given me the perfect opportunity to get them out of the castle, and I knew I couldn't let the chance slip away.

Despite their passionate declarations of love and devotion, it was clear to me Jax and Tannin's allegiance to their pack went deeper than our mate bond. I couldn't trust them to protect me, or what remained of my kingdom.

Standing in front of my parents' graves had reminded me of the sacrifices they'd made for their people and for me. And although it had destroyed me to do it, I'd known that turning my back on the two men I loved was the best way to honor their memories.

So, I crept away and bolted.

My feet had barely touched the cobblestone paths when Tannin called my name. Panic had shot a jolt of energy through my limbs, propelling me even faster.

But they were chasing me now. I looked over my shoulder, and two massive black wolves were darting across the cemetery at a terrifying speed.

I screamed at the top of my lungs, pushing my legs harder. I had to get to the entrance before they did. Jax and Tannin loved me in their human forms, but the beasts they'd become didn't look capable of love or anything other than brutal violence.

I didn't want to know what would happen if they caught me before I sealed the ward.

The light spilling from the open castle doors got brighter and brighter the closer I got. *Just a few more yards. Almost there!*

Vicious snarls sounded behind me, claws scraping against the stones frighteningly close.

Please, let me make it!

I hurled myself over the last few steps across the perimeter I'd made, then frantically scrambled for the sage braid beneath the rock. They were getting closer. Any second, they'd reach me.

"Flamare!" I screamed at the end of the sage gripped in my hand.

It caught fire in a blaze of flames, and at this point, I didn't care if the whole thing incinerated because its smoke was all I needed.

I waved it in front of me, the thick, dark gray cloud it emitted blocking out the charging figures of the wolves only a few feet from me.

"Parum nir alte tunak!" I cried.

The final section of the ward snapped into place, a pulse of energy radiating outward and blowing my hair back as the ephemeral wall flashed with every color of the rainbow for an instant before vanishing from sight.

The next second, the wolves leapt right at me, making me trip backward and fall hard on my ass. But they smacked into the invisible barrier with pained yelps, crumpling to the ground only inches from my feet.

The larger one rose back on its haunches, shaking its head and snarling at me.

"What is this?" Jax's voice, though much deeper and more grisly.

"A ward," I said shakily, staring at him with wide, horrified eyes. "I-it will only permit those I invite to cross it."

The smaller wolf cocked its head at me as it stood up, narrowing its eyes at me as if I'd physically wounded it.

"Why would you do that?" Tannin asked in a wolfish whimper.

I hesitantly climbed to my feet, and though my legs wobbled with the exertion of my sprint, I stood tall and held my head high.

"I heard you both this morning," I declared. "You've been lying to me ever since the moment we met."

Tannin's ears folded downward guiltily as he turned his head away.

Jax growled in frustration. "Then you know what's coming. Our pack will soon be here, and we're the only ones who can protect you from them."

I shook my head firmly. "The ward will protect me from them. Let your pack have my village, but they will never have my castle."

"That ward will not protect you for long," he insisted. "They'll find a way in eventually. Please, let us fucking help you!"

"Aliya, listen to us," Tannin pleaded. "We swear on our mate bond, on everything we are, that we won't let them hurt you. We'll reason with them. But you must cooperate. They will view this barrier as a declaration of war, and we won't be able to protect you from their wrath once that happens."

Their words had doubt festering inside me. Could their pack really break the ward? Were Jax and Tannin being sincere, and even if they were, would their pack listen to them?

Seeing the desperation in their eyes tugged on my heart, the bond urging me to let them in, to hold them and reassure them that everything was okay.

But I'd made my decision, and I refused to go back on it now.

A raspy snarl rattled behind me, and my breathing halted as a shiver of deepest dread ran up my spine.

Slowly, I looked over my shoulder.

Not one but *two* hideous, ash-gray monsters were prowling slowly toward me from the ballroom.

Cusith.

"Aliya!" Jax roared as one of them charged at me.

"Zepheren!" I yelled on instinct as I thrust out both arms, palms out, and a gust of air exploded from my hands and blasted into the creature, sending it flying across the ground.

But the other one lunged for me in the next instant, and I narrowly jumped to my right before its claws could strike me, and it slammed into the invisible barrier.

I didn't wait for it to recover, didn't stick around to watch as Jax and Tannin clawed and rammed into the barrier in their attempts to get to it. I just ran.

My feet hit the ground with a pounding thud as I trailed the castle wall within the ward, desperate to put as much distance between myself and those nightmarish monsters. But they were fast on my tail, one of them shredding the ground behind me, and the other one impossibly scaling the wall above me.

What was I going to do? There was nowhere to run. I had created the ward to keep monsters out, and I had inadvertently trapped two demonic beasts inside it that would stop at nothing to tear me limb from limb.

Why hadn't I learned more defensive magic? Dammit, I was such a fool! And now I was going to die for it.

"Aliya! Let us in!" Tannin barked as he and Jax ran along the outside of the ward, continuing their attempts to force their way through it.

"Don't make me watch you die!" Jax roared desperately.

But I couldn't hear their pleas, couldn't focus on anything but staying out of the cusith's reach.

The chicken yard loomed around the corner, an obnoxious obstacle in my path. Kicking my feet faster, I rushed at it, then hurtled over the fence, wind whipping around me as I flew off the ground for two heart-stopping seconds.

The tip of my boot caught on the top of the fence, stopping my ascent and forcing me face-down onto the filthy ground of the yard. The hens slumbering in the coop exploded into a frenzy of wing flaps and startled clucks at my rude arrival, and I frantically scrambled to push myself up.

But I'd lost all momentum, and the cusith scaling the wall flung itself off, dropping straight for me.

"Aliya, please!" Jax bellowed.

There was no more time to think. My brief, pitiful life flashed before my eyes in an instant, and I did the only thing I could.

"I invite you in!" I screamed, shielding my face with my arms as the cusith dove closer.

Two large black forms shot over the fence above me, one of them tackling the falling cusith into the wall, and the other catching the second cusith as it broke through the fence.

For a moment, I was too terrified to move, petrified into a turtling position. Finally, I broke free of my paralysis and jackknifed upward, watching in morbid fascination as the two wolves crushed the two cusith between gnashing teeth and powerful claws.

Blood sprayed out from their mutilation, splattering the wall of the castle and staining the wood of what remained of the fence. But Jax and Tannin didn't stop their savage assault until the beasts were nothing but pulp and shattered bone beneath them.

The two wolves backed away from their slain prey, panting and stumbling. Over the next few seconds, their forms shrank, their postures righting on two legs as their fur rescinded, and they once again became the two men I knew...and still loved.

Naked and covered in blood, they turned to face me, looking exactly as they had the night they'd come to me. Only this time, they had saved *my* life.

They both made a move toward me, and I ran to them without thought. They caught me as I threw my arms around each of their necks, wrapping their bodies around me and clutching me for dear life.

We held each other like that for a long time, and so many emotions were flooding over me that I couldn't name a single one.

I loved them. I hated them. I needed them. I couldn't trust them.

But right now, I didn't care about any of that. I was just glad we were all safe, and I was so overwhelmingly grateful to them for saving my life.

It was Jax who finally pulled away. "Come on. Let's get you inside."

I nodded, letting them each slip a hand into mine and guiding me toward the castle entrance.

"Where do we go from here?" I asked softly as we went through the large pair of doors.

"I don't know," Jax said. "But we'll figure it out together."

"Together," Tannin agreed.

They both looked down at me, and I could feel the love in those intense gazes. My fate was in their hands now, whether I liked it or not, and I had no choice but to have faith.

I nodded. "Together."

KINGDOM
OF THE WOLF

BOOK TWO

CHAPTER 1
ALIYA

A season of transformation had arrived for my kingdom, but I still wasn't sure if these new changes were for the better or the worse...

I was the heir to the throne of Varinya, the sole survivor of the plague that killed all my people. But for the first time in over a year, I wasn't alone. Jax and Tannin, the two wounded men I'd welcomed into my castle and nursed back to health also turned out to be my mates, a fact from which I was still reeling.

Jax was also a leader of the Black Wolves, the ancient enemy of my kingdom, one I'd believed had long died out. But they hadn't, and Jax and Tannin had journeyed here to eliminate me. Luckily for me, they'd recognized me as their mate and had waited before stopping my heart. Instead, they'd fallen me, and I for them.

Fate had woven quite the tangled web for us, and I was stuck right in the center of the biggest cosmic knot I'd ever seen.

I was also currently sandwiched in bed between those two men, Jax on my right, and Tannin on my left. After spending all night scouring the castle for any signs of more cusith, the hideous creatures that had nearly killed me, we'd collapsed into bed, exhausted and desperate for sleep.

But sleep evaded me, chased away by the worries that haunted my mind.

The entire pack of the Black Wolves was coming. They had every intention of occupying my kingdom and my castle, each of them demanding my death. My life had an expiration date, and the clock would start ticking the moment the pack arrived.

I believed that Jax and Tannin loved me, that they would do anything to protect me, but I wasn't sure it would be enough to save me from impending doom. The Black Wolves pack was still large and formidable. They were vicious and cruel, according to our folklore.

Would they forgive me for being the last princess of Varinya?
Doubtful.

I glanced over at Jax, savoring the cruel perfection of his face. In sleep, he looked more beautiful than brutal, with his black hair tousled over his forehead and curling around his ears.

As if aware of my attention, his eyes opened, and his body tensed. He turned his head toward me, his eyes meeting mine, and in his gaze were a thousand promises—and a determination to address the thousands of worries that filled me with dread.

"Good morning, beautiful," he said, cupping my face in his callused hand and leaning forward to brush a kiss on my lips.

As always, his touch stirred desire in my core. A huge part of me wished that he'd satisfy the need now growing inside me, but we had important matters to discuss and couldn't afford to lose ourselves in the carnal demands of our bond.

He sat up instead of continuing to kiss me, proving he agreed with my unspoken thoughts, and Tannin roused with a groan at being disturbed. He rubbed his eyes as he, too, sat up.

"Get your clothes on," Jax ordered him, throwing a fresh shirt and pair of trousers at him. "We have much to discuss and little time to do it."

With a sleepy nod, Tannin inclined toward me to kiss my cheek before climbing out of bed and stumbling into his pants.

I backed up right against my pillow, hugging my knees to my chest. "What are we going to do about your pack?" I asked, unable to keep the note of resentment from my voice.

Jax shrugged into his shirt and began fastening the buttons. "I think the only thing we can do is lie about who you are. We can claim that you're merely a servant... a maid, perhaps. If they think you're nobody, they'll care less about your fate."

Refusal whipped inside me like a solar flare. "You're suggesting I concede my throne completely? No." I shook my obstinately. "I won't do that."

Jax cut me a deadpan frown. "Is your pride so strong that you'd sacrifice your life for your title? If they know you're the princess, they'll demand your death."

"If they can't get into the castle, then what does it matter?" I countered with a catty smirk. "I'm not taking down the wards. Let them plot my death all they want. They won't be able to get to me."

Jax scoffed and shook his head. "Tannin, would you reason with her?"

Tannin, my green-eyed beautiful man, sighed as he finished buttoning his shirt, then sat on the bed beside me. "Aliya, Jax is right. The pack can't know your true identity, at least not yet. They need to believe you're not a threat. Give them a chance to get to know you so they can see what we do."

I glared at him. "Do you really think who I am on the inside will stop them from hating who I am on the outside? You two were mated to me and you still wanted to kill me."

Both frowned and looked down, their shoulders slumping with the weight of their remorse over that reminder. I almost felt bad for playing on that guilt, but I still hadn't fully forgiven them for their deceptions. They'd manipulated me and lied to me over and over, pushing me away only to pull me back in so many times. That wasn't something I could easily forget, even with this maddening mate bond making me crave them and clouding my judgment.

"All the more reason for us to keep your identity secret," Jax said. "They don't have the mate bond to open their eyes and force them to see the real you beneath your title. We're lying about who you are, and that's final."

I huffed. "And what, we lie about the mate bond too?"

"For now," Jax replied. "After the dust settles, we can *discover* the bond. The elders will confirm it, and once the pack has accepted you, they won't be able to harm you over the truth."

"Do you really believe that?" Tannin asked before I could.

"Yes," Jax said with a growl in his throat, though his eyes held a hint of doubt.

I shook my head, clenching the sheets at my ankles. "I don't like it. I don't want to lie."

"You did a pretty convincing job of it last night," Jax muttered. "Flirting with us and batting those lovely lashes of yours, all while plotting to lock us out of the castle. How long did that ward take you to build?"

I narrowed my eyes on him, his tone making me want to slap that pretty face of his. "About as long as it took you both to realize you didn't actually want to kill me."

Jax's nostrils began to flare, a rumble rolling his chest.

"This arguing isn't helping," Tannin chided. "We all did bad things, and we've all forgiven each other for them, right?"

I clenched the sheets tighter, and the line etched between Jax's eyebrows told me he harbored the same resentment. What wrong did I commit? I was just protecting myself, and I only started constructing the ward after I found out they were lying to me. I was innocent in all this.

"We need to be united going forward," Tannin insisted. He put his hand on one of mine, loosening my grip on the sheet. "Aliya, we're deeply sorry for the misconceptions we came here with, and for letting them skew our perception of you. We love you, we're devoted to you, and we will do everything in our power to protect you. But you have to let us do that. We know the wolves and how they think, and we must do this our way."

The sincerity in his words and the conviction shining in his eyes cooled my anger. Tannin always knew how to disarm me. *Dammit.*

I sighed. "Fine. But what are you going to tell them about the ward? You told me last night that it would be considered a declaration of war."

Jax nodded as he finally sat on the bed on my other side, his features relaxed after Tannin's words. "I thought about that too. You hid in the castle the first night we came, letting us think it was empty. You heard us talking about what we are, and while we were outside sending my moon song, you put up the ward. We didn't know about your existence until then, and because of the ward, we didn't yet know about the mate bond we both share with you."

Tannin tilted his head from side to side, pursing his lips as he mulled it over. "That's pretty good, actually."

Jax smirked. "That's why I'm the Alpha."

I rolled my eyes. "You really are an arrogant twat."

He waggled an eyebrow at me, giving me a look that made my thighs squeeze together. "But I'm *your* arrogant twat."

He leaned toward me and brushed his lips teasingly over mine. I tried to keep my lips pressed in a flat, stubborn line, but the soft warmth of his mouth melted my resolve, the yearning that burned in my core urging me to give in.

I opened my lips, swooning when his tongue pushed inside to caress mine in a sinful solicitation. A needy whimper squeaked through my tight throat, and he slowly pulled back the sheet as he deepened the kiss.

"Seeing as you're still naked, Tannin and I might as well take advantage while we still can," he purred. "Let your mates make you come one last time."

He's right. We should take advantage of this time while we still have it.

My pussy throbbed with need for them. I unbent my legs, spreading them in invitation. Jax slid his hand between my thighs, running his fingers between my sensitive folds, making me suck in a gasp.

"So wet for me already," he said. "That's my good girl."

My eyelids fluttered at his dark, sensuous tone, and I reluctantly admitted to myself that I loved it when he talked to me like that.

Tannin kissed down my neck as Jax's fingers slid up and down my center, his hand kneading my right breast as his mouth found my left and began to suckle. I cried out at the triple assault, my body a symphony of sensations. Between Jax's mouth devouring mine, his fingers tormenting my clit, and Tannin's masterful play of my breasts and nipples, I was drowning in a sea of wanton bliss.

I pushed my hips up in a silent plea for Jax to enter me. I needed his finger inside me, not just teasing me on the outside. He had to satisfy the crippling tension their affection was building in my core. But he didn't give me what I wanted. In fact, he evaded my tactics, chuckling into my mouth as he continued to merely tease me.

Asshole. I wasn't going to tolerate him toying with me. Not today.

I bit his bottom lip in warning, gently holding it between my teeth. A dark, raspy laugh rumbled up his throat as he slowly pulled it from my grasp.

"Our little kitten has teeth," he purred. "I like that."

At the same moment as he descended on my mouth like the hungry, powerful wolf he was, he pushed his finger into my entrance, forcing a moan from me that was swallowed up by his ferocious, dominating kisses.

His treatment of my sensitive opening was rough and demanding, his palm pressing hard against my clit as he dove his finger into my pussy, and fuck, it was amazing! The speed and friction drove me quickly up the pinnacle and forced me over the edge. I screamed in ecstasy into his mouth, bucking beneath Tannin's suckling against the intense pleasure of everything they were doing to me.

They continued their fondling until my tremors and cries subsided, but I was far from finished with them. I needed to give them the same pleasure they'd just given me.

Reaching down, I blindly clawed for the clasp of Tannin's pants, my fingers fumbling in their desperate attempt to free his cock.

Suddenly, they ripped their mouths away from me all at once, their ears perking as they stared wide-eyed at each other in alarm. I cried out in frustration, stretching out my arms to them. "What's wrong? Come back."

They turned their heads toward the open window, seemingly unable to hear my words.

"W-what is it?" I panted, my chest still heaving from my desire.

"They're here," Jax snarled, his jaw clenching. "Our pack is here."

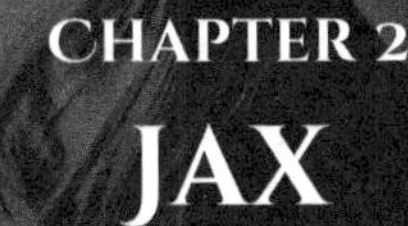

CHAPTER 2
JAX

As soon as I'd heard the distant footsteps in the forest beyond the village, I jumped from Aliya's bed. There was no time to waste. Grabbing Tannin's arm, I dragged him behind me as I darted down the stairs and out the back kitchen entrance.

The pack couldn't know we'd been in the castle. Our entire plan—our hope for salvaging the bond between us and Aliya—would be doomed from the start if they had an inkling of what we'd been up to.

Luckily, we made it out the door and around to the front of the castle as the first of our people emerged from the shelter of the trees. I took a quick inhalation of breath and plastered on my victorious Alpha smile to greet them as they began flooding the vacant cobblestone path in droves.

Young pups skipped ahead of those pulling caravans and carrying bulky canvas bags on their backs. The sight of the excitement on their adorable childish faces made my smile a little more authentic.

This was the moment I'd been dreaming of my whole life—the moment I brought our people out of exile. After generations of scraping by and living in shacks and hovels in the forest, I was the Alpha who finally brought us home.

Though the circumstances of that were so far beyond what I'd ever imagined.

The expectation was that we would find a thriving kingdom full of our enemies and we'd spend months infiltrating and plotting to destroy them from the inside. Instead, Varinya was empty, abandoned, and just begging for occupation by our people.

But it wasn't all silver lining for us. Being mated to the lone survivor of the royal family meant there may still be a fight yet—one against my own kind.

No, it won't come to that. I'll make sure of it.

"Welcome, Black Wolves, to your forever home!" I called out, raising my hands like a showman. "The houses and shops are all completely empty. Please, take your pick and make yourselves right at home."

The children let out jubilant yips as they began to run up and down the alleys filled with various buildings. Chatter broke out as the adults set down their belongings to peruse potential houses to call their own.

As the multitudes dispersed, the eight elders came up the cobblestones towards us. My muscles bunched aggressively at the sight of Coda striding alongside them.

It was no secret that Coda envied my position as Alpha, and while I hardly considered him a threat, my hackles still rose in his presence. And judging by Tannin's proximity at my side, the arrogant wolf had the same effect on him.

Coda had yet to challenge me, and after my triumph in bringing the pack home, I was certain he never would. At least two elders must consent to a challenge, and he'd never get that now. I would be beloved by our people, my name going down in history as the savior of the Black Wolves. And if he ever made the idiotic mistake of presuming to challenge me, I would take great pleasure in destroying him.

"Pretty impressive," Coda said as he approached, his chest puffed out like a posturing rooster. "How did you manage this?"

I shrugged casually. "I can't exactly take all the credit. A plague apparently wiped out nearly the entire kingdom. Fate seems to have been working in our favor."

"A plague?" asked Esther, one of the most respected matriarchs of the elders. "Does it still linger?"

"To the best of our knowledge, it has long since passed," I replied. "The last of the infected died over a year ago, and all the bodies were already either buried or incinerated before we got here. Tannin and I have been here nearly a week, and we haven't developed any symptoms, so I have no reason to believe that sickness is a danger to any of us."

The elders nodded as they looked around with wary gazes, as if expecting their old enemies to jump out from behind the closed doors and lay siege to us.

But Coda's narrowed eyes were fixed on me. "How do you know what happened here if the last of the infected died over a year ago?"

The anger in my blood began to simmer. I might just destroy him regardless of a challenge.

"Yes," interjected Droger, one of the male elders. "I believe you said the sickness killed *nearly* the entire kingdom. Were there survivors?"

Alright, I guess now was as good a time as any to rip off the Band Aid.

"Yes, there is one survivor," I said, injecting remembered irritation into my voice. "A young woman who was a servant in the castle. She rather reluctantly told us what happened here."

"There is a survivor?" Coda asked, folding his arms over his chest. "As in you let her live?"

A low rumble sounded deep in Tannin's chest beside me, but I clandestinely grabbed his wrist in silent warning to stand down. The last thing we needed was for him to expose any sign of our allegiance to Aliya.

"Well, there has been a complication of sorts," I began to explain, keeping my tone calm and confident. "You see, when we got here, we explored the castle and found no one. She was apparently hiding from us, and when we came outside to call the pack under the full moon, she cast a ward around the perimeter of the castle. We can't get in."

Coda rolled his eyes and snorted. "We'll see about that."

Before I could say anything to dissuade him, he burst into his wolf in an explosion of shredded clothing and galloped straight for the castle. I turned and watched him, full of anticipation. The jerk deserved this. The loud thud that preceded his pained yelp as he fell to the ground before the castle's entrance gave me no small amount of satisfaction.

I barked a laugh and crossed my arms over my chest. "Like I said, it's warded. Based on my limited knowledge of magic, no one can get in without the wielder's invitation."

The cocky wolf shook off the surprise of the impact, sneering at me, and the elders approached the spot to inspect the invisible barrier.

Esther lifted a hand and gingerly pressed it forward, sending a rainbowy ripple across the ward at her touch.

"This is powerful magic," she mused, then looked over her shoulder at me. "How do you know the girl is merely a servant?"

"That is what she told us," Tannin said. "When we tried to re-enter the castle after calling the pack, she was standing just within the ward. She'd overheard us talking about what we were and our intentions, and the moment she got the chance, she locked us out. Though her masters are dead and gone, she's apparently still loyal to their memory."

Esther nodded, seeming satisfied with Tannin's explanation.

"Have you spoken much with the girl?" Droger asked, tapping the ephemeral wall in various places as if testing its consistency.

"She only talks to us sparingly," I said. "That first night after locking us out, she came to talk to us, and a few sporadic moments after that as we scanned the perimeter looking for a way in. All she's told us is that her name is Aliya, she was a servant, and she's been alone in the castle for over a year after everyone died from a plague. We don't know much more than that."

"I see," said Wilda, my great-aunt. "But Esther is right. This level of magic takes either great skill or great power. It's hard to believe that a mere servant would have enough of either to form such a ward."

"I highly doubt this girl is a powerful wielder," Tannin scoffed. "If she were, she'd have blasted us with magic rather than just warding us out of the castle. My guess is that her year of solitude gave her the opportunity to study books of magic that were previously unavailable to her, and that this ward was a last resort to protect herself."

Ah, very clever, Tannin. Downplaying Aliya to lower suspicion against her. It was times like this that I was proud to call him my beta.

"I suppose that makes sense," Esther agreed. "Why shield when you can attack? So you two have no reason to believe she's a threat?"

I confidently shook my head. "None whatsoever. She truly appears to just be a lonely, frightened girl."

"Does she ever leave the perimeter?" Coda's wolf snarled. "She has to come out sometime. We can wait her out, then rip her wicked throat out."

I had to swallow hard to keep the menacing growl from rolling in my chest. "If she dies, we'll never get into the castle. Magic doesn't die with the wielder, you ignorant mongrel."

He sneered at me, his upper lip twitching dangerously.

"You are right about that," Droger said. "We can't harm the girl until she lowers the ward."

"We won't harm the girl at all," I declared, my voice ringing with authority. "She's an innocent who is simply misguided and scared. She's been told lies about us her whole life. Our quarrel isn't with her. Those are already dead."

"Then what do you propose, *Alpha?*" Coda hissed my title mockingly.

"Tannin and I have been working on that, and we'll discuss the matter at length during an official pack meeting tomorrow morning," I said. "In the meantime, I suggest you all claim one of the many houses and settle in."

The elders slowly moseyed on to do just that. But Coda, who shifted back to human form, was standing naked in the same spot, eyeing me with hatred blazing in his obsidian eyes. I held his glare, daring him to step out of line.

Give me a reason, asshole.

Finally, his nostrils flared, and he turned his back to me, striding off to chase a family out of one of the nicer houses, no doubt.

Tannin and I exchanged a tenuous glance. The worst was over for now. Our explanation had appeased the elders, and the pack was more than happy to start their lives in their new homes.

But the worst was far from over. Coda was going to be a problem. And I had a feeling I'd just made Aliya the target of not only his hatred, but his suspicion as well.

CHAPTER 3
ALIYA

My stomach was like a nest of snakes coiling into a thousand knots as I watched and listened from the window of the library just above the castle's front doors.

Despite the happy chatter of those moving about the village, I was able to pick up nearly every word being spoken between my mates and the wizened pack members I assumed to be the elders.

The way Jax and Tannin had referred to me made me feel small and helpless. I understood the good intentions behind their words, but I really hated being thought of as a lowly commoner. I was the princess of this kingdom. The last living heir to my family's legacy, and it felt like a betrayal to pretend to be something other than what I was.

But when I considered what my parents would tell me to do if they were watching me from the afterlife... I knew they'd want me to go along with Tannin and Jax's plan. They'd want me to do whatever it took to protect myself, and as long as the pack thought I was a nobody, they'd be less determined to see my head on a pike.

Except for that black-haired guy who shifted and charged at the ward. I nearly fell backward in fright when he slammed into it. He was eager to kill me regardless of my standing, and just from the small exchange I witnessed, I got the impression he wasn't too keen on following orders from Jax.

He was the embodiment of everything I'd always assumed Black Wolves were. Angry, bloodthirsty, ruthless. Jax and Tannin might be able to protect me from the pack as a whole, but what about outliers like him? Wolves who followed their own agendas, their own hatred. Wolves who harbored hidden rivalries for my two mates.

"What are we going to do, Tabitha?" I asked my orange cat, who was currently scratching the leg of my favorite armchair. She still continued to hide most of the time that Tannin and Jax were about the castle, though I'd seen her watching us on occasion.

"Mwwwrrrr," she said as she continued to scratch.

I nodded. "You're right."

I couldn't rely on the protection of Jax and Tannin alone. I had made the mistake of avoiding training in harmful magic before, and it nearly cost me my life against the pair of cusith. I wasn't going to make that mistake again. I needed to know how to defend myself, if not against the wolves, then at least against the cusith. And fire was the most obvious choice for destroying either.

"But where can I practice?" I debated aloud. "There's no way I'm going outside with the pack infesting the kingdom."

"Rawwwr," Tabitha replied.

"Oh, that might work," I agreed, rubbing my chin as I mulled the idea over. "But I'll have to clear things out first. The last thing I need is for the castle to go up in flames with me trapped inside it."

"Meow fft," she snorted in approval.

With a new plan in mind, I picked up the book with instructions for offensive spells and scurried down the stairs. Once I made it to the ballroom, I assessed the space. It really was a massive room, and by design, it had no objects in its expansive, open center. There were a few buffet tables along the walls for holding drinks and food for grand parties, and those would be a problem if something went wrong.

The biggest risk was that I'd get the fire spells wrong and burn myself alive. Barring that, I was pretty safe. And I could take precautions against missing my targets.

So, I spent the next hour or so moving the sparse furniture items out of the ballroom and piling them up against the side wall of the staircase beside the den. It was a lot more difficult than I anticipated.

The buffet tables, while narrow and seemingly delicate, were actually solid wood and very heavy. I had to drag each of them, taking little pauses to catch my breath and relieve my burning arms every few minutes. All the while, Tabitha merely sat on the fireplace mantle, watching me with idle curiosity.

By the time I was halfway done, my heart was racing, and my breathing was more labored than it should be.

"I don't feel well," I said, stumbling toward the staircase to brace myself against the handrail.

My whole body was flushed and damp with cold sweat, and my stomach...

"Oh, gods." I darted to the nearest bathroom and dropped down in front of the toilet, trembling as nausea burned my throat.

Any minute now, I was sure the contents of my stomach would lurch up and force its way out, so I hovered over the porcelain bowl, waiting and struggling to breathe against the sickening burn.

Nothing came up, but my mouth watered for what seemed like an eternity until the nausea subsided.

After a while, Tabitha wandered into the bathroom and came to lay beside me, the purr rumbling from her body oddly soothing. I took all the comfort I could from her presence and from the concern that led her to come look for me.

Was this a hangover? I did have a lot to drink last night before I tricked the men into leaving the castle. But I'd felt fine until I started lifting things. Had I just overexerted myself?

And why did I feel so weak? The trembling in my limbs and torso wouldn't go away. That couldn't be from just pushing and pulling a few pieces of furniture.

What if it was...

No. I'd seen enough people fall ill to the plague and eventually die. It didn't start with nausea. And why would the sickness affect me now, over a year since I had tended to so many who were dying?

No, this had to be something else—certainly something far less sinister. I was just being paranoid because of the pack being right outside the front door of the castle. Surely the trembling and nausea was from my extreme anxiety over that fact.

I only had three more tables to move. If I went slowly and took my time, I'd be fine... or so I hoped.

I picked myself up, chugged a glass of water in the kitchen, and continued with my task, much more slowly this time than before.

As if sensing my unease, Tabitha followed me as I moved each table. While I appreciated the sweet gesture, I almost tripped over her four times, and her watchful nature was becoming annoying. Suddenly, I wished she was still just watching from the sidelines.

Finally, the ballroom was completely empty of furniture. There was now nothing in the whole room that could ignite, Thanks to the stained-glass designs of the windows, there weren't even any curtains hanging over them.

Now I needed a target. I tapped my foot against the marble floor where I stood, brainstorming what I could possibly use as a target.

Suddenly, I remembered that there was a dress form mannequin in my mother's room.

I stared down at the cat pressed against my leg as if she'd been the one to give me the idea. "Tabitha, you're a genius."

I ran up the stairs—more winded than normal—and found the dusty old dummy standing in the corner of my mother's room. It still wore the same dress my mother had last put on it, which was beautiful. I took a moment to admire my mother's style, then carefully slid the dress off the mannequin, revealing the fabric torso and the metal stand it stood on.

The fabric on the torso was a thick, rough burlap. But I knew that wouldn't save it from burning. I hated the idea of purposely destroying one of my mother's cherished items. She'd probably had a nickname for the mannequin, one I'd long since forgotten.

But I didn't have many other options. The metal frame beneath the burlap was sturdy, and the perfect shape for practicing offensive spells against a human body. I knew my mom would say that my safety and that of the kingdom's legacy was worth the sacrifice of a burlap dummy.

So, I tucked the mannequin under my arm and awkwardly carried her back down the stairs to the ballroom, setting her a few feet from the wall that separated the ballroom from the den.

"Meow." Tabitha regarded the mannequin.

"Oh, that's a good point," I said.

I went to the kitchen and filled a bucket with water. Regardless of my success or failure today, I couldn't have any object freely burning inside the castle, not even the empty ballroom. I'd need to be able to douse the flames immediately and also have the ability to douse myself if needed.

I shivered at the thought of setting myself on fire, then carried the bucket to the ballroom. *Hopefully, it won't come to that.*

At last, my practice space was ready. I sat down in the center of the floor and flipped open the book in search of the simplest offensive fire spell, which happened to be a fireball.

I knew I could start a fire without a problem—I'd done it to light the sage braid for creating the ward—but wielding the destructive element was a completely different thing. And the warnings accompanying each of these spells didn't inspire much confidence. If I did a single hand movement out of order or said the words wrong or didn't channel the proper intention, the results could be devastating.

"So, I guess that's where the term 'Backfire' comes from," I said.

"Raww," Tabitha agreed from where she burrowed against my right thigh.

I stood and practiced the hand gestures until I knew I had them mastered. Hands were supposed to be flat and perpendicular to the ground, starting pressed together at breast level, and then crossing them to opposite shoulders with the right hand on the outer side from the body. Then you cross them again with the left hand on the outer side of the body, then extend them straight from the breast with palms facing out.

The hardest part was making sure my hands stayed flat and perpendicular. I repeated the routine over and over, until it felt natural and I stopped mucking up my hands and lowering my arms beneath the correct level throughout the sequence.

The second part was intention and emotion. Fear or anger would lend too much control to the fire itself and take it away from the wielder. That was easy to do now, when I was alone and safe inside the castle, but I'd need to be able to silence those intrusive feelings in the moment. I imagined myself running from the cusith from last night, and all the wild emotions that had taken hold at the time. I closed my eyes and practiced trying to block them out and quiet them.

It wasn't the same as being in the dangerous situation of last night, but I was successful. Hopefully, with enough practice, I'd be able to do it when the situation was truly dangerous.

Now I just had to put it all together with the incantation. Easy peasy, right?

I read over the incantation again and again until I had it memorized. *Incendia malé.*

Then I ran through the sequence a few times, adding the incantation in my head at the end. Even without saying it out loud, I could feel the magic pulling in my stomach, could feel the heat building against my palms. It was invigorating, and I was ready to do this thing for real. No more dipping a toe in the water, it was time to jump in.

I carefully executed the hand gestures and silenced my mind. Then I said the words as I extended my arms with my palms out.

With a roar of combusting air, flames burst to life in my palms and formed into a spherical shape that almost looked like it was liquid. I stared wide-eyed at the ball of fire, amazed at how the heat of it only felt like a gentle caress against my skin. The fire wasn't actually touching my palms, but instead seemed to float above them mere millimeters away.

Carefully, I willed the burning sphere to transfer into the control of my right hand, and when I lowered my left hand, the ball stayed levitating in my right.

"This is so cool," I breathed.

Tabitha snorted, as if bored by this whole thing.

Taking aim at the poor, defenseless mannequin, I drew back my arm and hurled the fireball at it. My aim was terrible, but thankfully, magic didn't depend on the physical prowess of the wielder. The ball left my hand and shot straight for the chest of the dummy, slamming it so hard the dummy toppled over and clattered loudly on the marble floor.

"Holy shit!"

I sprinted to the spot and bent down to inspect it. The mannequin wasn't on fire as I'd expected. Instead, the fireball had burned a massive hole straight through the fabric, leaving glowing, charred edges in its wake.

The acrid odor had my throat closing against the smoke, making me cough. And just like a light switch flipping, my nausea came back full force, and I vomited all over the floor beside the destroyed dummy.

Tabitha came up behind me and let out an irritated hiss.

I sighed. "Well, on the bright side, I already have a mop bucket."

As I went about cleaning up the mess I'd made, I was ultimately satisfied with what I'd accomplished. If the worst that happened from my incredibly dangerous training session was that I threw up, I should count myself lucky.

I definitely needed more practice before I could try applying it in the real world. But first, I desperately needed a nap. And maybe I could find an anti-nausea potion in one of these books.

My kingdom for an calm stomach.

CHAPTER 4

TANNIN

With the elders placated for the moment, and Coda licking his wounds in some corner somewhere, I went in search of my own little family within our pack—my mother and little sister.

While I hadn't been eager for everyone to arrive, I was grateful that my family was here and that they were safe. More than anyone else, they needed me, even if they would never know just how much.

Following my keen sense of smell, I tracked my mother's comforting floral scent to a modest house nestled in a cul-de-sac to the west of the main road that split the town. It was a small white cottage with burnt orange shingles on its angled roof, and paint flaking in quite a few places on the outer walls.

Leave it to my mother to choose the least assuming abode to call home.

I knocked briefly to announce myself before opening the front door, and as soon as I stepped into the living room, a familiar small form leapt into my arms.

"Tannin! You're here!" Twila squealed as her arms squeezed around my neck. "I missed you so much!"

I laughed as I closed my arms around my little sister and savored the feeling of her warm body. "I was only gone for a week."

Her arms tightened around my neck. "A week was way too long," she replied woefully.

I hugged her closer. "I know. I missed you too."

Mom appeared in the archway from the kitchen, and she leaned against the frame and smiled as she watched our exchange.

I planted a kiss on Twila's cheek and set her down in front of me. She immediately grabbed my hand and began to tug me toward the hall.

"Come on, I want to show you my room. It's so big!"

"I will, but first, I want to say hi to Mom," I told her.

"Aww," she lamented, still clinging to my hand.

"Soon. I promise," I said with a nod.

She huffed a sigh. "Okay." Then she scampered off down the hall.

I turned to my mother, who came toward me with arms outstretched, and I greedily welcomed her embrace.

"I am so proud of you," she crooned.

I didn't respond to her praise. All I'd really done since I got here was fight to keep the last living enemy of our pack alive, then lie to the elders about all of it. Though I knew it was the right thing to do, I wasn't so sure my mother would be proud of me if she knew the truth.

"How was the journey here?" I asked instead. "Any sign of cusith?"

She stiffened and released me from her hug, pulling away enough to look at me. "No, thank Luna. The journey was long, especially with poor Twila being hungry and tired. But we're here now, and that's all the matters."

I smiled. "I agree. And I'm glad you haven't encountered any cusith. Jax and I eliminated a pair of them only yesterday. They're getting bolder."

Concern struck her face, and I immediately regretted mentioning that.

"Do you think it's safe here?" she asked, wringing her fingers in front of her.

"It's a lot safer here than in the forest, and Jax and I will make sure the cusith won't be a threat," I assured her.

She nodded, though the worry didn't leave her eyes.

I looked around, eager to find a change of subject. "This house is so small. There are more than enough empty houses that are much larger and more comfortable. I'd be happy to help you find something more suitable."

She frowned and waved a hand at me as she headed back into the kitchen. I followed her. "This house is perfectly suitable. Two bedrooms are plenty enough for Twila and me. Leave the bigger houses for bigger families."

I sighed and watched as she began going through cabinets, reorganizing their contents. "But your status is higher now, Mom. You're the Alpha's family, and you deserve to live in luxury."

She scoffed and shook her head. "After a lifetime of sleeping on dirt with only patchy log walls surrounding me, this house is luxury. It has everything we need." She opened the pantry and beamed over her shoulder at me. "And look, there's enough canned food in here to last us months! Like I said, everything we need."

I rolled my eyes. My mother never knew or respected her worth, but I also knew that once she'd made her mind up, there was no changing it. She was stubbornly humble. I wouldn't be able to convince her to move somewhere better for her and Twila.

And I kinda loved her for it.

"Ah, tomato soup," she sighed as she turned a can over in her hand. "I haven't had this since I was a girl. I'm going to heat some up for the three of us."

"Oh, but I—"

"Nonsense," she interrupted. "You can stay and have a meal with your family. Why don't you go play with your sister for a moment, and I'll call you both when it's ready."

She began rifling through the kitchen drawers and plucking out pots and pans. I happily accepted that this was my fate for the afternoon. Breaking in the new house with a family meal sounded like a great idea, and though I knew I had a plethora of duties to attend to, they could wait for a couple hours.

I left my mom to her kitchen endeavor and ventured into the hall to find Twila. It wasn't difficult, the hall from the living room had only three doors, two of which were bedrooms and the other a bathroom.

Twila's voice trailed from behind one of them, and I pushed open the door to find her sitting in the middle of the floor, playing with toys that had been abandoned by the child who'd lived here before. Judging by the pink walls and dolls that scattered the floor, a little girl had once called this room hers.

"Wow, this is a nice room," I said.

Twila paused her imaginary game and grinned at me. "It's even better than I could have dreamed! Look at all these toys! Wolfy is going to have so many new friends." She held up the raggedy, tattered wolf Mom had sewn for her from an old pair of pants and whose sand stuffing almost constantly leaked out.

"He sure will," I said as I plopped down to sit next to her. "Have you come up with names for any of them yet?"

"Not yet," she said with a frown, then her eyes widened with an idea. "Maybe you can help me."

I chuckled, my heart warming at the idea of this game with my sister. "Sure. Let's see, who should be first." I scanned the dozen or so stuffed animals and dolls, then picked up a stuffed yellow bunny. "I think he looks like a Sunny. What do you think?"

She tilted her head and scrunched her nose, then nodded. "Yes, I think she looks like a Sunny."

"She?" I asked.

She rolled her eyes dramatically. "All stuffies are she, Tannin," she said matter-of-factly.

"I see. Even Wolfy?"

"Obviously," she said, and I stifled a snicker.

"Why are they all girls?" I asked, truly curious about her thought process.

"Because they're pretty and soft," she explained. "Boys aren't pretty or soft. Boys are mean."

I watched as darkness crossed her features and her eyes became distant, and like a knife driving into my gut, I knew where her mind went.

She blinked and then turned to me. "But not you, Tannin. You're nice. And I guess you're sorta pretty."

I let out a small laugh, even though my humor had been dampened by the memory. "Well, thanks, I guess."

I wanted to tell her that not all boys were mean, that plenty of us were good and kind. But after what she'd witnessed at such a young age, I selfishly appreciated her prejudice. It would safeguard her from getting hurt the same way our mother had.

Looking down at the newly named Sunny, I noticed a layer of dust on her, which only became more obvious when I gave her a shake, and a cloud of dust filled the air.

"Hey, why don't you give your new friends a bath?" I suggested as I waved the dust away. "I'm pretty sure they haven't had one in a long time, and it looks like you could use one yourself, little missy."

"Oh, that's a great idea!" she said.

"Great. You go get yourself and them clean, and I'll work on your room," I said. "We wouldn't want you sleeping on dusty sheets."

She shrugged. "Okay." Then she gathered her new toys in her arms and carried them out of the room.

The sound of water running in the bathroom soon followed, and I got to work removing the sheets from the bed. Then I went into the other room and did the same. My mother had enough to worry about without adding cleaning the beds to the list.

I took the bundle out the back door and was relieved to find an empty water basin and hanging lines for laundry. I filled the basin and scrubbed each sheet and blanket against the washboard, then hung them up to dry. Once that was done, I went back inside the kitchen to look for a broom and dustpan.

"Lunch is ready," Mom said as she filled three bowls with freshly heated soup.

"Okay, I'll fetch Twila from the bath," I said.

"Oh, a bath would be lovely," she said. "I haven't had a proper bath in years."

"Well, how about after lunch, you have yourself a nice, long bath while Twila and I get things cleaned up," I offered.

She gave me a loving pout, then cupped my face in her hands. "You are the sweetest boy."

She kissed my forehead, and though a patch of moisture clung to the spot on my skin, I didn't wipe it away. I loved my mother with everything that I was.

And I could only hope that she'd forgive me when she found out about Aliya and our mating bond.

I went to the bathroom and hastened Twila out of the tub while Mom set the table. She fussed about me interrupting her game, but she got over it as soon as she smelled the hot soup that was waiting for her. I handed her a towel so she could dry herself off. Then I sent her to the kitchen while I gathered her toys and hung them outside as well.

Our lunch together was like something out of a fairy tale. Sitting around a table in an actual kitchen surrounded by solid walls, a plaster ceiling and hardwood floors. It was surreal and so blissfully pleasant. We should have been living like this all along, and I was glad that I was part of the reason they now could.

When we finished, I insisted Mom go take a bath and volunteered Twila to help me clean up. She only whined a little, then easily fell into doing the simpler tasks like dusting and washing dishes.

"Tannin?" she asked after washing the last bowl.

"Yeah?" I said without turning from scrubbing down the counter.

"Do you think Mama will ever marry again?"

I stopped what I was doing altogether, every muscle in my body tensing. I swallowed before saying, "Why do you ask?"

There was a pause before she finally replied, "Because I don't want her to."

Pain lanced my heart, and I let go of the rag and crossed the kitchen to drop to my knees so that I was at eye level with her.

"Hey, no matter what happens in the future, I won't let anything bad happen to either of you."

She nodded without looking at me, so I took her face in my hands until her gaze finally met mine. "No one is ever going to hurt Mama again," I swore with every ounce of conviction I felt.

That finally seemed to reach her, and she wrapped her arms around my neck. "Thank you, Tannin. I love you."

"I love you too."

Sometimes I wondered if she knew what I'd done all those years ago. She'd watched her father—my stepfather—abuse our mother for years while I was gone helping Jax defend the pack and make trade deals. I hadn't been there to protect our mother from the worst of it. But I was ultimately the one who made it all stop.

And if another man came into her life and laid even a finger on her in anger again, I'd happily dispose of another body. And just like before, no one would ever know.

CHAPTER 5
CODA

U*nbelievable.* This whole situation was completely unacceptable. We were supposed to arrive to an empty king-dom, ready and waiting to welcome us into its dominion. Instead, some lowly peasant had evaded notice and locked down the castle. What a shit show.

Leave it to Jax to fuck even that up.

I knew I should've been the one to accompany him. I wouldn't have missed the scent of a Varinyan whore. I would have sniffed her out and slaughtered her on the spot. Then I'd be living in the castle, where I deserved to be.

Instead, I was forced to live in a townhouse like a commoner.

After a detailed scan of the village, I found the only one that came even close to what I needed. A three-story villa semi-adjacent to the castle, with tall windows from which I'd have constant view of my target. A lower ranking family of the pack had dared to attempt its occu-pation, but I made quick work of dismissing them. It would do for now, until we found a way to get that little bitch out of the castle.

"Coda, I really don't think we need such a big place," my mother said as we dropped our bags on the spacious living room floor. "It's just the two of us."

"Nonsense, Mother," I replied. "For too long, we have lived beneath our status. I am the rightful beta of this pack, and I demand we start acting like it. No one would respect us if we lived in one of the smaller houses."

"Well, I guess," she said. "But there's so much to clean."

"Well, now that you no longer have to forage, you'll have much more time on your hands."

I took a good look at the place I'd be calling home for the foreseeable future. Every surface was covered in a fine layer of dust. My mother was right. There needed to be a lot of cleaning done to get this place into acceptable shape.

"I don't understand why Jax and Tannin didn't spend more time clearing out the houses to prepare them for us," I said.

My mother sat on one of the couches, then waved off the cloud of dust that puffed up from the cushion. "Well, there are so many houses, and they were only here for a few days before us. Maybe they were able to get to a few."

I scoffed and put my hands on my hips. "Well, if *I* had gone on this mission, I would have seen to it that everything was prepared for the pack's arrival. I should be the pack's beta. Father was beta, and it is my right to follow in his footsteps."

She came over to me and put her hand on my shoulder. "Oh, I know, dear. You'd make a much better beta than Tannin. Why Jax can't see that is mind-boggling to me."

"It's because he's a fool," I growled, clenching my fists at my sides. "It wouldn't surprise me if they were harboring some unnatural romantic relationship. It's disgusting."

"Ugh, if only the elders knew," she said, shaking her head. "Such a thing would open up the right to challenge for sure."

I nodded, considering that for probably the thousandth time. Jax and Tannin had always been eerily close, since the night I cornered Tannin on the cliffside. I should have killed him before Jax showed up to defend him. Then I'd be beta right now. Mine and Jax's family had been beta and Alpha duos for generations. That Jax chose Tannin over me was something I could never and would never forgive.

But no matter. For a long time now, beta was no longer my goal. I wanted to be Alpha. And I was determined to prove that Jax was unfit to lead.

"I'm going to explore the house and choose my room," I declared. "Would you put on something for lunch before you start cleaning? I'm going to need my strength for the tasks at hand."

"Of course, my sweet boy." She kissed my cheek, patted my shoulder, and then disappeared into the kitchen.

I strode up the stairs and wandered through the upper stories, inspecting each room for size and furniture quality. There were three master bedrooms on the third floor, and though the one I chose was slightly smaller, it had windows facing the castle. The décor and clothing were clearly for a woman, but I'd have Mother rearrange things while I was out later to make the room fit for a man like me.

Now that the hard work had been done, I needed to find Jax and Tannin. They were hiding something—something even more devious than their torrid love affair—and I needed to find out what it was.

Any fault I could find in their actions would be of benefit to me and fit into my long-term plan. If Tannin proved deviant, the elders would have to dismiss him as beta and possibly even exile him, and I was the obvious next-in-line for beta. Then I could get close to Jax and either challenge him or see to it that he came to some unfortunate accident.

No matter what, I would reclaim the glory I so rightly deserved. I just had to bide my time and wait for the opportune moment.

After lunch with my mother, I went off in search of my two nemeses. I tracked Tannin to a shabby cottage in the heart of the village. Pathetic. The place looked only marginally better than the shacks we built in the forest. It was hardly suitable for the beta.

I scanned the perimeter, honing my keen sense of hearing to listen in on what was going on inside. His mother and sister were in there. The place only had two bedrooms.

This wasn't where Tannin was living. He was only visiting and apparently helping them with the cleaning. Ugh! Cleaning was a woman's job. Tannin was hardly a man at all.

So then where was his home? Surely, he and Jax had been living somewhere in the time since they'd been barred from the castle.

I briefly considered waiting Tannin out and following him, but he was a total mama's boy, and I didn't have time to waste sitting around listening to him fawn over his family, so I decided to locate Jax instead.

The so-called Alpha was harder to find. His scent was everywhere, leading me from house to house that pack members now occupied, especially the elders. I finally found him just before sunset helping Esther get set up in her new home.

While I hated his chivalrous tactic, I wished I had thought of it first. Catering to the elders like he was some kind of nurse maid was smart. Alphas weren't supposed to be so soft and pandering. They were supposed to take action and get things done. But it was his faux charm and attentiveness that made them love him so.

For a moment, I debated adopting a similar tactic, but I immediately thought better of it. Love and respect were two different things, and I preferred the latter. Love was fickle and weak. With respect came power, and I would need both to become Alpha.

I strolled inside the open front door and smiled at the two of them where they stood in the living room. "I'm glad to see you're making yourself at home, Esther. I just wanted to check in on you and see how you're settling in."

"Oh, I'm doing just fine. Thank you," she said as she slowly lowered herself into an armchair.

Feeble old crone.

"Jax was such a big help," she added as she relaxed into it, beaming up at him like a love-sick pup.

"It was my pleasure," he said. "It's the duty of all the pack to care for our elders."

I fought the urge to roll my eyes. "Of course. My dear, sweet mother requires so much attention, and I had hoped to assist the elders, but I see Jax has already taken care of it. I suppose not having living parents of his own to care for frees him up to help others."

Jax ignored my comment, but the sharp gaze he cut at me told me I'd hit the nerve I was aiming for.

"Actually, Coda, I could use your assistance moving Droger into the house he's chosen," he said with a sly tilt to his smile. "Now that you seem to be done aiding your mother."

"Oh, well, I—" I stammered.

"I think that's a great idea," Esther said. "Droger is such a stubborn old coot, and he hates accepting help, thinking he can do everything on his own. But he's going to hurt himself one of these days. He could really use two of our strongest wolves to help him."

"We'd be happy to, right, Coda?" Jax slapped a hand on my shoulder hard enough to sting and gave me a daring smirk.

Well played. Bastard.

"Of course," I said. "Let's go find the 'stubborn old coot.'"

With his hand roughly squeezing my shoulder, Jax followed me out the door. Not a word passed between us as we walked to Droger's house, and as much as I loathed being manipulated into doing a charity project, I reminded myself this was a good thing.

Play along and stay close to Jax. Find out what he's hiding. And then take him out.

<h1 style="text-align:center">CHAPTER 6</h1>

<h1 style="text-align:center">JAX</h1>

With each inch the sun dropped in the sky, I became more anxious. How did Aliya feel about all of this? Was she frightened? Was she doubting our devotion to her? I needed to see her.

I hated that tending to the elders was keeping me from her. I hadn't thought it would be this difficult for me to leave them. I felt responsible for the elders, in fact, for every member of the pack.

My father had been a great Alpha. He'd been kind as well as just. He went out of his way to make sure everyone he governed was happy and safe and healthy. Sometimes that meant foregoing eating so that the less fortunate wolves wouldn't starve or staying at a dying wolf's bedside so they wouldn't be alone in their final moments.

He taught me what it meant to be a good leader, and I felt compelled to live up to his example.

Before now, I'd never questioned my loyalty to the pack. It had come naturally. But after meeting Aliya and having this choice thrust upon me, my loyalties had changed. Now I found myself being pulled in two opposite directions, and I hadn't anticipated how difficult it was going to be.

Tannin found me as Coda and I were finishing Droger's move-in. Coda seemed oddly inclined to hover, which I didn't trust, but when I suggested he help Droger to his room, he suddenly *remembered* that his mother needed him and took off.

"He's a real piece of work," Tannin muttered as Coda disappeared into the night.

"I think the term you're looking for is 'Piece of shit,'" I corrected, and we both laughed.

"Are you about done here?" Tannin asked in clandestine tone, taking a look over his shoulder at Droger, who was perusing the books on the bookshelf. "We have that other matter to attend to."

Somehow, knowing that Tannin was just as eager to see our girl soothed the knot of anxiety in my gut. It was strange, but I was grateful that Aliya had him to care for her if I was otherwise unable.

I nodded, then turned to Droger. "You okay for the night, old man?"

Droger frowned at me. "I'm fine. I didn't need your help anyway."

Tannin and I chuckled under our breath, and I waved at Droger as we went out the door.

Now that night had fallen, the village was quiet. Not in the way it was before the pack had arrived, of course. That silence had been empty and eerie, echoing with the pain and sorrow of lost souls. This silence was full and peaceful, the sound of contented people who finally found home and were resting after a life-long journey.

Nevertheless, I was fully alert for watching eyes as we made our way through the streets toward the castle. It was of the utmost importance that no one saw us head that way, that no one questioned where we were going. Sneaking into the castle was a huge risk, but we couldn't leave Aliya alone in there with enemies at her gate.

She needed us, and we needed her. It was worth the risk, and we took every precaution to minimize that risk.

Thankfully, the kitchen entrance was on the opposite side of the castle from the view from the village. We made sure no one was watching or following as we made a wide arc around the back of the castle and finally crossed the ward to get inside.

The lights were off in the kitchen, and she didn't appear to be in there. In fact, as we entered the den, the lights were off there as well, and in the ballroom.

"What the hell is up with that?" Tannin jutted his chin toward the stairs, making me aware of the dozen or so buffet tables pushed up against the side wall.

I frowned. They looked like the tables from the ballroom. What were they doing out in the hallway? Following my curiosity, I poked my head into the darkened ballroom. Sure enough, the tables were all gone. What had Aliya been up to?

The only thing left in the ballroom was some sort of form on the floor. A woman's form...

"Aliya!" I rushed into the room toward her, but as I approached, my eyes adjusted, and I realized the figure was nothing more than a mannequin.

Tannin knelt on the other side of it and gingerly touched the wide hole in the fabric chest. He ran his fingertip over the blackened edges and then brought his hand up and rubbed his fingers together.

"Soot," he said. "I think our little princess has been playing with fire."

The soft pad of footsteps sounded from the stairs, and I looked up to see Aliya cautiously peering through the archway. I stood and stepped into the moonlight flooding in through the closest window so she could see me.

"Jax," she whispered, then skipped the rest of the way down the stairs and ran to me.

I caught her in my arms and held her tightly. The press of her body against mine soothed the deep ache in my soul that had started when I'd left her this morning. I wanted to hold her forever, but she pulled away so she could grace Tannin with her delicate affection. I begrudgingly let go.

"I'm so glad you're here," she whimpered as she drew back from him. "After you told them you weren't allowed in the castle, I didn't know when or if I'd see either of you again."

"Nothing and no one could keep us away from you," I vowed, taking her hand in mine.

A smile rose and fell on her face as her brows pinched together. "Is it safe?"

"We made sure no one saw us," Tannin said.

"And the pack are all so grateful to have real homes, I don't think they're paying attention to anything else," I said, then added, "Not to mention they're all exhausted from their travels." Hopefully, that was truly the case.

She nodded, though her face was still torn with worry and doubt.

"Come, my love. Let's go to the den and sit in front of the fire for a while." With a firm but gentle grip on her hand, I guided her to the loveseat in the den.

Tannin turned on the fireplace, then came to sit on her opposite side. She snuggled up between us, fitting so perfectly. With the room warming and lit only by the flames in the hearth, I could pretend for a moment that it was just the three of us in our private getaway, like it was before.

"Speaking of fire, what's with the incinerated mannequin and the empty ballroom?" I asked in a playful tone, arching a knowing eyebrow at her.

She shrugged and looked down at her lap. "I just figured I should learn how to protect myself."

The serious note in her voice made my spirits sink a little. I wanted to tell her that we'd protect her, and she didn't need to worry about learning how to fight. But I couldn't. Not in good conscience. The pack was a threat, but not the only one our princess had to deal with. She'd nearly been eaten by two cusith last night.

Granted, she wouldn't have gotten nearly as close to dying if she hadn't put up the ward...

But that was our fault, too. We'd both lied to her and manipulated her. We hadn't given her much reason to trust us, mate bond or not. I just hated the fact that she needed to know how to defend herself, because that meant I was failing her.

"And how did it go?" Tannin asked, keeping his tone light.

"Oh," she said, seeming to be pleasantly surprised by the interest behind his question. "Uh... I think pretty good. I was hesitant about learning to wield fire, but I didn't burn myself or anything else, so I'd call it a win."

Tannin chuckled, though I could tell his heart wasn't behind it. He was just as bothered by our joint inadequacy as I was.

"You'll have to show me some time," he said.

A flattering pink bloomed in her cheeks as she let out a nervous laugh. "Maybe not just yet. I need quite a bit more practice. And I wouldn't want to burn you by accident."

"I'm a Black Wolf. I'll heal pretty quickly," he said. "But I'd love to watch you grow with your magic. The idea of wielding has always fascinated me, and I've always secretly wanted to see it up close—as long as I'm not the target. The elders perform rituals from time to time, but only with potions and powders acquired through trades. We can't wield magic ourselves, so it doesn't really count."

She cocked her head at him. "What kind of rituals?"

"Mostly mating rituals when a couple pledges themselves to each other," he explained. "The ritual is meant to enhance fertility, I believe."

I'd only been to one of those as a young boy. The only thing I remembered from it were bright flashes of red and pink from powders splashed into the fire as the newlyweds mated in front of everyone. After that, I avoided all rituals altogether.

I'd been raised to fear wielders. Magic came from wielders. Magic killed my father and couldn't save my mother when she was dying from cancer. I'd been taught that magic couldn't be trusted, and I'd always found it hypocritical for us wolves to use it.

And yet, here I was, mated to a wielder with apparently great magical potential, according to Esther.

"Before I tried, I'd never seen magic before," Aliya said. "I wasn't even sure I could do it, to be honest. I only started learning the day you two showed up."

"Sounds like fate to me," Tannin said as he began trailing his fingertips up and down her arm.

She smiled and nestled her head against his shoulder.

"What does it feel like?" I asked, trying to separate myself from my many prejudices and be open-minded.

She pursed her lips in thought. "Um... It feels warm but also cool at the same time. It feels almost electric but soothing. I guess it feels like I'm connected to something bigger than myself."

I nodded, trying to imagine the contradicting sensations she was describing. The last part I understood deeply. Being the Alpha of a pack was the epitome of being connected to something bigger than oneself.

"So, what you're saying is, it feels magical?" Tannin teased, flaring his eyebrows.

She giggled and slapped his arm lightly. "Exactly."

She readjusted herself so that she was laying across us, her head in Tannin's lap and her creamy legs draped over mine. Tannin combed his fingers through the roots of her hair and began massaging her scalp.

"What's going to happen from here?" she asked, her voice holding slightly less worry than before.

I started lightly tracing my fingers over her shins, raising goosebumps in their wake. "Tomorrow, we're going to have a meeting with the elders to decide what to do."

"About me," she interjected.

"Yes," I said. "Tannin and I will convince them you're not a threat and claim to be attempting to make some sort of deal with you. During the course of our faux negotiations, we'll realize we're mate bonded to you. Then we can decide what to do about the ward around the castle."

"I'm not taking it down," she asserted.

I nodded in acknowledgment of her feelings, but I didn't reply. It was my hope that given enough time, this whole ward business would become a thing of the past. But I wasn't about to die on that hill right now, not when our time with her tonight was so short and precious.

"Let's not worry about that now," I soothed as I continued lightly caressing her legs. "Everything will work itself out. I'd prefer to continue where we left off this morning."

I crept my hand teasingly up her thigh and under her dress. She parted her legs to give me more access.

"Would you like that, baby?" I cooed darkly.

She breathed the word that was fast becoming my favorite syllable. "Yes."

CHAPTER 7

ALIYA

These men were going to be the destruction of me.

With an achingly light touch, Jax slowly ran his fingertips up the inside of my thigh, raising goosebumps on every surface of my flesh. As his fingers slid over the sensitive folds between my legs, Tannin's massaging of my scalp grew deeper and more sensuous, roaming to my ears to gently caress my earlobes.

I closed my eyes and melted into their touches, my problems and worries evaporating in the steam of their masterful play.

Tannin's free hand crept over my chest, slipping beneath the fabric of my dress to cup and knead my breast, all the while Jax continued to circle his fingers teasingly around my center. I squirmed and swiveled my hips to encourage his entrance, but he seemed intent on toying with me, and the frustration was becoming intolerable.

I bucked my hips upward, and his fingertip slid lower, grazing over the forbidden spot between my cheeks, and I gasped in surprise, my eyelids snapping open.

"Do you like that?" he murmured, dark temptation in his eyes.

I didn't know how to respond, mostly because I did like it and I felt guilty for that. Was something wrong with me?

Tannin's stiff cock twitched beneath my hand, and he lowered his

201

head above me. "It's okay if you like it." He planted a kiss on my forehead.

"It—it is?" I breathed, searching both of their faces.

He nodded.

"Let me show you how good it can feel," Jax rumbled.

Just as he had been doing to my pussy, he lightly circled his fingertip around the puckering flesh of my anus, and it felt so good in an entirely different way. I gasped at the unexpected pleasure of it, conflicted with what this meant about me.

But as his other finger entered my pussy as he continued to rub my most forbidden spot, the sensations were so overwhelming that I couldn't care what it meant. Individually, both places felt amazing, but together? There was so much I didn't know about my body, about the pleasures of the flesh. A thrill shot through me knowing my mates were determined to teach me all of it.

Suddenly, Jax removed his hand and lifted my legs so he could climb off the couch. "Take off your dress," he ordered as he unbuttoned his pants.

My pulse spiked with excitement as I stood up and did as he said, pulling my dress over my head with frantic hands and bated breath. He kicked off his pants but left his shirt on, devouring me with his eyes.

"Lay over the arm of the couch beside Tannin," he instructed.

The husky and commanding tone of his voice made my insides clench and melt in equal measure. I rushed to obey, starting to believe I'd happily do just about anything he told me to when he spoke to me that way.

I looked to him for confirmation as I bent over the arm of the couch, resting my belly on fabric and bracing my hands on Tannin's lap. The position was awkward, my ass up in the air, but he smiled in approval.

"Unbutton his pants and suck his cock," he said.

Desire erupted inside me, and my mouth began to water. I glanced up at Tannin as I started to unbutton his pants. The lust that weighed his eyelids encouraged me forward. He readjusted his posture as I lifted his hard cock and gripped the shaft in one hand.

I spread my lips over the tip and closed my eyes as I began to nibble and lick teasingly, eliciting a strained gasp from him.

"Perfect, baby," Jax praised from behind me.

I heard him come around, each step building my anticipation until finally, his thick cock pushed into my wet entrance. With slow but deep thrusts, he fucked me from behind, and I instinctively matched the rhythm of my mouth over Tannin's cock, loving the feel of his smooth skin against my tongue and lips.

And then Jax's thumb rubbed over my anus, and I whimpered at the sudden stab of pleasure in my core. How could this feel so insanely good? I feared I'd disappear into the incredible sensations forever and cease to exist. But at the same time, I never wanted it to end. I was their toy, their queen, and I would never get enough of the three of us worshipping each other like this.

The pressure of Jax's thumb increased as his thrusts intensified, his other hand spreading over my ass cheek and grabbing and squeezing. My muffled moans mingled with theirs. Soon, I couldn't distinguish over the others. We were simply a symphony of sin, lust and love.

I took Tannin deeper into my mouth, grateful that at least for this moment, my nausea was nowhere in sight. And all the while his hand was lost in my hair, massaging my scalp and adding to my whole-body euphoria, gripping my roots now and then in a way that hurt so good.

Jax's thumb slid into my back entrance, and the mix of pain and pleasure sent me over the edge in an explosion of ecstasy. My body tightened then began to convulse as bliss obliterated me, a deep moan rumbling up my throat and vibrating around Tannin's cock.

"Oh, fuck!" Tannin hissed as his seed spilled onto the back of my tongue.

His sudden release pulsed another wave of delight through me, extending my orgasm as I greedily swallowed.

"Yes, yes, yes!" Jax grunted, then he pulled his cock from my clenching pussy and pressed the tip into my tight asshole as he came, his hot cum shooting into my entrance and dripping down my thigh.

I continued to gasp and whimper until his groans subsided and his tip left my anus. I never imagined that pain could add to pleasure, and my whole world was spinning at that revelation. As spent and useless as my body was now, my brain was filled with new ideas. Could his cock actually fit inside my ass? All the way in?

A shiver of desire skittered down my spine at the sinful thought.

And then another even more wicked thought invaded my mind. *Could I have both of them inside me at the same time?*

My core tightened so painfully, I had to force the thoughts from my mind, or I would surely come again and how would I explain that?

I unsheathed my mouth from Tannin's still semi-hard cock and pushed myself up, finding my legs wobbly and weak. Jax scooped me up off the floor and carried me back to the couch, setting me between him and Tannin once again. I nestled into both as much as I could, and for a while, there were no sounds except for the whispers of the dancing flames in the hearth.

"I wish you could stay," I lamented, burrowing deeper between them.

"I know," Tannin said as he caressed the top of my head. "I wish we could as well. But it's too risky for us to stay the night. If anyone saw us…"

"I know," I said with a sigh.

"And we have to figure out where we've been living all this time," Jax added. "Coda is already suspicious that we haven't spent any time cleaning any of the houses for the pack. If he finds us in an abandoned house that clearly hasn't been lived in, he's going to cause problems."

I nodded, though I wasn't happy about having to say goodbye to them. "Who's Coda?"

Jax huffed a sigh. "He's the asshole who charged at the ward this morning."

"Oh." Nice to have a name for the guy I already didn't trust.

"Will you be okay here on your own for the night?" Tannin asked.

I looked up at him from beneath my lashes. "I spent every night for the last fourteen months alone in this castle. I'm sure I can do it again." Not that I wanted to, of course. But could I? Absolutely.

He chuckled at my sarcastic tone.

"We'll come back as soon as we're able," Jax said.

"Okay," I said reluctantly.

They both rose and took turns kissing me, then quietly went out the kitchen door. I hated knowing they were out there with people like Coda, who obviously had it out for them. I just hoped they'd be okay, especially since there was not a damn thing I could do to help them beyond these walls.

CHAPTER 8
ALIYA

A powerful wave of nausea rudely woke me from what had been a blissfully deep sleep. I rolled onto my side on the couch in the den and propped myself on my elbow, sure I was going to throw up all over the carpet.

After a few agonizing minutes of clutching my stomach and holding my breath, the wave subsided, and I let out a long, shaky breath.

Yuck, this was terrible. I wanted to believe this was some kind of food poisoning from poorly cooked chicken or infested fruit, but that kind of sickness didn't come in sporadic spurts.

The fruit... What if I was somehow making myself sick with magic? I'd used magic to make the vegetables grow bigger and faster. Could that be it? Or maybe the fact that I was attempting to wield more powerful magic than I could handle was having negative effects on my body?

Whatever it was, I just wanted it to go away, and I really wanted to go back to sleep.

The den was still dim, the fireplace the only light source, though I could see a faint blue tinge in the sky out the window to the east. I still had time before daybreak.

Laying back down, I closed my eyes and tried to fall back into the heavy slumber that had swallowed me for the first time in days. But without the feeling of my mates' bodies to comfort me, I couldn't silence the thoughts that were soon racing through my mind.

The pack meeting was today. Decisions would be made about and without me. Did anyone see Jax and Tannin coming or going last night? And what would happen to them if they had? What would happen to me?

Ugh. I guess I'm done sleeping.

I groggily pushed myself up to sit on the couch, and Tabitha meowed to me from her coil on the armchair.

"Were you laying there all night?" I asked, remembering the wonderful, sinful things Jax and Tannin did to me on this couch.

"Meowwwrrr," she affirmed.

"Perv," I muttered.

She snorted and tucked her head back beneath her hind leg.

"Nice to know someone can go back to sleep," I grumbled with a sigh. "Well, I guess I can get an early start on practicing."

As soon as I said the words, my stomach twisted painfully, a surge of nausea sending a tremor across my shoulder blades. I gripped the arm of the couch and braced myself.

"On second thought, maybe I'll just wait."

I sat there for a moment, waiting for the nausea to subside like it had before, but it didn't go away. It seemed to fluctuate like the tide, rising and falling infrequently, but never completely receding. So, I just curled up against the arm of the couch and tried to distract myself by watching the flickering flames in the fireplace.

Outside the castle, the sun rose, and before long, the buzz of happy chatter sang to me through the window. Such a strange sound. So foreign, yet so familiar. It was a sound that had been nothing more than a memory playing in my head for over a year, and now it was real once more.

But it wasn't the same as before. Beyond these walls was a whole community of thriving people, but I was still alone. I was the only insider surrounded by a kingdom of outsiders. What a surreal state of being. What a sad and desperate one, too.

I turned away from the golden light streaming through window, and my stomach growled angrily and pathetically. How could I be hungry when I felt like I was going to blow like a volcano at any minute?

I hung my head. Well, maybe if I ate something, it would ease some of my discomfort, not to mention give me strength for more wielding practice later.

Gathering my strength, I slipped off the edge of the couch and stood, bracing myself on the arm for a moment to make sure what little was in my stomach stayed there. When nothing came up, I proceeded with overly slow, cautious steps toward the kitchen, catching the edge of the counter like it was a life raft in stormy waters.

As I hovered there, I looked around at the counters and cabinets, which only made my nauseous hunger worse. Nothing sounded good. The thought of eating just about anything stored in here made my mouth water with sour distaste. Meat, eggs, bread... it all sounded terrible.

I glanced at the now empty vegetable basket on the counter near the door to the garden. Tomatoes were the only thing that sounded even remotely appetizing, but I didn't have any in here. If I wanted some, I'd have to go to the garden.

Outside...

I knew my apprehension was irrational. It wasn't the castle walls that protected me from the pack, it was the ward. The garden was within the ward, and I'd already witnessed multiple times that the wolves couldn't breach it.

But still, the thought of leaving this castle made me feel so painfully exposed that I considered foregoing eating at all.

My stomach growled again, this time twisting in a painful cramp, making me buckle forward as I grimaced.

Fine!

I pulled myself along the edge of the island counter, snatched the vegetable basket, and hobbled to the door to the garden. Opening it a crack, I peered outside, scanning what little my view allowed of the area. The space beyond the garden seemed vacant, and the voices of those in the village were distant.

Deciding it was safe enough, I slipped through the door, closing it quietly behind me—as if it mattered with the ward in place, but my paranoia was at an all-time high.

The air in the garden was muggy and thick with herbal fragrances.

Sparrows were flitting around, hopping along the fence posts and pecking at the remnants of the destroyed scarecrow.

Everything looked more or less as it always had, but I still rushed to the tomato plants and urgently plucked the juicy fruits loose without discrimination over color or ripeness, tossing them in my basket.

A twig snapped beyond the fence to my right, and I startled so dramatically that I dropped the basket and all the tomatoes spilled and rolled in all directions over the moist soil.

"You must be Aliya."

I snapped my head in the direction of the smooth male voice to see the last person I wanted to encounter casually strolling toward me on the other side of the barrier.

Coda.

Fear urged me to abandon my efforts, run inside, and slam the door, never to step out here again. But this was my kingdom, my castle, and the worst he could do to me from where he stood was intimidate me, which, at this point, honestly wouldn't take much.

"I am," I said, righting my basket and beginning the chore of re-collecting the scattered tomatoes.

He stopped directly across from me, the tip of his boot kicking the base of the ward and making rainbows ripple throughout the invisible barrier. He put his hands in his front pockets and smiled at me. Up close, he didn't seem so scary. He was handsome, and the charm of his smile was oddly disarming.

"I'm sorry for frightening you," he said. "It wasn't my intention. I only want to talk."

I focused my eyes on the tomatoes as I replied, "About what?"

"Just that I can't imagine what you've been through," he went on. "Living alone in the castle for over a year. It's no wonder you acted so rashly when a pair of big bad wolves came along and tried to take your home from you."

I didn't respond, not wanting to say anything that would contradict the story Jax and Tannin told the pack.

"What were you before the plague hit?" he asked in a conversational tone.

I could just ignore him. I was almost done collecting the tomatoes, and I didn't owe him a single answer. But wouldn't it be a benefit for me to confirm what he was already told?

"I was a servant," I replied, hoping my clipped tone came off as irritated rather than anxious.

"What kind?"

"I was handmaid to the princess," I lied, figuring it was the easiest story to go along with.

"Ah." He kicked at the ward again. "Are servants customarily taught to wield? I find it surprising that a handmaid, especially one so young, could conjure such powerful magic as this ward."

I cleared my throat and shook my head. "No. In fact, wielding hadn't been practiced in Varynia for generations. But as I was all alone and had nothing but time, I studied the ancient books and began practicing on my own."

I knew I was talking a lot, but I figured it was better he not perceive me as much of a threat. A servant who studied magic on her own for a year wasn't much to fear, especially against a whole pack of Black Wolves. And though it wasn't far from the truth, it was less menacing than a princess who could wield, period.

His eyebrows flared in surprise. "Oh. That's actually very commendable. You're an impressive young lady."

Dammit, why is his flattery making me blush?

"I'm sure you were raised on stories about my kind being the villains," he went on, "but I was raised on stories where your late employers were the enemy. I don't think the truth is so black and white. I hope that over time, you will come to see that we aren't so bad. You've been alone for so long. We could offer you community, protection, even a well-matched marriage—which is something I'm sure you wouldn't have gotten in your previous life."

His eyes lingered on me, the heat of his gaze a balm on my skin. I knew that look, had seen it from Jax and Tannin so many times, but receiving it from him made me feel dirty. He wanted me, even though I was sure he would just as soon kill me as fuck me.

I rotated my crouch so that my back was to him as I picked up the last of the tomatoes, giving him less to look at.

"I'm not asking that you take down the ward immediately," he said. "I'm just asking that you consider what's best for you. You could use a friend among the Black Wolves, and not all of them are as kind and understanding as me. I would protect you."

Yeah, right.

I rose, holding my full basket securely, and strode for the kitchen door without another word.

"Think about it," he called as I disappeared through the door.

Once inside, I pressed my back against the door and sucked in several heavy breaths that did little to calm me.

Coda was the epitome of the old phrase "A wolf in sheep's clothing." He had a handsome face and friendly smile, his words laced with honey and promises. But I could see through his façade. He was a wolf in every sense of the word, and I would never give him the opportunity to sink his canines into me.

<h1 style="text-align:center">CHAPTER 9
TANNIN</h1>

Whoever coined the term *No rest for the wicked* clearly didn't understand how much more work it took to do the right thing.

After our visit with Aliya, Jax and I spent the night covertly choosing a home suitable for our station and cleaning it up to make it appear both tidy and lived in. I got maybe three hours of sleep before Jax woke me to help him notify the pack leaders and elders that we would hold the pack meeting at our house.

Luckily, I found a tub of coffee grounds in the pantry, and by the time pack members began showing up, I was wide awake—perhaps too much so.

Like many things, coffee had been a rare luxury when we lived in the forest, and apparently, I'd forgotten how potent its effects were. I downed two cups, one after the other, without a second thought. I wasn't sure which was worse—being too groggy to focus or being jittery and anxious during one of the most important meetings of my life.

"Make yourselves at home," I said to Droger and Esther as I welcomed them inside. "There's fresh coffee in the kitchen."

"Thank you, Tannin," Esther said as she entered the living room. "But I'm afraid this old heart wouldn't survive. Perhaps a nice cup of tea instead."

"Sure thing." I rushed to the kitchen and began fumbling through the cabinets for tea packets, my heart racing until I finally located some.

Then when I went to fill a pot with water to boil, my shaking hands nearly dropped the full pot, forcing me to catch it awkwardly and splash water all over my shirt.

I'm never drinking coffee again.

When I returned to the living room with Esther's cup of coffee, everyone had arrived and filled the couches and armchairs. They were chattering lightly as I handed the mug to Esther and pulled up a chair from the dining room to sit next to Jax at the head of the makeshift circle.

"Now that we're all here, how is everyone settling in?" Jax asked the group as a whole.

"I slept like a baby for the first time since I can remember," Esther volunteered, smiling as she took a sip from her mug.

"Fine, I suppose," Droger muttered grumpily.

Esme, one of the deltas, raised a hand. "A scurrying rat woke me in the middle of the night, and I've heard from several families this morning of similar occurrences. I think we need to address the rat problem quickly."

Jax nodded. "Thank you for bringing that to our attention. I'm sure it's nothing we can't handle."

"Do you think the rats still carry traces of the plague?" asked Rubios, another delta.

"We can't know for certain," Jax replied after a moment of consideration. "It's been over a year since the last of the kingdom died off, and even if we assume the rats are immune to the plague, it's unlikely that any carriers still survive. But we will begin extermination immed—"

"I thought the purpose of this meeting was to discuss the matter of the warded castle," Coda interrupted. "Not to quibble over basic housekeeping."

Jax tensed in irritation at the interruption and narrowed his eyes at Coda for a moment. "I'd hardly call an infestation of possibly disease carrying rats a topic of basic housekeeping. As a majority of the pack won't be occupying the castle anyway, it's important to discuss their safety and health first."

"Well said," Esther agreed with a nod.

"Since the matter has been brought up, what do you intend to do about the girl barricading herself in the castle?" Droger asked, followed by a hacking cough.

Jax and I exchanged a glance, and Jax sighed as he turned back to the gathering.

"Tannin and I have been working on developing a rapport with her," he said. "Like it or not, we have to accept that she holds the power over the ward. We can't break it by force, and we can't intimidate her into lowering it."

He paused to let that sink in, and heads nodded reluctantly. All but Coda, who merely rolled his eyes.

"We have to show her that we are not her enemies, convince her that we can be a safe place for her," he continued. "She's been alone in that castle for over a year, and I think she's sad and frightened. I propose we offer her a promise of security and community in exchange for her cooperation—and we live up to it. When she lowers the ward, she will be given amnesty, and she will not be harmed by a single member of this pack."

"That sounds reasonable," Wilda mused, and others hummed in agreement.

"It's only reasonable assuming she is, in fact, nothing more than a servant," Coda said. "How can we be sure that's all she is?"

I eyed him with a look of bored tedium. "That is what she said she is, and we have no reason to believe otherwise."

"Then you have obviously been too distracted by her feminine wiles during your so-called *rapport* sessions to notice what was obvious to me after only a brief conversation," he countered with an arrogant smirk.

My already turbulent pulse spiked with fear.

"What are you talking about?" Jax asked, failing at masking his suspicion with exasperation.

The group turned to Coda with intrigue and curiosity lighting their faces.

"You spoke with the girl?" Esther asked.

"When? How?" Esme asked.

Coda shrugged. "I spotted her in the garden behind the castle about an hour ago. She was understandably reluctant to talk with me, but what little she did say was enough to give me doubt."

It was all I could do to keep my eyes from wandering to Jax's face, to keep my rising panic from my twitchy features. Coda had spoken to Aliya. If she had taken so much as one step beyond the ward, she could be dead right now. I wanted to shred Coda limb from bloody limb just for the possibility.

"What was said?" Rubios asked.

"She explained that she was handmaid to the late princess, and that she only began studying magic once the castle was empty," Coda explained. "But despite the dirt covering her clothes and hands, she carried herself like a noble, and she spoke with far better diction than I've ever heard from a servant."

Dammit. Why had Aliya spoken to him at all? Why didn't she just run inside and ignore him? She was a proud and stubborn woman, and in this circumstance, that might mean the ruin of her—and us.

"What are you implying?" Jax asked, and though I was close enough to hear the low, threatening rumble in his chest, I couldn't make any moves to calm him without attracting attention.

Coda leaned back in his armchair and slung an arm over the back of it, obviously savoring his current spotlight. "Just as I said. I think she's some manner of nobility. A debutant, perhaps. Hell, with her knowledge of wielding, she might even be the daughter of a sorcerer, or a sorceress in training."

I scoffed. "If that were the case, she could have done a lot worse to Jax and me than merely put up a ward to keep us out. She hasn't displayed a single act of offensive magic against us, nor has she attacked any of the pack since your arrival. That girl is no more a sorceress than I am cusith."

He glared menacingly at me. "Whatever she is, we can't just assume she isn't a threat. She has access to books on wielding within those walls, and just because she hasn't used magic against us yet doesn't mean she won't."

"That's a good point," Droger said gruffly. "Whatever the girl's status, she's a Varynian, and we can't trust a Varynian."

Mutters of agreement rose from the group, and I couldn't stop my heel from bouncing with nervous energy. I looked at Jax, hoping he could find some way to douse their hostility.

"Everyone, please," Jax said, raising both hands to silence them. "If we victimize this girl just because of her patriation, then we are no better than the Varynians. Our enemies are dead and gone, and I think our grievances against them should be buried with them. The girl in that castle isn't a Varyian anymore, and she hasn't been for over a year. She's an orphan... a lost soul without a people. We should treat her with the kindness we ourselves always deserved. If we don't, then we never deserved it in the first place."

The group fell utterly silent, the meaning behind Jax's speech ringing in solemn space.

"Jax is right," said Litta, a delta who had been quiet until now. "The generations-long war is over. Now is a time for peace. I agree with the Alpha's proposal of amnesty in exchange for access to the castle. Let's build a new kingdom, one our pups can be proud of."

The elders and deltas nodded, and I slowly let out the breath I'd been holding as a tide of relief washed over me.

"Thank you, Litta," Jax said. "I couldn't have said it better myself."

She smiled and nodded in response.

Coda, whose hackles had been rising over the turn the discussion had taken, leaned forward and puffed out his chest. "Perhaps the best solution toward peace would be a more formal alliance with the girl. A marriage, perhaps. She is quite beautiful. I wouldn't mind taking her for myself."

My head snapped in his direction with almost audible sound, my eyes narrowing to slits as I glared at him.

And he noticed, matching my glare with a challenging curl to his lips.

"You would actually consider marrying a Varynian?" Droger barked in outrage.

"She won't be a Varynian after I'm done with her," Coda replied, keeping his eyes locked with mine.

The men in attendance laughed and snickered, while the women scoffed and snorted in disgust. The latter had the right idea.

Jax cleared his throat, both a warning to me and a distraction for the pack from my hostility. "I think we can all agree it's far too early for marriage talk. Tannin and I will continue to work on negotiations with the girl. It might not happen overnight, but I'm confident that peace will be found before long. Until then, we have the security and maintenance of the rest of the kingdom to address. Let's return to the matter of the rats."

The meeting continued with talk of pest control and securing the borders from future cusith attacks, but it was difficult for me to concentrate. I didn't like Coda's interest in Aliya, whether murderous or lascivious—though, for Coda, I doubted there was much of a distinction. He was a brute in every way, and I didn't want him anywhere near my mate.

I needed to see her. Needed to make sure she wasn't too rattled by her interaction with him. And I could hardly wait for the meeting to be over so I could ensure she was alright.

CHAPTER 10
CODA

I only paid mild attention to the rest of the meeting. All this talk of getting rid of the rats in the kingdom was a waste of my valuable time. Were we not Black Wolves? Had we not lived in the forest surrounded by all manner of rodents for hundreds of years? We weren't timid humans who ran away at such things, we were the ones to be feared.

And as for defending against future cusith attacks again, I wasn't worried. I'd slaughtered dozens of cusith single-handedly. Let them try and come at me.

What I was interested in, however, was Tannin's behavior. The way he'd reacted when I suggested taking the supposed servant girl as my bride was telling. He wasn't merely angry about it, not the way Droger had been. No, that was jealousy I'd seen in his bloodthirsty eyes.

He fancied the girl. Maybe that was why he and Jax were so adamant about sparing her life, determined to convince the pack that she wasn't the threat I knew she could be. He wanted her for himself.

I could certainly understand why. She was a lovely little thing, with skin as pale as milk and probably just as smooth. And that witty mouth of hers would look great wrapped around my cock. I'd have the last laugh.

Let them take her in like a stray pup. I would charm her, woo her, and then when she was mine, I would greatly enjoy bending her to my will until she broke beyond repair. I could even use her magic to my benefit, which would help me greatly when I came into my true role as Alpha.

My dick hardened as I thought about all the ways I would destroy her when the time came. She was young, so she'd be physically strong enough to put up a good fight. Or so I hoped.

But one thing was for certain, I didn't trust Tannin. For the remainder of the ridiculous meeting, he didn't so much as glance in my direction.

What are you hiding from me, mongrel?

Whatever it was, I was determined to find out.

When the meeting finally ended, I was the first one out the door. Crossing the street, I lingered behind the trunk of a thick tree, watching as the rest of the pack leaders filed out. Jax led a handful of deltas down the road, off to catch themselves some rats, no doubt. But Tannin didn't go with them, which was strange. He barely left Jax's side for a moment.

A wave of satisfaction rolled over me. I was onto something here. I stood waiting outside the house, and for a second I had a moment of doubt. What if I was wrong and Tannin was living with Jax? Perhaps, he wouldn't come out at all. Instead, he'd be washing the dishes like the good house bitch he was.

How long was I going to wait for him?

Just as my impatience began to grow and I considered going home, the would-be beta emerged from the front door. He scanned the road along both sides before rounding the side of the house and turning down the alley.

Jackpot.

I abandoned my hiding spot and began my pursuit, trailing far enough behind him that I could easily duck out of sight if he looked over his shoulder. Which he never did. Some beta he was. He had no idea he was being followed. I would've known immediately.

Just one more reason he wasn't fit to be second-in-command.

He stuck to the alleys and back streets, weaving his way through town until he had emerged on its eastern edge that nearly touched the tree line of the surrounding forest. As soon as he was off the beaten path, he jogged across the grass into the trees.

Where the hell was he going? Maybe he was aware of his tail after all, and was leading me on a wild goose chase.

Nevertheless, I went in after him, treading as lightly as possible over the fallen thistle as to not make a sound as I hovered several dozen yards behind him.

He didn't go deeper into the forest. In fact, he seemed to be scaling the edge of it...toward the castle.

He was trying to avoid being seen heading in that direction. Unfortunately for him, I was watching him like a hawk.

He continued along the forest's edge as it rounded the back of the castle. Only once he was out of sight of the village did he emerge from the tree line. Crouching behind a bush, I watched as he crossed over the grass toward the garden where I'd found the little welp this morning.

Was he hoping to find her out here so he could pine over her? *Pathetic.*

But he didn't stop as he approached the ward, and then—

Holy hell! He passed through it!

I blinked in shock several times after he crossed the invisible barrier like it didn't exist at all. And then he opened the door she'd gone through earlier and went inside the castle like he'd done it a hundred times.

I wanted to feel triumph over this discovery, but all I felt was fury.

The only way Tannin could go through the ward was if the girl had invited him. She had invited him, but not me?

That was why he'd reacted so sharply to my quip about taking her for myself. He already had her. And there wasn't a doubt in my bones that Jax knew about it. They'd both been lying to everyone from the start.

I wasn't going to stand for it. This was the highest of betrayals, and I was going to make sure the entire pack learned of it.

The sound of a door closing made me jump so hard I nearly fell off the couch in the den. My heart shot up into my throat, and white-hot panic splashed over my face and neck.

Someone had somehow gotten through the ward. But who? Was it Coda?

Gripping the top of the couch's back, I peered over it with wide eyes, preparing to use whatever magic I could to defend myself as footsteps grew louder and closer.

Tannin's face came into view as he stepped through the archway from the kitchen, and the tension in my body left me so suddenly and violently that my muscles felt like mush.

"Tannin, what are you doing here?" I asked when I finally found my breath. "It's daylight. Someone could've seen you. Someone could have—"

"Hey, it's okay," he said in his soothing tone that never failed to settle my anxiety. "I made sure no one saw me. We're safe."

I let out a shaky breath as he came around the couch to sit beside me, putting a comforting hand on my knee.

"I just had to come and see you after hearing at the pack meeting that Coda confronted you," he said, concern furrowing his eyebrows. "Are you okay?"

I shrugged, not wanting to tell him that I wasn't okay, but I couldn't lie either. My interaction with Coda had left me shaken and even more certain that the pack couldn't be trusted. And those fears only intensified the turbulent knot that continued to twist and grow in my stomach. I'd eaten a few of the tomatoes I'd gathered today, and they'd helped for a short while, but it didn't take long for the pain to return. I didn't want to worry him with that, either.

He frowned at my non-response. "What did he say to you?"

I looked down at my lap, picking at the fabric of my dress. "He asked about my history, who I was before the plague. He asked about my magic and if I'd had training. I told him I was the handmaid to the princess because it was the easiest lie I knew I could play along with. And as for the wielding, I told him pretty much the truth—that I'd only started teaching myself from the books here after everyone died. I figured that little speck of truth could only help make me seem less threatening."

He nodded with tight lips, exhaling through his nose. "Okay. I think you said the right things, though he's still not convinced."

I shifted in my seat, my pulse picking up speed. "Why? What did he say about me?"

His jaw ticked. "He said your posture and speech are too proper for a servant."

I balked at that, my lips twisting in a deep frown. "He clearly doesn't know what he's talking about. The castle servants were taught to present themselves in a manner befitting the crown. Hell, some of them spoke more eloquently than I did."

He shook his head. "I know. Coda hasn't been around anyone but traders his entire life, so he assumes that anyone who isn't a noble would behave like a peasant, like him. But his opinion matters very little. The rest of the pack bought the story we sold them."

My spine straightened. "And? Was anything decided?"

"Yes," he said with a nod, taking my hands in his. "They've agreed to give you sanctuary if you lower the ward."

I had expected to feel relieved by such news, and the weight of doom to be lifted off my shoulders. But instead, the weight I carried only changed, bringing with it a whole new slew of concerns and fears.

If I accepted the offered deal with the Black Wolves, I would never be the princess of Varynia again. They would demand that I forsake my entire identity, playing the role of a nobody for the rest of my life, while allowing my kingdom's most ancient enemy to make the castle their home. My parents' legacy, my home, would never truly be mine again. Could I ever sleep peacefully again knowing I'd made that choice?

"Aliya?" Tannin asked, his green eyes glowing in the dance of firelight.

"I don't know. I just... I wish there was another way. An option that didn't mean abdicating my throne completely."

"Hey, it won't be forever." He squeezed my hands. "Once our bond is made known to the pack, you'll be the Alpha's wife. You'll become queen of the new kingdom anyway. This farce is only for a short while, I promise you."

I looked off to the side. "I suppose."

But that was assuming that everything went according to plan. If the Black Wolves found out that Jax had lied about my heritage, would he be de-throned also? I trusted Jax and Tannin, but their pack was a problem for me. The Black Wolves didn't know me, nor would they want to get to know me once they found out who I truly was.

I really didn't think that pulling down the only thing that was keeping me safe—the ward—was smart for me. Or my men.

"Look on the bright side," Tannin continued. "You'll never have to be alone again. You'll be part of a community built on the deepest loyalty, and they're going to love you as much as Jax and I do once they see the beautiful, kind, incredible person you are."

He was being too optimistic, but that was part of Tannin's attraction.

"I hope so," I said with a sigh, though his flattery did help lighten my spirit a little. "So, where do we go from here? I can't just lower the ward without a fight. That wouldn't seem real."

I didn't want to lower it at all, and I truly hated even discussing it. Some dark part of me hoped the pack would change their mind about the deal, then I'd never have to lower the ward. I'd have an excuse to keep the ward up, to stay locked inside my cold, hollow bubble that I'd grown oddly accustomed to, and nothing would have to change.

But I knew that wasn't realistic. If an agreement couldn't be reached, it truly would be war. They'd find a way to get me out of the castle or to cross the ward, and I wouldn't have any leverage left to bargain for my life.

This was the only way.

"No, we'll draw the negotiations out," Tannin said, and my tight chest muscles loosened. "When we're ready, we'll make a show before the pack leaders of coming to an agreement and making promises. That way everyone will know the exact terms of what's been decided. And you'll be safe."

"Okay," I agreed, relieved beyond belief that I still had time. To adjust, to accept, or come up with an alternative, however unlikely that might be.

"Come here."

He pulled me into his arms, and I let myself relax against the firm comfort of his chest.

"What were you doing in the garden this morning, anyway?" he asked. "There's plenty of food in the kitchen. Even with the ward up, I don't feel good about you going outside where the pack can see you."

"I know," I said, debating for a beat whether to tell him about my recent decline in health. "I've just had an upset stomach the past couple days, since the pack arrived. I think my nerves are getting the better of me. Nothing in the kitchen sounded good, and I didn't think it would hurt to quickly grab something fresh from the garden."

His body stiffened beneath me. "Are you sure that's all it is? You don't think it's the..." He broke off, as if even suggesting it would make it true.

"The plague?" I finished for him. "No. I treated so many of the infected toward the end, and mild indigestion wasn't how it started. I really do think it's just anxiety."

Maybe if I say and think it enough times, I'll actually believe it.

His arms tightened around me, and he placed a soft kiss on the top of my head. "I'm so sorry we put you through this. I'm sorry about everything. You should never have gone through all the loss, loneliness, and fear you've endured. But it'll be over soon. Jax and I will make sure you get the life you deserve."

His promise was touching, taking the edge off the worries that plagued me. If nothing else, I believed in Tannin and in Jax. What we had was messy and complicated, but it was stronger than steel and more glorious than anything I could have dreamed up for myself. It was the best thing that had ever happened to me.

As long as I had them, I knew everything would be okay no matter what else befell us.

Tannin and I held each other like that for a long moment, and I was aware of each second that ticked by because I knew that any one of them could be the last. I didn't want him to go. I didn't want to be left alone in the castle with wolves prowling outside, plotting my demise and waiting for me to make a single wrong move.

But the moment inevitably died, and Tannin sat up. "I should get back out there before anyone notices my absence."

I nodded mutely as I peeled myself from his embrace. He rose, and I followed him into the kitchen.

"Let me at least check outside first and make sure it's safe," I said. "Make sure no one is around to see you leave."

"Okay," he said, hovering by the edge of the counter.

I went to the door and pushed it open, poking my head out of the gap and looking in every direction. I didn't see anyone, didn't hear any footsteps or distant voices.

"Alright, it's safe," I said, beckoning him forward with a wave of my hand.

He rushed toward me, taking my hand as he lowered his face to mine to steal one last kiss. It was bittersweet and far too brief. The worst part was wondering when I'd feel his lips again. It could be tonight, or it could be days or weeks from now. I hated the uncertainty most of all.

Finally, he slipped away from me and went out into the garden. I lingered in the doorframe, watching as he clandestinely hopped the fence, then looked both ways before crossing through the ward.

I let out a breath of relief.

Suddenly, three men emerged from the shade of the trees, storming right for Tannin with Coda in the lead.

"Traitor," Coda hissed before he sucker-punched Tannin in the face.

Pressing my hands over my mouth to cover my scream, I watched with wide, terrified eyes as the men restrained Tannin's flailing arms and legs and carried him away.

"Tannin," I whispered, stretching out a hand to reach for him. But there was nothing I could do about it.

CHAPTER 12

JAX

fter setting rat traps in various places in the fourth house, I decided to break for lunch. There were still a lot more houses left, but I was running on empty since last night, and I needed to eat to be at full focus and strength.

As I stepped out the front door of the house I'd just finished, a ruckus in the distance caught my attention. Lots of voices were shouting a few blocks away, but not in fear, as if a cusith had attacked. They sounded angry, like a riot had begun.

What fresh hell is this now?

Following the cacophony, I hurried into the village square in front of the castle, preparing myself to break up some sort of dispute over property. A crowd had already gathered around the instigators, and I had to push through from behind.

When I got through the hollering bodies, what I found was the last thing I would've expected.

Tannin was being forced to kneel on the ground, with Coda's lackies —Tywen and Hollis—gripping his wrists at awkward angles to keep him in place. He jerked in his attempts to break free of their hold, pain contorting his face into a grimace.

"What the hell is going on here?" I demanded, my voice radiating power and authority.

"Tannin is a traitor and a liar," Coda declared with a snarl from where he stood beside his captive. "And I move for immediate exile."

More shouts erupted from the crowd.

"On what grounds?" I barked loudly above the noise, my knuckles aching with the pure, unadulterated desire to beat Coda's cocky face to a bloody, unrecognizable pulp.

"He's been lying to us. To everyone," Coda said. "He can cross through the ward. He's been conspiring with that little bitch in there this whole time."

My heart thudded with panic, but my face remained a mask of fury. "What evidence do you have to support your ridiculous claim?"

"We saw him with our own eyes," Hollis said. "We saw him leave the rear entrance of the castle and pass through the ward like it was nothing."

My fury didn't wane at this information. Instead, it changed targets. My eyes fell on Tannin's face, and he peered a pleading gaze up at me.

Fucking idiot! Why on earth would he go to her in the middle of the day? He just put everything we'd been working toward in jeopardy.

"And I'm pretty damn sure he's not the only one allowed inside that castle," Coda added, stalking toward me like a predator about to pounce. "There's no way you wouldn't have known about your beta's alliance with the girl when it was just the two of you here waiting for us. So, either you knew about them and decided to keep it from the pack, or you're both in on some scheme with that wielding Varynian whore."

"Don't call her that!" Tannin snarled, bucking against his restraints.

Shut up, Tannin!

"You're treading on dangerous ground, Coda," I said in a low, warning growl. "This is not the way we handle those accused of a crime. If Tannin did indeed enter the castle, then he deserves the right to explain himself. You know that he and I have been working on building a rapport with the girl. It could very well be that he gained her trust enough for her to allow him inside today, in which case, he should be commended rather than condemned."

The shouts died down, replaced by curious whispers and mutters of agreement.

But Coda was unphased by the shift in public opinion. He folded his arms over his chest and smirked at me, snorting a laugh through his nose.

"Do you deny my accusation of your treachery with the girl?" he asked.

"I deny every accusation of treason," I said boldly. "And your mudslinging is a waste of everyone's time."

Coda tutted, shaking his head. "That's not what I asked. Do you deny keeping secrets for the girl in the castle?"

The chatter of the crowd died down as everyone was eager to hear my response.

"Yes," I asserted. "I deny this whole charade you're putting on in your pathetic attempt at a power grab."

Coda's smirk grew, and he unfolded his arm and reached into his back pocket, pulling out a small glass vial filled with purple liquid and holding it up for all to see.

"Then you won't mind taking this truth serum, would you," he said, dangling it in front of me.

Fucking snake. That was a dirty trick to pull.

My muscles seized, and my blood ran cold. As much as I tried to maintain my confident façade, I was fucked now. If I refused to take the serum, it would be viewed as an admission of guilt. But if I did take it, there was no beating Coda's challenge. I'd have no choice but to honestly answer every question—and I kept more secrets than just Aliya, even if some of them weren't mine.

"The use of such magical tonics is reserved only for serious cases, like murder," I countered. "We're not wielders, and we only resort to their tricks when absolutely necessary."

Coda pushed the vial even closer to me. "I'd call treason a serious case. I think the elders might agree."

I looked around at the faces of the elders, the pack leaders, and the families we protected. Loyalty and trust were on several, but doubt was creeping in to more expressions than I would have liked.

"Jax, just take it so we can put the matter to rest," Esther suggested.

"Yeah, my lunch is getting cold," Droger rasped grumpily.

Coda smirk spread to a full-on sadistic grin. "Take it."

"No," I hissed low behind gritted teeth.

"Take it," Esme said, and when I turned to look at one of my most loyal deltas, her expression was hard with suspicion.

As was every other face looking back at me.

I'd never taken truth serum before, never even seen it used. Maybe I could withstand its effects. I was Alpha. I was strong. And I had no choice.

I snatched the vial forcefully from Coda's hand, jerked the cork off, and tossed the liquid into my mouth. It was thinner than water, with a floral flavor, like lavender. And when I swallowed it, it sent a cooling sensation all the way down my throat and into my belly.

"Now then." Coda clasped his hands behind his back, regarding me with a look of smug triumph as if he had already won. "Did you know that Tannin was permitted through the ward?"

The truth tugged at my soul like a fishing hook had snagged it, being reeled out of me by the question asked. I clenched my jaw with painful force against the urge to speak the damning word, grasping and clutching desperately for the willpower to say the opposite. But there was nothing to reach for, nothing but me and the truth inside the shell of my body.

"Yyyyesss," I grunt-hissed despite my full-body refusal.

Gasps rose from the crowd around us.

Coda's lips curled wickedly, his eyes narrowing. "And are you also allowed through the ward?"

The compulsion to confess was stronger than anything I'd ever felt. I closed off my throat, determined to hold my breath until I passed out. Perhaps the serum would wear off by the time I regained consciousness.

But the cooling chill the serum had left in my throat turned into an unbearable itch, scratching and tickling until my eyes watered and tears blurred my vision.

I couldn't take it anymore! I gasped and hacked against the excruciating itch, each couch a choked, "Yes," as it escaped my lips.

Sharper gasps pierced the air, which was now thick with tension and betrayal.

"Why?" Coda interrogated. "Why are the two of you allowed through the ward?"

I glanced at Tannin as I struggled to fabricate some way to fight this compulsion. His green eyes held a dim resolve, an acceptance of defeat, somehow giving me permission to stop resisting.

I sighed as the itch vanished without a trace. "We're mated to her."

Several dozen "Whats?" scattered around the gathering. But I didn't look at any of their reactions, focused on Coda's. His eyes narrowed, his irises bright with possessive rage, his jaw clenched, and his nostrils flaring.

Just seeing the jealousy he expressed made me want to murder him right where he stood.

"What do you mean 'We'?" Esther asked.

"Tannin and me," I clarified, puffing up my chest with the clarification. "We're both mated to her."

"Liar." Coda spat, and I couldn't help but laugh at him.

"I can't lie." I spat back at him. "It's the truth. She's our mate."

"But... that's impossible," Droger argued. "Mate bonds don't form between more than two people."

"Actually, that's not true," Edith said. "It has been known to happen, but it's incredibly rare."

"And how do we know that it's a true mate bond and not just some spell?" Esme prompted. "It's far more likely that the girl enchanted both of you for her own protection."

"That's not what happened," I refuted. "When we showed up here, we were wounded, me fatally so. She healed us, not knowing who or what we were. Tannin and I were both aware of the bond even before we decided to kill her, but the bond was too strong to let us even attempt it."

The truth was flying out of my throat now, and I wouldn't have held it back, even if I could. Perhaps the truth would set us free.

"Why did you decide to kill her after she healed you?" Esther asked.

"Because she's the princess."

I didn't have time to even think about trying to stop myself from telling the truth. The words flew out of my mouth before I consciously decided to respond, skipping my brain entirely. And as soon as they left my lips, the weight they carried crushed down on my heart and soul like an anchor hitting the sea floor.

All eyes were on me now, wide and disbelieving. Their trust was slipping through my fingers so fast, it practically left rope burn. I couldn't let this get any farther out of control than it already was.

"Yes, I lied about who she was, and about the mate bond," I said, owning the authority I still had as Alpha. "But I did so for the prosperity of the pack. Aliya is my mate and future female Alpha. Killing one's mate, no matter their lineage, is a crime against the pack. I can only respect that the reason Fate bonded me to her was because she will make our pack stronger. As Alpha, my decision still stands. Aliya will lower the ward, and she will not be harmed."

Wilda stepped forward between Coda and me, then turned to face me. "Lying to the elders about such a serious matter is treason, regardless of your reasons for doing so. An Alpha must be trustworthy, or he is not worthy at all."

Esther came up and put a hand on Wilda's shoulder. "We will deliberate on the matter and announce our verdict tomorrow morning. In the meantime, Jax and Tannin, you will be placed under confinement at your home with guards posted around the clock."

Several pairs of hands grabbed me from behind, twisting my arms behind me in the same manner as Tannin's, but I didn't struggle. I let them push us toward the house we'd claimed without a word of refusal.

The pack was and always would be my responsibility, handed down to me by my father and his father, as well as far back through the generations as we could know. I was not going to run from this. I was going to find a way to fix everything and ensure that both Aliya and the pack came out ahead in all this.

Or I would die trying.

CHAPTER 13

ALIYA

Ll I could do was yell and scream at the glass of the window in the library as I watched Jax and Tannin being forcibly dragged from the village square. Tears were streaming down my face and neck, soaking into the bodice of my dress.

"No! No, no! Leave them alone. Please."

What was the pack going to do to them? Would they be executed because of me?

Nausea flared in my gut so suddenly, I didn't have time to get to a trash can before acid erupted up my throat, and I threw up on the once beautiful ancient rug beneath my feet.

I collapsed beside the putrid puddle, only crying harder as I wiped my mouth with the back of my arm.

It was impossible to just stay here inside the castle and do nothing. They'd risked their lives for me, and now they might die for the same reason. I couldn't let that happen, I just couldn't. But how was I going to save them? I was so sick, I could barely move a few steps without throwing up again.

And even if I could move freely, the pack would surely kill me if they saw me step even one foot beyond the ward. I was fairly decent with my fire and wind wielding now, but against a whole pack of Black Wolves I didn't stand a chance.

243

Going out there would be suicide, especially in my current state.

I sat on the ground for a long moment, gathering my bearings and just breathing through the storm of emotions and physical discomforts assailing me.

Tabitha hopped down off the couch and sauntered toward me, sniffing at the puddle and then snorting in disgust. Then she sat beside me, looking up at me with those big green eyes.

"Meow?"

"I know, Tabitha," I said, patting my hand down her head and back. "I'm no good to anyone like this. I think, unfortunately, I have to help myself before I can even attempt to help them."

She blinked, then turned and pranced to the most recent spell book I'd been studying on the arm of the couch. She swiped her paw at it insistently.

"Oh, good idea!"

I had healed Jax with a spell that first morning, brought him back from the brink of death. Surely, whatever was wrong with me wouldn't be as difficult as that. And if I could use my magic on someone else, I could use it on myself.

Ignoring my mess for the moment, I crawled on my hands and knees to the couch, pulling myself up enough to reach the book and dragging it along the front of the cushion, down to my lap.

I opened it, flipping through the pages for the section on healing spells. Wounds, missing limbs, broken heart, blah, blah—here! Spell to cure illness.

I had no idea what was actually wrong with me, or what illness I had, but this spell was broad, intended for a wide array of common sicknesses, from intestinal upset to chronic migraines and influenza. If I had some form of food poisoning or a stomach bug, this should fix it.

The instructions were similar to the healing spell I'd performed on Jax. *Place hands over the afflicted region, focus on the intention to heal, and recite the incantation.* I studied the ancient words and repeated them in my head a few times until I was confident I wouldn't have to look at the page to remember them.

Then I set the book down and sat up straight. I placed my hands on my belly, closed my eyes and took a deep breath, blowing it out slowly. I emptied my mind, focusing my will only on my intense, desperate desire to be free of this affliction.

"Exos mallum nostra tyehrn," I said.

The warm-cool tingling sensation I'd become so accustomed to filled my chest, spreading up my shoulders and down my arms to my hands. I could feel the pulse of magic from my palms over my belly, and hope flared in my heart.

But then the pulse withered and evaporated, rescinding up my arms and settling in my chest, dormant once again.

I opened my eyes, frowning down at my body. Nothing had changed. I didn't feel any better or any different at all. My stomach still ached, my limbs still trembled, and acid still burned in my throat.

Why didn't it work? Was I really so weak at the moment that my magic was no longer effective? Or had I somehow messed it up? Maybe I said one of the words wrong.

I read over the incantation again and sounded out the words in my mind, even though I was certain I'd said them right the first time.

"Okay, I'll just try it again," I decided out loud. It wasn't like it could hurt.

I repeated the process, this time saying the words loudly and slowly, enunciating each syllable as clearly as I could, pushing my will even harder than before.

Once again, magic stirred inside me, blossoming like an ephemeral rose and spreading down my arms. And just like before, when it reached my palms, it seemed to bounce off my belly, pulling back up my arms like rain falling in reverse.

"Dammit!" I cursed, slamming my fists against the floor on either side of me.

I needed this to work. I needed to be rid of this condition so I could help the men I loved. Why wasn't the spell working? Unless...

What if this wasn't some common sickness? What if the plague really had mutated and come after me? Or maybe this was something entirely new. Which begged the question... would my mates be safe being in contact with me?

Intuition snapped an answer deep in my gut. I'd already been in pretty close proximity with them after I started feeling this way. If they were going to catch whatever this was, it was already in their system.

And if I didn't get to them soon, the pack would kill them anyway, and my worry over this sickness would be for naught.

No, quarantining myself in this castle wasn't an option. I'd free them of their confinement, and then we'd deal with this sickness together.

"But how am I going to get to them like this?" I lamented. "I need to be better to even have a chance."

"Rowr," Tabitha said.

I turned to look at her, and she turned her head toward the row of shelves to my left. An idea formed in my mind.

So far, I'd been solely focused on defensive and offensive spells, with brief forays into healing—however unsuccessful. I hadn't even bothered to look into potions.

"Now you're thinking, Tabitha."

I rose to a stand on wobbly legs and approached the bookshelf with labored steps. Scanning the titles on the spines, I let my intuition guide my gaze. About a foot above my head, the title *Potions for All Maladies* caught my eye.

"Perfect."

Stretching on my tiptoes, I reached my hand up, gripping the base of the spine and inching it out until it just about fell on my face. "Ah!" I called out, scrambling to catch it. The jostling upset my stomach, and I stilled for a long moment until the pain passed.

Once I was stable, I hugged the book against my belly and carried it to the couch. My body sang with relief to sit in comfort again, and I looked down at the tome in my lap.

There had to be something in here that could help me, if not to cure whatever was wrong with me, then at least to make the nausea go away temporarily. I had to get into fighting shape fast. It didn't matter if it lasted, but it was imperative that I got to my mates in time.

Turning the cover, I followed the table of contents to the section on medicinal potions. As I flipped through the pages, I got the sense that potion-making was a last resort, mostly used by those that didn't have a strong grasp on wielding. After all, what could a potion do that a spell couldn't? A potion couldn't reseal a mortal flesh wound in seconds.

But seeing as I had little knowledge of spells and no time to invest in locating the correct one to fix me, a potion was a good last resort. I just hoped it worked.

Ah, there it is. Nausea remedy. A look through the ingredients made me sigh in relief. I had all those herbs and spices in the kitchen, thank the gods!

Ginger root, sprig of mint, cinnamon stick, and water for the base.

Invigorated by the prospect of relief from this hell, I climbed off the sofa and strode down the stairs and into the kitchen. I pushed through the pain that gnawed in my gut as I got to work collecting the items.

Filling a pot with the exact amount of water, I set it on the stove, watching it intently. Finally, it began to bubble and boil. I dropped the herbs in the order and amounts instructed. I stirred the concoction for thirty minutes, until the water turned honey brown.

The potions book said to remove the pot from the heat and say the incantation so that the magic could fortify the potion as it cooled.

So, I turned off the stove and set the pot to the side, immediately reciting the short verse with my hands held just above the rising steam.

"Imbuee magi conter."

Magic flared in my chest and spilled down my arms, glowing a pale, beautiful green as it left my palms and absorbed into the liquid. I was so grateful that my magic didn't retreat this time that I wanted to cry, but the tightening of my throat triggered my nausea, and I swallowed against it, stifling my happiness.

Besides, the true test would be if the potion worked, which I wouldn't even be able to test for another thirty minutes when it had completely cooled.

I sat at the island counter, reading through the book of potions as I waited. But despite trying my absolute best, I couldn't really retain what I was reading. My eyes kept glancing at the timer, which only made me more frustrated.

"Ugh!" I groaned.

When the chime finally rang, I slid off the stool and practically sprinted around the counter to the pot, spurring a fresh wave of nausea up my chest with urgency.

"Not this time," I croaked as I scooped a spoonful of the concoction. "Please, not this time."

Just as the burning stung my throat, I closed my mouth around the full spoon and quickly swallowed.

The change was instant. The burning in my throat vanished, the urgency to vomit completely gone. My stomach no longer twisted and cramped, and the sweat cooled from my brow and neck. Even my limbs felt stronger, the trembling now nonexistent.

"Thank you," I whispered to whoever could hear me.

Now I had a chance. And without the distraction of my body's misery, I could think more clearly. Night was my best opportunity to get to Jax and Tannin. It would give all of us more cover from suspecting eyes.

That's when I would make my jail break.

Hold on, guys. I'm coming.

TANNIN

The air in our temporary house was so thick with hostile tension, I could have sliced into it with my claws. Jax hadn't spoken a word to me since Coda's lackies shoved us through the front door. He just sat on the couch, glaring at the inactive fireplace, silent and unmoving as a stone.

"So you're just going to ignore me?" I asked when I couldn't take it anymore.

No response. Not even a glance in my direction.

"Look, I know I screwed up, but we need to figure out a plan if we have any chance of protecting Aliya," I urged.

"You didn't just screw up," Jax said in a low, dangerous voice that cut through the tension like a poison-tipped blade, his back still facing me. "You single-handedly destroyed our only opportunity to integrate our mate safely into the pack."

Though I was grateful the silence had finally ended, I shrunk inwardly in disgrace under the weight of his scolding words.

"You not only outed yourself and me as traitors, but you also outed Aliya as the last surviving enemy of our people," he went on, his voice growing in volume.

He turned to me then, eyes slit with rage. "You fucked all three of us!"

I flinched, wincing tightly. "I know. And I can never express how deeply I regret that."

He leaned forward so his glare could ensnare me. "What the hell were you thinking? Sneaking into the castle in the middle of the fucking day! Of all the idiotic, thoughtless, reckless—"

"I know!" I blurted, jumping to my feet. "But after hearing about how Coda interrogated her, I had to make sure she was okay. I was worried—"

"You don't think I was worried too?" he snapped, slamming his hand on the armrest so hard that the wooden frame beneath the fabric cracked. "You don't think I wanted so badly to race to her side and comfort her and find out the truth from her own sweet lips? She's my mate too. But I knew better than to do something so asinine. We agreed not to enter the castle during the day. Or did your dick make you forget?"

I put my hands up defensively. "Hey! I didn't fuck her, if that's what's got you pissed."

"No, what has me pissed is that you destroyed everything we're trying to build!" he roared, forcefully pointing his index finger in the direction of the castle—in the direction of our mate.

My shoulders sagged, and I shook my head. "I was so careful. I took every precaution to stay out of sight, sweeping through the back streets and following the edge of the forest until I got close to the garden. I kept an eye out the whole way, making sure I wasn't followed. I never would've put Aliya in danger intentionally."

His bunched features smoothed ever so slightly, and he leaned back against the sofa. "Well, you did. And now it falls to me to figure out what we're going to do about it."

I sighed, then went to sit on the other end of the couch with a respectful amount of space between us. "What are we going to do about it?"

He shook his head, bringing his hand up to rub his mouth and chin. "I don't know. That's what I've been deliberating."

I nodded, turning my head to gaze out the window across the room. A silhouette passed by, briefly blinking out the afternoon light.

"I've checked all the doors and windows of the house," I said. "There's someone stationed at every possible exit."

"That's fine," he said. "We're not going to flee."

"We're not?"

His gaze snapped at me, blazing with conviction. "I am the Alpha. Trying to escape would be an admission of guilt, and I won't have my people believing I abandoned them for an outsider."

Anger flared in my chest. "Your people just rejected you. They dragged you by force and threw you in this gilded cage only because they didn't have access to a proper dungeon. They don't accept you as their Alpha anymore."

"What they accept doesn't matter," he countered. "The Black Wolves are my responsibility, my sacred duty handed down to me by my father and his father before him. I love our pack, and it's my obligation to do what's best for them."

As much as his stubborn attitude chewed on my thinning patience, I felt the same. Mama and Twila were my responsibility. And no matter what happened with Aliya or the pack, I would rather sacrifice myself to a horde of cusith than abandon them.

They must be so worried right now. I couldn't bear to think about what Mama must be feeling knowing I'm being detained on the accusation of treason and facing a possible death sentence. And poor Twila... I was the only male role model she had left. I was her protector. Her hero.

Some hero I was turning out to be.

If I died, there'd be no one to watch over them. No one to help raise Twila and encourage her to make better choices as she grew up. No one to prevent Mama from marrying another abusive asshole.

No one to do what would be necessary and dispose of the body afterwards.

I thought about that when Jax was forced to drink the truth serum. I'd never told him about what I'd done, thank God. But the way he'd looked at me the night that Corbin's disappearance had been announced made me suspect he knew what had happened—what I had to do to save Mama and Twila from further abuse.

I'd walked into the house that night to see Corbin kicking Mama in the stomach as she curled up on the floor, covered in blood. Twila was huddled in a corner, silently sobbing, a purple welt on her forehead.

I didn't hesitate. And I've never felt guilty about my choice.

But that was information that could have damned both Jax and me if anyone had thought to ask him about it while under the influence of the serum. He didn't know for sure, of course, but that wouldn't have stopped him from answering honestly. Then my mangled corpse would have been tossed into the dark depths of the forest for cusith to find and devour.

I turned away from those thoughts and looked back at Jax. "If we're not going to flee, then what's your plan?"

He crossed his arms over his chest. "I'm going to try to reason with them. Coda and the deltas may be a bunch of impulsive hotheads, but the elders are wise. Esther and Willa will push the verdict in our favor, and from there, we can convince the pack that Aliya is not a threat but rather a blessing to our people."

I shook my head, the muscles of my shoulders clenching. He had so much faith in the fickle people he served. As the heir to the Alpha lineage, Jax had never experienced the cruelty of which they were capable. All he'd ever received was respect, and that was distorting his perspective.

Before he'd appointed me his beta, I'd been the subject of ridicule and brutality. I had seen first-hand the darker nature that all men harbored, and I knew better than to expect mercy from our captors.

"And what if things go differently?" I asked. "Are you going to let them execute me? Sentence you to death or exile?"

"It won't come to that," he declared.

"But what if it does?" I insisted. "Are you so blindly dedicated to your pack that you would let them turn you into a martyr and leave Aliya without a defender?"

The inner corners of his eyebrows twitched, and I could see his resolve waning.

"No," he said after a moment. "My allegiance is first to Aliya, and then to you. I won't let them harm either of you. If their decision goes in an unfavorable direction tomorrow, then... I will fight them by your side."

I offered him a small smile, taking comfort in his promise of solidarity. Hopefully, he was right about the elders and that when we were *escorted* back into the village square in the morning, the pack leaders wouldn't break his heart.

They'd broken mine a long time ago. And the next day's dawn would decide everything.

255

CHAPTER 15
ALIYA

I could hardly sit still for the rest of the afternoon, pacing through the castle and watching the light through the window slowly fade.

It felt good to be able to move freely again, and now that I could, I couldn't seem to sit still. I needed to take advantage of this period of good health while I could. I wasn't sure how long the anti-nausea potion would last. An hour? A day? Though so far, it had been several hours, for which I was grateful.

I filled a small vial with the potion and attached it to a string I secured loosely around my neck, so that if the sickness were to return while I was in the middle of my dangerous excursion, I could address it immediately. I didn't want anything to hinder my rescue mission, or to put the men I loved in any further danger than necessary.

When the sun had finally set, I ran to my room and began my search for the proper attire for such a mission. There was no need for a dress. The billowing fabric of a skirt would just get in the way.

Ultimately, nothing in my wardrobe proved appropriate, so I went to my father's room and grabbed a pair of black pants and a black shirt. Both were too big for me, so I improvised by stuffing the shirt bottom into the pants and fastening a belt tightly around my waist.

Then I took my mother's black scarf and wrapped it around my head so it covered my braided hair, nose and mouth. This was probably unnecessary as only Coda had seen my face, but I figured concealing as much skin as possible would help me blend into the night.

If someone from the pack were to catch me dressed this way, I could claim to be a pauper from a neighboring village to buy time to flee.

A quick glance in the mirror showed I looked like a gypsy. Though with my father's hunting dagger secured to my belt, I looked more like an assassin—if only that were the case.

Armed and ready, I crept down the stairs. There were only two doors that led in and out of the castle—the front doors that opened to the village square and the kitchen entrance around the back. As Coda had seen me use the kitchen entrance twice now—and assaulted Tannin on the second occasion—I'd be a fool to try it a third time. And the front doors were obviously a big, fat no.

So, I had to get creative.

All the windows on the ground floor were either fixed stained glass or blocked off by iron bars to prevent access to intruders. My forefathers had been wise when building this fortress, but they would never have anticipated anyone needing to escape from the inside.

There was only one other point of access I knew... the wine cellar. It had a small window at ground level that was just on the other side of the chicken coop from the garden. It wouldn't be easy to reach, and even harder to climb through. But it was the best option I could come up with shy of tying bedsheets together and scaling down the wall from one of the upper story windows like Rapunzel.

Opening the door to the cellar beside the kitchen, I quickly skipped down the stairs in the dimly lit space. The air was cool and moist, with only enough twilight haze to see the edges of the steps in front of me.

I gave my eyes a long moment to adjust to the darkness because I didn't dare bring a light or a candle, not wanting to attract any unwanted attention. The darkness was my only shield, and I couldn't do anything to break it.

After a few minutes, the outlines of the wine-filled shelves became clearer, and the meager amount of light coming from the night outside illuminated the glass of the window at the top of the wall at the back of the cellar.

As quickly and quietly as I could, I moved the bottles of wine from the slots beneath the window that I planned to use as footholds, shoving them into other empty slots on either side.

The gold foil on the top of the last bottle caught my eye, and I paused for a moment, holding it up to examine it.

This was the same wine Jax had brought out for our little ball. Had that really been only a few days ago? My lips curved into a bittersweet smile at the memory of the three of us dancing and drinking and laughing. How I longed for that privacy now. A kingdom for only Jax, Tannin, and me.

I shook my head to clear the reverie and grabbed the shelves and jerked outward, making sure the structure wouldn't fall forward with me halfway up it. The rack didn't budge in the slightest, didn't even creak. It was probably bolted into the wall.

Good. Well, here goes nothing.

With my hands still gripping the shelves, I inserted my right foot into one of the diagonal square slots. It was an awkward position, but the slot seemed the perfect fit for my foot. I hoisted myself up, grabbing a higher shelf and sticking my left foot in a higher slot.

The climb was easier than I anticipated, but that didn't stop my hands from trembling with each inch I gained. When I reached the ceiling, I gripped the wood even harder with my left hand, flattening my body against the shelf so I could use my right hand to manipulate the narrow window.

It was much narrower than I'd pictured in my mind, and I wasn't quite sure I'd fit. What if I got stuck? There'd be no one to help free me, and I'd slowly die of starvation and thirst if my men never found me.

But tonight, that was a risk I was willing to take. Tannin and Jax needed me.

The latch gave easily, and when I pushed the window open, a cool night breeze swept a handful of fresh earth right into my face, making me wince and resist the urge to cough.

Thanks a lot, nature.

I shook off the irritation and pulled myself up higher, pushing my head through the gap. The state of having my face at ground level while the rest of my body was pressing against a ceiling was incredibly disorienting, and panic spiked my pulse for a second. But I kept going, slipping one arm through at a time as I lifted one foot after the other.

Once I had my breasts through the gap, I clawed at the ground, dragging myself out inch by inch, grateful for the thickness and coverage of my father's shirt as bits of gravel scraped against it. Were I wearing a dress, I'd have dirt sandwiched against my breasts and belly. A shiver ran through me at the thought.

Finally, I had my hips through, and from there, I rolled onto my butt and scooted backwards as I pulled my legs out.

I sat there for a moment to catch my breath, knowing that this wouldn't even be the hardest part of my evening. But I wasn't about to stop now.

I climbed to my feet and dusted the dirt from my hands, shirt, and pants. Then I turned around to assess the best place to cut across to the forest.

My heart slammed against my spine.

"Hello, Aliya." Coda stood just on the other side of the ward, hands clasped in front of him, a wicked smirk on his face. "Or should I say, Princess."

I couldn't move. I couldn't even think, I was so paralyzed by surprise, fear...and defeat.

"See, I had a feeling you'd try to sneak out to rescue your little pets," he said, his smirk growing into a grin. "That's why I took precautions." He gestured to his right, then to his left.

My head rapidly snapped from one direction to the next, spotting a pack member several yards away on both sides.

"We have you surrounded," he boasted. "We may not be getting in, but you're definitely not getting out."

My pulse got to such an insane speed, I could hardly even feel the beat anymore. My belly cramped, and nausea stirred in my stomach.

Dammit, not now!

I clutched my stomach on instinct, then thought better of it and hugged myself with both arms to make it look like I was merely frightened and not physically impaired.

"You don't understand," I said in a pleading tone. "I don't want war with your pack. Mating with Jax and Tannin has taught me that both our sides have had it wrong all this ti—"

"Bullshit," he spat. "Don't think I can't see right through you, girl. You bewitched those two with your powers, put them under some kind of spell. The Jax I knew would never have let a Varynian live, and he certainly never would've fallen in love with one. Tannin, perhaps, but not Jax."

He smiled and began to pace along the edge of the ward. "I suppose I should thank you, though. Whatever magic you used on him has made him weak, and it gave me just the leverage I need to eliminate him once and for all."

"No!" I shouted. "Please, don't hurt him. Don't hurt either of them. I didn't use magic on them, I swear. Fate did this to us, and my love for them is just as much against my will as theirs, but just as strong."

He threw his head back and laughed loudly, his cackling echoing in the night. "Ah, that was good. You're a skilled actress, I'll give you that. You almost had me going there for a minute."

My mind began to race along with my pulse. What was I going to do? There were three men that I could see, and who knew how many more nearby, waiting for their chance to strike. I couldn't take them all on.

This was hopeless. I had no cards left to play.

"As a thank you gift for your help in raising my status, I'll be sure to deliver your lovers' heads on a silver platter," he said with a sneer. "I'll leave them just outside the ward so you can look at them always."

Like a match being struck in a mine filled with gas, a fury more powerful than I'd ever experienced erupted in me, and with a piercing shriek, I threw my hand out, hurling a blast of fire at him.

He jumped out of the way just in time, the ball of fire singing the sleeve of his shirt as it sailed past him and exploded the trunk of a tree.

The two men guarding either side of the perimeter darted toward him, but he held up both hands.

"No," he ordered. "Hold your positions. We can't leave a gap."

"But the fire," the man to my right argued. "It could spread and take out the entire kingdom."

Coda got to his feet, glaring at me as he patted the charred patch of his sleeve. "Fine," he barked. "Olaf, go get help to douse the flames. I'll man your spot."

The man—Olaf, apparently—ran off into the night, and I struggled to rein in the volatile rage that scorched within me. I wanted to hurt

Coda more than I'd ever wanted to hurt someone before. I wanted to watch him burn to ashes.

But the little voice of rationality whispered in my mind. Coda's reflexes were far better than my aim. If I kept throwing fireballs recklessly at him, I could destroy the forest, and it didn't deserve my incinerating ire.

I needed a new plan. Standing here, listening to him taunt me wasn't going to get me anywhere, so I turned back to the castle and plopped myself back on the ground in front of the window.

"You'll pay for that, you little bitch!" Coda shouted as I retreated. "I swear to you now, my face will be the last one you ever see."

I ignored him, shimmying back through the window and making the climb down the wine rack, which was even more difficult than the climb up.

I wasn't giving up. I just needed a better strategy. If only I knew where to start.

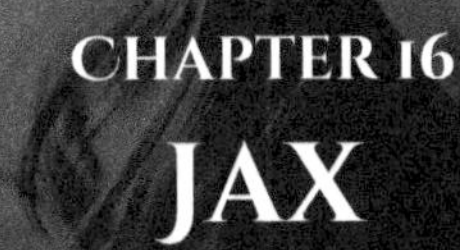

CHAPTER 16

JAX

I hadn't even bothered trying to sleep as the night slowly crept by. There was too much weighing on my mind, too many difficult choices looming just ahead. And I didn't trust Coda not to pull some stunt like sneaking into the house in the middle of the night and slitting our throats.

As much as I hated to admit it, Tannin brought up some good points yesterday. I was no longer entirely confident that the loyalty of the pack would remain with me. I'd lied to them and betrayed their trust. Me, the one person who was chosen to guide and protect them.

It didn't matter that I did it with no malice. They saw my actions as siding with the Varynian princess over them. Even after being divinely bonded to her, I still hated what she stood for. That hatred ran deep through the entire pack, and I couldn't expect them to just let it go on my account.

If they chose to execute Tannin and me, chose war with Aliya, could I really turn my back on them and fight alongside the woman I was destined to defend? The question felt like having to choose between having my left arm cut off or my right.

I wasn't sure what I was going to do, but I trusted that the answer would reveal itself to me when we heard the elders' verdict.

Shortly after sunrise, the fateful knock came at the front door.

I roused Tannin from where he'd been sleeping fitfully on the couch as Esme opened the door and hovered just outside.

"They're ready for you," she said. Her expression was unreadable, but I felt no animosity in her steady gaze.

"Thank you, Esme," I said with a nod, trying to convey my appreciation for her years of loyal service with that simple platitude. "We're coming."

Without a word, Tannin followed me onto the front porch, where four strong deltas immediately grasped both our arms roughly. I didn't reject the manhandling, and I was grateful that Tannin didn't either. We needed to cooperate. To show them we weren't their enemies. Most importantly, we needed to show them the grace of our positions, even under such duress.

I held my head up proudly as they escorted us through the village, offering nods and smiles of reassurance to the fearful faces of the families who watched as we passed.

"Tannin!" called a sweet young voice, and a small figure I recognized as Tannin's little sister pushed through the crowd and ran toward us.

She grabbed the arm of one of the men detaining him and began to yank angrily. "You let him go, you big meanie!"

"Twila, please stop," Tannin urged.

"No. I won't let them hurt my brother," she refuted, scowling at the man as she jerked him to no avail. The sight made my heart ache.

Feet slapped against the cobblestones, and Tannin's mother, Freya, came running to grab Twila and pull her away.

"Twila, please. You're going to get in trouble," she pleaded as the child squirmed in her arms.

"No," Twila began to cry, tears streaming down her cherubic face.

Our escorts paused their procession and tugged Tannin sideways so he could face her. He looked to the man on his right, a silent question passing between them, and the man nodded, loosening his grip to let Tannin lower to his knees.

Freya released her daughter, and Twila threw herself into Tannin's arms.

"I don't want to lose you," she sobbed. "Please don't let them take you from me."

"Hey, it's going to be okay," he soothed as he patted the back of her head. "Everything is going to work out, I promise. I'm never going to leave you."

"You better not," she warned through sniffles.

Tannin chuckled, though I could see the pain and doubt in his pinched features. He gave her one last squeeze before gently pushing her back and standing up.

"Be good for Mama, okay?"

She nodded as she wiped her eyes with balled up fists. Tannin patted her shoulder to encourage her to run back to Freya, and then his escorts locked their hands around his arms once more, and the procession continued.

The elders, deltas, and Coda were all gathered in the square as we approached, the circle of bodies parting to allow our entourage access. They towed us to the pinnacle of the assembly and turned us to face the crowd as it closed in, keeping their hold firm on our upper arms.

Esther stepped forward, and all the whispers and muttering fell silent so her voice could be heard.

"Alpha Jax and beta Tannin," she said, her voice ringing off the walls of the surrounding buildings. "You have been accused of treason against the pack. You have been cavorting with the last surviving heir of the Varynian throne, and you lied to the pack leaders about your involvement with her."

She paused, allowing those words to saturate into the hearts and minds of all who listened. Looking across the faces that stared back at me, I found a mix of sorrow, anger and faith. I absorbed them all, the three warring in my chest.

"Because of your devoted service to the pack, we have decided to overlook your transgressions," Esther announced.

My heart skittered with surprised relief as whispers scattered throughout the crowd.

"What?" Coda snapped, stomping into the center of the assembly. "You're just going to let him go? He betrayed us for our most ancient enemy! You can't just—"

"Let me finish," Esther interrupted, raising a silencing hand. "We will overlook your transgressions on one condition."

Coda seethed, growling menacingly.

"You must go into the castle and convince the princess to let down the ward," she said.

My breath caught in my throat, and I looked at Tannin beside me, the fearful caution in his eyes mirroring my own.

I swallowed. "What then? What will become of the princess?"

She raised her chin. "She will be given a fair and public trial."

Gasps rose from the crowd, though I could barely hear them over the rush of blood in my ears.

"A trial for what?" I asked, trying to keep my voice steady and calm despite my outrage and fear. "She has committed no crime."

"Her crime was being born of Varynian royalty," Droger grunted.

"That's not a crime," Tannin argued, jerking against the arms that bound him. "She could no more choose the blood in her veins than you could yours. You can't penalize someone for something they have no control over."

"Why not?" Coda barked. "Her kind have been doing that to us for centuries."

"And the crimes of her forefathers justifies killing her?" Tannin quipped angrily.

I cut him a warning glance, though I was barely able to contain my own righteous rage.

Esther raised her hand again and spoke loudly over the growing chatter. "As I said, she will be given a fair trial, during which the two of you are welcome to advocate for her."

"And if she's found guilty?" I pressed.

She held my gaze for a moment, the wrinkles in her wizened face seeming to deepen. "She will be punished in accordance with the laws of the pack."

My heart plummeted like an anchor through blood-stained waters as the truth of our situation sank in. They would never let Aliya live. No matter what we said or did, they were determined to kill her. And if we didn't comply with their demands, they would kill us too.

Which arm was I going to chop off?

I sighed. There wasn't really a question now. The pack had given us no option. The choice was crystal clear, and I felt no remorse or grief for the limb I was about to lose.

We could lie and tell them that we'd do as we'd been asked and just walk calmly into the castle. But no... they wouldn't allow that. There was really only one way to do this now. I turned to Tannin once more, and when our eyes met, I knew he understood the words I couldn't say out loud.

As one mind, we exploded into our wolves, the surprise and eruption of shredded clothing allowing us to knock our captors to the ground. We leapt over the crowd seconds before others shifted, chasing us as we raced toward the castle.

Howls and snarls filled the air as paws slammed on the ground inches behind our tails. A set of claws slashed at my ankle, making me whine in pain, but I refused to look back, refused to slow my desperate charge.

With one final leap, Tannin and I sailed through the glorious magic of the ward, skidding over the cobblestones and smacking against the castle doors. Breaths heaving and heart hammering, I looked behind me just in time to see a dozen or so Black Wolves slamming against the ethereal veil and falling to the ground.

They barked and snarled, spittle flying everywhere as they continued to ram and claw at the ward in brutal fury.

"Traitors!"

"Cowards!"

"Bastards!"

The barked curses chorused a deadly symphony as Tannin and I shifted back to human form and caught our breath as we watched their futile barrage. We were safe. Aliya was safe. For now, that was all that mattered.

"You were never fit to be Alpha," Coda growled as he tore at the barrier. "And now that you've shown where your loyalties lie, this is war!"

I patted Tannin's shoulder and nodded toward the door, turning my back on the pack I would have died to protect.

Coda was right. I knew where my loyalty lay... with the family Fate had chosen for me. And I'd never been more certain of my choice.

CHAPTER 17

ALIYA

As soon as I saw my wolves cross the ward safely from the library window, I raced down the stairs, skipping pairs of steps at a time in my haste to see them.

I got to the ground floor just as the large double doors opened, and the low morning sun shone behind the silhouettes of my mates like a glorious beacon. I sprinted across the ballroom and launched myself into their outspread arms.

"Oh, thank the gods!" I whimpered between kissing them everywhere my lips could reach as they held me tightly. They showered me with kisses in equal measure, fingers clutching and prying in grateful desperation.

"I was so worried," I said. "I was ready to charge out there and do whatever it took to save you."

Jax cupped my face in his hands and held it a breath away, his gaze piercing into mine. "Don't you ever put yourself in danger for us. Protecting you is our job, not the other way around."

I laughed through the thickness in my throat, too relieved to have him back in my arms to argue that I would always at least try to protect them, no matter the cost to me.

The howling and barking outside the walls only grew louder, interspersed with eerie, hollow booms from the wolves slamming against the ward.

"Come, let's go upstairs and get away from the noise," Jax said, releasing my face and slipping his hand into mine.

I nodded and took Tannin's hand with my free one, and together we strode across the ballroom and up the stairs.

Jax led our threesome to his room, and though it was unnecessary, he bolted the door behind us. From up here, the angry ruckus was muffled and distant, but there was still no ignoring it.

Jax pulled me to the edge of the bed and scooped me onto his naked lap, closing his arms around me, and Tannin sat beside us, nuzzling into my hair.

"What do we do now?" I asked after a moment of silently savoring their embrace.

"I don't really know," Jax said softly. "But I don't think we have to *do* anything."

I looked up at him curiously. "What do you mean?"

He shrugged. "They can't get to us. No matter what they try or how hard they slam, they can't get through the ward. We're safe in the castle."

"So...you're proposing we do nothing?" I asked.

"Exactly," he said. "For now, anyway. We have everything we need within the ward. Food, water, electricity. We could live off the chickens and the garden forever, the same as you did before we came here."

"So, we just live out our lives in solitude and ignore the pack of wolves surrounding us that want to tear us to pieces?" I asked, incredulous that he really thought that was an option.

I also didn't know enough about wards to know how long it would stay in place. Was it linked to my life force? If something happened to me, would the veil release?

"We don't really have another choice," Tannin said. "It's far from ideal, but at least we're safe and we're together."

"Yes," Jax said, then brushed a kiss on my forehead. "The pack will eventually tire of their banging and shouting, and in time, as long as we ignore them, they might just accept that this is the way it's going to be."

"You really think they're going to leave us alone?" I countered. "You guys came here to claim the kingdom for yourselves, and you were prepared to shed as much as blood as possible in the process. The castle is the heart of Varynia. They're not going to let this go. They're not going to just accept living next door to two traitors and the princess they detest forever."

"That's fine. Let them refuse to accept it," he said, and the calm he was maintaining was only serving to exasperate me. "Let them continue to batter and break themselves trying to get in. Thanks to you and your incredible wielding skills, there's nothing they can do about it."

Rationally, I knew he was right. The pack had no way of getting to us, and there was nothing we could do to make them leave. Neither of us was going anywhere. It was still a hard truth to accept.

Hiding behind the castle walls, knowing the wolves outside wanted me dead, had been incredibly difficult the past few days, making me literally sick with anxiety and dread. Could I live the rest of my life like that? Always looking over my shoulder and jumping at every sound?

But what choice did I have? Gods, how had things gotten so screwed up?

On the other hand, wasn't this more or less what I wanted? To have Jax and Tannin to myself, alone in the castle? We could still have a kingdom that was just the three of us, cut off from the rest of the world. Jax was right. We had food, water, and electricity. We would want for nothing. My men would be enough for me, even if we were surrounded by an army that hated us.

Jax curled his finger under my chin and tilted my face up to look at him. "How about we engage in a little distraction?"

The hunger and heat in his blue eyes sliced right through the angst that rattled me, igniting a welcome ache in my core and making me very aware of the fact that they were both naked after destroying their clothes in their escape.

"I think the three of us could do with a nice, hot shower," he purred, and his exposed cock stiffened and twitched against the back of my thigh. "After we get you all dirty, that is."

"Sounds like a great idea to me," Tannin agreed, tugging at the belt around my waist. "I would ask why you're dressed in men's clothes, but really, I just want you out of them."

Jax lifted me off his lap, and with eager, rough hands, the two of them stripped the shirt and pants off me. The shouts and bangs outside faded beneath the rise of my pulse and the heat of their lips and tongues as they descended on me.

The world became a blur of demanding mouths and grazing fingers, and I could barely keep up with what body part was whose as I blindly stroked a stiff cock with each hand.

"I have a fun idea we could try," Jax growled beneath my ear, scraping his teeth teasingly against my neck. "Are you up for trying something new, baby?"

"Yes," I breathed as a thrill stabbed through me.

"Good," he purred, then he inclined toward Tannin and whispered something in his ear.

The wicked curve that pulled Tannin's lips as they both turned on me made my pussy throb with burning curiosity. Moving as one, they backed me up against the edge of the bed.

"Lay down, beautiful," Jax commanded.

With a fluttering heart, I obeyed, splaying myself against the silky sheets. Tannin gripped my hips, pulling my butt to the edge of the mattress while Jax gently nudged my shoulders, angling me diagonally on the corner of the bed with nothing but Jax's hand to support beneath my head.

"Relax your neck, my love," Jax instructed. "I've got you."

I did as he said, gawking upside down as he fisted his stiff cock inches from my face. My mouth watered at the sight, and when Tannin's hand spread my legs, I widened them willingly, desperate for both my men to fill me.

"Do you want to suck my cock?" Jax asked, his voice heavy and raw with desire.

Something pressed against my clit and slid up and down the wet folds between my legs. I didn't have to see to know it was the tip of Tannin's cock teasing me.

"Yes," I murmured.

He chuckled darkly. "That's my good girl."

Those last two words had me clenching my thighs, eager to show him how good a girl I wanted to be for them.

Jax came closer, guiding his dick to my mouth, and Tannin's cock nestled deep into my opening. When I opened my mouth to moan, Jax gently slid his cock between my lips.

Oh, the feeling of having them both inside me! I would never get enough. My eyes rolled up into my head, and I closed my eyelids to savor the feel of their cocks inside me. The taste of Jax's dick was perfection, and the little gasps of pleasure they made as they began to sway their hips back and forth made me throb with desire.

Tannin's hands were clutching my hips, anchoring me as his thrusts grew deeper and more forceful. Jax's hands roamed my breasts, squeezing and kneading them as he buried himself deeper into my mouth.

I'd never been more grateful for the potion I'd made, or that I'd taken it just an hour ago. The tip of Jax's cock pressed lightly at the back of my throat. I wanted to take him all the way inside my mouth, wanted so badly to please him as fully as possible, but my throat wouldn't relax to allow him any deeper.

Though, judging by the breathy moans escaping him, he didn't seem to mind.

Their rhythms fell into sync, their cocks pushing into me at either end at the same, making my moans echo around Jax's cock.

"Fuck, her moans feel so damn good," he grunted, squeezing my breasts almost painfully, but that only heightened the tension coiling tight in my core.

Euphoria erupted inside me at hearing proof of his pleasure, and I let out a deep, guttural moan.

"Oh, gods!" Jax hissed, and his cum shot onto my tongue with his cock only halfway in my mouth.

Reaching my hands up and grabbing his ass, I amplified the pressure of my lips on his shaft, sucking hard as he continued to come. I swallowed his seed, then lapped and sucked more on his cock, not wanting his pleasure to be over.

I suckled and nibbled on him until, with a series of powerful slams, Tannin found ecstasy inside my pussy too.

Jax withdrew himself from my lips, then knelt beside me and devoured my mouth like a starving man.

"You are incredible," he panted.

Tannin pulled out, and the two of them helped me to stand back up.

"You're the best thing that ever happened to us," Tannin said before claiming my mouth for himself.

"Now, let's get our girl cleaned up." Jax smacked my ass, making me squeal in surprised delight.

As they pulled me into the shower, I hoped Tannin was right, because they were the best thing that had ever happened to me.

CHAPTER 18

TANNIN

By the time dusk fell, the three of us were completely spent. We had enjoyed the whole day playing in the bedroom and getting lost in each other. Jax and I had resorted to taking turns with our girl, and just the act of watching each other please her made our recovery time that much more fleeting.

Now we were sprawled across the bed, panting, covered in sweat, and thoroughly sexed out.

But none of us were at peace. The comfortable lethargy that should have followed after so many climaxes was nowhere to be found, only the dull gnawing in the pit of my stomach. I could feel the same restless energy radiating from Jax and Aliya as we lay in a heap.

As it turned out, the distraction only lasted as long as the act itself.

I wasn't sure when the angry barks and slamming against the ward stopped in the midst of our carnal frenzy, but everything was eerily silent now. Not even the wind howled outside the walls. All I could hear was our collective breathing and the frantic rhythm of my heart.

"I don't know about you two, but I haven't eaten since yesterday, and I could really use a hearty meal, especially after the fun we just had," Jax said, then he turned on his side, kissed Aliya's shoulder, and slid off the side of the bed.

279

"I'm not too sure I can eat," she said as she propped herself up on her elbows.

"Really?" Jax asked as he pulled his pants up. "Did Tannin and I not do a good enough job of draining your energy?" He waggled his eyebrows at her flirtatiously.

She breathed a short laugh, but amusement was short-lived on her pretty face as her features tightened with angst. "No, it's just...I guess I don't have much of an appetite."

I sat up, noticing that her complexion did look a little pale. The strain of the pack politics must have really been stressing her out. Jax and I shared a concerned glance.

"I know how you feel." I put a comforting hand on her bent arm. "With everything that happened today, it's a lot to take in. But we should all eat, keep our strength up. Maybe some protein will help us process the changes better."

"Well said, Tannin," Jax praised, shrugging into a white button-up shirt. "I think there might be some cooked chicken left. I'll make some stew, and we can all eat together in the dining room like old times."

A nostalgic smile tugged at the corners of my lips. Those precious meals we shared were only days ago, and yet it felt like a lifetime had passed since.

"Sounds great," I said, though my tone was flatter than I intended.

He gave me an understanding nod before leaving the room.

Aliya sat up all the way, tucking her legs up beneath her and looking down into her lap. "I'm really sorry about all of this."

I cocked my head at her. "What?"

"This." She waved a hand around, gesturing to the room as a whole. "You and Jax are stuck in the castle, cut off from your pack, possibly forever. And it's all my fault."

I shook my head and let out a breath through my nose. "Nothing about what's happened is your fault."

She snorted apathetically.

I took her hand and held it tightly. "Listen to me. You did nothing wrong. If anything, this is on Jax and me. You were minding your own business here, living a perfectly peaceful life. Then we showed up and turned your whole world upside down. We were the assholes who plotted to steal your kingdom from you, and it's our fault the pack came here at all. You are innocent of blame in all of this."

She sighed. "I don't know. I could have left when you told me to that first night. The only thing that kept me here all this time was my pride. Even when I was so lonely I fantasized about jumping from the window of the highest tower, my stupid royal pride kept me from going through with it. Maybe it would have been better for everyone if I had died in the plague."

Pain sliced through my heart as if she had plunged a dagger into my chest.

"Don't say that," I growled, my fear of losing her bringing out the beast in me.

But she didn't flinch at my wolfish tone, merely looked up at me with those wide amber eyes. "If I hadn't been here when you guys arrived, the pack's transition would have been smooth and painless, and you and Jax would be heroes. Instead, you have to turn your back on everything and everyone you know because of me."

"No," I argued, feeling irrationally angry with her for blaming herself, for even considering removing herself from this world—from me. "You have no idea how miserable I was before I found you. I've hated most of the pack for most of my life. I was the runt of my generation, and just when my fellow pups were about to eliminate me, Jax stepped in and saved me. My peers have always resented that, hated me for being given the beta position out of merit rather than birthright.

"Before I found you, I was just floating along, existing in a world of dull grays. Now my world is bright and filled with promise and joy. That is your fault. So, I don't want to hear any more talk of how I would be better off without you."

Her big eyes glistened as they bore into my face, and a tear fell from her lashes onto her thigh. Then she looked away.

"What about Jax?" she asked in a small voice. "He really cares about the pack, and he had to relinquish being their Alpha for me."

I squeezed her hand. "Yes, Jax cares deeply for the pack. The men in his family have been Alpha for generations, and he feels a great sense of responsibility for them. But you have made him so much stronger and wiser. He used to be such an asshole before he met you."

She blurted a giggle. "He's still kind of an asshole."

We both laughed.

"My point is," I went on, "you have added so much more to our lives than we've lost. Having to spend the rest of our time confined to this castle is going to be an adjustment, but you are worth any price. And I know Jax feels the same way."

She nodded, but she still didn't seem convinced. That was okay. I'd do my best to show her every day how precious she was to both of us.

"There really isn't anyone you'll miss from the pack?" she asked after a moment.

Her question struck a chord in my chest. I debated lying to her for a split-second because my admission might make her feel worse. But I'd lied to her enough for a lifetime, and I never wanted to betray her like that again, not even to ease her concerns now.

"Actually, there is," I confessed. "My mom and little sister."

Her brows puckered. "I'm sorry."

"Please, don't be," I insisted.

She twisted her lips, clearly struggling with the added guilt. "I didn't know you had a sister. What's her name?"

"Twila." I couldn't help but smile saying her name, her bright, cheerful face popping into my mind. "She's about eight years old."

Her smile mirrored mine. "I always wanted a sister or a brother. I always thought it would be fun, having that kind of bond with someone."

I nodded. "It is a powerful bond. I would do anything to protect her from harm."

I realized my mistake as soon as the words left my mouth, the guilty lines returning to Aliya's face.

"But she has our mother to take care of her," I amended quickly. "She's in good hands."

She didn't say anything, just stared absently down at her lap, and oh, how I wished I could take all her pain away.

I brought her hand up to my lips and placed a meaningful kiss on the back of it. "Come on. Let's go down to the kitchen and see if Jax needs any help with dinner."

She nodded. "Okay."

I put on some pants and a shirt as she draped a silk robe over her shoulders and tied it at the waist, and then, hand in hand, we made our descent down the many flights of stairs.

As soon as my foot landed on the ground floor, I could hear Jax cursing in the kitchen along with the sound of pots clattering.

"Shit," I hissed, releasing Aliya's hand and sprinting to the kitchen. Had they found some way in? Were we all about to die?

I burst into the kitchen to find Jax jerking on the faucet handles. There was no one else here, thank the moon. Jax was just having a tantrum.

"What's going on?" Aliya asked when she caught up to me seconds later, her voice sharp with worry.

"The fucking water," Jax snarled.

"What?" I asked.

"Those bastards!" he shouted. "They cut off the fucking water!"

CHAPTER 19
ALIYA

"Are you sure?" Tannin asked as Jax continued to roughly pry and twist the faucet handle.

"The plumbing didn't just stop working on its own," Jax tossed back. "Go check the other faucets. The bathrooms... everywhere."

Tannin dashed out of the kitchen and up the stairs to follow Jax's orders.

"Have you ever had issues with the water before?" Jax asked me.

"No," I said. "At least not in the time I was alone. Before that, I don't really remember. If there had been a plumbing problem, it likely would've been fixed before I noticed."

He pushed away from the sink and ran his hands through his hair, clutching his black locks tightly.

The fear that had been clawing at my insides the whole time they were being held captive returned with a vengeance, just in a different form. We wouldn't survive long without a water source. The pack was trying to kill us from the outside in.

Tannin ran back into the kitchen, breathy as he said, "No water. None of them. You were right."

"Aaggh!" Jax kicked the bottom of the island counter. "Fucking assholes couldn't just let us be! After everything I've done for them, they just—"

He broke off, and I could see the pain surface just beneath his anger. I felt so badly for him, discarded by the people he cared for. I wanted to do something to comfort him, but I had no comfort to give.

Tannin went around me and put his hand on Jax's shoulder. "I know, Jax. I know."

The heaving of Jax's chest slowly subsided, and he calmed a little, putting both hands flat on the countertop and leaning on it. "Okay, okay... we have to think this through rationally. How long can we live without water?"

Tannin folded his arms over his chest. "Three days, if we don't exert ourselves. And that's if we're lucky."

Three days. I'd never had to go without water or food for any length of time. Not even after everyone died. The water never stopped flowing, and the garden and coop provided everything I needed. I never had to imagine what it would be like to suddenly be without one or the other, or how long I could without them.

"Aliya, are there any water stores in the castle that you know of?" Jax asked. "Anything that could get us by for a little bit longer?"

I thought over every inch of the castle, every room and closet. I shook my head. "No. Just the wine and liquor in the cellar."

Jax pursed his lips. "Drinking that will only dehydrate us faster."

"We might be able to sustain ourselves off the juices of the fruits and vegetables in the garden," Tannin postulated. "But I'm guessing the garden is fed by the same water system. The plants won't last long either."

Jax chewed on his lip as he thought. Then he looked up at me. "Aliya, what about your magic? Is there a spell or something to create water?"

I frowned as I thought about that. Not that I was an expert on wielding, but from what I read so far, magic didn't create anything. It drew on and amplified what already was. Like wielding wind and fire, the magic just manipulated the air particles to either move with force or ignite. I now wished I had studied more about water wielding.

"I don't think magic can do that," I said. "Magic doesn't create, it just uses what's already there. But I can do more research."

Jax's face fell, and he sighed. "There's nothing we can do from in here to turn the water back on, and even we succeeded in some stealth mission to turn it on and come back here safely, they would just shut it off again. I think our only option for survival is to leave."

I'd known he was going to say that, and he was right, but those words stung something deep inside of me. I'd held on to this place so desperately, clinging to the echoes of the ones I loved and lost. And now I had no choice but to let it go. I would die if I stayed, and I'd been damning my mates to the same fate.

It was time.

"Okay," I said.

Tannin pulled me into his arms, and I soaked up every ounce of the comfort he offered.

"That brings up its own difficulties," he said as he rubbed my back. "How are we going to leave the castle? They'll have the perimeter heavily guarded, especially now that they're trying to smoke us out—or drought us out, in this case."

"Good point," Jax agreed. "Aliya, are there any secret passages out of the castle?"

"No," I reluctantly reported. "If there had been, I would have used it to get out last night. I tried to sneak out and rescue you, but Coda had every entrance covered, just as Tannin guessed."

Jax gave me a heartfelt frown. "I want to scold you for even considering such a dangerous thing, but I'd be lying if I said I'm not honored that you tried. I'm just glad nothing happened to you."

"Of course, I tried," I said. "You're my mates. Now that I have you, I don't want to live in a world without you."

His eyes twinkled with so much love that it cracked my heart to see it, and yet I couldn't look away.

"We feel the same way about you, love," he said. "That's why we will get you out. We just have to figure out how."

I thought back over my failed escape attempt last night.

"Actually, I might have an idea." I pulled away from Tannin's embrace so they could both see my face. "We could create some kind of diversion, a decoy maybe. Get them thinking we're sneaking out one way while we use a different route."

Jax cupped his chin. "Hmm, interesting thought. But that would mean at least one of us would have to lead the diversion, and I don't like the idea of any of us splitting up."

"Not necessarily," I said. "I've been practicing my magic on a mannequin. I could dress it up like me and wield air from a distance to make it move, make it look like I'm running away."

Both Tannin and Jax raised their eyebrows in consideration.

"That might work," Tannin said. "At least long enough to give us a few seconds of a window, which, if we're fast enough, is all we'll need."

"How close do you have to be to move the mannequin?" Jax asked.

I shrugged uncertainly. "I'm not sure. I haven't really tested distance, or any of this. But my guess is I would at least have to be able to see it."

Jax thought for a moment, then clapped his hands. "Okay, I've got it. I found a roof entrance to the second floor a few days ago, before the pack arrived. You can move the dummy through the kitchen door from there, lead the pack away, and then we'll jump right over their heads into the forest."

I blinked. "Jump?"

He nodded. "In our wolf forms, Tannin and I can easily make that leap. You'll have to ride on one of our backs."

I swallowed, and although the idea of riding one of them like a horse twenty feet in the air did scare the hell out of me, I was pretty sure the tightening in my gut wasn't from fear.

I was overdue for another dose of the potion. Crap, I'd forgotten all about that with these new developments. I only had enough potion left for a few days. When I ran out, I would slow them down. I'd only be a burden on them.

"Aliya?" Tannin asked, snapping me out of my worried daze. "Are you okay?"

"Yeah, just...overwhelmed," I lied—though, it wasn't completely a lie. I was terrified.

"I know, love," Jax said. "But this plan is a good one. We'll all get through this."

I nodded, forcing a smile to appease him even though acid burned the back of my throat.

"We'll do it tomorrow night," he said. "That will give us time to pack up a few days' worth of food and give Aliya time to practice moving the mannequin. We'll only have one shot at a stunt like this, because they won't fall for it a second time if we fail."

Tannin and I nodded.

"I'll work on squeezing some of the tomatoes into juice, so we have something to drink on the road," Tannin volunteered. "Just until we find water again."

"Good idea," Jax said. "I'll start packing food."

"And I'm...going to see what more I can learn from the wielding books," I said.

I ducked out as they got to work with their tasks, hastily uncorking the vial that hung around my neck and pouring the potion into my mouth. Relief swept over me, but only physically.

I didn't know what was wrong with me. What if I was dying from some degenerative disease? Some form of cancer? Or maybe some magical backfire?

Jax and Tannin would be risking their lives for nothing, and they would have thrown away everything they knew for an empty promise. I hated the thought of leaving them even more than I feared death itself.

But if we did make it out of here alive, we could go somewhere with trained wielders. They could find out what was wrong with me and cure me. Yes, everything would be fine, one way or another. We just had to get out.

I went to the library and began rifling through the books I'd read for anything that might help in our escape attempt and beyond. Sadly, I wouldn't be able to take these books with me. Even one might prove too heavy for trekking through the wilderness.

It broke my heart that I would have to leave them behind—that I would have to everything I'd ever known. There were so many memories that lived within these walls. I could still remember my father sitting in that armchair beside the open window and smoking his pipe on clear nights like these.

I looked at the spot, picturing him there, smiling at me as smoke wafted out the window to caress the waning moon.

Wait... Waning...

Oh my gods.

With how chaotic everything had been since the night Tannin and Jax showed up, I'd forgotten about the other visitor that hadn't—the one that had never missed a visit since I was thirteen years old.

Could it be? Could *I* be...

With new purpose, I flipped through my spell books again, this time with a specific spell in mind. Finally, after nearly tearing a few pages out with my frantic fingers, I found it.

Pregnancy Detection Spell.

My eyes darted over the instructions, and several times I had to force myself to slow down so I could absorb what I was reading.

The only thing needed was a dried chamomile flower. I was to ignite it and waft it over my belly. The smoke would turn blue if the result was positive, otherwise it would remain a grayish white.

Without hesitation, I ran back down to the kitchen. The staff used to make chamomile tea for themselves every night after dinner, and as I wasn't a fan, I hadn't touched it since they'd gone.

Tannin looked up at me from his tomato crushing as I opened the tea cabinet. "What are you looking for?"

"Just something for a spell," I said, scanning the many jars of herbs.

There! I pulled the jar from the back of the cabinet and withdrew one of the delicate, somewhat crunchy white flowers, careful not to break off any of the petals. Before Tannin could ask me anything further, I darted out of the kitchen and ran for the stairs.

I couldn't mention my suspicions to them, not until I knew for sure. They had enough to worry about without me crying wolf over possibly nothing.

Back in the library, I plopped down on the rug in front of the open book and read the instructions again to make sure I had it right. As I waved the smoking flower over my belly, I was supposed to say a short incantation. The smoke would either change, or it wouldn't.

"Okay, here goes nothing," I said to myself.

I leaned backward so that my torso was at an angle and opened my robe to expose my bare belly. Then I ignited the flower with magic just as I had with the sage braid, blowing out the flame so that it only smoked.

Waving it over my belly, I read the incantation out loud with a wavering voice. "Sunas gravi."

I held my breath as I watched the smoke, waiting for my fate to be determined.

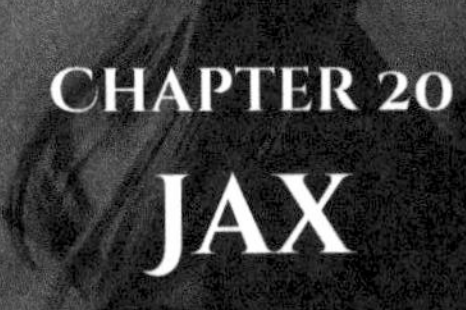

CHAPTER 20

JAX

I went into default Alpha mode as I stuffed food supplies into a sack, operating calmly and efficiently. If I just focused on the task at hand, I wouldn't have to feel the thousands of conflicting emotions clawing beneath the surface.

Some part of me had hoped that peace could still reign. That given enough time, we could find a solution with the pack that would make everyone happy. As long as we stayed in the castle and they stayed in the kingdom, there was still hope.

But, just as with every other opportunity this week, the pack disappointed me. They truly had turned their backs on us—on me. That hurt most of all. I had dedicated my life to leading and protecting them, and now they were giving me no choice but to abandon them as surely as they had abandoned me.

I tied the sack closed, then went on to filling another one. There were enough canned goods in the pantry to last us a lifetime, but I had to pack lightly, especially for Aliya's sake. She was much smaller and weaker than Tannin and me, and I didn't want to overburden her with too much weight.

I arranged the contents of each sack in order of weight, placing five cans at the bottom of the bag first, then a few fruits and vegetables, and

293

then a small loaf of bread. In the bags meant for Tannin and me, I also carefully arranged a pot for cooking and utensils.

My grief and regret had been simmering into anger, and as I tied off the last bag, that anger boiled over. I slammed my fists against the counter.

"What is it?" Tannin asked, pausing in his juicing efforts to look across the kitchen at me.

My fists unclenched enough to grip the edge of the counter. "I just feel so betrayed," I growled in a low voice. "I hate that they're making us do this."

Tannin lowered his head, and I could see the same weight of sorrow pressing down on his features. "I know. I hate it too." He let out a heavy sigh. "But we have a new pack to protect now—one built of just the three of us."

I nodded, and the truth of that slowly seeped into me. Tannin was my best and oldest friend, and Aliya was a precious gift given to us by Fate. I loved and trusted them both beyond measure. That could be enough for me.

It would have to be.

A sniffle sounded to my right, and I turned to see Aliya standing in the archway of the kitchen. The whites of her eyes were pink, and tears streaked down her cheeks.

The Alpha wolf in me leapt to the surface. "What's wrong? Did something happen? Did they get in?"

She shook her head slowly and wiped the moisture from her face. "No, it's not that. Um..."

She bit her lower lip, and though that gesture from her usually aroused desire in me, the deep sadness beneath this instance only made my heart ache.

I released the counter's edge and strode over to her, putting a hand on her shoulder as Tannin rushed over to put his hand on the other.

"What is it, my love?" Tannin asked softly.

"I...um...I've been feeling sick for a few days," she began in a pinched voice. "And, um...I-I realized that it's been over a month since my blood came in..."

She pursed both lips, looking up at us with big, wet, pleading eyes.

"Oh," Tannin said beside me, and when I looked to him, his eyes were wide with an understanding I hadn't yet grasped.

She sniffled again loudly. "So I-I found this spell to check for—you know—and... I'm pregnant." Her pitch heightened at the end, the final word coming out as a mousy squeak.

I stared at her dumbly for a long moment, her words, her dismay, failing to register.

"You're... Oh, sweet moon!" Tannin breathed.

I turned to him again searchingly, and a wide smile spread across his face.

"Aliya, that's amazing!" he burst out, pulling her into an excited embrace. Then he pulled away. "Wait, why are you crying? This is an incredible thing."

Her face scrunched up with pain, and she cried harder. "I can't leave like this," she sobbed. "I'm only going to slow you both down. I would have been a burden before, but like this...I'm going to end up getting one or both of you killed trying to take care of me. Of us." She pressed her hand to her belly and looked woefully down at it.

Tannin gave her a sympathetic frown. "Please, don't think of it like that. Yes, we would both die for you and the baby, but it won't come to that. I promise you. We survived in the wilderness our whole lives while protecting an entire pack of women and children. We know what we're doing. We will keep you and ourselves safe. You just have to trust us."

She nodded, taking in several deep breaths and wiping her face again. Then she looked to me, a conflicted question in her misty, blood-shot eyes.

"I need a moment," I said, then I slipped past them and strode out of the kitchen.

I didn't know where I was going as my legs carried me up the stairs, I only knew that I needed a minute to process all of this. My mind whirled as I continued to move forward blindly, and I didn't stop until I found myself on the roof of the second floor.

The night was deceptively quiet and still. Peaceful. The chirping of crickets was a low cadence, with an occasional staccato of a hooting owl. If I didn't know better, I'd think we were alone in the kingdom again, but I knew if I looked over the edge, I'd see a pack member skirting the perimeter of the castle.

I looked up at the sky, silently pleading the half moon above to give me an answer.

Aliya was pregnant. My mate was going to have a pup. I was going to be a father.

This news should have made me deliriously happy as it had Tannin, but I understood Aliya's grief. Traveling with a pregnant woman in cusith-infested wilderness was going to be treacherous, to say the least.

Yes, Tannin and I had successfully defended others against their attacks, but we had a whole pack to back us up. I wasn't so convinced that the three of us could survive on our own. We could fend off one or two cusith at a time, but the beasts had been getting bolder and more numerous lately. Not to mention the fact that our pack might very well hunt us down after they realized we'd left the kingdom.

I'd nearly died on our journey here, and that was with Tannin and me against three of the monsters. How much more devastating would that be with both of us distracted by our love for Aliya and the baby? One false move, one misstep, and it would be over for all three of us.

But what other choice did we have? If we stayed here, Aliya and the baby would die in a matter of days from dehydration. We all would. Our only option was to take our chances in the forest and get to a new town as quickly as possible and pray we didn't come across any cusith along the way.

Dammit! I hated feeling like this. New pups were always a celebration for the pack. How could they do this to us? How could they discard a woman who—

Wait.

My pulse sizzled with revelation. Holy shit, that was it!

Spinning on my heel, I sprinted back inside, skipping down the stairs as fast as I could. When I landed on the ground floor, Aliya and Tannin were standing in the den and turned to look at me with confused, expectant expressions.

"Jax?" Aliya asked in a small voice, taking one small step toward me.

I came up to her only long enough to take both her hands, bring them up to my lips, and place a quick kiss over both knuckles.

"I have a plan," I assured her. "Wait here." Then I strode confidently down the long ballroom to the castle's main entrance.

I unbolted the double doors and pushed one side open, stepping onto the pathway. Just as I expected, a pack member was standing guard across from me just on the other side of the ward—Esme.

Her eyebrows flickered as she watched me approach, hesitation, curiosity and regret playing on her face. She had always been one my most loyal deltas, and I could plainly see she wasn't happy about the turn of events.

I stopped a foot away from her, safe within the boundary of the magical veil.

She frowned at me, an expression both pleading and stern. "You know I can't let you go."

"I'm not asking you to," I said in an even tone. "I want to speak with the elders."

Her brow flared with surprise, then lowered in bitterness that teetered on pity. "Jax, they're not going to negotiate with you."

"I have new information that they'll want to hear," I said. "Please, call them all to gather here."

She frowned doubtfully, eyeing me as if suspecting I was trying to pull some kind of trick on her. Maybe get her to abandon her post so we could sneak out. But then a kind of acceptance smoothed her features, and she nodded.

It was nice to know some wolves hadn't fully turned their backs on me.

She backed up, then turned and jogged off to fetch the stubborn old bastards who had.

I waited patiently, clasping my hands behind my back. If this didn't work, if the pack still refused to accept us, then we would continue with our escape plan and make the best of it. Nothing would be lost by tugging on this one last rope. But I had faith in the pack, faith that they would be forced to make the right choice.

"Decided to give yourself up, have you?"

Coda emerged from the shadows to the right of the courtyard, strolling casually onto the path and stopping directly in front of me. His smile was smug and condescending.

"I didn't expect our little ploy to work so quickly," he went on. "I thought it would take you at least a day or two before you came groveling."

I narrowed my eyes at him. "A true Alpha doesn't grovel."

He arched an eyebrow daringly. "We'll see about that."

A group emerged onto the courtyard behind him, approaching with slow, labored steps. Esme led the elders this way, and she smiled and nodded at me.

Coda turned around, then stiffened when he saw the elders coming toward us. "What's the meaning of this?"

"That's exactly what I want to know," Droger commented grumpily as he hobbled to a stop in front of me.

"Good evening, Jax," Esther greeted, as if she hadn't labeled me an enemy of the state. "To what do we owe this late-night rendezvous?"

"You woke me out the first good sleep I've had in years," Droger sniped.

I straightened my posture and regarded them with the respect and authority I always had. "I apologize for the late hour, but this matter simply couldn't wait. There's been a new development that I believe will change everything."

"As if we're going to believe anything you have to say," Coda quipped.

Esther ignored him, giving me a calculating look. "Very well. What is this new development?"

"Aliya is pregnant," I declared loudly enough for everyone to hear.

Esther's brow rose, and the other elders gasped and whispered amongst themselves.

Coda puffed out his chest and folded his arms across it. "And?"

"And the oldest law of our pack is that a woman pregnant with a pack pup can't be killed," I said.

The murmurs grew louder, but all I could focus on was the surprise and fury brewing in Coda's heartless eyes.

"Bullshit!" he yelled. "This is obviously a lie to save his own fur."

"Not if I can prove it," I countered. I looked to Esther. "You have ways to tell, do you not? You're the pack midwife. You've confirmed every pregnancy since I was a child."

She nodded slowly, still analyzing me with her eyes. "Yes, I do have ways." She paused for a moment. "Alright, bring her out. We will see if you are still the virtuous man I believed you to be."

CHAPTER 21

ALIYA

I was a bundle of nerves as I waited with Tannin in the den for Jax to return—even more than I'd been since the pack arrived.

Jax hadn't taken the news well at all, just took off upstairs before stomping out the front doors. What was he doing? Did he not want this baby?

Not that I could blame him if he didn't. I wasn't too sure how I felt about it myself. I'd wanted to be a mother since I was a little girl playing with my dolls, and finding out I was pregnant should make me jubilantly happy. But this wasn't anything like how I imagined it to happen.

I was supposed to be happily married, secure and comfortable in my castle, and celebrating the wonderful news with my people. Instead, I was living in sin with not one but two men, my people were long dead, and I was being forced out of my castle by the pack of wolves that had taken over my kingdom.

How was this going to work? If we managed to escape successfully, would our baby survive the trek through the forest? Would I?

What if we didn't make it to a safe place in time, and I had to give birth in the woods? I knew very little about what that entailed, but I did know that women die in childbirth. I was nowhere near prepared to deliver a baby, let alone take care of one.

My mom should be here. I was supposed to have my mother by my side to guide me through this. At least to hold my hand and tell me everything was going to be okay.

Now, I couldn't imagine how anything would be okay.

Maybe that's why Jax went out there. Maybe he was making some sort of deal to hand me over. I was too much of a burden, mate bond be damned.

"What do you think he's doing?" I asked Tannin, my throat tight with worry.

He shook his head. "I have no idea. Maybe setting up some kind of trap to help with our escape? But he's right out in the open for everyone to see, so I just don't know."

"You don't think..." I couldn't finish the question. It felt like a betrayal of my love for Jax to doubt his love for me.

"What?" Tannin implored, rubbing my shoulder.

I chewed on my cheek, struggling for the right words. "Do you think he's angry about this?" I rubbed my belly.

Tannin looked taken aback. "What? No, he would never be upset about that."

"Well, he just looked so cold and detached," I said. "He didn't say anything about it."

Tannin nodded and shrugged. "Oh. That's just how Jax is. He tends to focus on resolving problems rather than dealing with the emotions that result from them."

I deepened my pout. "My pregnancy is a problem?"

"No, no, that's not what I meant," Tannin urged soothingly. "This whole situation is a problem, and you being pregnant just heightens the stakes. But I'm sure Jax isn't upset about the baby. When Jax cares, he cares deeply and unwaveringly. You've seen how hard he's tried to defend the pack even after they cast him aside. It's because he sees them as his responsibility. You and the baby are the priority now. Imagine how much more he will love that baby. Now that it's in existence, he will stop at nothing to protect it."

I nodded but didn't say anything. I knew so little about the men I'd been mated to. In my heart, I knew they were kind, virtuous and steadfast, and my heart at least trusted their love. But my mind still held doubts because this kind of devotion and passion defied all logic.

One of the front doors opened, and Jax entered, looking just as he had when he left. I was so relieved to see him in one piece. But his face was still a mask, and that made me uneasy.

He crossed the ballroom toward us, and behind him through the open door, I could see a gathering of people in the courtyard outside.

Oh, no. My breathing became shallow and weak. What had he done?

He stopped in front of me and held out his hand. "Come with me, my love."

I stared down at his hand, then back up at his face. Though his features were hard, there was a light in his ice-blue eyes that begged me to trust him.

"What are you doing?" Tannin asked, his voice sharp with alarm as he stepped closer to me. He had seen the people in the courtyard too.

"The most ancient law of the pack is that a woman pregnant with a pack pup cannot be harmed," Jax said meaningfully. "We're going to prove to them that Aliya is pregnant."

"How?" Tannin asked, skeptical.

"Esther has a way of confirming pregnancy," Jax replied. "She's the pack midwife, remember?"

Tannin frowned. "Okay, but then what? You prove to them that she's pregnant, and what... they'll just welcome her with open arms? Not a chance in hell."

Jax's gaze pierced into Tannin's. "Have faith, brother."

Tannin eyed him a moment longer, then sighed. "Fine. I guess it can't hurt." He looked to me and gave me an encouraging nod.

"Okay," I said, setting my hand in Jax's waiting palm, and he ushered me out onto the courtyard.

The crowd tonight wasn't near the size of the one this morning. Most of them were older people with white or graying hair, with a few younger adults off to the sides. Coda was among them, glaring at me as we approached. Well, almost everyone was glaring. The cold, hostile reception made my insides feel shaky and stiff at the same time.

"Princess Aliya of Varynia," Jax said when we reached the ward, his voice carrying across the night. "These are the elders of the Black Wolf Pack."

A few snorts rose from the group, and one of the old men who was hunched over his walking stick, spat on the ground.

I didn't know what else to do except lift my hand in a timid wave and awkwardly say, "H-hello."

"Princess Aliya." One of the old women stepped forward. "I am Esther. Jax has made the claim that your womb holds a pup of the pack. Is this true?"

"Y—Mmhmm," I cleared my throat. "Yes. I'm pregnant."

"And who is the father?" she asked.

I looked to my men on either side of me, finding uncertainty on their face that mirrored mine. I turned back to the old woman, fighting down the shame that wanted to rise up.

"I don't know for sure," I said honestly. "I have mate bonded to both Jax and Tannin, and they to me. The child could be either of theirs."

Gasps split the air, and I was pretty sure I heard some offensive female curses hissed under breaths.

"She's a harlot!" the hunched old man rasped. "She's bewitched them."

"Silence, Droger," Esther ordered with a raised hand. "We will assess the validity of the pregnancy before we address the legitimacy of the bond."

"Okay, how do we do that?" Jax asked.

"I will need a drop of the girl's blood," she said.

"What? Why?" Tannin asked in a guarded tone.

Esther gave a small smile. "I have a unique gift among wolves. I receive visions from the taste of a person's blood, mostly of current health issues, but even premonitions. I will even be able to detect who the father is, and whether it's even one of you."

I resented that remark. I'd been alone in this kingdom for over a year. Who else would I have been intimate with? Certainly not another member of the pack. Though I was pretty sure Coda would have taken me if given the chance.

"Tannin, give me your dagger," Jax said.

Tannin begrudgingly obeyed, pulling his dagger from the sheath on his belt, handing it across me to Jax.

"Aliya, may I have your hand?" Jax asked in a sweeter tone.

I looked worriedly up at him.

"Trust me," he said.

I did.

I held up my hand for him, and he turned it palm up and curled all my fingers, bracing my extended index finger.

"This is going to sting a little," he warned and as he held my gaze.

I nodded, all my fear and uncertainty melting in the love I found in his eyes.

He raised the dagger with his other hand, brought the point of the blade to the pad of my fingertip, and gently pressed it into my skin. Blood beaded from the small wound, and I hardly minded the pain. Jax turned my hand and scraped the rest of the blood with the front edge of the blade to get as much as possible.

Then he held out the dagger just enough so that the blade crossed the ward, making sure they couldn't get to him if they tried.

But no one did anything. They just stood and watched silently as Esther carefully accepted the dagger from Jax and brought the tip blade's tip to her mouth. Her tongue flicked out and licked the blood clean off.

We all waited as she seemed to savor the crimson droplets. I wasn't entirely convinced she could do what she claimed. I'd never heard of such a strange and specific ability—but then I didn't know much about the world of magic and wolves. Whatever she said would determine our fates, and the pack had shown me little to be optimistic about.

Slowly, her eyes widened, the wrinkles around them bunching and becoming more evident as her gaze settled on me.

"Sweet Luna," she gasped.

"What is it?" another old man asked.

"What did you see?" one of the younger women asked from the side.

"The princess is indeed pregnant," Esther announced without breaking eye contact with me.

"So what?" Coda asked. "Who's the father?"

"Jax," Esther said, "and Tannin."

The word "What" sprang out of the mouths of everyone gathered, even mine.

"Twins," Esther clarified with a surprisingly soft smile. "One child from each man."

Tannin, Jax and I exchanged wild, frantic glances back and forth. Twins? I was having two babies, from both of my men? Holy gods!

"That's impossible," Coda snarled. "She's bewitched you with her blood."

Esther whipped her head in his direction, glaring at him warningly. "Are you questioning me, boy?"

Coda narrowed his eyes but pursed his lips in begrudging compliance.

Esther turned back to the three of us and smiled again. "The mother of these pups will not be harmed," she declared.

I was so stunned by her words and change in demeanor that I couldn't react. She almost seemed to approve of me, which was something I just couldn't register after everything they'd said and done to us.

"So we're just going to let them stay in the castle?" Droger complained.

Esther patted the top of his hand that held his cane. "It's for the best. You will see."

"We can't stay in the castle," Tannin argued. "You guys have made certain of that."

Esther tilted her head curiously at him. "What do you mean?"

The three of us looked at each other again, confused.

"You turned off the water access to the castle," I volunteered.

Esther frowned, confused now. "We didn't turn off the water."

"I did," Coda said proudly.

"On whose authority?" Esther demanded.

"Mine," he countered. "I am the rightful heir to the beta position, and in the absence of the Alpha, the beta must take control for the sake of the pack."

"You are no beta," an elder woman said derisively.

"How dare you declare yourself leader," Droger grunted. "How dare you undermine the authority and wisdom of your elders."

He raised his cane and swung it at Coda's head, though he was several feet too far away to reach. I would have laughed at the comical scene if I wasn't so shocked.

The elders hadn't tried to chase us out, it was only Coda. And Esther had come through about the pregnancy in more astonishing ways than I ever could've imagined.

"We will turn the water back on at once," Esther assured us. "Perhaps then, we can work on making amends with each other."

Jax gave a small bow of appreciation. "Thank you, Esther. I knew we could trust your wisdom."

All was quiet for a moment, except for Coda muttering in the corner of the group with his tail between his legs.

"Well, now that we're done with this nonsense, I'm going back to bed," Droger rasped and turned to head back to the village.

Murmurs of agreement followed, and the group began to move toward a similar end.

"Wait," I called out, driven purely by a sudden surge of intuition. My rational mind didn't understand the choice, but I was quickly learning my mind didn't know everything.

The group paused and turned their attention back to me.

"As a sign of good faith and a gesture toward making a brighter future for the Black Wolves of Varyina," I announced, "I would like to invite a few wolves to move into the castle."

Jax and Tannin both grabbed an arm on either side of me.

"What are you doing?" Tannin hissed.

"Are you sure about this?" Jax whispered.

"Trust me," I told them both.

"That's a wonderful and generous offer, Princess," Esther said.

"Whatever," Droger grumbled. "I just want to go to bed, don't care where it is."

This time, I did snicker, as did Tannin and Jax.

"For now, I'd like to invite the pack elders to move in," I said. "You have waited the longest for a place to call home, and I don't think anyone deserves a room in the castle more than you."

For the first time, the murmurs that came from the group were positive and grateful.

"What about me?" Coda demanded, stomping his foot just in front of the ward as the elders began to pass through it one by one.

I ignored him, smiling at my new guests as my mates escorted them through the front doors. The rest of the pack members dispersed as the elders disappeared inside, but Coda lingered, glaring at me murderously.

I stood my ground, staring back at him with the blank, unfettered mask I learned from Jax. I had won. Coda couldn't scare me anymore.

"This isn't over," he growled, then stomped off into the village.

I smirked at his retreat, then turned around and joined the others inside my castle. I had no idea what would happen from here, but I felt that we were one step closer to peace. My mates and I were safe.

Now I just had to figure out how the hell I was going to handle having twin wolves.

HEIRS OF THE WOLF

BOOK THREE

CHAPTER 1
ALIYA

A year ago, everyone I had ever known died from the plague. They left me alone, the sole survivor and princess of an empty kingdom. I'd been devastated and lonely to the point of wanting to join them in the abyss forever.

But now, everything had changed. I was lying here beside my gorgeous mates, the three of us safe after making a tenuous peace with their wolf shifter pack. I couldn't help but count my blessings.

"I still can't believe there are *two* babies in there," Tannin said, tracing lazy circles over my bare belly with his fingertips.

"And that we're each the father of the one of them," Jax said, his hand flat on the other side of my stomach, his thumb rubbing lightly up and down.

"I know," was all I managed to say, though my heart was full.

I wasn't sure if I'd ever get over the shock of that revelation, nor the stress and worries of the past week. I'd realized I was pregnant just as we'd been planning to go on the run through monster-infested wilderness. Then we found out I was having twins fathered by *both* my mates and were offered amnesty by the pack because of it less than twenty-four hours later.

What were the odds of all this happening? Getting pregnant by two men at the same time? It felt like a cosmic joke. But so did a wielder princess becoming mate bonded to not one but two Black Wolves.

Both were now staring at me, wearing curious, slightly concerned expressions.

"Are you unhappy about it?" Jax asked, his gaze searching my eyes.

I chewed on my bottom lip for a moment. "I don't know how I feel at the moment. I know I should be thrilled, but the timing of all of this is so weird and honestly terrifying. Just last night the pack wanted to kill us, and now some of them are living in the castle."

Jax nodded in understanding. "I know how frightening this has been for you, but you have nothing to worry about now. The elders have accepted you, declaring you untouchable, and no wolf would ever hurt a woman carrying unborn pups. You and our babies are safe." He planted a kiss on my forehead that was meant to be both reassuring and dismissive I suspected.

I wasn't as convinced as he was, though.

"I'm not so sure about that," I hedged with a frown.

"What do you mean?" he asked.

"Coda?" I reminded him. "He hates us. I don't trust that he'll follow the normal pack rules. He'd do whatever he can to hurt us." He'd gone behind the elders' backs to shut off the water in an attempt to scare us out, which was enough to convince me he'd do anything to punish us for having what he wanted.

"I don't trust him either," Tannin said, hostility flaring in his green eyes. "He's a power hungry, self-entitled coward, and that makes him dangerous."

Jax's jaw clenched, and he looked away. "Yes, he's definitely a problem. He'll need to be dealt with. But in the meantime, he can't get to you, and Tannin and I will make sure he can never harm you or the babies."

He bent over and kissed my belly, looking fondly down at it as if he could see the little creatures within.

"Is there something else you're worried about?" Tannin asked, gazing at me almost like he could read my mind.

Jax looked up at me expectantly, and I felt shame for the answer I'd been struggling with all night and morning.

I sat up so I couldn't see either of their faces, and they couldn't see mine. How did I put into words how terrified I was? Taking a deep breath, I tried to put my thoughts into words.

"I'm afraid I'm not going to be a... good mom," I confessed, my voice small. "I always saw this happening so differently when I was growing up. I thought I would have my mother by my side the whole time, walking me through it. And now, knowing there are *two* of them depending on me... I'm scared I'm going to fail. Them and you."

"Are you kidding me?" Tannin pushed himself up to sit next to me. "You are the sweetest, kindest, most loving person I've ever met. You are going to make an incredible mother. Our little pups are so lucky to have you."

Pups... Oh, God, I had so many questions. Were they going to shift like Jax and Tannin?

"And you won't have to go through any of it alone," Jax said, putting a comforting hand on my back. "We will both be there with you, supporting you, protecting you, and showering the three of you with all the love you deserve."

I smiled at him. He was so good at reassuring me. I loved Jax and Tannin so much, and I was grateful to have them. Most people went their entire lives searching for this kind of deep, abiding love, and I had somehow found it two-fold.

"You're both going to make amazing fathers," I said, turning a loving gaze on each of them.

"Exactly," Jax said with a proud grin, tugging me back down on the bed. "So, let's not worry about the what ifs and just try to enjoy this time. We'll figure out the rough patches together as they come."

I snuggled up into the crook of his neck, savoring the heat of his skin against mine. "At least we have nine long months to prepare for them."

Tannin chuckled as he stretched out on my other side. "More like three, love."

"What?" I angled my head over my shoulder to give him a quizzical look.

"Wolf pregnancies are much shorter than human," he said. "I guess I forgot you wouldn't know that."

My eyes widened as a tight knot formed in my gut. "Three months? Three!"

I'd thought my belly was too big for this early stage, but I'd assumed it was just because I was carrying twins and added water weight or something.

Three months? No way! This was just too much, too fast.

Jax closed his arms around me, pulling me snuggly against his chest. "Hey, hey, hey, it's going to be okay. Don't freak out. This is a good thing. We're focusing on the positives, remember?"

I took a few steadying breaths as he held me, savoring the strength of his muscular chest and arms around me. He was right. Freaking out about this wouldn't make it easier to endure. I had to be strong, even if I felt like I was falling apart.

Would the pack help? Were there women that could guide me in all this? I was so lost. Who could I even trust?

"What are some of the positives about this?" Jax asked, cupping my chin and tilting my face up towards his. "Tell me one."

The love in his eyes softened some of the tension inside me, and the heat in them pierced me in a way that spurred a different kind of tension.

I smiled. "We're together and we're safe inside the castle."

"Good." He grazed his lips teasingly over mine. "What else?"

"The elders have accepted me and the babies," I said quickly, my breath hitching in my throat as I tried to chase his lips.

"Mmm hmm." He bit and licked my bottom lip. "What about the fact that you have two powerful wolves devoted to you who think you're the sexiest woman on the planet?"

Tannin began to kiss my shoulder blades, and I became very aware of his cock pressing against my ass cheek. "And that, for the next three months, we have you totally and completely at our mercy."

Jax finally claimed my mouth, pushing his demanding tongue between my lips with a groan, and I kissed him back like a starving woman. He pushed me onto my back but stayed lying beside me as he fucked my mouth with his tongue and teeth, while he pinned my wrists over my head.

Tannin rolled on top of me and pressed his lips to my neck, kissing down my body. When he got to my belly, he gripped under my knees and pushed them up, exposing me. The heat of his breath bathed my pussy as his mouth closed over my clit, making me gasp and arch up into his touch. His tongue was like magic against my flesh, pressing and circling over and between my sensitive folds.

I broke the kiss with Jax to moan and gasp for breath. Never would I get enough of this... their mouths devouring me at the same time, their bodies working together to simultaneously worship and destroy me.

Tannin slipped a finger into my opening as he nibbled and suckled on my clit, slowly teasing at first, then suddenly pumping his fingers into me. I whimpered into Jax's mouth as he pulled me back for another kiss, bucking my hips at the relentless pounding of my pussy, desperate for more.

The pleasure was sharp and powerful and was quickly becoming too much. But with Jax clutching my wrists against the pillow above me, and Tannin firmly holding my knees against my belly, I was well and truly at their mercy. I moaned deeply into Jax's feverish kisses against this sweet torment that I both hoped and feared would never end.

I couldn't stand it, I couldn't—and just as I was about to scream to them to end the torment, my core shattered in ecstasy that had my eyes rolling up into my head. Tannin removed his finger and stuck his tongue inside me, lapping and sucking at the juices, groaning in hunger the whole time.

Before the waves of bliss finished pulsating through me, he pushed my legs apart as he got to his knees, propped my ass up on his thighs, and drove his cock into my still quaking pussy.

With the same ferocity that he had pumped his finger, Tannin slammed his cock into me, drawing out the ripples of my orgasm. Jax swallowed my screams as he kneaded my breasts, and I blindly reached for his cock, stroking it, desperate to please him too.

Panting hard, Tannin stopped suddenly and pulled out of me, slapping Jax on the shoulder. Jax didn't hesitate. He broke our lip lock and situated himself between my legs as Tannin came around to the side of me once more.

Before I could work out what they were doing, they'd swapped places. Tannin bent his head to suck on my breast, and Jax took off right where Tannin left, thrusting into me.

"Oh my..."

My screams of pleasure filled the room, and I couldn't even consider whether any of our new occupants heard me, let alone care. It was impossible to be silent with the masters of pleasure working my body like it was their own personal instrument.

Jax fucked me hard and fast until he got close, his breathing ragged and gasping. I reached for him, assuming he'd fill me with his seed, but instead he pulled away and tagged Tannin back in.

"Fucking hell," I gasped out as my empty flesh was once again filled and pulsing.

My men continued this game of taking turns fucking me over and over. I lost track of the orgasms they coerced from my flesh, the pleasure unending. I wasn't sure how much longer they could keep this up, or how much longer I could withstand the blissful torment.

Finally, they fell at my sides, and I had a moment to catch my breath. My chest was heaving, and my beloved men were still touching me. They kissed my neck and breasts languidly, then rolled me onto my side facing Tannin, who lifted my leg to drape it over his hip, and he slid into me, thrusting slowly.

Jax curled up behind me, and a thrill shot through me at what I suspected—hoped—he was planning to do. The tip of his cock rubbed up and down between my butt cheeks, and his teeth scraped against the back of my neck.

"Is this what you want, my dirty girl?" he asked, his voice rough and deep.

"Yes, yes, yes," I pleaded, arching my back to present my ass to him even as Tannin slowly fucked me.

His resulting groan was delicious, and his tip pressed against my tight opening, nudging in a teasingly gentle rhythm that drove me insane. It hurt a little, but in a way that thrilled me and that I wanted so badly to explore further.

The head of his cock entered me, and a deep, raw groan escaped me as my entire body stiffened against the intrusion. But he didn't push any further, just held his cock right there, barely inside me, and began to squeeze his shaft.

Tannin's breathy moans grew louder and sharper, and with a final thrust, he buried himself deep inside me, filling my pussy with his warm cum. The pulsing called on my own body's orgasm, and I shuddered as a wave of pleasure washed over me once more.

Jax sank his teeth into my neck, stroking harder and faster, pushing into my ass just a bit more as he reached his long-awaited climax with tight hisses against my skin. The feeling of his cum spilling into me there was alarmingly tantalizing. Even though I was thoroughly exhausted and sore everywhere now, I couldn't help but wonder how it would feel to have him buried fully in me there.

We lay in a sweaty heap for several long moments, continuing to pet and kiss each other wherever our spent hands and lips could reach.

As I was catching my breath, I became aware of the fact that the elders were most likely awake and would be getting hungry soon. As much as I didn't want to leave this bed, I did want to make a good impression on them during my first full day as their hostess.

With no small effort, I sat up in bed and rested my back against the headboard.

"I would like to host a welcome dinner for the elders tonight," I announced, still panting from all the exertion.

Jax lazily rolled his head in my direction. "I think that's a great idea. It will give them a chance to get to know you, and you, them."

"Perfect." I turned to Tannin. "And I was thinking we should invite your mother and sister to live in the castle too. I know how important they are to you, and it might be nice to have a little help with meals and things."

"Oh." His brows flared in surprise, and his eyes lit with gratitude. "That would be wonderful. Thank you, my love. I'll go tell them the good news now." He tried to curl upward, then flopped back onto the sheets with a huff. "Well, I will as soon as I can get out of bed."

I giggled. "You two are going to be the ruin of me."

Jax waggled his eyebrows at me. "Keep talking like that, and we might have to go for round two."

Oh, no way!

I hastily scooted down the mattress and slipped off the edge before he could grab my arm. "I don't think I could survive another round like that."

My mates chuckled, and I fled to the bathroom for a quick shower before dressing. I had a big day ahead of me, and I couldn't afford to let them lure me in with their dark promises. I could only hope the elders found me half as charming as my mates did.

CHAPTER 2
TANNIN

I stood in front of the castle's main double doors for several minutes, frozen with indecision. I was thrilled about the prospect of having my mother and Twila living in the castle. After everything they'd been through, it would be a dream come true for them, and I'd feel much better about their safety with them residing within these walls.

I wanted to say I was surprised that Aliya offered such a wonderful invitation, but I wasn't. Her sweetness and generosity knew no bounds. I meant what I'd said to her regarding what an amazing mother she would make, probably more than she understood or believed.

What had me staring at the doorknob was my lack of faith or trust in everyone else. Most of the pack adored Jax, but they'd still turned on him like the tide during a full moon. I wasn't nearly as popular. So even though the elders had pardoned us completely, I wasn't expecting a parade when I walked through the village to fetch my family.

There were clearly some among the pack who wanted me dead, Coda most of all. And Aliya had made a valid point this morning. For all I knew, he was just waiting for one of us to step outside the castle so he could catch us unaware and discreetly dispose of us.

But if he tried, I would not go down silently. I refused to live the rest of my life in fear of betrayal. And if I were to sneak around or show fear,

I would be perceived as weak, an easy target. That was not going to happen.

I straightened my posture, put on my best cocky Jax impression, and strode out into the courtyard.

The morning was beautiful. The sun's rays were warm on my face, countered by a cool, gentle breeze. No one was standing guard outside, waiting for me to come out. At least not that I could see. But if they were, I was prepared to shift and tear them to pieces.

Children were playing on the main road ahead, their giggles and shouts skittering off the cobblestones and walls of the homes lining the path. Smoke danced from the chimney of the once abandoned bakery and the aroma of cinnamon in the air proved to me that someone had decided to claim it as their own.

I took a long, slow inhalation of breath as a wave of calm washed away my fear. This was the kingdom we were building, one of peace and prosperity. Everything was going to be okay. Fate clearly had its claws deep in our lives, and I had to trust that it would not disappoint me.

The house my mother had chosen as her own was only a few minutes' walk from the village square, so I set off on the path. Seeing the flaking paint on the exterior and the handful of shingles dangling from the edge of the roof as I approached made me even more excited news the news I was soon to deliver.

Finding a patch of wood that wasn't splintered, I knocked on the door. The slapping of little feet sped to respond on the other side, and Twila's large blue eyes peered through the gap in the door as she slowly opened it.

"Tannin!" she squealed, throwing open the door and jumping into my arms like a little spider monkey.

"Twila!" I said, trying to mimic her reaction despite the surprisingly strong grip of her arms and legs around my neck and ribs. Seriously, this kid was going to make a formidable wolf.

At the high energy of our voices, my mother came to the door and gave me a smile that looked on the brink of tears. With no small effort, I peeled my sister from my torso and set her down so I could embrace my mother.

"I was so afraid for you," she whispered into my ear as she squeezed her arms firmly around my chest.

I grunted against the pressure. "Between you and Twila, I'm going to end up breaking a rib."

She released me, and we both laughed.

"Well, it'd be your own fault for making us worry like you did," she said, glancing up as if to keep tears from falling.

"I know, Mama," I said with a hint of guilt. "But neither of you has to worry again because I come bearing news directly from the princess."

My mother straightened in surprise, and Twila peeped, "Oooh, what is it? What is it?"

I knelt down to her level and put my hand on her shoulder. "Princess Aliya has invited you and Mama to come live with us inside the castle."

Her eyes widened, and her mouth formed a long O as she sucked in a loud breath. "I get to live in the castle like a princess?!"

I chuckled and ruffled the top of her hair. "That's right. Go get your things, and we can leave right now."

With a sharp squeal, she ran off to her bedroom, leaving me to laugh as I watched her go. I stood back up to meet my mother's disapproving frown.

"Tannin, we can't move into the castle," she chided, as if correcting a child on the color of the sky.

"Of course, you can. And you will," I countered with an unphased grin.

"No, no, no," she said as she turned and wandered back into the house. "The castle is for royalty and nobles."

"And the families of royalty and nobles," I said as I followed her into the kitchen. "I am the pack beta and mate to the princess. That gives you status by relation."

She picked up a towel on the edge of the sink and resumed drying a dish, an act that my arrival had obviously interrupted. "But Twila and I don't *need* to live in the castle. This house is perfect for us. We have everything we need right here."

I looked around at the modest accommodations. "Mama, this house is barely a step above the shack we shared in the forest."

"But it *is* a step above," she said. "We have solid walls around us and a roof over our heads."

"A roof that will surely leak when the rains come," I argued. "Half the shingles are missing."

"And we have a kitchen," she went on, gesturing to the space around her. "An actual kitchen with running water and electricity. I have my own room. Twila has her own room. No, this house is our home now."

I clenched my teeth. I should have anticipated that my mother's stubborn humility would be a problem. She refused to accept more than she believed she deserved, which was a very low margin. I'd have to approach this differently, in order to convince her.

I took the towel and dish from her hands, set them aside, and held her hands in mine.

"The truth is, you'd really be doing me a huge favor by moving into the castle," I said in a forced confessional tone—though it wasn't really a lie. "You must have heard that Aliya is pregnant with twins, one fathered by each Jax and me."

A bright smile split her previously stern face. "Yes! What wonderful, incredible news. I'm so happy and proud of you." She cupped my cheek, pinching it a little.

"Yes, it is incredible," I said. "But it's also going to be a lot of work. Aliya has been so ill with morning sickness the past few days, and now with having to feed and care for the elders on top of being pregnant, she's feeling very overwhelmed."

She gasped suddenly, then realization dawned. "Oh, the poor thing. She shouldn't have all that extra responsibility on top of growing her babes."

I nodded sympathetically. "I know it would be asking a lot of you, but she could really use the help of someone she can trust. We all could. And with her own mother gone, she's afraid that the lack of maternal energy in the castle will reflect poorly on her own ability to mother our children. So—"

She cut me off with a wave of her hand. "Say no more. Nothing would give me more joy than helping the mother of my grandchildren cope in these difficult times. Just let me pack up a few things."

And just like that, she hurried off to her room.

I really should have led with that angle. My mother was nothing if not a perfect, selfless woman. She may not live in the castle for her own comfort, but she'd come willingly if it meant helping another.

And while everything I'd said was true, my main reason for wanting them both in the castle was for their safety. I'd never lived more than a few feet away from them.

With the current arrangement of us living separately, if something happened, I might not know. They could be in trouble, and I would be far too late to help them. With Coda's unpredictable animosity, that was a massive problem. I needed them close, where I knew they'd be safe, and there was nowhere safer than inside the castle.

After a few minutes of waiting, they were both ready. Twila's bag consisted of the few clothes she owned and her favorite dolls and toys that had been left behind by the previous occupant.

My mother was a different story. She had two large sacks, one filled with her previous clothes and everything in the closet, and the other almost overflowing with canned goods from the pantry.

"Mama, you won't need all this food in the castle," I complained as I hefted the heavy bag over my shoulder. "There will be plenty of food—"

"Nonsense," she said as she led the way out the door. "There's no such thing as too much food, especially when there's an entire castle of people to feed. And here, it would just go to waste. What's my number-one rule?"

I rolled my eyes and deadpanned, "Never waste food."

"Exactly," she said with a grin.

I sighed and shook my head, but I couldn't help but smile as I brought up the rear behind them. I was just glad this was all working out, and if I had to carry fifty pounds of cans on my back to get her out of that run-down hovel, it was well worth it.

As we rounded the corner toward the village square, I saw Coda leaning against a lamp post with his arms crossed, eyeing us menacingly.

My shoulders bunched with tension that had nothing to do with the weight they were carrying, and I readied myself to discard it the second he made a move. But he didn't budge, only continuing to glare as we crossed in front of him toward the castle.

"Where are you going?" he barked when I finally turned my back on him.

I stopped and cast a disdainful, smug glance at him over my shoulder. "To the castle."

"And them?" He jutted his chin at my mother and sister, looking down his nose at them.

I turned to face him, puffing my chest out. "Also to the castle. Aliya has invited them to live there."

A muscle at the corner of his nose began to twitch, and he kicked away from the lamp post, making my every muscle stiffen protectively.

"She welcomed *them* into the castle?" he seethed.

"Have a good day, Coda." *Or better yet, fuck off.*

I turned my back on him again and urged my family through the ward ahead of me. Twila squealed as she ran ahead, and even my mother moved a little faster.

His outraged roar followed me through the ethereal veil, and though part of me savored the smug satisfaction at his frustration, another part of me hardened ominously. We were poking the bear, and it was only a matter of time before his teeth and claws truly came out for everyone to see.

CHAPTER 3
ALIYA

I never imagined how difficult and stressful it could be to cook for so many people, and all I'd done so far was make a massive amount of scrambled eggs, toast some bread, and set out various jams for the elders to have for breakfast. Next on my list was the big dinner I volunteered myself to make for them tonight. *Oh, boy.*

I took a moment to breathe as I leaned against the kitchen counter after serving the food in the dining room, trying to collect myself before starting on the next big project.

Tabitha leapt onto the counter and perched beside my bent arm. "Rawr."

"I know, it's a lot," I told her, scratching the back of her head. "But I'll be okay. I just need a little break."

Her body rumbled with her satisfied purr as she nuzzled into my hand, but I took that as a nod of agreement.

For the last year—though it had felt like an eternity while I'd been alone—I'd only had to worry about preparing food for myself, which usually consisted of fruits, a few vegetables, and whatever canned soup or chili I could heat on the stove. And with no one around to scare them off, there was no shortage of rats for Tabitha to catch.

Before the plague, having enough to eat had never been a concern for me. The kitchen staff had always baked delicious snacks for me, and they'd cooked gourmet dishes for every meal. Oh, and the cakes! I missed their cakes.

I'd realized how much I took them for granted after they'd died, but now I was learning just how much work they actually did. Cooking for just Jax, Tannin and myself had been a big production on its own, but now I was going to cook for a dozen or so disgruntled elderly people whose favor I desperately needed to win.

No pressure or anything.

I wasn't even sure where to start. The only meat I had access to was chicken. Did they like chicken? What vegetables would they like? Should I attempt to make a cake and risk it being a disaster, or would they be fine with pie? And what flavor of pie?

My stomach did a somersault just thinking about so much food, making me buckle and clutch my too-round belly. Ugh, I did not need this right now.

I plucked the vial of anti-nausea potion from my skirt pocket and stared at it, debating. This was the last of the batch I'd made a few days ago.

"Meh," Tabitha complained when I stopped petting her, glancing at me with impatient irritation.

"I don't have time to make more right now," I explained. "Hopefully this will last until I do."

She snorted and flicked her tail against my shoulder.

I uncorked the vial and spilled the contents into my mouth, holding it above my tongue to let every last drop fall. I swallowed, and relief immediately soothed the chaos writhing in my gut—or at least the part that was due to the two little lives I was carrying.

Three months. Only three months. Oh, my goodness. Well actually, some time has already passed, so it's closer to two and a half...

I mentally stomped on that train of thought, unable to afford to let my thoughts downward spiral about that now. Just focus on the task at hand, that was all I could do.

"Okay, Tabitha," I said, running my hand down her back one last time. "Let's go catch some chickens."

As I lifted my foot in that direction, sunlight momentarily streamed across the ballroom floor through the archway, and then the heavy front doors closed with a resounding boom.

"Wow, it's even prettier than I dreamed it would be," a small, girlish voice echoed off the marble floor.

I gasped in excitement. *Tannin's family.*

I rushed to the archway of the kitchen to see Tannin, a middle-aged woman who looked just like him, and a little girl that looked nothing like him. They were walking across the ballroom carrying large patchwork sacks.

Tannin smiled as he caught sight of me and steered them toward me, setting down the sack he was carrying and leaning it against the wall. "Mom, Twila, this is Aliya, princess of Varynia."

Holding her pinched fingers out to the sides as if spreading out the skirt of an invisible dress, Twila bent her knees outward in a bow so deep she nearly fell forward. Then with cheeks reddened by embarrassment, she righted herself and beamed up at me.

"I've never met a real princess before," she said in the most adorable voice. "I'm so excited we get to live with you. Does this mean you're going to be my sister? I always wanted a sister."

I couldn't stop the giggle that trickled up my throat. "I've always wanted a sister too, and Tannin tells me you're the best sister in the whole world."

Her blush grew brighter, and she looked down as she shuffled her feet. "Well, I don't know about that."

We all laughed, then his mother stepped forward and put her hands on my upper arms, wearing a big, motherly smile.

"I'm Raya," she said. "But you can call me Mom—if you want to. I am so proud that my Tannin mated to a princess. And you are more lovely than I imagined. Welcome to the family."

Then she pulled me into a hug, catching me off guard so that I only got to pat her back before she drew away.

"Now, Tannin tells me that you need some extra help since the elders have moved in," she continued, her tone all business now. "What can I do for the mother of my grandbabies?"

"Oh... er... uh," I stammered.

"Mama, why don't you get settled in first?" Tannin suggested, giving me a conspiratorial wink. "At least put your things in your room."

"Ah, yes," she agreed, glancing at the sacks. "We can't just leave them here to clutter the ballroom and make more mess for the princess. Come along, Twila."

"I've already chosen rooms for the two of you," Tannin said as he led them toward the stairs.

"Nothing too ostentatious, I hope," her voice trailed off as they began their ascent.

I grinned as I watched them go, relieved that his mother at least seemed to like me. That had been just one of the many things I'd been stressing over this morning. And I was grateful that she was so willing and eager to help me, as it would make preparing dinner much easier.

I turned back to the kitchen. "Come on, Tabitha. Let's get those chickens."

"Mew!" She hopped off the counter and followed me outside.

I used to hate letting her come to the coop with me whenever I fetched eggs because she made a game out of chasing and terrorizing the poor chickens. But today, I figured I could use it to my advantage.

Just as I knew she would, she dove at the smallest hen, sending the two of them zooming around the yard and scattering the rest of them.

I watched the melee for a moment, noting the reactions and paths of the hens that flitted away from their feline foe. Then, as Tabitha chased her reluctant prey around the corner, I bent down and snatched one of the hens that fled my way, trapping it against my chest and arms.

It took some maneuvering, but I eventually got hold of its feet and held it upside down, and it fell limp in my grasp.

"I'm not going to like this part," I grumbled to myself.

Taking a deep, steadying breath, I gripped the chicken's neck and twisted it with the flick of my wrist, cringing at the sharp *crack* that resulted.

"Yuck." I set the dead chicken on the ground on the other side of the fence. "Okay, one down, one more to go."

Catching the second chicken was harder and took twice as long as the first, and by the time I had it in my hands, my clothes and hands were covered with dirt and God knew what else. I snapped its neck too and headed for the gate.

"Alright, Tabitha, play time is over," I called to her as I opened the gate and bent to pick up the other chicken.

I saw her slowly coming over to me in my peripheral vision and looked up at her. The neck of the small chicken she'd been chasing was firmly clenched in her teeth and she was clumsily dragging its body between her paws.

I sighed. "I guess we're cooking three chickens, then." Though the one she killed was hardly large enough to feed Twila.

With my free hand, I scooped both her and her bounty off the ground and carried all four animals back into the kitchen.

Raya was already sitting on a stool at the island counter, chopping potatoes.

She paused at my lumbering entrance and looked at me timidly. "I wasn't sure what you had planned for the menu, but I figured potatoes go with everything."

"Oh, they definitely do. Thank you." I hefted the two dead hens on the counter near the sink. "I wasn't fully decided on anything, so I am definitely open to suggestion."

She grinned like I just gave her a prize. "Wonderful, because I found a recipe for a casserole in that cookbook that sounds delicious!" She tilted her head towards the open book at the top of the stack on the side table against the wall.

"Perfect," I said.

I had only looked through those books a couple times in the first days of my solitude, ultimately deciding that attempting any of the recipes was pointless without anyone to cook for. I had all but forgotten about them until now.

Tabitha slipped through my arm, running for the archway as fast as she could with her trophy getting in the way.

"No, no, nope," I blurted out, rushing after her.

I caught her and wrenched the poor bird from her mouth, then tossed her a little less than gently into the open space between the den and ballroom.

I held up the mangled, bedraggled thing, grimacing at it. It was hardly worth eating, let alone cleaning, preparing and cooking.

"You were probably a good egg layer, too." I sighed again and went to work scalding and plucking the three chickens.

When I had the smaller one mostly plucked, feet shuffled into the kitchen. I turned to my right in time for Esther to open a cabinet next to me, frowning as she searched apparently in vain.

I set the chicken down. "What do you need?"

"Where are the glasses, dear?" she asked. "I would just like a glass of water. That is, if Coda hasn't shut if off again," she added in an irritated mutter.

I wanted to ask more about that topic, but I needed to focus on dinner and didn't want to accidentally shatter this tenuous peace, so I just hummed in response, washed my hands, and reached into the cabinet above my head for a glass. I filled it and handed it to her.

"Thank you." Her eyes lingered on me as she took a drink.

I wasn't sure whether to wait to see if she needed anything else or continue my feather plucking, so I just sat there awkwardly.

She lowered the glass, holding it in front of her large bosom, and gave me a warm yet somehow mysterious smile. "How are you and the little pups doing today?"

My breath hitched in surprise. Pups. They weren't just regular human babies, they were Black Wolves. What if they shifted inside me and tore my belly wide open?

I swallowed, mindlessly putting my hand over my bump. "We're fine," I lied.

I mean, I was fine right now, but how long would I stay that way? And that was just physically. Mentally, I was a writhing pit of snakes, all my emotions knotting and hissing and striking at each other.

Her expression softened, and she put a hand on my forearm. "I know you feel overwhelmed right now, but everything is going to work out the way it's supposed to. Fate has you in its favor—both you and your little ones."

I frowned in curiosity as I looked into her wizened gray eyes. She had gone from wanting to execute me to treating me like I was *her* princess. Did she know something about my babies that I didn't?

I opened my mouth, but she spoke before I could.

"Oh dear, that is not how you pluck a chicken." She frowned down at the scrawny, nearly bald bird in front of me. "You're missing all the pin feathers. Here, let me show you how it's done."

She pulled the bird toward her and began pinching the small needle-like feathers that stayed stuck in the skin, showing impressive dexterity for a woman her age.

"Oh, no, you don't have to do that," I objected, reaching for the bird. "This dinner is for you."

"Yes, and I don't want to choke on pin feathers while I eat it," she said without pausing. "So you can start plucking the large feathers off the next bird, and I'll take care of these smaller ones."

I could see why she was such a respected pack leader. She spoke with a matriarchal kind of authority that one would be reluctant to question or deny. And on the bright side, I could definitely use her keen eye for those damn needles.

I pulled over the next chicken and started pulling out feathers by the handful, and as we worked together in concentrated silence, I couldn't help but wonder what she had seen in the drop of my blood.

I hadn't expected to be nervous about this dinner. Anxiety wasn't an emotion I usually experienced. But as I set the table in the dining hall while Aliya got herself clean and dressed up, my movements were clumsy, my fingers fumbling in their attempts to arrange the silverware properly.

I didn't like it. I had faced countless life-or-death situations without breaking a sweat, and yet a single dinner where I wasn't even the one in the spotlight had me shaken.

Why though? I had the elders' favor, and after Esther's prophetic proclamation, my new family was untouchable, our previous status restored and secured.

But I had to admit, I cared what the elders thought about Aliya. I wanted them to like her—no, *love* her—and for them to accept her as not only their Alpha's mate but also their queen. I wanted Varynia to be a kingdom again, one that was both prosperous and joyous, ruled this time by both wolves and wielders.

That all hinged on this stupid dinner going well. So, I set each dish and piece of cutlery with stubborn precision, brought out the food platters and arranged them in the most visually appealing way, interspersed by short vases of fresh cut flowers. Then, for the final touch of ambiance, I set candelabras along the table and side tables, lit each candle, and dimmed the lights.

The end result was a feast table fit for a king, the sweet perfume of the flowers mixing with the savory aromas of roasted chicken and vegetables, all amplified by the gentle warmth from the candles.

"Looks perfect," Tannin said, patting me on the back.

"Thanks," I said gruffly. Table setting wasn't exactly something I'd trained for. "Would you let the elders know that dinner is served?"

He frowned at me. "Shouldn't we wait for Aliya."

I smirked and shook my head. "I want her to make an entrance."

He returned my smile and left the room with a skip in his step.

I went to the entrance, leaning against the archway, ready to greet each guest as they appeared, like the Alpha host they deserved.

To my surprise, the elders arrived in style, dressed in elegant gowns and handsome suits I assumed they found in the wardrobes of their new rooms. Albeit several items were too big or too small—the buttons of Droger's shirt were barely hanging on for dear life—but the joy on their faces said that didn't matter.

They'd lived their entire lives in second-hand rags or garments they made themselves out of animal skins and old linens. These fine clothes, left by the previous occupants, were their first experience with true finery, and it made me smile from ear to ear to see them enjoying their over or under-sized couture.

After half the elders had taken their seats, I ducked into the kitchen and waved Twila over. She left her mother's side, who was putting the finishing touches on a freshly baked pie, and skipped to me with a grin bunching her cheeks.

"I need you to do me a favor," I said in hushed tone.

"Yeah? What?" she asked, mimicking my low register.

"Can you go tell Aliya it's time for dinner?" I asked.

Her nostrils flared. "Yes!" Then she ran to the stairs and bolted up the steps.

I couldn't help but laugh as I watched her. I often felt like she was my little sister too, just as Tannin was my brother. And now, because of Aliya, we were going to become an even closer, bigger family. My heart swelled with a joy that took the edge off my nerves.

Everything is going to be fine.

I ushered Raya with the pie into the dining room as Tannin escorted the last of the elders to her seat.

"Thank you all for joining us for what I hope will be the first of many meals we share together," I announced. "You all look so elegant, I hardly recognize you. Especially you, Droger."

The old grump grunted and adjusted the lapels of his suit jacket as the rest in attendance chuckled.

"Aliya worked very hard all day to prepare this meal, and I hope you will appreciate it." That didn't come out quite the way I intended, but I couldn't help myself. I wasn't sure I'd be able to restrain my temper if any of them dismissed her efforts or treated her poorly after all she had done.

She was born and raised a princess, after all. The expectation that she should also cook and serve was a little strange, but she was exceeding everyone's expectations so far, and I couldn't be prouder.

"Huh-huh-hum," Twila dramatically cleared her throat to make her presence know as she preceded Aliya into the dining room.

All heads turned to her.

"May I present Princess Aliya," she declared, stepping aside and gesturing theatrically to Aliya as she came forward.

I didn't know how it was possible for our girl to take my breath away every time I saw her but tonight was no exception. She was an angel in her rhinestone-studded silver gown, her honey hair done up in a series of braids that coiled at the back of her head like a crown.

But to me, her beauty wasn't determined by the clothes she wore. Even when she'd been dressed in a dirt and blood-stained slip, she'd still been stunning. Her inner beauty shined through everything else.

Only a few of the elders clapped along with Tannin, his family, and me. I went to Aliya's side and led her to the chair at the head of the table, where she belonged. Then Tannin and I took our usual seats on either side of her, me always on her right, and Tannin on her left.

"Alright, everyone," I said. "Dig in."

They might have been dressed like nobles, but they were still wolves as they broke into a feral frenzy to serve themselves. Rather than chastise anyone, I decided instead to lead by example.

Calmly and gentlemanly, I sliced a leg off the nearest chicken and scooped a spoonful of vegetables onto a plate, then I set the plate in front of Aliya.

"Thank you," she said.

I leaned forward and planted a chaste kiss on her cheek, then began to fix a plate for myself.

The lesson landed, for some, at least. The bickering and rivalry over preferred items quieted, and for a moment, all that could be heard was the clinking of cutlery on porcelain. And the sound of Droger tearing into his chunk of chicken with his bare hands and chomping jowls.

"Aliya, the chicken is delicious," Esther praised as she delicately cut into a breast with a knife and fork.

"Thank you," Aliya said graciously. "But I couldn't have done it without your help."

"Oh?" I asked, turning to Esther, who was down the table to my right.

"All I did was pluck out the pin feathers," Esther explained. "Aliya took care of the rest. I honestly don't remember the last time I had meat that was so well prepared. So full of flavor."

"Mine's a little dry," Droger grumbled with his mouth full.

"Then drink some water," Wilda snapped at him.

He muttered something incoherent and continued to chew.

Wilda sighed and turned to Aliya. "You'll have to forgive us, Princess. We've been in the forest for a very long time, and apparently some of us have lost our manners."

Aliya smiled and paused the cutting of her chicken leg. "I know it's not the same, but I was completely alone for over a year after the plague. Civility can leave one pretty quickly under destitution."

I couldn't help but smile. That was very well said.

"I'd hardly call living in a palace destitution," Droger complained, earning himself a few glares around the table while others nodded in agreement.

Tannin's jaw clenched across from me, and although I was also losing my patience with the old bastard, I gave Tannin a warning look not to retaliate.

"It's true," Aliya said. "I was fortunate to have such strong walls to shelter me, just as you were fortunate to have such a strong community to shelter you. We all do the best we can with the tools we are given."

Droger frowned, either unwilling or unable to argue her point. I wasn't sure, but my bet was on the latter.

"I couldn't imagine what it must have been like for you to be here all by yourself for so long," Esther commented. "Even in a castle, I think many of us would have found it hard to survive, pack creatures that we are. How did you manage it?"

Aliya shrugged. "One day at a time, just like you all did. Although I must give credit where credit is due. Tabitha, my cat, saved me from truly going insane from loneliness."

She went quiet for a moment, and the whole table was hushed, waiting for the next thing she would say.

Aliya went on, "I often wondered why the plague didn't take me too. Everyone said I was blessed to be immune to it, but after they all died, I thought maybe I was cursed instead. The loneliness was crushing."

She paused, and I swore I saw hints of pity in several pairs of eyes.

"But now I see that Fate had a plan for me," she continued with a lighter note to her voice. "And I'm very grateful for where it's taking me." She put her hands on one of mine and of Tannin's, gracing us each with a loving smile.

Aliya's vulnerability turned out to be the magic key to unlocking the stubborn lips and minds of the elders. Throughout dinner, some asked her questions about her solitude, while others asked about what the kingdom was like before the plague. Soon everyone was sharing their own stories, some of which I was surprised to learn I'd never heard before. Even Droger opened up about a torrid love affair he had with a gypsy from a neighboring village when he was a young man.

The evening was going so much better than I anticipated or hoped. And though a fraction of the elders seemed to still hold some animosity toward Aliya, they were at least treating her with respect.

As I glanced around the table, my heart singing, all I could think was, could things actually work? Or was our fragile peace doomed to break?

CHAPTER 5

ALIYA

My nerves didn't settle until dinner was over and the last of the elders retired to their rooms for the night. It seemed to have gone well, but I wasn't certain. More of the elders seemed to have accepted me over the course of the meal, but the fact that some clearly didn't bothered me. Rationally, I knew trust wouldn't happen overnight, but I couldn't help but be disappointed.

How ironic that I was so desperate for the approval of the people I'd been raised to hate.

Once the dining room was empty, Raya and Twila helped me gather all the dishes and take them into the kitchen. I turned on the faucet so I could start to wash them, but Jax reached over me and turned the water off.

"Leave it for tomorrow," he said in my ear in that husky tone that instantly made my insides clench. "I want to reward you for all your hard work."

I looked up at him, and Tannin was standing just behind him, giving me the same hungry look. Heat flushed across my body, and I didn't protest as Jax gripped my wrist with just the right amount of gentle force and tugged me away from the sink.

I muttered a quick goodnight to Raya and Twila as I scurried up the stairs with my mates chasing me. As soon as we got to our room, I let them catch me, and they descended on me with starving kisses and ravenous petting.

"You were amazing tonight," Jax crooned between gruff kisses on my neck as Tannin trapped my lips with his.

Tannin hummed his agreement into my mouth as he deepened our kiss. I couldn't help but respond, sliding my tongue against his, and grabbing onto whatever anchor I could find.

"There's something I've been wanting to teach you." Jax ran his hand down the center of my back, sliding his finger between my butt cheeks and applying a pressure that shot a thrill through me. "Are you ready to learn?"

"Yes, yes," I panted through wet kisses, arching my back to push my ass into his hand.

"Good girl," he growled, then playfully bit my earlobe before dragging the straps of my dress over my shoulders.

Tannin pushed the dress down as I shimmied out of the snug, unforgiving fabric. He kissed down my chest and torso as each bit of me was revealed. As soon as my bottom was free, Jax's hand returned, venturing lower to cup my pussy from behind and pressing his thumb against my ass at the same time.

I hissed a sharp whimper at the duet of sensations, both touches contrasting yet complimenting each other.

The dress pooled around my feet, and Tannin knelt in front of me, licking my aching clit while Jax's finger pushed into me, his thumb rubbing teasingly over my back entrance in time with the slow rhythm of his finger's penetration.

I melted into their arms. What they were doing to me was so perfect. If it weren't for Tannin's hands gripping my hips, and Jax's hand hooked between my legs, I would have crumpled to the floor.

"Come with us, my love," Jax cooed, withdrawing his masterful fingers and pulling me toward the bed.

Tannin pressed a kiss to the front of my pussy and rose to his feet so that Jax could draw me away. Then my two mates slowly removed their clothes, almost as if creating a show for me, and with bated breath and bitten lips, I watched as every glorious, chiseled inch of their bodies was exposed.

Finally naked, Tannin lay on the edge of the bed with his legs spread and feet planted on the floor, his eager cock standing at attention.

Jax came up behind me and put his hands on my shoulders, bringing his mouth close to my ear as he said, "Straddle him. Take him all the way inside and lay down on top of him."

My pulse skittered like a thrown rock skipping over the surface of a lake as I moved to follow his instructions. I climbed onto Tannin's lap, my limbs trembling with anticipation, and took his cock inside me, slowly lowering down his shaft until he filled me completely.

I began to sway my pelvis to amplify the sensation, but Tannin's hands moved to my hips, pinning me in place on top of him.

"Don't," he said with a strained gasp. "Lay on top of me." His fingers trailed up my sides as he gently encouraged me forward, and though confused, I did as he said.

Jax positioned himself behind me and cupped my ass cheeks, his palms pressing into my flesh as his fingertips teasingly caressed.

"Gods, you're so fucking beautiful," he said with a groan, and all I could do was remain poised with my ass exposed to him and wait as he kneaded my cheeks.

Finally, the warm tip of his cock pressed against my ass, and my eyelids fluttered as I gasped.

"We're going to take this very slow," Jax said. "It's only going to work if you relax completely. Don't fight it."

I nodded, trepidation and excitement mingling with a need I couldn't resist.

Tannin tipped my chin up so I could look at him. "If you want to stop, we'll stop. Just say the word."

"Okay," I breathed nervously, squeezing my pussy walls around his cock in a silent caress.

He hissed out a breath, kissed my lips, then gently positioned me so that the side of my head rested on his chest.

Jax's hand moved up my back, his thumbs and fingertips kneading into the muscles along my spine. It felt like heaven, and I began to let go of muscles I didn't know I was clenching.

Until his cock pushed deeper into my ass. I flinched under the sharpness of the pain, my body tightening against the intrusion.

"It's okay, beautiful," Jax said in a soothing tone as his fingers worked harder on my muscles. "Just relax. Let me in." His hips were gently rocking back and forth, not pushing forward, yet helping me to relax.

I'd never felt such a contradiction of emotions or physical sensations. I really wanted this, but at the same time, I wanted to stop. The thought of them both inside me simultaneously was unbelievably intoxicating, but the practice was much less comfortable, and I started to think it was impossible. Jax could never possibly fit.

But he entered me further, inch by achingly slow inch, massaging my back, hips, and shoulders the whole time as Tannin's fingers gently massaged my scalp and neck. I did my best to relax, to resist the involuntary urge to clench. Their touch felt amazing, and I focused on them, willing my body to melt into them.

After a while, the discomfort started to fade, the pressure of him filling me melding with the desire their hands had been stoking all along. I didn't realize Jax's cock had gone so deep until I felt his pelvis pressing against my ass cheeks, and that suddenly ignited my core like a raging inferno, sending a pulse of overwhelming lust radiating through my entire body.

I squeezed my pelvic muscles, and they both groaned in pleasure. But they both stayed very still, and I couldn't take it anymore.

I moved slightly forward, testing this new position, and they hissed as their bodies stiffened even more beneath and behind me. It was obvious they were both incredibly turned on and didn't want to come too fast, but I couldn't handle much more.

My mates were both finally inside me, and I could hardly bear how perfect it was. The sensation of rocking my hips teased me, hinting at the pleasure I so badly craved. I needed more.

I swayed back, arching my ass toward Jax, and the change in pressure had a deep, guttural moan slipping out of my throat.

Planting my hands on either side of Tannin's head, I pushed myself up and craned my neck over my shoulder to look at Jax. His features were strained, his face and chest glistening with sweat.

"More," I begged.

"Oh, baby," he grunted. "Are you sure?"

I nodded, gasping out as Tannin's cock thickened inside me.

Jax gripped my hips once more, then slowly, he drew back, his cock dragging a fire against my tight inner walls that made me groan again.

I looked down at Tannin, locking his gaze with mine. "Please."

He didn't need clarification. Lowering his hands to my waist, he lifted me up, holding my hips aloft as he began to thrust his cock up into me over and over again.

My eyes rolled back in my head. The feeling of them both filling and stretching me in tandem was utterly explosive and almost too much to tolerate. They were going so agonizingly slowly, I thought I would die from the pleasure overload assaulting my body and soul.

They found their rhythm, plunging and receding in unison, and I couldn't contain the moans that were forced out of me with each of their thrusts. It was so intense, and I felt so unbearably insatiable that tears started to stream down my face.

Tannin froze, the restraint seeming to cause him physical pain. "Oh fuck, are we hurting you?"

"No, don't stop!" I cried out. Oh, God, I'd die if they stopped now.

"Are you sure?" he asked, his gruff voice uncertain.

"Yes, yes!" I cried out.

He buried himself inside me again with more vigor, and I exploded with a piercing shriek. Blinding ecstasy ripped through me with so much force, I feared my heart would burst. All my inner muscles quaked and squeezed around both their cocks, their unceasing thrusts intensifying my orgasm to even greater heights.

Tannin lost it. With a loud groan, he pressed his pelvis against mine as hard as he could, the heat of his seed spilling against the deepest part of my core. Small but sharp whimpers escaped him as the power of his orgasm had his cock pulsing inside me.

Jax followed almost immediately behind him, driving hard into me with one final thrust. I screamed again as his cum filled me, the finality of the end of this interlude incredibly bittersweet. I'd never wanted it to end, and yet I'd felt like I would die if it didn't.

I collapsed onto Tannin's chest, not caring that it was covered in my fallen tears and his sweat. My body was so torn with bliss, I could barely stand it, and yet I couldn't wait to do this again.

Jax slowly withdrew from my ass, leaving me feeling strangely empty and cold. With shaking limbs, I rolled off Tannin, and together the three of us scooted to the top of the bed and fell into each other, lazily kissing and petting one another.

How could something so insanely sinful be so beautifully heavenly? These men were corrupting me in every possible way, and damn me for loving every dark, precious minute of it.

CHAPTER 6

JAX

"I still don't think this is a good idea," Tannin grumbled, leaning over the kitchen counter of our temporary house with a slumped posture.

I was tired of this argument, but I maintained my cool exterior as I waited beside the front door. "It's been three days since the elders pardoned us, and we haven't spoken to any of the deltas since. This meeting is long overdue."

"They betrayed us," he argued. "Why don't we just appoint new deltas and be done with it?"

I sighed, pretending to dust lint off my sleeve. "They only did what the elders told them to do, which means they are loyal. And loyalty shouldn't be punished."

"Not all of them were just following orders." His boot tip knocked against the bottom corner of the counter as he idly kicked at it, I assumed to distract himself from his misplaced angst. "At least, not from the elders."

"Are you telling me that you're actually worried about Coda?" I retorted snidely, arching my eyebrow mockingly.

His kicking grew louder. "I'm just saying we shouldn't underestimate him. He wants to be Alpha, and he'll stoop as low as necessary to accomplish that."

"And he'll be reprimanded for his actions," I assured him. "But right now, having an open discussion with all the deltas is the only thing that matters. It will give them a chance to air their grievances, so we can move forward with building the kingdom we all want. Like it or not, we can't do that without them."

He huffed but didn't argue, though the incessant knocking of his damn foot was grating on my nerves.

"Will you stop doing that?" I snapped.

With a glare at me, he straightened his leg and planted his foot with a decisive stomp.

When a knock sounded from the door, my temper flared for an instant before I realized it hadn't come from Tannin. Plastering on a magnanimous smile, I turned and opened the door.

Esme was the first to arrive, with Cameron and Hayden coming up behind her.

"Nice to see you, Alpha," she said, giving me a respectful nod before entering the house that had briefly served as my and Tannin's jail. I figured holding the meeting here would deliver a message—nothing and no one could hold me down.

One by one, the twelve deltas arrived. I studied each as I greeted them, gauging their demeanor toward me. Most showed reverence as Esme had, but a few seemed to just go through the motions.

Tywen and Hollis, however—the two who'd dragged us to this very house after Coda exposed us—refused to make eye contact as they passed through the door. I told myself not to hold that against them. They'd been misled. Now they would get a chance to state their cases and make a choice.

Coda was the last to show up. Typical. Neither of us said a word as we locked eyes on the doorstep. How he could still wear such a smug expression was beyond me. All the arrogance of a spoiled prince with the grace and charm of a mangy street dog.

I stepped aside to let him enter, then finally closed the door to begin. I had no idea how the conversation was going to go, but it needed to be done. And I wouldn't shy away from discussions about our *new normal* any longer.

The deltas filled the empty space in the small living room, most choosing to stand in typical delta fashion. While I appreciated the shrewd vigilance that came in handy as they were always our scouts, on this one occasion, I wished they'd just sit.

"Good morning, everyone," I began, my voice loud and clear. "I know things have been a bit chaotic since we settled here, more so than we could have anticipated. And I know that many of you are hesitant about the mate bond to the princess that Tannin and I share, which is only natural after the long, dark history of our two peoples."

Almost every face stiffened, every pair of ears pricking with hostility.

"But Fate, in her endless and incontrovertible wisdom, has decided to intervene," I continued. "I am and always will be your Alpha. And while I believe this alliance will only make our young kingdom stronger, I understand your reticence to accept the elders' decision."

There were some furtive glances and side eyes now, but I continued, "So, I'm going to offer each of you a choice. If anyone no longer wishes to follow my command, you may resign from your position as a delta of the pack, with no chance of reinstatement."

I paused to let that sink in, studying the reactions around the room as utter silence fell. I waited, hiding my concern that they all might get up and leave behind a stalwart mask. But no one moved, not even Coda.

"No one?" I asked, baiting them.

Stances relaxed, and I could practically see their inner wolves ducking in submission. Confidence swelled in my chest.

"Very well. But if you choose to maintain your post, I expect each of you to follow my orders without question from here on out. You will treat me with the respect your Alpha deserves, and you will treat Princess Aliya with the same honor you'd give your Alpha's mate. Any slights will be severely punished. There will be no second chances. Do you still wish to stay?"

The silence in the room was so loud, you could have heard a pin drop, and the tension that had previously been thick in the air melted like butter in the summer sun.

Movement caught in the corner of my eye, and I shifted my gaze to Esme as she moved forward. For a moment, my heart split. She was going to leave? Of all my deltas, she was the last person I expected to—

But then she knelt in front of me, placing her fist over her chest and bowing her head. "I'm with you, Alpha."

For a beat, all I could do was stare down at her, pride and humility filling me in equal measure.

Slowly, the others began to follow her lead. I stole a glance at Tannin in the kitchen, and he looked just as shocked as I was.

Tywen, Hollis and Coda were the last to kneel, each of them with increasing reluctance. I caught Coda glaring off to the side as he bowed his head. He clearly wasn't staying out of any sense of loyalty. He just didn't want to lose the small amount of power he had.

Tannin's right not to trust him.

I had half a mind to strip him of his position here and now and be done with him, but that wouldn't bring him to heel. He needed to be broken like a stubborn colt. He needed to be made an example of.

"Thank you all," I said, waving them up off the floor. "But there's still one more matter that must be dealt with."

I waited for them to rise, drawing out their anticipation as their full attention fell on me.

"There's one among you who went rogue, who took matters into his own hands and acted with intent to harm on his own authority."

I didn't have to look at the perpetrator to offer anyone clarity. All eyes shifted to him, and his eyes narrowed on me.

"That is not the way of the pack," I went on. "Our strength lies in our unity, our harmony, each of us working together like the cogs of a clock. When one cog begins to spin in a different direction, the clock can no longer function and eventually breaks if left unchecked."

I turned to Coda, fighting back the satisfied smirk that tugged at the corner of my lips at the flash of fear in his eyes.

"Coda. You went around the elders and shut off the water to the castle without regard for the well-being of the pack. Your actions could have had lasting repercussions that went far beyond simply forcing Tannin, Aliya and me out into the open.

"So, it's now your responsibility to visit every single residence in the kingdom and ensure that the plumbing wasn't damaged. You will check every faucet and spicket, clean out every drain, and if there is so much as a leaky pipe, you will fix it."

His eyes widened in indignant horror. "What? You must be joking. That will take weeks!"

I let the smirk spread my lips. "Then I guess you'd better get started."

He shook his head. "Ja—*Alpha*, this is absurd! I'm a warrior, not a handyman. I don't know the first thing about plumbing."

"You obviously knew enough to turn off the water supply to a major complex." I stepped closer to him, looking down my nose at him. "You will do as I have ordered, or you can resign right now."

He gritted his teeth so hard the grinding was audible. "Yes, Alpha."

I smiled wider, savoring his angry, bitter compliance before stepping back to address the whole group. "Does anyone have anything else to share or address before we adjourn this meeting?"

Hayden, the youngest of our deltas and still a little wet behind the ears, raised his hand. "Yes, Alpha. Cam and I caught sight of a cusith while patroling the village perimeter this morning. And I saw a couple yesterday as well."

"So did I," Esme added.

I nodded in careful consideration. I hadn't seen or scented one of the monsters since the night two of them attacked Aliya before the pack arrived. I had assumed the large number of people filling the town had scared them off. But nothing could keep them away for long.

"What were they doing?" I asked. "Did they try to attack?"

Hayden shook his head.

"We only saw a glimpse of it running through the trees about a hundred yards out," Cameron informed me.

"And the couple I saw yesterday were about the same distance away," Hayden added.

"Do you think they're afraid to come too close?" Esme asked.

I frowned. In my experience, cusith weren't afraid of anything, only cautious and calculating.

"I don't know," I said. "But for now, it seems they're keeping their distance. We need to heighten security around the border. Esme, I'm putting you in charge of organizing a tighter patrol schedule."

She nodded. "I'll get right on it."

"In the meantime, Tannin and I will work on an emergency plan for everyone in case an attack arises," I said. "They need to be prepared."

"We may want to consider recruiting more deltas," suggested Shyla, one of the older deltas. "The border of the kingdom is much larger than our camp in the forest. Even with all of us patroling around the clock, we won't be able to see everything."

She was right. I didn't want them all exhausted and unable to fight if the need arose.

"Okay, that's a good idea," I said. "We'll announce open recruitment to the pack, and Shyla, I'd like you to be the one to train the new deltas."

She bowed her head in agreement.

"Alright, you all know what to do," I said. "We'll reconvene in a week's time."

With nods and mumbles of affirmation, they began to file out of the house.

"Oh, and Coda." I stopped him with a firm hand on his chest before he could stomp past me. "I will be checking on you. Do a good job."

His gaze begrudgingly met mine, but his lips were tightly pressed.

I withdrew my hand, and he strode quickly past me, closing the door behind him.

"Well, that went better than expected," Tannin commented as he strolled out of the kitchen toward me. "Though I had hoped you'd give Coda a physical punishment."

I snorted a laugh. "Forcing him to do hard labor that he will hate every minute of will humble him far more than even a hundred lashes could."

"Perhaps," Tannin said with a shrug. "But this will make him hate you even more."

I didn't think that was possible, and at this point, I was done coddling him. "As long as he learns his place, he can feel however he wants."

Tannin sighed. "I hope you're right about that."

We left the meeting house together, and as we walked back to the castle, a sinking feeling in my stomach settled in deeply.

I hope I'm right about Coda too.

CHAPTER 7

CODA

Filth. I was completely covered in filth, and I could barely contain my rage and disgust as I finally trudged home around nightfall.

I had assumed following Jax's order would be a cake walk. I'd go only to the houses and businesses that were occupied, fiddle around, do the minimum, and be done with it all in just a few days. And all the while, I'd play the hero, pretend I was doing voluntary public service, and gain the favor of the people.

Jax was going to regret assigning me this chore.

I started at the smallest house first, the one the widow Sage chose. She fawned over me for my kindness and generosity because her water pressure was, in fact, low. Great. Into the basement I went, and after hours of fiddling around with the pipes with no success, one of them burst, spewing a fowl sludge all over me and the basement floor.

Fucking pipes had a build-up of rust and gods knew what else that was clogging up the system. I had to patch up the pipes in my soiled clothes, wreaking like death, then clean up the mess before I could leave.

I'm going to kill him. With my bare fucking hands. Slowly. Torturously!

But first, I absolutely had to get clean.

I was finally at the front door of my house. I kicked off my soaked

357

shoes and stripped out of my grimy clothes, not caring who saw me. I had cleaned enough shit for one day, and I was not about to make a mess of my new home.

I pushed the door open and stomped inside.

"Sweet Luna, what happened to you?" Mom gasped from the rocking chair where she was reading a book.

"I'm not in the mood to talk," I growled, charging toward the bathroom.

"Oh, my poor boy. Let me get you cleaned up." She closed her book, sprang off the chair, and rushed after me.

"I don't need your help," I said.

"Nonsense." She squeezed around me into the bathroom and turned on the faucet of the bathtub. "You haven't been this filthy since you were a pup, and it's a mother's job to clean her pup."

I rolled my eyes but didn't argue. After the long, miserable day I'd had, I deserved some pampering. And I was just grateful that we weren't in our wolf forms, and she wasn't licking my pelt clean like she used to.

I tapped my foot impatiently as she filled the tub, periodically testing the temperature of the water with her fingers and adjusting accordingly. Luckily, there didn't seem to be a water pressure issue in this house.

When it was finally full, I stepped in, the water so hot it nearly scalded my skin. But I didn't care. I lowered myself all the way down, savoring the delicious heat as it ate away at the ache in my muscles and the grime on my skin.

"Ahh," I sighed, reclining into the bath and letting my tight limbs relax.

I didn't complain as my mother immediately soaped a washcloth and began scrubbing my caked arms. Yes, I deserved to be cared for. And she lived for taking care of me. Really, I was doing her favor.

"So, are you going to tell me how you got this dirty?" she nagged as she scrubbed under my fingernails.

I sighed gruffly. "Jax. As punishment for turning off the castle's water, he's forcing me to go to every house and check the plumbing for damage. At the first house I went to, a pipe burst, and I had to work all day covered in this shit."

"Aww, that sounds awful," she crooned, dipping the cloth back into the water to rinse it of clumps.

"It was, Ma," I said, momentarily lifting the back of my head from the tub's edge to look at her for emphasis. "It's so unfair. All of this. They even let Tannin's worthless family move into the castle. Tannin! And his slut of a mother. While we're stuck in this shithole, living like peasants."

"Ugh, that woman." She grimaced. "She's been basically an omega since we were pups. It's no wonder she spread her legs for every man that came along."

"I hate all of them," I groaned. "I don't know what the fuck the elders were thinking pardoning Jax and accepting that Varynian whore into the pack."

She shook her head as she reached into the water to hoist my leg up. "I bet that girl bewitched the elders, too. I bet whatever Esther saw in her blood was some kind of trick."

I rested my head back against the tub. "That girl's magic is a problem, and she needs to be dealt with."

She paused and looked up at me from her work on my foot. "How?"

"I don't know. But I will *not* let this stand."

I rubbed my chin to help me think, but my fingers ran over wads of crud covering it, so I cupped handfuls of water onto my face and rubbed vigorously until it was all off.

"I need to talk to the guys." I pulled my foot back into the water and snatched the cloth from her to finish the job myself. "You can go now."

She gave me a sad pout, lingering where she sat on the edge of the tub for a moment before finally leaving me to clean myself in peace. She was so lucky she had me. I didn't know what she'd do without me.

But I had to think of myself right now.

I made quick work of scrubbing down the rest of my body, then climbed out and dried off. I threw on a blissfully fresh set of clothes and went out in search of my personal betas.

It didn't take long to track down their scents, which led me to an abandoned pub. Tywen and Hollis were standing behind the bar, filling glasses with beer from the tapped barrel for what smelled like not the first time.

"Enjoying yourselves?" I clipped low in irritation.

They jumped and spun around to look at me, beer sloshing from their full mugs.

"Hey, where have you been?" Tywen asked.

"We were looking for you," Hollis said. "Thought we'd offer you a hand with your task from *Alpha*." His voice theatrically mocked the last word.

"Well, I guess you didn't look hard enough, did you?" I strode up to the bar and climbed on a stool across from them. "Give me a beer."

Tywen pushed his mug toward me, then picked up a new one to fill for himself. I took it and chugged down half. It may have been warm, but damn, did it taste good. Beer was a luxury we only got to enjoy during treks to trading villages, and I had dearly missed its crisp bite down my throat.

"This place is pretty cool," Hollis said as he sipped his. "There's a loft upstairs. I think I might move in here."

I choked and spit a short spray of the beer in my mouth. "No! Our place is in the castle. Have you given up on that?"

Hollis faltered. "Er, well... I mean, it's not like we have a choice. Jax has solidified his place as Alpha, and we don't have access to the castle."

"And that's good enough for you?" I demanded. "You've just accepted Jax as your leader? Accepted that witch as your princess? You can't be fucking serious."

Tywen made a disgusted grimace. "What? Of course, not."

I set my mug down loudly on the dusty bar top. "Then let's do something about it."

"Like what?" Hollis asked. "What *can* we do? The elders made them both untouchable."

"Then we'll go over their heads, just like we did with the water supply," I said, the hint in my tone a threat to force their hands.

They both ducked their heads guiltily. They were lucky I didn't rat them out for the parts they played, though why I'd stayed silent, I would never understand. They should have been punished just as severely as I had.

But now... they owed me. And I liked that.

"There have to be other members of the pack that hate Jax, or don't trust the princess, and don't give a fuck what the elders think," I said.

"You two are going to help me find them. If enough of us side against them, they won't stand a chance. They'll have to bend to our will."

"But how?" Hollis asked. "With the ward up, we can't get to them, and the princess never leaves the castle."

I took a slow sip of my warm, bubbly beer as I considered, plotted. "Things won't stay this way forever. Eventually, they will open the castle to the whole pack. Jax knows as well as I do that he won't keep the pack's trust by keeping them shut out."

Tywen set down his mug, leaving a mustache of foam over his lip, and nodded thoughtfully, looking utterly ridiculous. "Okay, so we gather supporters, build an army, and when the opportunity presents itself, we strike."

My lips spread in a wicked grin, and I raised my glass to his. "I have taught you well, my beta."

He clinked his glass against mine, grinning with far too much enthusiasm over my praise. They were both pathetic, but I needed them to accomplish my goals.

I lowered my mug and straightened my posture. "Until then, we'll lay low, play along, and let Jax think we've fully bent the knee. We'll show them we're not a threat and gain their trust. And in the meantime, you two are absolutely going to help me with the plumbing bullshit."

And by that, I mean you're going to do it all by yourselves while I watch.

"Yes, Alpha," they said in subdued stereo.

Ah, it felt so good to be called by my rightful title.

I finished my beer and shoved my mug toward Tywen. "Another."

He hastily worked to fill my mug and hand it back to me.

I lifted it in the air in front of me. "Cheers to our new plan, boys."

"Cheers!" they shouted, lifting their mugs in kind.

Jax, you'd better watch your back. I'm coming for you, and after I've finally slaughtered you, your pretty little bitch is going to be mine.

CHAPTER 8
ALIYA

People always say that pregnant women have a radiant glow about them, but the naked girl looking back at me in the mirror wasn't glowing. She appeared pale and too skinny, save for the bump in her belly that seemed twice as big as yesterday.

The speed of all this frightened me. Compared to women I'd watched throughout the years before the plague, I looked three months along, and it had only been a few weeks. I wasn't ready for this.

But, then again, life never happened when you were ready for it. I wasn't ready for the plague that killed everyone I had ever known and loved. At least this change would be a positive one.

I hope...

I put my hand over my belly, surprised by how tight it felt. Hard to believe there were two small creatures growing inside me. What would they be like? Would they look like their fathers? I'd been having nightmares of them coming out like mutant puppies, and the worst were the dreams of them clawing their way out of me.

I shivered as I stomped that memory down. It wouldn't work like that, right? Raya had given birth to Tannin, and she was still alive and healthy.

Ah, that was it! Raya had gone through this twice. She would be able to answer my questions, and I trusted that she would do so honestly and hopefully, without hesitation.

Scrounging through my wardrobe, I finally found a dress with an empire waist that fit. Anything with a corset would be out of the question for the next few months. Then I brushed out my hair and coiled it up into a simple bun before going off in search of Tannin's mother.

I found her in the garden, picking vegetables with Twila as they sang a song in a foreign language that was unfamiliar.

"That's a really pretty song," I said as I walked out into the bright sunlight beside them. "What is it?"

Raya paused her work and smiled up at me. "It's called Luna's Lament, a lullaby in the ancient language of our people."

I knelt beside her to help gather sweet potatoes.

"The song is about the tragic romance between Luna, the moon goddess, and Apollo, the sun god, forever doomed to be separated."

I pondered that for a moment. The celestial bodies as living, feeling beings. One master of the day, and one mistress of the night, only able to look over at each other through the vast distance above the earth, longing but never meeting. The idea touched me deeply. I couldn't bear it if I were doomed to be forever parted from either of my mates in that way.

"That's so sad," I said softly.

"It is, but she chose to reign over the night to protect us," she explained. "The song is a reminder of her deep love and devotion to our people... that she chose us over her soul mate."

My heart squeezed inside my chest at the bittersweet story. "Is that what you truly believe?"

She shrugged thoughtfully. "I don't know, but it's nice to think that someone is watching over us, and that she cares enough about each of us to have made such a sacrifice. It's certainly better than the alternative."

I nodded. I knew very little of the gods of old. Such beliefs weren't really practiced by our kingdom, at least not for a long time. My mother had told me about Fate and an afterlife that waited beyond this one, but the details were always vague. It would be nice to think that there was a being above with a plan for us... for me.

Though if there were, was the great loss I suffered part of their plan?

I wasn't sure I liked the idea of that. It seemed like some twisted joke, of which I was the butt.

"How are you doing this morning?" Raya asked, her brow creasing with concern. "You look troubled."

I swallowed and cleared my throat. "Actually, I was hoping to ask you some questions about...um... about what to expect when I..." I looked down at my belly.

"Oh." Her brow flared in surprise for a moment, then her expression melted to one of maternal indulgence. "Of course, dear. What do you want to know?"

My cheeks burned, and I suddenly felt foolish for the words I was about to speak. "So, I know that a wolf pregnancy is a lot shorter than a human one. I guess I'm wondering what else is different."

She pursed her lips in thought. "Well, I don't really know. I haven't had many opportunities to meet pregnant women not of the pack. But I imagine it's very similar."

I nodded, my embarrassment growing to the point I was reconsidering my next question. But ultimately, I just had to know.

"When the time comes for giving birth, how do they come out?" My stomach knotted, triggering my nausea despite the potion.

She gave me a pitying frown. "Oh, you poor dear. Did your mother never explain to you how it works?"

"No, I—yes, she did," I stammered, getting increasingly flustered. "I just mean, do they come out looking like us?" I waved my hand around at the three of us. "Or do they come out...in a different form?"

"Oh." Her eyes widened, and then she started laughing.

My mortification knew no bounds, and I had the ridiculous urge to cry.

"Is that what you've been worried about?" she asked, reaching out to put her hand over mine. "Well, let me ease your mind. Your babies will come out just like any others, without fur or teeth. Our kind doesn't shift until around age five. That's when the mayhem really begins."

She winked at me, and I let out a nervous laugh as relief washed away the worst of my fears. So there would be no mutant births or monsters clawing their way out of my stomach. I was being so silly. Everything was going to be fine.

Suddenly, something moved inside my abdomen, a little flutter that felt entirely new.

I rushed my hand to my belly and gasped. "I...I think I just felt one."

"Really?" she gasped, clapping her hands together excitedly. "That's so wonderful!"

The tears that had threatened before sprang forward and trickled down the side of my face. But they weren't tears of fear or embarrassment. Joy swelled inside my chest to the point of bursting, and for the first time, I no longer felt any dread about what was to come.

"Ah, there you are."

I hastily wiped my face and looked up at Jax standing in the kitchen doorway.

He smiled at the two of us. "Would you mind if I borrow my mate for a while?"

"Of course," Raya said cheerfully. "Twila and I can take it from here." She gave my hand a reassuring squeeze before letting it go and returning to her task.

I stood up, dusting dirt from my skirt, and joined Jax inside.

He took an apple from the basket on the counter and used the bottom of his shirt to polish it. "The meeting with the deltas went well. All of them reaffirmed their loyalty to my leadership."

"That's great," I exclaimed, relief and joy becoming a powerful force in my chest. I knew he'd been worried about that, and so had I.

Maybe everything really was going to work out for the best.

He brought the apple to eye level and examined it. "But a few of them voiced concerns about cusith sightings around the borders of the kingdom. I was thinking it would be a good idea to have you officially meet them and help with securing the border." He bit into the apple as he studied my reaction.

Unease and hesitation deflated the happy pressure in my ribcage. "A-are you sure we can trust them?"

"There's not a doubt in my mind," he said around the crisp mouthful he was chewing. "Besides, I will be right by your side the entire time. You have nothing to worry about, my love."

As memories of those very deltas ramming ferociously into the ward flashed into my mind, I wasn't so sure.

He must have seen the apprehension on my face because he pulled me into his arms. "I can understand your hesitation and concern. But meeting them will alleviate that on both sides. Once they see that you are willing to use your magic to protect the pack, they will know that their suspicions are unwarranted, and you will see that they are good people."

I relaxed into his embrace, savoring the feel of his strong body around me. I may not trust the deltas, but I trusted Jax completely.

"Okay," I said, pulling away. "The most important thing is protecting the kingdom from cusith. I can begin putting up a ward around the borders."

"That's an excellent idea." He kissed my forehead, then bent his arm in invitation. "Shall we?"

I looped my arm around his and let him lead me out into the courtyard.

The day was so beautiful, it was hard to hold onto my anxiety as we strolled arm in arm down the main road. I hadn't been out here in weeks, and the village was vastly different from my last visit.

For too long, it had been empty and deathly silent, a literal ghost town. Seeing it so filled with life, kids running around and laughing as they played, had raw emotion pushing behind my eyes for the third time today. It was almost as if the plague had never happened.

Except for the way my new subjects looked at me as we passed by. There was no reverence or adoration on their faces, only wariness and cold stares, some even shooing their children away while also giving Jax the smiles they refused to give me.

I hoped Jax was right about this. I so desperately wanted to prove to them that I wasn't their enemy, and I could only hope that using my magic for their benefit would accomplish that.

By the time I finally returned to the castle in the late afternoon, the potion had completely worn off, and I was shaking with the rush of sickness that assaulted me.

I knew I should have left sooner, or at least as soon as I felt the first signs of the potion waning, but I was too impassioned with my task to stop before it was absolutely necessary. Now that I was running to the kitchen and heaving with the urge to vomit, I was strongly regretting that decision.

"Dammit," I cursed when I found my supply diminished.

I had completely forgotten that I was almost out. Now I'd have to rush to make more while I could barely move.

With stumbling feet and fumbling hands, I gathered my supplies and ingredients, hunching over to fight the pain twisting in my stomach and clawing up my throat. I really, *really* should have stopped sooner.

The day had gone so much better than I'd expected, and I hadn't wanted to cut it short. Jax introduced me to the six deltas on patrol duty around the perimeter—Esme, Cameron, Hayden, Mira, Lucius and Kai.

Unlike the people in the village, the deltas greeted me with the same respect they greeted Jax, bowing their heads and smiling. There was no hostility in their demeanor or tone, and they seemed eager to hear what

I had to say. They were especially thrilled when I proposed putting up a ward around the kingdom, praising me for my kindness and power.

Esme was my favorite. Her loyalty to Jax was tangible. She stayed with me as I began building the ward along the most northern part of the kingdom's boundaries. She chatted with me and asked questions about my life while sharing stories about hers. When Jax got called away, I wasn't worried. Esme stuck to me like glue, keeping her eyes forever on the horizon in search of a threat.

Somehow she won me over immediately, and I knew that she would keep me safe if a threat came our way.

I had covered only a small fraction of the perimeter before my nausea overcame me. The ward around the castle had taken me three days to put in place. This ward would take me several weeks at least, but it would be well worth it. I only hoped I could finish before the cusith could get any bold, deadly ideas.

My stomach clenched tighter as I impatiently waited for the water to boil in the pot, and suddenly, I couldn't hold it back any longer. I rushed to the sink as acid rushed up my throat, bracing myself against the counter's edge even after the flood had passed.

"Sweet Luna, are you alright, child?"

I didn't have to look up to know that it was Esther, and even if I did, the tears stinging my eyes would have blinded me to her. She came closer and put a comforting hand on my back, her gentle rubbing making me feel slightly better.

I coughed up and spat out the lingering acid, then pushed myself away from the sink and wiped my mouth with the back of my hand, blinking away the fog from my vision.

"Yes, I'm okay," I lied. "I just can't wait for this part of the pregnancy to be over."

"I remember that," she said, nodding sympathetically. "I went through it three times in my younger years. In my experience, the morning sickness only lasts for the first few weeks. Hopefully, yours will end soon."

"I hope so," I sighed.

The gurgle of bubbles sounded at the pot on the stove, and I rushed back to it to add the ingredients before it could get too hot.

"What is this you're making?" Esther asked, peering into the pot.

"It's an anti-nausea potion," I said, dropping in the mint leaves and giving it a stir. "I discovered the recipe shortly after the pack arrived, before I knew I was pregnant. I wouldn't be able to function without it."

"Wow, magic really is miraculous," she said with a note of admiration in her voice. "We had to make rather expensive trades for such potions, and yet you can just create them in your own kitchen without any sort of training. You are a very resourceful young woman."

I offered her a tentative smile. I never would have thought of myself as resourceful. I just drew at random straws to survive, never really knowing which straw would come through.

"Is there anything I can do to help you with your potion?" she asked. "I'd be very interested to learn how it works."

"Oh, well, sure."

I walked her through each step as I continued to brew it, explaining the importance of each ingredient. Then, when it was finished, I recited the spell to give it its magical potency, and she watched with awe as the glow flowed from my hands into the concoction.

"The ingredients on their own don't have much effect," I said. "But the spell at the end amplifies their natural properties."

"How fascinating," she said in wonder. "I would love to help you brew more potions. There are several people in the pack that have chronic health conditions, and your brand of medicine would be a godsend to them. Such an olive branch would go a long way toward getting them to see you as their rightful queen."

My breath hitched, the nausea pausing for an instant. "Esther, that's a fantastic idea. I would be honored if you would help me make the potions the pack needs."

With another set of hands working with me, I could do so much more.

She beamed at me and clapped her hands in satisfaction. "Wonderful! But first, take care of yourself and drink some of your potion before your lovely complexion gets any greener."

I giggled as I spooned a serving of the potion and put it in my mouth. Soothing comfort washed through me as I swallowed, the magic dissolving my nausea altogether and restoring my strength.

For the next several hours, we studied the potion books for remedies to the ailments pack members suffered and began brewing. Gout, arthritis, diabetes, mostly for the elders and older members, but there were apparently a few children who suffered from things like epilepsy and scoliosis.

I was so relieved to be considered useful and able to create these things for the people who now depended on me, I couldn't believe the rush of happiness that filled me. Since bonding with the deltas and starting to build the ward, I was realizing how responsible I was for the pack, and how much I could do to help them.

"Esther, how much do you know about what happened between our two peoples?" I asked as we began brewing the third potion. "There wasn't much taught of our history as I was growing up. All I was told was that the Black Wolves were our enemy, but I know we had an alliance at one time. I just want to know what caused that to change."

She sighed and nodded as she stirred. "It is told that centuries ago, the Black Wolves were the guardians of Varynia. Wolves and wielders lived in harmony with mutual respect for one another, fighting side by side. Together, we forced the cusith back into the shadows from whence they came, and the kingdom enjoyed a long period of peace."

I blinked in surprise. "You were once our guardians? Against the cusith?"

She nodded.

I shook my head curiously. "I don't understand. I'd never heard of the cusith before Jax and Tannin arrived."

"That doesn't surprise me," she mused, turning the spoon round and round in the pot. "The battle against the cusith was hundreds of years ago. It wasn't until the last few generations that the creatures began emerging from the depths once more. I suspect they know our alliance was broken, and they are testing how strong we are independently."

I swallowed, my heart thudding. "You think there will be more attacks?"

She slid a wary gaze to me. "I believe the battle against the monsters is only just beginning." Her tone held the same ominous ring that I'd heard before, like she knew more than she was willing to say.

Establishing the ward had to be my top priority.

"So, what happened between us to break the alliance?" I asked, getting us back on track.

She turned the stove down to a simmer. "An ancient king's daughter fell in love with the Alpha's son. The king refused to give his blessing for the union, so the young lovers snuck off and eloped in secret."

"That's so romantic," I said, putting my hand over my chest. I couldn't help but see the parallels to my own story.

"When the king found out that his daughter was pregnant with a wolf child, he saw it as an abomination," she went on. "Our two kinds were not allowed to mix, and a wielding wolf would be more powerful than both."

I looked down at my belly. Would my children be that powerful? Did the wolves see them as an abomination? Would my parents have if they were still alive?

As if they could hear my thoughts, two little flutters tickled inside my abdomen, and all I could feel was love. *No, you're not an abomination.*

"The king slaughtered both his daughter and the Alpha's son, which, as you can imagine, started a vicious war. The wielders' magic was too strong for us, and we were ultimately forced out of the kingdom, doomed to survive the woods on our own. The Alpha was determined to get vengeance on the king, and that hatred has been ingrained in our blood ever since."

She released the spoon and turned to face me. "Aliya. I believe that your mating to our Alpha and beta is Fate's way of correcting the mistakes of the past. And I am ashamed of myself and my peers for almost making the same mistake again."

Her words humbled me deeply, and I pitied the guilt she clearly felt. But I held no bitterness or animosity toward her or any of the pack, for that matter. The hatred between our peoples had strong, stubborn roots, and it took a lot of courage and wisdom to sever them.

"But you didn't make the same mistake," I said softly. "You chose a different path, and our kingdom will be so much stronger because of it."

She smiled. "I believe so, too."

We shared a long, meaningful glance, then she looked back at the potion. "I think it's ready for you to say the incantation."

I nodded and spoke the spell, imbuing the diabetes potion with the necessary magic. Together, we poured the potion into jars for each of the afflicted people. Tomorrow, I would deliver our concoctions to the pack members, and I'd feel good about it, whether or not it bought me their favor.

It had been my ancestors that destroyed the alliance, and it was my responsibility to mend it.

CHAPTER 10

TANNIN

Now that the day was finally over, I couldn't wait to see my girl. My spirits were heavy, and I just wanted to escape from the weight of my worries, if only for the night.

Jax had put me in charge of checking on Coda to ensure he was working on his task. I found him at Esme's house, surprisingly conducting a thorough analysis of the plumbing system. He had recruited his two lackies to help him—no surprise there.

What was the most remarkable was the cordial way he spoke to me. At first, I thought it was a joke, a form of sarcasm, but there was no menace or mocking in his tone. If I didn't know any better, I would think he'd learned his lesson and actually respected my position.

But I didn't buy it, not for one second. People don't change overnight, especially not someone like Coda. He was up to something, I was sure of it. And I didn't like the gnawing feeling in my gut over what that might be. I wanted to let it go, to unburden myself, but I knew that only my beautiful mate could ease my anxiety.

I looked all around the castle but didn't find her in her usual places. She wasn't in the kitchen or the garden. No sign of her in the den or the library. When I found her old room empty, I began to worry all over again.

Jax had requested she construct a ward around the kingdom. What if something had happened to her? What if that two-faced, maniacal Coda got to her when no one was watching?

With growing panic, I burst into our room. She wasn't here either. Fuck, fuck—

The tinkle of her laughter caught my ear, immediately melting my paranoid fears.

I followed the sound that had a tight grip over my heart to the room Twila and my mother shared. Aliya was sitting on the floor with my sister, playing with dolls while Tabitha rubbed against Twila's side. I hung in the doorway for a moment, not wanting to interrupt their fun, and wanting to watch them from a distance.

"I think she likes you," Aliya said with a giggle.

Twila picked up the orange tabby and held her tightly against her chest. "I like her too."

Tabitha snorted at being squeezed too hard and began to wriggle out of my sister's arms.

"I know, Tabitha," Aliya said. "But she's a child, and she just wants to give you love."

Twila frowned and released the cat, who quickly scampered away to hide behind Aliya's back.

"Can you actually hear what she's saying?" Twila asked in wide-eyed wonder.

Aliya shrugged as she twisted around to pick up Tabitha and place her into the hollow of her pretzeled legs. "Sometimes I think I can. But I really don't know. I was alone in this castle for over a year, with Tabitha as my only company. I got so used to talking to her and imagining her responses that I guess it's hard to stop."

Twila nodded matter-of-factly. "Well, I think you really can hear her. You're magical. Maybe understanding animals is one of your powers."

Aliya laughed, and I couldn't help but snicker too, which betrayed my presence.

My mate and sister both turned to smile up at me.

"You two are getting along, I see," I said as I entered and joined them on the floor.

"You mean three," Twila corrected, reaching for Tabitha again, who recoiled deeper into Aliya's lap.

"Ah, yes. Of course," I agreed, biting back my amusement at the way the poor cat had slumped reluctantly in my sister's hold. It didn't take magical powers to know what the cat was thinking in this particular instance.

I picked up one of the dolls, a much nicer one than those Twila had taken from the other house. "What are we playing?"

"Castle, of course," Twila informed me. "That's the princess, and she's about to meet Prince Charming at the ball."

I looked at the assortment of dolls, all of which were girls. "And which one is Prince Charming?"

"It's you, silly," she said, then exploded into a fit of girlish laughter.

Aliya leaned over to plant a chaste kiss on my lips. "Obviously," she whispered.

The brush of her lips on mine made me hungry for more, but I restrained myself from attacking her in front of my sister.

"Actually, this game gave me an idea, and I was wondering what you might think," Aliya hedged, picking up another doll and patting down the back of its hair.

"Oooh, what is it?" Twila asked, her eyes wide with intrigue.

"I was thinking that we should throw a ball of our own, for the entire pack," Aliya said, looking into my eyes to gauge my reaction.

"Yay, yay, yay!" Twila hollered. "I'm going to go find my dress right now!" She sprang up off the floor and darted to the closet.

Caution doused the joviality that had begun to settle my soul. "Here? In the castle?"

"Of course. Where else would we host a ball?"

"You want to take down the ward and let everyone in?" I almost couldn't believe what I was hearing.

She blushed slightly under my incredulity, but it didn't seem to hamper her conviction. "I was talking to Esther this evening, and she told me what happened between our people. A Varynian princess fell in love with the Alpha's son, and when the king found out, he had them murdered. That's what started the war and the hatred between our people. But we were always meant to live in harmony as one kingdom. I want to show the pack that I trust them, and in turn, I hope that they will come to trust me."

I looked down at the doll I still held as I considered all the information Aliya had shared. I hadn't heard that story before. All I had known was that we were banished from the kingdom and I never questioned why.

I appreciated Aliya's desire for unity. It was the same as Jax's. I wanted to feel it too, but I didn't have the same faith in my pack that they seemed to share. I had never been given much reason to.

But I had faith in Aliya. She was destined to be the queen we always needed, and I had to believe that whatever course of action she pursued was the correct one.

"Okay," I finally conceded. "If you think it's a good idea, then I do too."

"Yes!" She threw her arms around my neck, and I caught her with a surprised chuckle.

"We'll have to discuss it with Jax first, of course," I said. "And the elders. And we'll need weeks to plan it."

"Of course," she agreed. "I can arrange the whole thing, and I'm sure I can recruit your mother and some of the deltas to help me."

"Don't forget about me," Twila called from the closet. "I would love to help decorate!"

Aliya and I laughed.

"Absolutely," I said. "We couldn't organize a grand, royal ball without you. You're the guest of honor."

Twila squealed with delight, clutching a dress to her chest.

"We'll bring the matter to Jax at dinner," I said.

"What matter?"

Aliya and I turned to see Jax peeking into the room from the hallway.

"Ah, excellent timing, as usual." I waved him into the room and got to my feet. "Aliya was just telling me that she'd like to a throw a ball for the pack... and she'd like to take down the ward around the castle."

He flattened his mouth as he nodded in consideration, then gave an appreciative smile. "I think that's a great idea."

Of course, he did. Some secret part of me had hoped he'd shut it down, but I should have known better.

Twila clapped with unbridled enthusiasm and began to jump up and down.

"How long do you think we need to get things prepared?" he asked Aliya.

She shrugged, pursing her lips in an excited smile. "Maybe two weeks?"

Jax flared his eyebrows and grinned. "That'll be just in time for the next full moon."

"Oh, that's perfect!" Aliya jumped to her feet. "I'll get started right away. I'll write the invitations and plan the menu and the music. This is going to be so much fun!"

"Even better than the private ball we had a few weeks ago?" Jax asked teasingly.

Aliya blushed and drew close to grace him with a gentle kiss. "Well, it'll be a close second."

"You guys already had a ball without me?" Twila complained, snappily folding her arms over her chest and glaring at us.

Jax, Aliya, and I shared amused looks before I turned back to my baby sister.

"Trust me, sweetie, we'll never make that mistake again," I assured her.

"You better not," she grumbled.

Jax put his hands on Aliya's waist, giving her a serious yet affectionate look. "Just please don't overextend yourself. There's a lot going on, what with you single-handedly putting up a new ward around the kingdom and now the ball. Are you sure you can handle all of this?" He looked down at her rounded belly.

"I promise I won't overdo it," she said, putting her delicate hands on his chest. "And I'll make sure to ask for plenty of help."

He leaned forward to kiss her again. "Tannin and I will be here for whatever you need. Just tell us what to do. You get to be the boss."

She arched an eyebrow and tapped her chin with her index finger as she glanced back and forth between us. "I kind of like the sound of that."

Jax snickered with a low, hungry growl beneath, and the way he gripped her hips teased my own desire.

But before he could lure her into our room, she slipped out of his hold and ran to Twila.

"Would you do me the honor of helping me create the invitations?" she asked with a dramatic bow to my sister.

"YES!" Twila howled. "Let's go find some paper!" She grabbed Aliya's hand and dragged her out of the room.

Jax and I just stood there, laughing as we watched them go.

"Do you really think this is a good idea?" I asked when we were alone. "Taking down the ward and inviting everyone in? Is that safe?"

He patted my shoulder. "Things are finally working out the way we always dreamed. The elders have accepted Aliya, the deltas have fallen into line, and soon, the entire pack will love Aliya just as much as we do. I strongly believe that this ball will be the start of a glorious new way forward for our kingdom. You worry too much, brother."

I nodded and followed him out of the room, and I really hoped he was right.

CHAPTER 11
ALIYA

It had been over a year since I'd had to present myself in an official capacity to the public, talking face to face, and I was out of practice. Granted, these people were entirely different and they hated what I represented, but I did everything possible to make myself look and act like the princess they deserved despite my frazzled nerves.

When I was finally ready—at least on the outside—I shouldered the pouch full of invitations and met Twila and Raya at the double doors of the castle.

"You look lovely," Raya gushed as I approached. "They are going to love you."

I offered her an uncertain smile. *I really hope so.*

I cleared my throat. "Do you have the potions?"

"Right here." She patted the satchel that I hadn't noticed hanging against her hip.

"Oh, good," I stammered. "A-And you remember who each of them goes to?"

She reached out to give my shoulder a comforting squeeze. "Stop worrying, dear. Everything is going to be fine."

I let out a long breath and nodded, then pushed the doors open and stepped into the bright noon sun.

"Just remember, I get to hand out the invitations," Twila said as she laced her little hand into mine. It felt so nice to feel her fingers against my skin. Reassuring in some way.

"Yep," I said, handing her a stack of the painstakingly illustrated cards.

It had taken us three days, but Twila and I wrote out all two hundred and fifty invitations by hand. There was a bit of a learning curve that involved me trying to teach her calligraphy with ink and a quill, and then a lot of me privately correcting her mistakes, but the final product was an announcement card that I could be proud of.

I just hoped they looked official enough to appease the recipients.

Raya led our trio to the bakery, the first building on the left of the main road where the warm fragrance of sweet pastries filled the air.

"Lance and Jora are the ones running this bakery," she informed me. "They have two children, one of whom has epilepsy." She rifled through her satchel and handed me a jar of the appropriate blue potion.

I took the jar and nodded, then took a deep breath before entering the shop.

A woman with long dark hair and an apron covered in flour stood behind the display case that housed several dozen varieties of pastries. She looked up to greet her new customers, but her smile faltered when she realized who had come to call.

"Hello. You must be Jora," I said in my best dignified tone.

She didn't say anything, just looked me up and down with suspicion. That didn't stop Twila, however.

"We came to invite you to a ball," she said, running up to her and waving an invitation in the air.

Jora couldn't seem to help but smile at Twila's adorable enthusiasm, and she accepted the card.

"A ball?" She read over the details on the card, then looked up at me. "You're throwing a ball? At the castle? For everyone?" Her tone grew more humble and less hostile with each word.

"Yes, in a week and a half," I confirmed with a nod. "I can't wait to see you and your lovely family there."

She looked it over again. "Will there be food?"

"Of course," I said. "And drinks and music. A true ball to celebrate the Black Wolves' return to Varynia."

"Hmm," she hummed, still seeming a bit dubious.

It was time to hit her with the clincher.

"And, as a sign of good faith, I wanted to offer you this gift." I held up the jar and brought it closer to set it on top of the display case in front of her.

She eyed it with surprised curiosity.

"I hear that one of your children struggles with epilepsy," I said. "So, I have brewed this potion to treat and prevent his episodes."

Her eyes widened as they darted between me and the jar.

"It won't cure his affliction, but it will make it more manageable," I explained. "I will see to it that you're provided with a regular supply of this potion until we can find a more permanent solution."

Her mask of animosity shattered into an expression of misty-eyed gratitude. "Thank you so much, Princess. You don't know how much this means to me. How can I ever begin to repay you?"

The smile that bunched my cheeks was authentic and unbridled. "Your presence at the ball will be payment enough."

"Yes. Yes, we will all be there," she swore, dipping behind the case in a curtsy I could hardly see. Then she took the jar and hugged it to her powdery apron. "Thank you again."

With a happy nod, I bid her good day and led my trio out of her bakery.

"See, that wasn't so bad," Raya commented supportively.

"No, not bad at all," I agreed, continuing to the next house with more confidence.

The next few houses went about the same. My offer was received first with apprehension, then gratitude when I delivered the potions for their specific ailments. Of course, those who didn't need a potion only accepted the invitation with silence, but I could only hope their walls would lower by the time of the ball.

After word began to spread, the need for door-to-door visits became unnecessary. An animated crowd soon gathered around us halfway down the main road, everyone eager to receive their own invitation.

The three of us hastily handed out the cards, and I couldn't have been more pleased by this turn of events. The pack was actually excited to attend, and it began to feel like nothing had changed from before the plague.

It was a struggle to distribute the right potions to the right people in the crowd, but Raya did an excellent job of remembering who needed what. And when others saw the magical gifts being handed out, they requested potions for things I wasn't aware of. I was more than happy to oblige them, promising each of them a delivery within the week.

By the time the crowd dispersed, we had a quarter of the invitations left, and still a few jars to deliver.

"Any chance you remember who's left?" I asked Raya playfully.

"For the potions, yes," she said. "The invitations, not so much. Things got so hectic there for a moment."

I nodded, then looked up at sun's westerly position in the sky. It was mid-afternoon, and I still needed to work on the ward for at least a little while before the sun set.

"I'll go with you to drop off the last of the potions, but after that, would the two of you mind handing out the rest of the invitations on your own?" I asked. "I have another task to attend to before the day is over."

"Absolutely," she said, patting Twila's head. "We'd be happy to finish for you, wouldn't we?"

"Definitely," Twila trilled.

Raya guided us to a neighborhood in the western part of the village, and I was surprised to see Tannin standing in front of one of the houses.

"What are you doing here?" Raya asked as she hugged her son.

"Babysitting," he said with a snort. "How's the delivering going?"

"Better than expected," I informed him cheerfully. "We just have a few more potions to hand out."

"And this happens to be one of our stops," Raya added, gesturing to the house we stood in front of. "Is Manu home?"

"Yes, he's in the living room while Coda and his pals are fixing the kitchen faucet," he said.

"Coda?" I asked. I had forgotten that he was supposed to be doing door-to-door plumbing, but it might prove fortuitous. "Well, I suppose that'll save us a trip to his house."

Raya and Twila made their way inside, but Tannin held me back a moment.

"Be careful with him," he cautioned. "And if he makes even the slightest move to hurt you, I'm right out here."

I nodded. "I'm sure I'll be fine. Besides, he wouldn't do anything in front of your mother and sister."

"Perhaps," he said, glaring into the house.

I cupped his cheek and gave him a kiss. "I'll be right out." Then I swept away before he could stop me again.

Raya was already chatting with the older man in the living room, her and Twila telling him about the ball. I made as graceful of an entrance as I could with the jar in my hands.

"Good afternoon, Manu," I greeted. "I see Raya has told you about the ball. I would be so thrilled if you would join us. And as a gift, I brewed you a potion to help with your arthritis."

After repeating the same words so many times to so many different people, it was beginning to feel tedious, but I hoped my demeanor came off as genuinely as I intended.

"Really?" he asked, accepting the jar and studying it. "This will fix my aching joints?"

"Yes. Just drink a spoonful every day, and I will ensure that you get a regular supply from now on."

"Well, how can I pass up the opportunity to dance, especially now that I'll actually be able to?" he said with a laugh. "Perhaps you'll save me a dance, Princess?"

"It would be my honor." I bowed my head indulgently.

"Then I'll be there." He disappeared into the kitchen with the jar to try it out for himself.

"Would you save me a dance as well?" Coda appeared from around the corner, wearing a wolfish smirk that was disarming despite my best efforts to resist.

I straightened my posture as I regarded him with neutral expression. "I suppose that could be arranged."

He sauntered up to me, clasping his hands behind his back, and I couldn't help but stiffen defensively.

"Good," he said in a sincere tone. "Because I'd really like the chance to apologize for my earlier behavior. I was wrong and I made many mistakes. But I assure you, that will not happen again, Princess. I want to be of service to you any way that I can, and I hope you will forgive my misplaced aggression."

"Oh." This was the last thing I'd expected from him, and I didn't really know how to handle it. Everything about his tone, his expression, his posture, seemed genuine, and his natural charm made me want to believe him.

"So, will you save me that dance?" he asked in a voice that melted my resistance.

"Sure. Just don't be alarmed if I step on your toes. It's been a while since I've had a proper dance," I joked to lighten the mood.

He chuckled. "As graceful as you are, I'm sure you're very light on your feet."

Heat flushed up my cheeks, and I cleared my throat. "Yes, well... we have a few more stops to make."

"Then, have a pleasant evening, Princess." He gave me a curt bow.

I spun on my heel and rushed out quickly, then waited on the doorstep for Twila and Raya to follow.

"Did he bother you?" Tannin asked.

"No, not at all," I said. "He was surprisingly courteous."

He frowned, glaring at the door again. "I don't like it."

"Come along, Aliya," Raya encouraged. "We have two more stops."

With a brush of my hand over Tannin's chest, I continued to the next house. But I couldn't deny that the encounter with Coda left me feeling confused and uncertain. Could he really have changed his stance?

Could I really trust him?

CHAPTER 12
CODA

The night was still and quiet as I trod through the empty streets to the pub. It irritated me when I found Tywen and Hollis there that first night, but it had worked in my favor, because the pub served as the perfect location for meetings such as this.

The light coming from the windows was low and dim, but still too bright for my comfort. I looked in all directions for watchful eyes as I approached. Though Jax and Tannin had retired to the castle hours ago, there could be deltas sniffing around.

Only when I felt certain I wasn't being spied upon did I stealthily enter the old pub.

My betas sat at a table in the far corner with four male newcomers who I recognized as lower ranking members of the pack, all of whom turned to gaze at me beneath the heavy shadow of their wary brows.

I wasn't sure how I felt about the recruits as I strode across the pub to join them. They had no standing, no notoriety among the pack, each easily forgettable.

But perhaps that would prove beneficial. They had no loyalty to the false Alpha, and I wouldn't have to worry about double agents. Not to mention these nobodies would be the last people Jax would suspect of plotting, much less implementing a coup.

"Good evening, gentlemen," I said in a low register, taking the last empty seat and lacing my fingers on top of the table. "I assume you all know why we're here."

The men exchanged surreptitious glances around the circle before returning their beady eyes to me.

Hamish, a wooly, middle-aged man who served as a lumberjack during our time in the forest, leaned low and forward, as if he might be lashed for voicing the words he was about to speak.

"We were told that you wanted our help in restoring the kingdom to us in the way we were promised," he said in a hushed but gravelly voice.

My lips curled in a satisfied smile. "That's exactly right. But before we begin, I need to be positive about where each of your loyalties lie. Do you reject Jax and his Varynian concubine and swear fealty to me as your true Alpha?"

One by one, fists pounded loudly against chests around the table, a fierceness in each of their eyes as they beheld me. My chest swelled with pride that was more fulfilling than any other sustenance, and my wolf salivated for righteous bloodshed inside me.

"Excellent," I purred, then I snapped my fingers at Tywen. "A round of drinks for the table."

"Right away, Alpha," he muttered, then clambered out of his chair and rushed to follow my orders.

"I'm sure you all received one of these." I held up the stupid card announcing the ball, quietly savoring the scent of the princess that wafted into the air as I did.

Some nodded, others held up their own copy.

I slammed it onto the table with my palm pressed over it. "*That* is when we strike. The ward will be down, and they'll be completely defenseless. The entire pack will be in assembly, everyone drinking in the crowded ballroom. The false Alpha will be so blinded by his own bullshit that we'll take him completely unaware."

Faces melded into apprehensive frowns.

"But there are only seven of us," said Chase, a ripe young boy in his late teens, not quite a man, but not still a pup. "How will we possibly stand a chance against the entire pack?"

"You forget that more than half of the pack consists of women and children," I pointed out. "And very few of the men are fighters. Nevertheless, your jobs over the next week are to bring more people to our side—quietly!"

I pointed a warning finger at each of them in turn. "Only speak a word of this to those you know you can trust. Otherwise, be ready to kill them if they reject the idea. Do any of you have prospects in mind?"

Hamish nodded and raised a hand. "My brother and his wife."

"Cane," Allistar said. "He would follow me to the ends of the earth."

A few more names were muttered around the table as Tywen set fresh mugs in front of everyone.

"Good," I said, sitting back in my chair. "We will build an army that not even Jax can defend against."

"What about the elders?" Chase asked nervously.

I snorted. "Those wizened old farts have far outlived their fighting days. They will have no choice but to come to heel. And if they don't, we don't need them."

A solemn silence fell as everyone considered what I was suggesting. Whimsical fools. Their morality would be *my* undoing.

"Look, would you rather do nothing and follow a Varynian queen, or would you like to go down in history as the heroes who restored the Black Wolves to glory?" I said in a purposefully harsh voice. "Every war has its casualties. Some must perish for the greater good. My question is, are you willing to do what's necessary to accomplish that?"

I took a long pull of my beer as I studied each of their wavering expressions, and it pleased me to watch them all solidify into firm resolve. Mumbles of consent rose around the table.

I smiled and lifted my glass above the center of the table. "A toast, gentlemen, to the kingdom we were always promised."

"Here, here!" Hollis raised his glass as well, and everyone else followed suit, the clinks so vigorous that beer splashed onto the table.

"What do we do about the princess?" Chase asked. "We can take on fellow wolves, but we can't defend against magic."

I nodded, rubbing my chin with my free hand as I mulled it over. And then the perfect solution came to me. "Leave that to me. I have something in mind to nullify the threat she poses."

"And then we kill her," Tywen declared, raising his glass again.

"No!" I snapped, making him cow in subservience. "No one will touch the princess."

"I—I don't understand," Tywen frowned.

Letting out a frustrated sigh, I pinched the bridge of my nose. I was dealing with imbeciles. "In order to be a legitimate kingdom that rivals our neighbors, we need a legal claim to the throne. I will take the princess as my bride and become the true king of Varynia."

Surprise flashed in every pair of eyes that was fixed on me, some with reverence, some with doubt.

"I don't just want the Black Wolves to be a kingdom," I clarified, my voice booming with passion. "I want us to be an empire—the greatest empire the world has ever seen."

I paused to watch wonder play on the faces of those around me as they imagined such a possibility.

"Varynia is just the beginning. Once I am king, we will go on to conquer the kingdoms to the north and the west. With the princess' magic firmly in check and bent to our will, we will be unstoppable. We will have everything that was stolen from us and much, much more."

I leaned over the table and cast a stern glare around at my compatriots. "If anyone amongst you isn't willing to do what's necessary for that to happen, leave now."

Waiting, I watched them all as the ticking of the clock on the wall counted each second, but no one moved.

I sat up straight. "From here on out, you are all part of the rebellion, and I promise you, your efforts will be greatly rewarded. Riches and land beyond your wildest imaginings, your names in the history books for centuries to come."

I could practically see their egos inflating as their chests puffed out, their mouths spreading in hopeful smiles.

Hamish lifted his glass for another round of toasts. "To our new Alpha and the empire he will build!"

"To the Alpha!"

"To the empire!"

"To Coda!"

With a flood of invigorated determination, I downed the rest of my beer and slammed the empty mug onto the table before pushing away and standing.

"We will reconvene the night before the ball," I declared. "In the meantime, there is something I must do." I looked toward Tywen and Hollis. "If I'm not back before dawn, cover for me."

Driven by purpose, I strode from the pub before they could ask any questions. I knew what my next step had to be, and I wasn't going to waste another minute.

~

It was nearly dawn when I finally caught sight of the castle peaking over the trees in the distance. Sprinting in my powerful wolf form, a journey that should have taken two days took me only one night. And though I was exhausted to my very bones, it was well worth it.

The precious trinket I acquired from the gypsy outpost was tucked safely away in the pouch secured around my neck. This was going to change everything. The potion I'd acquired was the key to securing my victory and rendering the princess helpless. She would become my pawn, ripe for molding however I saw fit.

From that first moment when I'd seen her in the garden outside the castle, I'd known she was destined to be mine. I didn't believe for a moment that she was mated to Jax or Tannin. No one mated to two people. It was utterly ridiculous. Jax seduced and manipulated her, and of course, had gotten Tannin to go along with it.

It was disgusting the way they shared everything, but sharing a woman, especially a luscious woman like that... it was the greatest crime of all. When she was finally mine, no man would ever touch her again.

My body tensed with desire as I dashed through the forest. In less than a fortnight, I would claim my bride. I could hardly wait to taste her, to dominate her, to hear her screams of pleasure when she realized I was her true mate.

Just a few more days.

A twig snapped in the distance to my right, making my ears perk as I continued to run. Probably just a rabbit or squirrel—

Bam!

Something large and heavy smacked into my side, rolling over the forest floor with me until we smacked into a tree. Claws slashed down my sides and dagger-like teeth snapped and gnashed inches above my face as I struggled to push it back.

A cusith. Its haggard breath and slimy drool assaulted my face as it desperately, viciously tried to rip into my throat.

"Not today, asshole," I growled.

With a powerful thrust of both my fore and hind legs, I launched it off me. I rolled onto my paws and charged at it before it could recover, clenching my jaw onto its neck and tearing my claws over its abdomen.

The beast let out an ungodly whine that pierced my eardrums, but I didn't let up. I clamped my jaw harder over its neck, tasting the foul, sickly sweet blood that trickled into my mouth. It tasted like death. Like rotting meat and disease, pure pestilence.

The taste hit the back of my throat, and panic gripped me in my refusal to swallow, forcing me to release my bite and hacking the inky substance out.

The creature wobblingly righted itself, shaking its head against the pain I'd inflicted. And just when I thought it was going to lunge for me again, it turned tail and leapt into the darkness of the trees.

For a moment, I just sat there, catching my breath.

It would take more than a lone cusith to get the better of me. I was the true Alpha, and clearly the beast sensed that. That was why it ran rather than face my wrath a second time.

Sudden fear had me reaching my paw up to my neck. I exhaled in relief. The pouch was still there, its contents whole and unharmed.

Good. This attack only confirmed what I already knew. Nothing was going to stop me from fulfilling my destiny.

CHAPTER 13

JAX

I sat in front of the softly crackling hearth and despite the whiskey I was nursing and the knowledge that every inhabitant of the castle was sleeping peacefully, for some unknown reason I couldn't relax.

The pack was joyous since hearing the news of the upcoming ball. Aliya was happy and healthy in her pregnancy, growing increasingly beloved by my people each day. And all the preparations for our extravagant gala were going smoothly. There hadn't even been a cusith sighting since the meeting with the deltas.

Everything was perfect. And for some reason, that made me uneasy. I had never known a time of peace. My entire life had been a battle for survival and defending my pack, a cloying race to get to where we were now. I was waiting for the next shoe to drop, for the inevitable storm to obliterate the calm.

The last log in the fireplace snapped, and the flames began to dim, a subtle sign that I should go to bed. But I wouldn't be able to sleep. Not yet.

So, I got up, threw another log on the fire, and sat back to sip my whiskey as I continued my staring contest with the dancing flames.

"Can't sleep either?"

I smirked, keeping my gaze on the hearth as Tannin came to sit next to me on the couch. My beta had always been more in tune with my soul than anyone. "I'm restless, I suppose. What about you?"

He ran his hand through his hair in my peripheral vision. "I don't know. I just feel like things couldn't possibly be this good. Everything seems so perfect on the surface, and I guess I don't trust it."

I looked up and offered him my glass. He gratefully accepted it and took a long sip, then let out a low hiss against the burn.

"I feel the same way," I confessed. "Our lives have been like a changing tide since we got here, one turbulent wave after another—some that we barely survived. Now that the waters are clear, it's hard not to anticipate the next tempest."

He nodded, idly turning the glass in his hands as he stared at the fire. "I've been thinking a lot about something Aliya said."

Curious, I pulled a bent leg onto the couch and turned to face him.

"The reason she came up with the idea of the ball was because of a story Esther told her about our history," he went on. "That an ancient princess fell in love with an Alpha's son against the king's wishes, and when the king found out, he killed them both."

He turned his head in my direction, looking into my eyes. "Did you know about that?"

With a frown of intrigue, I shook my head. "No. All I heard growing up was that we were banished from Varynia. I didn't think anyone knew why. I assumed that knowledge had been forgotten."

Something shuffled in the darkness by the stairs beyond the fire's glow, and I immediately tensed in preparation as I turned in that direction.

"His name was King Solomide," Esther said as she emerged into the firelight.

I relaxed with her presence, settling back against the cushion of the couch as she lowered herself into the armchair opposite us.

"My grandmother was a girl when the great war divided our two people," she went on. "She had adored Princess Bronwyn, so when the king had her brutally and publicly executed, it left a deep wound inside my grandmother. She would tell me the story often so that I would never forget where we came from."

"What happened?" I asked. "Why did this king kill his daughter?"

"As I understand it, the Black Wolves were the soldiers of Varynia, fighting alongside the kingdom's wielders to fend off the cusith," she explained, looking into the flames as if the story was playing out within them. "The two factions were supposed to be equals, but the king always favored the wielders, viewing the wolves as primitive and less worthy.

"Marriage between the two factions was forbidden, but there's no accounting for young love. Princess Bronwyn fell in love with Janus Gray." She turned her head and gave me a meaningful gaze. "The eldest son of your ancestor, Quintus Gray."

My breath hitched. My great-great-great-grandfather, and the Alpha that led the pack to safety after our exile.

"Bronwyn pleaded with her father to let her marry Janus," Esther continued. "To let their two people be officially united as one in the eyes of the kingdom. But Solomide forbade it and put her under house arrest until he could find her a suitor of his choosing.

"What he didn't know was that Bronwyn was already pregnant with Janus's pup. One night, she snuck out of the castle, and the two eloped. As you can imagine, such news didn't stay secret in such a large kingdom, especially with how short wolf pregnancies are.

"When Solomide found out his daughter had not only gotten pregnant out of wedlock, but also with a wolf's child, he decided to make an example of them. He had them burned at the stake in the village square for all to see, locking the wolves in place with his wielders' magic so they were forced to watch."

I took a long pull of my whiskey, horrified by the awful mental images her words invoked. "I can't believe he killed his own daughter just for loving one of us."

She shook her head. "It wasn't because she loved a wolf. Solomide feared the potential power of a wielder wolf. He was convinced that the progeny of our two people combined would be stronger than both. He feared losing his kingdom to a force beyond his control."

The image of Aliya lovingly patting her round belly flashed into my mind. Her babies—our babies—would be both wielder and wolf.

Tannin leaned over his bent knees, looking at Esther with concern. "Do you think that's true? Will our children be the powerful force the king feared?"

"What did you see when you tasted Aliya's blood?" I added.

She let out a slow breath and returned her gaze to the fire. "This union was always destined to happen. Prejudice stopped it long ago, and prejudice almost stopped it again. But we can't let history repeat itself. Wielders and wolves must sit on the Varynian throne. Together."

Tannin and I looked at each other, and a pulse of fate sent a shiver over my entire body.

"That's what's been niggling at me the past few days," I said with bated breath. "Varynia has its princess, but it needs its queen."

"And its kings," Esther added with an arched eyebrow.

"Kings? Plural?" Tannin asked.

She nodded, and understanding settled deep within my soul.

"We both mated to her," I said. "That makes us equals in the eyes of Fate. I'm not your Alpha, and you're not my beta. We are *her* kings."

Humility softened Tannin's eyes as he smiled at me. He had never truly been my subordinate. In many ways, he was superior to me, and even a better man than I. He was my brother, the light to my dark, my polar and necessary opposite. And it saddened me that I had never really expressed that to him.

I reached for his hand and gripped it. "Tannin, will you do me the honor of being my partner husband to our girl, my tandem king to our queen?"

His smile widened. "I thought you'd never ask."

I chuckled, and Esther laughed, which turned into a coughing fit.

"And I know the best time to make it happen," I said as the idea sprang into my mind. "Let's turn the ball into a surprise wedding."

Tannin's features stretched with excitement. "That's a brilliant idea. The whole pack will already be there for a massive party."

"I think that's a fabulous idea, Jax," Esther said with a nod of approval. "I will speak with the other elders and get them on board. We wouldn't want one of Droger's grumpy riots to ruin the celebration."

"Thank you, Esther," I said, trying to convey the depth my gratitude for everything she'd done with my tone and gaze. "For so many things. Could I ask one last favor of you?"

"Of course."

"Would you be willing to officiate the wedding for us?"

Her lips spread in such a wide smile that every single wrinkle in her face was exposed and highlighted by the fire's glow. "Nothing would bring this old heart greater joy."

With no small amount of effort, she rose from the chair and stepped slowly over to me. She patted my shoulder and cast a motherly smile down at me.

"I am so proud of the man you've become." She then turned her smile to Tannin. "Both of you. You are the leaders we always needed."

Tannin returned her smile, and I put my hand affectionately over hers until she pulled it away.

"Well, if you'll excuse me, these old bones need some sleep."

"Good night, Esther," Tannin and I said in unison.

She shuffled towards the stairs, leaving us alone in front of the whispering fire once more.

"I love this plan, truly," Tannin began, "but are you sure it's a good idea to spring it on everyone like that?"

I debated that for a moment. Yes, there were likely still plenty of people who didn't trust Aliya, but over the past few days, I'd watched everyone warm up to her, from the deltas to the lower ranking members. I'd even seen some of the pack children run up and hug her while their parents stood back and smiled. She had shown them her kind heart, and they couldn't resist falling for her just as we had.

"I understand your concerns," I said. "But this feels right. And just imagine the look on her face when we get down on one knee before her in front of everyone."

I couldn't contain the joy that filled me at the thought of it. Declaring my love and devotion to her to the world. What could be better than that?

Tannin nodded, wearing a pensive look. "This does feel right. And the pack have been surprising me over the past week. Could we really have everything we ever wanted?"

"I think we can," I said with a wide grin. "Now, come on. Let's go to bed before Aliya notices we're both missing."

I put out the fire and followed Tannin up the stairs. Though I could barely contain my smile as I made my way up, I still couldn't shake that feeling that there was another shoe hiding in the shadows, just waiting to drop.

CHAPTER 14
ALIYA

The day left me pleasantly drained. From sunup to sundown, I had worked tirelessly to bake cakes and prepare the food to be cooked for the ball tomorrow night. Thankfully, I'd had help from Raya and a few of the female elders. My skin was powdered with flour dust, and my muscles hummed from too much standing, too much smiling, and too much pretending I wasn't nervous about the ball.

Night had fallen, and though there was still so much left to do, I was spent. I wandered toward the room I shared with my mates, my fingers absently smoothing down the front of my gown. My belly felt taut, heavy, but the twins were mercifully still.

Only when I pushed open the door and found both my mates waiting did I remember just how awake my body could become.

The fire had been stoked high in the grate, shadows licking across the stone walls. Jax leaned against the bedpost shirtless, his blue eyes glinting with something feral. Tannin lounged in the armchair across the room, sprawled like a king on his throne, his green gaze dragging over me until heat flushed my cheeks.

"You've worked hard today," Jax said, his voice like rough velvet. "So, we've come up with a little something to reward your efforts."

The dark promise in his words stole the air from my lungs. My hand lingered on the doorknob, half-tempted to retreat and half-tempted to throw myself at them both.

"Don't look so shy, love," Tannin murmured. "You've earned every bit of what we're about to give you."

I swallowed. "And what is that?"

"Something new," Jax said. "Something we've wanted to try for a while. Seeing as the castle will soon be public access, tonight may be our last chance."

He pushed off the post and stalked toward me, the muscles in his shoulders flexing like a predator ready to pounce.

"Do you trust us?"

My pulse fluttered like hummingbird wings against my throat. After everything we'd already shared, the answer was easy. "Always."

"That's my good girl." He tilted my chin, kissing me tenderly yet possessively.

Tannin rose from the chair and came up behind me. His warm breath teased the nape of my neck as his voice rumbled low in my ear. "Tonight, we want to show you the pleasure of surrender."

Despite my earlier exhaustion, my core tightened with anticipation. "Surrender?"

"Yes." Jax brushed his thumb over my lower lip. "You are our queen. But before you can master control, you need to learn how to relinquish it completely."

Tannin's hands suddenly closed around my wrists, pulling them behind my back and locking them in place with speed and force that made me gasp in surprise.

"Surrender control to us, and let us worship you," he purred into my ear.

My mouth went dry as I realized just how helpless I was, trapped between these two powerful men. Though my heart was racing, I desperately wanted to be stretched out, under their control.

"I surrender," I whispered.

Jax's grin turned wicked. "Strip for us."

Tannin released my wrists and came around to stand beside Jax, both watching me with the same hungry expectation.

My hands trembled as I untied my dress and let it slip to the floor, leaving me bare and flushed under their stares. They exchanged a heated glance, and Jax gave Tannin a subtle nod.

Tannin moved to the bed, uncoiling a length of black rope that sat atop the sheets. He tested it between his palms with a predator's patience, and my pulse quickened at the knowledge of what it must be for.

"Get on the bed," Jax said, his voice a sensuous command.

With shallow breaths, I obeyed. I climbed onto the mattress and lay flat on my back as they loomed over me.

Tannin's strong hands lifted my wrists above my head, his lips brushing the inside of my arm before looping the rope around my skin. The rope was softer than it looked, almost like silk. The strands slid around my wrists, snug but not biting, circling until my wrists were bound together. He secured the rope to the top of the carved headboard, leaving just enough slack that I could move slightly—but not enough to escape.

"Our little goddess," Tannin murmured, stepping back to admire me, his cock already straining against his trousers.

I tugged experimentally, the restraint making my pulse skitter. I couldn't move, there was no way. I was utterly exposed to whatever they wanted to do to me, utterly theirs.

Jax sat on the bed beside me, bringing a long strap of black silk toward my face.

I gasped, but I didn't dare even move as he draped the fabric over my fluttering lashes. He lifted my head and tied the strap to secure it in place, leaving me completely blind.

For a moment, panic gripped me. I couldn't move or see. I'd never been more helpless. I forced myself to take a quick breath and focused on centering myself, staying calm. I could feel their presence, and their scents filled the air, soothing my primal fears.

When lips brushed against mine, I was startled.

The owner of those lips chuckled above me. Jax's voice. I willed myself to relax.

My lips parted, and I tilted my head up once more, inviting him in as he kissed me slowly and deeply. His warm hand cupped my breast while the other skimmed down my belly to the slick heat between my thighs.

"Look at you," he murmured against my lips. "Already soaked."

A whimper escaped me as his fingers teased my folds, circling my clit, then plunging into me with delicious force. I arched against the rope, helpless to grab him, helpless to control the rhythm. My fingers reached for him, but I couldn't do anything more.

"That's the point of all this," he purred, his voice raw. "You don't get to touch. You don't get to choose. You just feel."

Sheets rustled on my other side as new weight settled on the bed, and another mouth claimed my nipple. I gasped out loud, and Jax deepened our kiss. Tannin's tongue swirled as he suckled me, teeth grazing just enough to make me hiss. His hand landed on my hip, steadying me as Jax finger fucked me harder, each thrust designed to wring another moan from my throat.

"Please," I gasped, my body trembling.

"Please what?" Jax purred between kisses.

"Please...fuck me."

He pulled his hand away, leaving my swollen pussy clenching around emptiness. "Not yet."

Tannin chuckled low, his lips wet against my breast. "Patience, love. You'll have both of us soon enough."

I writhed against the ropes, against the unbearable need that threatened to shatter me. The rope bit deliciously into my wrists as I twisted, desperate to touch them, desperate for more. But all I could do was lie bound and trembling while my mates hovered over me like wolves playing with their prey.

The bed shifted beneath me as their hands and mouths left me completely, the sounds of moving fabric and drawn zippers heightening my anticipation. The inability to see their bodies as they disrobed was its own form of agony, but the uncertainty of watching them move and knowing when and where and *if* they were going to touch me was the worst.

Just when I thought I'd go mad with caged need, a pair of hands gripped my thighs, spreading them wide as a weight settled between them. I bucked my hips as I presented my drenched center, a silent plea for release.

The hands moved up my thighs, thumbs dragging toward my mound, but stopping just shy of where I so desperately needed to be touched.

The words I wanted to beg died in my throat as something moved across my chest, and weight settled on either side of my head. My imagination was running away with what might be happening, but as smooth, supple skin brushed against my lips, certainty found me with renewed desire.

"Open your mouth, beautiful," came Tannin's gentle, growled command.

I obeyed instantly, parting my lips and greedily sucking as he slid his thick length across my tongue. His guttural groan was my reward, encouraging me to take him deeper. I lifted my head, but he withdrew, making me blindly chase him.

"Give in, my love," Tannin instructed. "Surrender."

Frustration tightened every muscle in my body, and I wanted to cry. But I knew there was only one way I was going to get what I craved, so I let my head fall back against the bed, resigning myself to finally do what they said. I surrendered.

"That's it," Tannin praised, slowly pressing his cock further into my mouth.

Something hard and warm rubbed against my entrance between my legs, making me moan around Tannin.

"So wet," Jax growled, circling the head of his cock over my folds as if savoring the feel of my juices.

I fought the urge to squirm, to rise my hips to meet him, and just lay as still as I could, letting his teasing torment add to the feeling of Tannin gently fucking my mouth.

At long last, Jax pressed his cock into my opening, easing inside me inch by inch until I was stretched full.

The sensation was overwhelming, and I inadvertently tugged against my restraints as my muffled cries vibrated around Tannin's cock. But my masters didn't seem to notice, losing themselves to their own ecstasy.

"Fuck, she feels incredible," Jax snarled, gripping my hips to hold me still as he thrust deeper, his cock dragging against every sensitive nerve inside me.

Tannin cupped the side of my face, thrusting slowly and steadily into my mouth. "That's it, love. Take us both. Let go."

I couldn't move, couldn't control the pace, and the loss of power was intoxicating. Every thrust of Jax's cock had me writhing, every pump of Tannin's filled my throat, and all I could do was surrender, drowning in them.

Jax's rhythm grew harder, faster, his hips slamming into mine as he pinned me to the mattress. The rope squeaked against the headboard as I strained against it, tears leaking from my eyes—not from pain, but from sheer intensity.

Tannin groaned above me, his fingers tightening in my hair as he drove deeper, entering my throat.

"Gods, I can't take it," he hissed.

I moaned in answer, the sound vibrating down his shaft and making him shudder around me.

"Not yet," Jax barked as his thrusts came harder and faster, making me scream around Tannin's cock as their sweet dominion drove me closer to the edge.

"It's too incredible," Tannin grunted, slowing his pace. "I can't."

"Come for us, Aliya," Jax demanded. "Come as you swallow him."

The words detonated inside me. I shattered, convulsing around his forceful thrusts and screaming around Tannin's shaft as waves of pleasure wracked me.

"Fuck, yes." Tannin's grip on my hair tightened to the point of pain as he buried his cock in my throat. "Take me. Take me!"

His cum shot into the back of my throat, hot and salty, as my muscles flexed to swallow around his tip. He let out a symphony of clipped groans and grunts as he spilled into me, his legs trembling around my face.

"Oh, fuck," Jax snarled with a final slam, his seed flooding my pussy as the last pulses of my orgasm squeezed him tight.

Tannin removed his cock, and I sucked in a breath of air as waves of pleasure continued to wash through me.

Even after Tannin pulled off the blindfold, the world was a blur as they untied the ropes, kissing the angry marks on my wrists where the bonds had held me.

They collapsed around me, and I lay limp and spent between them, every muscle trembling, my body still humming with aftershocks.

They had called me their queen, their goddess, but until my dying day, I would be their willing sacrifice.

CHAPTER 15

ALIYA

The ballroom looked like a fairytale wonderland, fully decorated with lavish flower arrangements, streams of cream lace and silk adorning the walls, and every candle in the chandeliers and candelabra were lit.

But even though it looked truly perfect, I couldn't stop obsessing over every detail.

"Put the roast chicken in the center of the sides, that way it looks like a centerpiece," I instructed Tannin. We were going to need to start outsourcing the hunting for our meat. I was running out of chickens to kill, and I still wanted fresh eggs. There were deer in the woods nearby, perhaps the guys wouldn't mind hunting some? "Oh, and let's get those vases on either side of the buffet table."

I rushed to fetch the flower collections on the floor to rearrange them myself, but Jax stopped me with a gentle hand on my upper arm.

"Ah-ah, no bending over," he cautioned, glancing down at my large belly.

I huffed a frantic breath. "Okay. You're right."

He picked up the vase for me and set it on the edge of the buffet table lining the wall. It still didn't look right, so I turned it, trying to find just the right angle to show off the best view of the roses.

Jax chuckled. "My love, you're driving yourself crazy. Everything

415

looks beautiful, and everyone is going to be blown away by what you've put together."

I let my shoulders fall slightly. "I know. I just want this night to be perfect."

He leaned in and kissed my cheek, then whispered, "It will be."

"In the meantime, have a drink and just relax." Tannin handed me a flute of fruit punch. "Guests will start arriving soon, so enjoy yourself and try to have a little fun."

I nodded and took the flute from him, indulging in a little sip. He was right. They both were. And worrying over every little detail was going to give me a heart attack. It was already upsetting the little bundles I was carrying, making them fidget restlessly in my belly. I needed to calm down, for all our sake.

"Aliya!" Twila called at the foot of the stairs as she came running toward me. "Mama found this dress and did my hair. What do you think?"

She looked like a little princess, wearing a lacy pale pink dress I had worn as a girl. Her hair was done up in dozens of small braids atop her head with the back left flowing down her neck.

"I think you'll be the most beautiful girl at the ball," I cooed.

She looked around at the empty ballroom. "But nobody's here yet."

I laughed. "You'll still be the most beautiful girl, even after the room is full."

"Second most beautiful," Jax whispered behind me.

I blushed and smiled at him over my shoulder. Then I turned back to Twila and held out my hand. "Okay. Are you ready to help me greet the guests?"

She took my hand and gave a firm nod, and together we walked across the ballroom floor and out the main doors.

Though the sun had not yet set, dozens of people were already gathered just beyond the ward, dressed in the finest clothes at their disposal and eagerly awaiting their chance to enter the castle.

I took a moment to brace myself. Once I did this, there was no turning back, no undoing it. And though there was apprehension and fear in my chest, there was also hope and faith. This was the right decision for everyone and seeing the excited anticipation in every pair of eyes watching me, my doubts melted away.

I lifted my hands out and above my head, closed my eyes, and spoke the incantation loudly and clearly for all to hear.

"Moerus dissipo."

The air between the people and me shimmered, pearlescent ripples vibrating across the ward as it slowly evaporated and fell away. My heart swelled and shivered as the magic returned to me, filling me for an overwhelming instant before flowing back into the world around me from whence it came.

The people watched with mystification as the barrier separating them from the castle dissolved, their smiles growing. And when the last of the ward disappeared, they erupted in cheers.

"Welcome to the first of many balls, Black Wolves of Varynia," I announced.

Those at the front of the crowd stood hesitantly for a moment, slowly stepping forward to test if the ward was truly gone. When nothing hindered them, they burst forth like a flood through a broken dam.

The happy chatter around me was so deafening, I could hardly hear the praises and greetings of those who passed me on their way inside. I was so full of joy that I wanted to cry, but I held it back so as not to smudge my makeup. Still holding Twila's hand, I turned and followed the happy crowd inside.

Classical orchestra music was already playing on the victrola, and the pack wasted no time at all enjoying the food and drink we'd prepared.

By the time night fell, the entire kingdom had finally arrived, and the ballroom was packed with people eating and toasting, laughing, dancing. Even Droger was waltzing on the dance floor with a young lady who seemed to be obliging him out of pity. It was quite amusing to watch.

I lost count of the number of men I danced with on request. Though Jax and Tannin were very gracious about loaning me out, they never took their eyes off me for a second until each dance was over. How could I be so lucky to have found them?

Dancing so much eventually proved too much for me, and I stole away to sit in one of the chairs against the wall. The moment my butt hit the thin cushion, I closed my eyes and let out a contented sigh of relief. My feet were very sore, and it felt amazing to give them a break.

I nursed my glass of wine and watched those around me having the time of their lives.

"I never thought I'd have this again," I whispered down to my babies, patting my belly with my free hand. "I can hardly believe this is happening. Sometimes I fear this is all a crazy, wonderful—sometimes terrifying—dream. Maybe I'm really just going mad with loneliness, and Tabitha is curled up next to me while I sleep?"

I glanced around again, and a huge smile lifted my lips. No. This wasn't a dream. This was too real.

The chime-like sound of Twila's giggling made me turn. Tannin was holding her hand up above her head as she twirled around like a ballerina. Then he picked her up, tossed her into the air and caught her, spinning them in circles as they both laughed.

It warmed my heart to see them so happy.

"And if this is a dream," I whispered, rubbing my thumb over my navel as a tiny foot nudged beneath it, "then I hope I never wake up."

A shadow fell over me as the tips of polished black shoes entered my peripheral vision. I looked up to see Coda smiling roguishly down at me, wearing a dashing black suit that appeared tailored to flatter his muscular physique in all the right places.

"Good evening, Princess," he said with a short bow of his head. "I was hoping you might have room on your dance card for one more."

Out of sheer politeness, I pressed my feet to the floor, attempting to get up, but they throbbed in rebellion.

"Actually, I think I just need to sit for a while," I said apologetically, bending to the side to rub my ankle.

"Ah, of course," he said. "You've been on your feet all day. You deserve a chance to sit back and enjoy the fruits of your labor." He turned to his side and looked fondly over the gathering. "You did a magnificent job setting this up. You've truly outdone yourself."

"Thank you." I offered him a tenuous smile, still struggling to reconcile this version of him with the one that threatened to deliver the heads of my mates on a silver platter just two weeks ago.

He glanced at the glass in my hand. "At least let me get you another drink."

I flitted my gaze to it, finding it nearly empty.

"Perhaps the fruit punch? Thank you." I handed him my flute, and he disappeared to the buffet table.

He returned quickly with a glass in each hand and gave one to me.

"Thank you," I said as I took it and held it over my lap.

"Would you mind if I keep you company while you sit?" He gestured to the chair to my left.

"Oh, no—I mean—sure, be my guest," I stammered.

With a chuckle, he lowered into the chair. Then he lifted his glass between us. "A toast. To you, the princess who restored Varynia."

A mixture of embarrassment and pride washed over me at his surprising gesture, but I recovered quickly and raised my glass as well, drinking some of it just to end the uncomfortable moment of being in his spotlight.

He grinned around the rim of his own glass as he watched me drink from mine.

"Excellent," he purred, his voice catching and echoing in the small hollow of his glass.

"Aliya," Jax greeted as he and Tannin emerged from the crowd in front of me.

"Coda," Tannin said flatly, giving him the side-eye.

"Can we borrow you for a moment, my love?" Jax extended a hand, the secretive smile on his face and the twinkle in his eyes sparking my intrigue.

"Yes?" I said, the word lilting into a question.

I put my hand in his and let him pull me to my aching feet. Tannin took my other hand, and together, they guided me through the bustling ballroom floor to the front of the large space, where Raya stood, beaming at me with a smile that was bursting with love.

When we stopped at the head of the room, Raya tapped a metal knife against the top of her wine glass, making a sharp *tinking* sound that called the attention of all in assembly and encouraged them to quiet their chatter.

"Ladies and gentlemen of the Black Wolf Pack," Jax announced.

What is he doing?

"I have a confession to make," he went on in his booming, authoritative voice. "This ball is not just a celebration of our return to Varynia.

It is the dawn of a new age for our kingdom, and tonight we would like to make it official."

He and Tannin released my hands and moved in front of me, facing me with their backs to the crowd. I frowned at them curiously, but they only smiled in return. Then, as everyone watched with the same keen interest as me, they lowered to kneel in front of me.

My breath caught in my throat, my heart skipping.

"Aliya, princess of Varynia," Jax said, the deepest love and devotion pouring from his blue eyes.

"Fate gave us the greatest gift any man could receive when she mated us to you," Tannin said, the same love shining on me from his simultaneously intense but soft gaze.

Jax removed a small black box from his pocket and held it in front of him.

"Will you marry us?" they asked in unison.

Jax opened the box, revealing a stunning princess-cut diamond set in a white gold ring.

My entire body froze, and for the briefest moment, I thought I would die on the spot from jubilant shock.

Finally, I found my voice, and uttered the single greatest word known to mankind. "Yes."

CHAPTER 16
CODA

My ears roared with the rush of my flash-boiling blood, and it was all I could do to maintain my cool façade as I glared through the bodies of the crowd at my two nemeses kneeling in front of *my* future bride.

I flicked my gaze to those around me, expecting the same roars of outrage that I wanted to bellow. They were Black Wolves. They would never bow to a Varynian queen, never accept the betrothal of their Alpha and beta to a wielding vixen. Surely, they would rebel and over-throw the lot of them without the need for my intervention.

But rather than shouting obscenities, they cheered. Everyone in the ballroom was fucking cheering.

Traitors, all of them.

They'd allowed themselves to be bewitched by the princess just as Jax and Tannin had, just as the elders had. Well, her days of magical deception were over. And as her so-called mates rose and toasted their imminent nuptials, her emptied glass sealed her fate.

I curled my fingers around the empty vial in my pocket, satisfied that its target had downed its contents. I'd nearly died to acquire it, but it was worth the pain to nullify her powers.

Or at least, it would be.

Now was the time to act. We had to strike before this sham of a wedding could happen. *I* was destined to be the new king, not the two great pretenders. *I* had to be the first to wed her. The *only* one to wed her.

I had hoped to wait until the gathering was sufficiently drunk—especially Jax and Tannin—and for some of the lesser, bothersome members to retire home for the night. But the attack couldn't wait. It had to happen now.

I caught Tywen's gaze from across the room, then Hollis's, then Hamish's hulking form near the doors. Though their faces were stony masks, I could see the fury they shared with me burning in their eyes.

A subtle nod was all it took.

They moved as one, melting into the crowd to quietly alert the others of our motley crew that it was time to act. Little by little, each man slid into his assigned place while the pack were all too distracted with joy as they watched Esther join the throuple, announcing that she would officiate their union.

Once I'd dispatched Jax and Tannin, she would be my next victim. She'd been the one to demand clemency for Aliya. She'd been the one to pardon Jax and Tannin despite their treason. I would not allow her to corrupt our pack any further, and her blood would be mine to bathe in.

In mere breaths, my men were stationed around the ballroom. Tywen and Hollis blocked access to the kitchen. Hamish and Avery stood guard in front of the double doors. Chase and Allistar were positioned at the head of the ballroom behind Esther so that no one could flee upstairs. And the other six members of my rebellion were spread throughout the crowd.

Slowly and silently like a serpent, I pushed through the assembly, making my way to the front row and readying myself to shift. The act would destroy the fine suit I had chosen for this occasion, but once the night was over and I took control of the castle, there'd be no shortage of designer clothing to replace it.

"Ladies and gentlemen of the Black Wolves," Esther began in her dry, wizened voice. "Tonight, we stand witness to the blessed union of our Alpha and beta to Princess Aliya..."

She blabbered on about Fate and correcting mistakes of the past, but I refused to listen any of it, eager to silence her—and them—once and for all.

An ear-splitting shriek sliced through the walls and the night beyond, and every pair of eyes widened in fear as Esther finally shut her yap.

Each of us knew that sound to our bones, and as one, we all turned to look at the double doors in the direction from whence it came. The doors exploded inward, knocking Hamish and Avery face-first onto the floor as shards of wood shot across the ballroom like arrows.

A cusith sailed into the space, knocking over pack members in their finery like bowling pins. Another charged in, and then a third, and the crowd dissolved into chaos as people scrambled from the snapping jaws and slashing claws.

Screams tore through the ballroom. Wolves leapt for the shift, clothes ripping as bodies warped into fur and fangs. Glasses crashed, tables overturned, and the scents of meat and wine soured in the overwhelming rotting stench the beasts brought.

Tywen shoved his way toward me, his complexion pale with fear and desperation. "What do we do?"

This wasn't the plan. This wasn't my moment. My followers glanced at me, waiting for the signal, torn between fight and flight.

"Hold!" I barked, my voice nearly drowned out by the screams, cries and roars. "Do nothing until I command it!"

But even as I shouted, a cusith tore into Hamish's shoulder, dragging him down in a spray of crimson.

Chaos had stolen my stage. Fate had spit in my face. But I wasn't going to let it conquer me. In fact, I was going to use it to my benefit.

Scanning the frantic crowd, I locked eyes on my prize. Nothing was going to stop me from taking her. Not even an army of monsters. And if I was lucky, they would take out my enemies for me.

CHAPTER 17

JAX

The moment the doors shattered, the world went red.

I was shifting before the first cusith's claws scraped marble, my body breaking and remaking itself in a rush of agony and power. Bones stretched, muscles tore and mended, and fur erupted across my skin as my wolf ripped free. My howl was a battle cry that shook the chandeliers.

These abominations had no right to break into Aliya's castle and threaten the lives of my pack. Not today, not any day. But definitely not on our wedding day.

The ballroom was chaos. Wolves threw off their finery and exploded into fur, gowns shredding, suits splitting at the seams as my people answered instinct with fangs. The air filled with screams and roars, the high-pitched screech of cusith mingling with the bone-crunching sound of impact as they hit the crowd like a storm.

The one that had burst through the doors first righted itself and set its sights on Aliya, lunging for her in the next blink.

I didn't think, I just leapt to save her, more swiftly and viciously than I knew I was capable of. My teeth sank into the beast's throat, crushing bone and spraying its foul blood across the marble tiles. Its body convulsed, but I held my jaws tight until it went limp, then flung it aside like a putrid husk.

"Protect the women and children!" I barked, my wolf's snarl ringing loudly over the melee.

Tannin's answering growl was immediate, sharp with protective rage. He howled, and the deltas rushed to gather the weaker members of our pack, forming a protective shield around them.

I spun, already leaping for the next cusith. Its claws raked across my flank, searing pain that only fed the fire in my veins. I slammed into it, jaws snapping, and together we rolled across the ballroom, smashing through a table in an eruption of splintered wood and spilled wine. I ripped its belly open, entrails steaming in the candlelight, but another was already on me, talons digging for my eyes.

A mighty jaw tore it off me—Esme, silver fur bristling and eyes alight with fury. She ripped the creature's ear clean off and spat it onto the floor. It shook off the attack like it was nothing more than a bug bite and launched itself at the nearest wolf, but Esme leapt onto its back.

My desperate eyes searched through the chaos for my mate, needing to see that she was okay. I found her pressed against the wall, one hand cradling her belly, the other lifted as if to summon magic—but nothing came. Her eyes were wide, frantic, and my gut dropped.

She can't use her power.

The crunch of bone announced the death of the last cusith in the ballroom, spurring me into command mode.

"Everyone out of the castle," I ordered as I tentatively shifted back to human form. If there were more making their way into the castle, we needed to get out. My people were sitting ducks inside.

Those who had shifted turned back to human, climbing to their feet as their rescinding fur exposed deep slices and bite marks. The party was over.

We should never have taken down the ward.

I should have encouraged Aliya to keep it up and grant the pack access instead, but I'd been a fool. I'd been so distracted by own happiness, made arrogant by my hope for the future.

Our guests collected themselves, and Tannin and I, along with the deltas, escorted them into the courtyard. We needed Aliya to finish the ward around the castle as soon as possible. We could not afford another attack. We—

A shriek split the night as the moon herself hid behind a cloak of dark clouds.

I looked out into the darkness and froze where I stood.

The forest at the edge of the village swarmed. Dozens of glowing eyes blinked back from the tree line, each pair set in a nightmarish face.

"Get back." My voice came out like a hoarse whisper, my throat momentarily cinched by terror. "Get back!" I roared at the top of my lungs. "Everyone, back inside. Now!"

Cusith poured from the darkness like an avalanche of fur and fangs, their shrieks shaking the very stones beneath my feet as they charged up the main road. Their numbers were staggering—one of them for every five of us at least. We'd never encountered such an onslaught of them.

This wasn't just a scout mission or a handful of rogues looking for blood. No, it was a calculated attack.

"Form ranks!" I bellowed, the command vibrating through every wolf's bones. "Every able-bodied fighter remains in the courtyard! Hold the line!"

One by one, the males and deltas of my pack filed alongside me, Tannin right by my side. In a gruesome symphony of snapping bone, we shifted once more, hunching low in preparation for battle.

In the corner of my eye, I saw Aliya lingering behind me.

"Get inside," I demanded over my shoulder.

She blinked at me, her face pale but set with determination.

"Get the women and children to safety," I said, my words more of a plea than a command. "And keep yourself safe, no matter what happens."

A tear trailed down her cheek and finally, she gave a reluctant nod before rushing inside.

With a fearful heart, I turned back to face the tide of monsters charging toward us. We had to win. For her, for our children growing inside her beautiful belly. We could not fail.

I would not fail.

The first wave of cusith hit, and the courtyard exploded into carnage. Claws met claws, jaws snapped, and blood sprayed across the cobblestones.

A young, newly recruited delta whose name I hadn't learned yet went down screaming, his throat ripped out before I could reach him. I tore into the beast that killed him, ripping its leg clean from its socket.

Everywhere I turned was blood, fur, and teeth.

The wall we'd formed grew holes as our individual fighters got taken out. But our trained deltas held firm, intercepting and killing those cusith who managed to get past us before they could enter the castle's destroyed front doors. Even a few of the untrained women ran out to join the fight.

Tannin and I worked in perfect unison against them, my beta standing at my back so that no one could take advantage of my blind spots. When one beast would come at me from behind, he was right there to crush its spine with his powerful jaws. When another leapt at him from the side, I pounced on it to crack its skull against the cobblestones.

Our fight became a bloody, synchronized dance, as if we'd practiced for this our entire lives. We shared the same purpose, the same all-important goal: protect Aliya and our unborn babies.

Before we'd even finished defending against the first wave, the second wave of cusith came charging toward us. But beyond the drove of snarling beasts, I noted that there were no more glowing eyes hiding in the shadows.

We had a chance. A small but lingering chance. And as the next batch of creatures crashed down on us, I hoped I would survive, if for no other reason than to see my mate's face one more time.

CHAPTER 18
ALIYA

I could barely hold back my burning tears as I rushed back into the castle. I hated leaving my mates to battle the horde of cusith without me. I wanted to stand alongside them, fight with them, but my magic wasn't responding, and without it, I'd only be a liability.

Still, the only thing keeping me from charging back out there was the fact that I carried two defenseless lives inside me. I couldn't risk my life, because theirs were linked to mine, and they were far more important than anything else.

My mates would lay down their lives for us, but they'd never forgive me if something happened to our babies. I could never forgive myself either.

And with so many of the young women running out to join the fight, I had the lives of all their children on my shoulders as well.

"It's okay," I said to a pale blonde who looked woefully out the shattered doors as she shielded her two small sons. "Go. I'll take care of them."

Her worried gaze lingered on me for a moment, then on her frightened boys, then flicked back to the courtyard. Finally, she nodded. She dropped to her knees, kissed each of her sons on the cheek, then darted outside.

The other mothers surrounding the group of children looked at me with hope and desperation. They couldn't stay here in the ballroom. They were too exposed. I needed to get them somewhere safe—safer than here, at least. And there was only one place within the castle walls I could think of.

"Come on!" I urged, waving them toward the passage behind the kitchen. "Everyone, this way."

"Where are you taking us?" asked a petite brunette.

"The wine cellar," I said hastily. "It's below ground, and the only access is the door behind the kitchen. The cusith will have a much harder time getting to you there."

The mothers nodded, following behind me as they herded their children in front of them. The elders hovered in the archway of the den, looking after us with apprehension.

"You're coming too," I insisted, beckoning them forward.

They looked at each other. "Save the young ones first."

I shook my head rapidly, urgency making me impatient. "There's room in the cellar enough for all of you. Please. Your lives are important too."

Reluctantly, they left the shadow of the den and rushed after the group as fast as their stiff joints would allow.

Everyone descended the stairs, and we herded the wide-eyed children down the steps two and three at a time. Twila clung to my skirt with one hand and her doll with the other, her face chalk white. Behind us, Raya carried a toddler who sobbed into her shoulder, while a pair of older women shoved more little ones ahead with frantic urgency.

We reached the cellar, the cool, damp air splashing over our sweat-caked faces.

"Hurry, everyone in," I urged, shoving the heavy oak door open. "Stay together. Stay quiet."

The children scrambled inside and huddled on the floor with their mothers, some whimpering, some stone-silent with shock. My heart twisted. They were too young for this. Too young for blood and monsters. But death cared little for age or innocence. I knew that better than anyone.

Please, don't let this happen again. I can't lose another kingdom. I just can't.

I helped the last of the elders down into the cellar, being as careful as possible in my panicked haste. Every single pair of eyes looked up at me as if I were the answer to their prayers, the one who could somehow save them. My gut told me to stay with them, protect my unborn children, but someone had to protect everyone else.

"Lock the door from the inside," I told Raya. "Don't open it for anyone but me, Jax, or Tannin."

She blinked in fright. "What? You're not staying with us?"

I shook my head between shoulders that shook with the weight of the burden I carried. "Someone needs to stand guard on the other side. I have my magic. I can use it to protect you all."

Her eyes brimmed with fear, but she nodded, tightening her hold on the child in her arms.

I turned and darted back up the stairs, planting myself in front of the door as it closed and locked behind me. My belly felt heavy, the twins restless inside me as though they sensed the terror outside.

My palms sparked faintly, magic begging to be unleashed, and I prayed it would be enough. Maybe I'd just been stunted by fear earlier, because I still couldn't explain why I'd failed when my kingdom had needed me the most.

Perhaps it had been a momentary lapse in my powers, and my magic would respond when I really needed it? I just had to find my calm, to center myself, and everything would be okay.

It had to be.

The silence stretched too long. Every sound in the castle had become suspicious—the creak of beams, the drip of condensation, the faint shuffle of rats in the walls.

Just breathe, I told myself, feeling for the well of magic inside me. *Stay calm. Don't panic.*

A clicking rattle sounded around the corner to my left, practically freezing my body to stone. That definitely wasn't a rat. I kept my eyes trained on the passage, and my heart leapt into my throat as a low, hulking shadow painted the opposite wall, growing larger as claws scraped the marble floor with each step.

The eerie rattling deepened, and I realized with dread that it was the sound of its breathing.

I tugged harder at the well of magic in my core, but it had gone cold and thin. Trying to grab hold of it was like grasping at smoke.

No, no, no. Come on!

The cusith emerged around the corner, low and creeping, its eyes the brimstone red of the fires of Hell as they fell on me...its next victim. I didn't even dare to breathe as it stalked slowly forward, sizing me up. It shrieked, the sound drilling into my skull, and charged.

I thrust my hands forward, summoning the words, the fire, the power that should have answered me. "Ignis—"

Nothing.

The spark inside me sputtered and died like wet tinder. The magic was gone.

"No!" I gasped, horror chilling me to the marrow. I tried again, screamed the spell, clawed at the vacant well in my core, but it was useless. Nothing came.

The cusith leapt.

I threw up my arms to shield my belly, certain the next moment would be my last.

Instead of death, warm blood sprayed across my face. Not mine, the beast's.

Coda's blade tore through its throat as he slammed into it, snarling like a man possessed. He wrenched the dagger free and drove it into the monster's skull again and again until the shrieking stopped. The body collapsed at my feet, twitching, foul blood pooling around us.

Coda turned to me, chest heaving, his face spattered with gore. His eyes gleamed—not just with victory, but with something darker.

"You're safe now, Princess." His voice was low, almost tender.

I backed against the cellar door, nausea boiling in my throat. "W-what are you doing here?"

"Protecting you." He sheathed the dagger and stepped closer, extending a beckoning hand to me. "Now, come on, we have to get you to safety."

I shrunk back against the door, shaking my head. "No. I must protect them. The children. The elders. They're down there."

He frowned, his eyes growing more intense. "Your scent will only lure more of them here. If you want to protect the children and yourself, you need to come with me."

My legs were rooted to the floor. I promised them I would stand guard. But maybe Coda was right. At least in the cellar, the aroma of stale wine and dust might shield the wolves' scents. And without my magic, I was little more than a limping gazelle drawing the cusith straight for them.

Ultimately, I couldn't do it. I couldn't abandon them. They were *my* pack now.

I shook my head. "I can't leave them."

His tender, protective expression twisted to one of cold anger. "Your magic's gone, isn't it? How are you going to protect them or yourself without it?"

Fear thrummed like a dark chord echoing in my chest.

"How did you know that?" I asked, my voice low, my breathing shallow. "How did you know my magic was gone?"

He loomed closer, his lips curling between a smirk and sneer. "Because I put a magic-blocking tonic in your drink."

My memory flashed to earlier at the ball. Coda offering to refill my drink. Me accepting the glass from him. The sweet yet sour taste of the punch as I swallowed.

Oh, gods, no.

He reached out, curling his fingers around my wrist before I could jerk away. His grip was iron. "We can't risk you hanging around down here like a trapped lamb. If the cusith breach the cellar, you and the pups are finished. I can't allow that."

"Let me go!" I hissed, trying to pull free. But he was so much stronger than me, his grip pressing on my bones and threatening to snap them.

"Never." His smile was cold and triumphant. "You're too important. You belong to me now. And when your wolves fall, you'll understand."

Before I could scream, he dragged me from the cellar door, picking me up and hauling me down the corridor. My feet scraped against the stone, my protests swallowed by the clash of distant battle. I scratched and pried at his hands, his arms locked around my waist, but he didn't even react. My efforts might as well have been love taps.

We mounted flight after flight of stairs, climbing higher, his grip unyielding no matter how violently I fought.

At last, he pushed through the roof access door and shoved me onto the rooftop. The night spread before us, alive with fire and slaughter —

wolves and cusith locked in brutal combat across the courtyard below, their howls and shrieks rising to the sky.

Coda yanked me against his chest, one arm banded tightly around my middle as he brought me to the roof's edge.

"Look at them," he snarled, his mouth at my ear. "Your precious mates are bleeding for nothing. They'll die, and when they do, you'll stand beside me. You'll be my bride. My queen. Together we'll rule what's left of this kingdom."

I thrashed against him, fury and terror warring in my veins. "Never!"

He laughed, harsh and hungry, pressing his mouth to my temple. "You will. Because you have no choice. You belong to me now, and there's nothing you can do about it."

As the battle raged below, I realized he was right about one thing. Without my magic, without Jax or Tannin here, I was utterly helpless.

CHAPTER 19
TANNIN

The sound snagged my heart like a fisherman's hook. Even through the snarls of the wolves fighting alongside me, through the shrieks of the cusith whose numbers were slowly dwindling, a sound reached my ears and stole every quantum of my attention.

Aliya's scream.

I whipped around, catching only a glimpse of Aliya's flailing feet before she was dragged up the stairs and out of sight.

Someone—or some*thing*—was hauling her away against her will. Fear squeezed my heart, threatening to crush it into pulp. At the same time, that fear wrung pure, protective fury from my soul flooded my entire being.

Driven by the most primal instinct a wolf could have—love for his Fated mate—I abandoned the battle and charged into the castle as fast as my paws could carry me.

The floors were slick with blood and chunks of cusith body parts, causing me to slip and slide, but I didn't give up. Aliya was in trouble, and nothing, not even a horde of blood-thirsty cusith, was going to keep me from getting to her.

I reached the bottom of the stairs, finding them dark and empty.

There were no signs of blood, and the only scent of cusith came from the blood matting my fur. She hadn't been taken by one of the beasts.

I exhaled a breath of relief, but it was short-lived. Just because it wasn't a cusith that took her didn't mean she wasn't in serious danger. Someone from the pack had dragged her away, and I knew exactly who the culprit was.

I leapt up the stairs, all the while keeping my ears trained for her voice, my nose keen to her scent.

Where had she been taken? And why? If someone wanted to kill her, why drag her away from the monsters who would happily take on the task? Unless her death wasn't what they wanted.

Floor after floor, I climbed, darting down hallways in the desperate search of my mate, only to lose her scent and double back. Each second that passed without sight of her made me more and more frantic, panic growing in my chest like a living parasite.

"Aliya!" I howled on the landing of the third floor.

No response, not even the shuffling of feet or a muffled breath.

"Aagh!" I roared in agitation, slashing my paw at the wall and sending hunks of painted drywall raining down the hall behind me.

Suddenly, a sequence of muffled thuds caught my pricked ears. I stilled, forcing my heavy breaths to slow so I could hear more clearly. They came again, sounding like footsteps on the floor above.

Without hesitation, I rushed up the stairs that would take me to the fourth floor, scanning every inch above with visual, auditory and olfactory precision.

Her scent grew stronger with each handful of steps I bound over, the thudding louder and sharper. I followed them up and onto the fourth-floor landing, where the tether of her smell led me to a door that was almost camouflaged into the wall.

There was no time to waste on shifting just so I could turn the knob. I took several steps back, then rammed into the door, my weight and force smashing it in an explosion of splintered wood.

I found myself outside, on the roof, surrounded by cool night air and the miasma of distant howls, snarls, and shrieks from below.

A scream sounded from around the turret from which I'd just emerged, drowning out all other sounds, all other thoughts.

Aliya.

I tore around the turret just in time to hear her cry out in furious terror from where Coda had pinned her against the parapet. His filthy hands gripped her wrists, his mouth on her neck, his hips pressed indecently close to her swollen belly.

Red. All I saw was red.

"Get your fucking hands off her!" I roared, charging toward him.

Coda spun, his eyes blazing with sick triumph. He shoved Aliya aside like a rag doll, and she crumpled against the stone wall, clutching her belly.

In an explosion of shredded clothes and sprouting fur, he shifted and dove at me.

We collided with the force of thunder, claws raking, teeth snapping. I sank my fangs into his shoulder, ripping free a mouthful of fur and flesh. He howled, the sound torn between rage and agony, and he slashed his claws across my ribs. Hot blood spattered the roof tiles.

I didn't feel the injury. All I felt was fury. All I saw was Aliya, trembling on the roof behind him, her gown torn, her wrists bruised where he'd gripped her.

I lunged again, driving him back, but he met me with equal savagery. His jaws clamped around my foreleg, bones grinding. I roared and hammered him with my free paw, claws tearing through his face until his grip broke.

"You don't deserve her!" he snarled, blood streaming from a gash across his muzzle. "Not you or fucking Jax. And once I force out your bastards, I'll take my sweet time claiming her as mine!"

"The fuck you will," I snarled back, my voice warped with the guttural echo of my wolf.

I slammed him into the parapet, stone cracking under the impact. He clawed for my throat, but I twisted, sinking my teeth into his neck. He thrashed, his claws gouging my side, and hot pain tore through me, but I didn't let go.

Aliya's voice pierced the roar of blood in my ears. "Tannin!"

Coda's claws raked across my back, but her cry fueled me. With a final savage jerk, I tore his throat open.

The whine that escaped him was wet, bubbling, and pathetic. His body convulsed once, twice, then went slack in my jaws. I spat him onto the stones. Blood spread in a dark pool beneath him, steaming in the cold night air.

Silence fell heavily around us, broken only by the screams of battle below.

I shifted back, my body aching, bleeding, trembling from the exertion of the fight. My breath came in ragged gasps as I staggered to Aliya.

She was on her knees, tears streaking her face.

I gathered her against me, my hands running frantically over her arms, her belly. "Are you hurt? Did he—"

She shook her head, sobbing. "He didn't...but Tannin, I tried to use my magic, and nothing happened. It's gone."

I froze, dread crawling over my skin. "What do you mean *gone?*"

"I tried," she whispered desperately. "When the cusith came. I said the words, but nothing...nothing came. Coda said he put some kind of magic-blocking tonic in my drink."

My gaze dropped to Coda's corpse. His suit lay in rags a few feet away. I strode to the strewn mess, dropping to my knees to feel around the fabric. My palm landed on something hard and small in what used to be the top of a pair of trousers. I dug my hand into the pocket and closed my hand around the glass vial, then pulled it out and up to inspect it. Not even a drop remained inside.

Fucking evil bastard. This wasn't just something he had lying around. He'd gone out of his way to get this. He planned on disabling her ability to wield before this attack even started.

She stood and slowly padded toward me. "It's true, isn't it? My magic is gone." Her voice was broken and strained.

"No, not gone," I said, turning to face her. "At least, not forever. No tonic can take away a wielder's magic forever. It should wear off."

Aliya's lip trembled. "What if it doesn't?"

I didn't know what to say. The truth was, I wasn't so sure what would happen now. I knew very little about potions and tonics. And though the words I was saying felt true, I couldn't be certain.

I cupped her face in my bloodied hands, forcing her to meet my eyes. "We'll figure it out in time. Right now, the only thing that matters is you're safe, and he can't hurt you again."

She nodded, still shaking, and pressed her forehead to mine. "I was so scared."

"I know." I kissed her fiercely and desperately. "But you're safe now. I'll always keep you safe."

Below us, the howls rose louder. Not howls of pain or death. Howls of victory.

I strode to the edge of the wall and peered down. A small handful of cusith were fleeing down the main road toward the forest, chased away by Jax and three deltas. The battle was over. The pack had won, but at a cost I didn't want to imagine.

I pulled her close and stood, one arm braced around her waist. "Come. We must go down. They'll need us."

We descended together, leaving Coda's body cooling on the rooftop.

When we reached the courtyard, the sight stopped my heart.

There was blood everywhere. Wolves sprawled across the stones, some still twitching with what life they still held onto, some gone forever. There were many cusith corpses laying in grotesque heaps, their blackness seeping into the cracks of the castle's foundation. The survivors licked their wounds, eyes haunted.

Victory tasted like ashes.

Aliya clutched my hand, her eyes wide with horror. "So many..."

I tightened my grip, my jaw hardening. "This isn't over. But as long as we stand together, we will survive."

I looked over the crimson desolation and prayed the words were true.

CHAPTER 20
ALIYA

The courtyard smelled of ash and blood.

I stood in the ruins of what should have been a celebration. Lace and roses were trampled into filth, and wine goblets were shattered under claw marks. The marble tiles were slick with black and red. The cries of the wounded echoed from every corner, and wolves howled in mourning as bodies were carried inside.

I couldn't breathe past the weight in my chest.

It was my fault. All of it.

If I had finished the ward around the borders, the cusith never would have gotten close enough. If I had trusted my instincts instead of waiting. If I had worked faster, harder...

When that beast had come for me in front of the cellar, I had nothing to defend myself. No magic. Nothing to save the children, nothing to protect myself or the babes in my belly. Just fear and failure.

Now the pack was paying for my weakness. Too many dead. Too many grieving.

I wrapped my arms around my belly, shuddering with feelings of loss and grief. The twins shifted within me, restless, as if they sensed my guilt.

"I'm so sorry," I whispered to them. "I should have protected you. I should have protected all of them."

"Child." Esther's voice was rough but steady as she hobbled toward me, her robes darkened with blood at the hem, but her eyes sharp as ever. "Do not take burdens on your shoulders that belong to Fate."

Tears burned behind my eyes. "If I had finished the ward—"

She lifted a gnarled hand to silence me. "You are one woman, not a goddess. Even a queen cannot be everywhere at once. The attack was not your fault."

"But my magic," I lamented. "It's gone. What if it never comes back? How can I protect anyone without it?"

Her gaze softened. She touched my cheek, then let her hand drift to my belly. "Your little ones are strong. I felt their heartbeats myself, steady as drums. And your magic will return when the potion leaves your blood. Do not let Coda's wickedness make you doubt your own power."

I swallowed hard, my vision blurring. "He almost—" My throat closed around the rest, the memory of his hands still burning my skin.

"I know." Her voice cracked, but only for a heartbeat. "But he's gone and can never hurt anyone again. The pack will not honor his name."

I nodded, though her words didn't deliver the comfort they'd intended.

I turned away and busied myself with cleaning what I could. My mates, with the help of the surviving deltas, were struggling to gather the bodies of the fallen wolves for a massive funeral pyre, and seeing how I wasn't strong enough to help them, I needed to feel useful. Thankfully, Raya and the other mothers joined me in my efforts.

Come dawn, the majority of the destruction and blood had been cleared away. One might never know the ballroom had seen such loss and pain to look at it. But the echoes of the screams would haunt me forever, and I would never be able to look at this once cherished space the same.

The dead had been collected and laid in rows across the courtyard beside the massive fire. Their fur was brushed clean, their eyes closed, their bodies wrapped in the remnants of silks torn from the ballroom. The pack surrounded them in a great circle, heads bowed, the silence deeper than any prayer.

Jax stood on one side of me, Tannin on the other, both still bruised and bloodied from the battle. Their presence was the only thing holding me upright.

An elder lifted his voice, a long, low howl that carried grief into the pale morning sky. One by one, others joined, the sound swelling into a keening chorus that rattled my bones. I tilted my face upward, tears streaming freely, and added my voice—not a howl, but a raw cry, torn from a throat too full of sorrow to hold it in.

When the last echoes faded, the bodies were carried to the pyre. Firelight licked across every tear-stained face. Smoke curled heavenward, carrying the souls of the fallen.

Coda's corpse was not among them. He had no pyre, no honor. His body had been dragged from the castle, left in the woods for carrion to pick clean. No one spoke his name. His betrayal would be remembered but not sanctified. If he had any help within the pack, no one had stepped forward to mourn him.

Even though he was gone, his shadow lingered. I felt it in the suspicious glances that slid toward me in the way some wolves whispered in corners. He had planted poison deeper than any tonic—a great distrust now grew.

Later, when the fires burned low, and the mourners drifted back to their homes, I remained in the courtyard alone. Every stone seemed stained with blood that would never wash away.

Such a strange funeral tradition, this pyre. It reminded me of the mass burial pyres at the height of the plague. I understood the need for it then. Fire had been hoped to halt the spread of the disease, and the numbers had been so high, ground burial would have been implausible.

When the last of my loved ones fell to the plague, I couldn't burn them. I'd dragged them to the field and dug their graves myself. My last-ditch attempt at holding onto them in some way. I wished I could hold onto those we lost last night, but now they were nothing but ash and smoke.

Tannin found me, brushing his knuckles across my arm as he came to stand beside me. "We survived."

Jax came up behind me, his hands warm on my shoulders. "But we can't pretend this is over. More will come."

"I know." My voice was hollow. "And I don't know if I'll be ready. I don't even know if I'll ever get my magic back."

Jax turned me, forcing me to meet his eyes. "Listen to me... you are more than your magic. You held this kingdom together with your heart, not just your power. That's what makes you our queen."

I wanted to believe him, wanted to feel strong. But all I could think of was the way my spells had fizzled into nothing when I needed them most.

I pressed both hands to my belly again, clinging to the only certainty I had left. "Another attack will come," I whispered. "And I don't know if we'll survive it."

The fire crackled before us, consuming the last of the dead, and for the first time since the plague, I wondered if Fate's plan for me was not to survive, but to sacrifice.

⁓

Night had fallen again by the time the courtyard was finally cleared. The last embers of the pyre smoldered like dying stars, their smoke curling into the heavens as if to remind the gods of every life lost.

I stood at the edge of the courtyard, the cool stone biting into the soles of my bare feet as I stared out at the forest beyond. It was silent now, too silent, as though the trees themselves were holding their breath.

But silence no longer meant safety.

The ward I had begun to build hummed in the distance, beckoning me, ready and waiting for a completion that might never come. My magic remained a void inside me, a well gone dry.

I pressed my hand to my belly, whispering a promise to the restless life within. "I'll protect you. Somehow."

Behind me, Jax and Tannin argued in low, urgent voices with Esther and the elders, debating strategies, speaking of patrols, rebuilding, preparing for another assault. The weight of leadership pressed heavier than ever, and yet none of us truly knew what we faced.

Then a sound drifted on the night wind. Not the cry of a wolf, not the screech of a lone cusith. An eerie, rattling song, like the blow of a death horn. Deep. Resonant. Inhuman and un-wolf-like.

It rose from the northern woods, a call and an answer, echoed by another in the west, then another in the east.

I froze, my blood running cold. That was no accident. No random beasts.

An army.

The cusith last night had been scouts. Testing us. We had survived their trial, but the true war was only beginning.

I tightened my grip on my elbows as the calls faded, replaced by the hush of a forest waiting for the next command.

Fate had brought me this far, had taken everything from me only to give me a new, unlikely kingdom in return. But if my magic didn't return, if I couldn't finish the ward, if I couldn't protect my people...

Then Varynia would fall, and with it, the last hope of uniting wolves and wielders.

The twins stirred within me, fussy, impatient, a reminder that time was slipping through my fingers.

And for the first time, I whispered the thought I had been too afraid to voice.

"What if Fate chose the wrong person to save?"

BABIES OF THE WOLF

BOOK FOUR

CHAPTER 1
JAX

The sun climbed over the peaked roofs of Varinya, heralding the start of a new day. Our surroundings appeared peaceful, as if we hadn't lost dozens of our wolves to the cusith last night, and we weren't waiting for them to attack once more.

The night rain had rinsed the cobblestones clean, glazing the courtyard in a crisp sheen that mirrored the sky. But sound has a memory that stone doesn't. I still heard the shrieks echoing inside my head. I still smelled the blood so deeply inside my nose, I could almost taste it.

Every place my gaze landed—a stair tread, a drain, the angled lip of a fountain—wore the ghost of a moment from three nights ago when the cusith came for us like a living avalanche.

Morning meant safety. The monsters hated the light, sulking in the shadows, all teeth and too much patience. Then dusk arrived and pulled a dark blanket over their backs, giving them courage to move once more.

The knowledge that we were currently safe should have steadied me. It didn't. Instead, I stood in the den, spine tight as a drawn bow, forcing my lungs to count to four on every inhale, reminding myself of the simplest truth I had left—I was the Alpha. These were my people. We needed a plan.

The den filled in slow tides. Elders first, their steps careful on the marble—Esther, calm and flinty-eyed, Wilda with her hawk's profile,

Morain in a shawl too fine for war, and Droger, who could curdle milk from twenty paces with a single grunt.

Then the surviving deltas, lean and gray around the edges from sleeplessness—Esme in the doorway, arms folded like a barricade, Amara at her shoulder, Aldric, the youngest, trying to make his fear look like focus. A few others we were used to seeing were simply...gone. Their chairs remembered them. Our hearts did, too.

No one took the Alpha's chair. Fine. I couldn't have sat if I'd tried.

"Thank you for coming," I said, and was stupidly proud when my voice didn't crack. "I know you're exhausted. We all are. But we don't get to be broken today, we get to be useful."

"Useful," Elvira echoed, a sting in the sugar of her tone. "Useful would have been the princess finishing the ward when she promised."

A murmur like dry grass in wind scraped around the room.

Tannin stepped up beside me, every muscle tight and a warning. "You know damn well Coda slipped her a magic-blocker before the attack," he said, each word clipping close to the bone. "If you want to be angry at anyone, you need to be angry at the traitor."

My hand found his wrist and squeezed once. I didn't need him setting fire to the tenuous bridge on which we all stood.

"Aliya's magic is suppressed," I said evenly. "It's not a choice, and it isn't permanent. When the tonic wears off, she'll complete the ward around the kingdom. Until then, we build stopgaps that work in daylight and hold through the night."

I let the silence sit. It was heavy, making us all listen.

Aldric raised his hand halfway, like a schoolboy. "What about a wall?" he offered, flushing when Droger's mouth already twitched. "Stone or wood maybe? It wouldn't stop them forever but—"

"But it would slow us down," Droger cut in, rolling his eyes. "You want to give the beasts furniture to smash? By the time you finish, we'll all be bones."

I lifted a palm. "I appreciate the thought, Aldric, but Droger's right. The cusith would simply ram the barrier or climb, and we don't have months. We barely have days."

Morain cleared her throat. "A moat, then. They can't swim. I remember that much."

"You also remember our water situation," I said, gentler. "We couldn't fill a moat big enough to matter. And even if we could, we'd drown half the village digging it."

The room sagged. That was the thing about hope. Too much of the wrong kind just made you more tired.

Aldric's hand lifted again, slower. "Not a wall. Not a moat. A...shelter? Underground. A place for the children and elders when the howls start. A panic room with earth for armor."

Droger's snort tried to bulldoze him, but a stern glare from Esther nailed the old wolf to his chair.

I weighed the simple idea in my mind. Aliya had hustled our non-fighters into the wine cellar during the attack, and the stone held.

"As a last resort, yes," I said. "We'll survey basements and tunnels. But wolves don't win wars under floors." I let my gaze rake faces. "We win them together, above ground."

"What we need is steel in hands," Esme said from the door. "Bows on the parapets, spears at the gates, knives where knives belong. We need fighters."

"More deltas," Amara added. "Twice as many as we have."

The argument I'd been shaping jolted clear, simple as a name. "Not just deltas," I said. "Everyone."

The word hit like a thrown plate. Heads jerked, and a few mouths opened and forgot what they planned to say.

"Everyone?" Esther asked, eyebrows tipping up.

"Everyone," I repeated. "Every wolf old enough to shift learns to fight, starting today. Those who can't shift or can't hold steel learn something else—to lay traps, to sound alarm horns, to shoot from a distance, to carry the wounded without dropping them. We don't separate the pack into fighters and fragile. We don't have fragile. We have wolves. We act like it."

"You mean to send children to war?" Elvira demanded.

"I mean to make sure no one stands in a courtyard screaming with empty hands while monsters pour through the streets," I clarified with authority. "Prepared isn't the same as expendable. Kids will never meet a cusith alone. They'll be in teams, with me." I lifted my chin. "You want to debate? Debate with me tomorrow, after we make it through tonight."

Silence rang again. The listening kind, not the sulking kind. Then came the chorus of exhales that meant the decision had settled.

"Bows and arrows," Esme said, recovering first. "There's an armory in the east tower. I saw racks."

"Good," I said. "You and Amara are with me after this. Count fletched arrows, count heads, and make a list of anything we can sharpen into spears."

"Consider it done," Amara replied.

I nodded and scanned the room. The other thing we had to say was uglier, and it would curdle in the shadows if I didn't haul it into daylight.

"One more matter," I said, feeling Tannin's attention sharpen beside me. "We left Coda's body at the edge of the village. Someone checked this morning." I let the beat land. "It's gone."

The words rolled around the den, hitting ribs and finding old bruises.

"Scavengers," Droger said quickly, like an amulet against worse possibilities. "Wolves, boar, carrion birds."

"Maybe," I allowed, and I wanted to believe him. "Or maybe one of the night things dragged him off to eat later. Either way—he's not our problem anymore."

The pack wanted to spit on his grave. They couldn't if there wasn't one. I could feel the unease tightening throats and fists.

"Listen to me," I said, pushing steel into my voice. "Dead is dead. What matters is the living. We lock each entrance point at dusk. We move in pairs. We keep a count on the children at all times."

That got me a few bleak smiles.

I straightened, and the room straightened with me. "Orders. Esme, Amara, survey the armory. Aldric and Hayden, round up the youth at the courtyard by third bell. They're with me. Wilda, you and Morain take inventory of basements and root cellars. Take note of any that could hold twenty breathing bodies without you fainting from the smell. Esther, I want elders visible on the training field. If the old fight, the young won't dare shrink. Droger—"

"Yes, Alpha?" He leaned back, suspicious of what job I would give him.

"Food stations," I said. "You'll organize them. I want broth and bread ready at sundown. Fighters need fuel."

He blinked, then harrumphed. "Broth, I can do."

"Good," I said. "Go. Bring me the pack by three."

They started to spill out in clumps, orders carried on their shoulders like burdens they could finally name. The den lightened by degrees.

Esther lingered, as she so often did. She squeezed my forearm as the last of the deltas brushed past.

"This is right," she said softly. "They need to see themselves as wolves again."

"We'll give them a reason to bite," I said, and only after she left did I let my jaw unclench.

Tannin waited for me to breathe, then shouldered me with fraternal irritation. "You were about three seconds from tearing out Elvira's throat," he muttered.

"I was about one from tearing out Droger's," I added. "Be honest. Did I sound like an arrogant ass?"

"You sounded like the Alpha," he said simply.

He shifted his weight the way he did when there was something he didn't want to say. "About Coda..."

"He's dead," I said, too quickly. Saying it made it truer. "I won't waste daylight worrying over a carcass. Not when there are hands to put bows in."

He grunted, which for Tannin meant we'd say more later, over whiskey or blood, whatever the day served.

The castle breathed around us. The hearth crackled, the distant clattering of pans sounded, and Twila's peal of laughter somewhere down a hall made something in my chest go liquid for a second.

This was what I'd dreamed of as a boy—our people in rooms that didn't leak, kitchens that smelled like butter and not smoke, elders who wore velvet because they could. Fate had delivered it with scars.

Esme reappeared at the threshold with Amara on her heels, both already dusted with tower grit.

"Armory's intact," she reported, efficient as always. "Three longbows strung, five needing new strings. A crate of arrows, two good quivers' worth. Spears are a lost cause. All the shafts are split. But there are halberds. And...a ballista crank."

"A what?" Tannin said, eyebrows pinched.

"A very large crossbow," Amara explained, her grin daring the day to fight back. "If we can find the rest of it."

"We'll make do," I said. "Get the bows oiled. Amara, find someone with hands gentle enough to restring. Maybe Raya, if she'll sit still long enough. We'll tie practice straw in the courtyard."

Amara nodded and strode off. Esme didn't move.

"What is it?" I asked.

She tipped her chin, eyes flinty. "You can't run every line yourself. If you're training the pups, you need lieutenants who can shout at adults without flinching."

"I have a beta," I said, giving Tannin a sideways look.

He smirked.

"You have one," she said. "You need five."

She wasn't wrong.

"Congratulations," I said dryly. "You've just promoted yourself."

She blinked and almost smiled. "I'll earn it."

"You already did," I said, and I meant it. "Go. Make a list of names. I want them on the field by three."

She nodded once and strode out, her shadow cutting long and sure across the floor.

When the door shut behind her, Tannin exhaled a low whistle. "You sure about that?"

"She's loyal," I said. "And smart. We need both."

"Still," he muttered. "Esme doesn't exactly...take orders quietly."

"Good," I said, rubbing the tension from the back of my neck. "The quiet ones don't win wars."

He laughed under his breath. "I guess that makes three of us."

For a heartbeat, it almost felt like peace.

I looked toward the window, where morning bled into gold across the courtyard, and muttered to myself, "Let's hope we last the day."

CHAPTER 2
ALIYA

The castle had lungs. Even when no one moved through the corridors, I could feel the silence breathing slowly, patiently, predatory.

The wind threaded through the cracks in the stained-glass windows, humming along the seams of the stone, and every strange musical note reminded me of the voices this place used to hold. Servants laughing in the kitchens. Guards barking drills in the yard. My mother's piano from the east wing.

Now there was only me. Well, me, Tabitha, and the faint pulse of two small lives turning inside my belly.

I traced my fingertips across the curve that rose just below my ribs. They were only weeks old, and yet I swore I could already sense their different rhythms—one steady and strong, the other fluttering like a curious bird. My twins. My two tiny miracles that had somehow survived the same darkness that devoured everyone else.

And I couldn't protect them anymore. Not without the power that was supposed to be mine. Even worse, taken.

The magic-blocker Coda had slipped into my drink still burned like a memory in my veins. When I reached for the familiar spark inside me, there was nothing. No warmth. No answering hum. Just a hollow ache under my sternum, as if someone had scooped out the center of me and left the edges to rattle like an empty tin can.

"Meow," Tabitha announced from her perch on the window ledge, her tail flickering once at me.

"I know," I told her. "I'm brooding again."

She stretched, unimpressed. Typical feline wisdom—eat, nap, survive. If only life could be distilled so neatly. I wondered if she had any idea of the danger that plagued the rest of us.

Down in the courtyard, the pack were busily preparing for something. Through the glass, I caught the echo of Jax's voice, low and decisive, and the softer counterpoint of Tannin's, threading reassurance between orders.

Even from here, I sensed the ripple of authority in Jax's tone, the way it filled the air and left no space for fear. He carried leadership like a torch. A bright, guiding light with dangerous potential.

And all I could do was watch from the sidelines. I felt like Rapunzel in her tower, but where she didn't have a choice other than to stay, I was here avoiding everyone. Ignoring the fact that I was now useless and in doing so, all but abandoning the people I was meant to serve.

The irony wasn't lost on me. A wielder princess guarded by the very beasts I'd been raised to fear.

I left the window and turned back to the library. On the reading table lay the books I'd been pretending to study. Volumes on magical detoxification, pregnancy in shifters, and a grimoire whose pages smelled faintly of smoke.

I'd read the same paragraph four times without absorbing a word. Every spell I tried to recite fizzled into nothing. My hands itched to do something—to matter—but the emptiness inside me swallowed each attempt.

Tabitha walked over to me, tail high, and sprawled across my open book. Her golden eyes blinked slowly, as if to say, "*Accept defeat, foolish human.*"

"Traitor," I murmured, scratching behind her ears anyway.

She purred, the sound a low motor that settled some nervous part of me I hadn't realized was trembling.

The door creaked, and I nearly jumped before Tannin's familiar scent reached me.

"Sorry," he said softly, stepping inside. "I didn't mean to scare you."

"You didn't," I lied, smoothing my hair.

He leaned on the doorframe, a smudge of soot along his jaw, shirt unbuttoned two notches from whatever task he'd abandoned. "Jax sent me to check on you."

"I'm fine." I turned toward the shelves to hide the tremor in my hands. "Just restless."

"You don't have to keep proving your strength to us," he said. "You've already done that a hundred times."

"Tell that to my magic." The words came out sharper than intended. I softened my voice. "It's like having a limb missing or something. I can feel where it should be."

Tannin crossed the room and stopped beside me. Our reflections stood shoulder to shoulder in the mirror, his green eyes catching the afternoon light. "Then we'll bring it back. Esther thinks the blocker will burn out in a few more days."

"And if she's wrong?"

"Then we keep you alive until she's right."

I almost laughed. "That's your solution to everything."

"It's worked so far."

He brushed a stray lock of hair behind my ear, his fingers lingering just long enough to anchor me. The simple touch broke through the numbness I'd been clinging to. I wanted to lean into him, to draw strength from his calm certainty, but half the pack already doubted my right to exist. I couldn't allow myself a moment of vulnerability.

Still, I didn't step away.

He dropped his hand first, clearing his throat. "We found something you should know."

"What is it?"

"Coda's body." His voice lowered. "It's gone."

For a heartbeat, the world tilted. "Gone? As in?"

"As in not there. Jax thinks the scavengers got to him. Esther says the forest takes back what it's owed." He rubbed the back of his neck. "I don't like either answer."

Neither did I. The memory of Coda's death was still raw—the flash in his eyes before they went dull. I'd thought that was the end. Now the idea of that body going missing made every hair on my arms rise.

"Do you think...could he have survived?"

"No." Tannin's reply was immediate. "I watched the light leave his eyes, heard his heart stop beating."

"Then something else moved him."

"Maybe." His tone said he didn't believe it was anything we could name.

I hugged my arms, suddenly cold. "If the cusith dragged him—"

"Then he got what he deserved," he said gently.

I looked past him to the table, to the small object I'd left near the grimoire. The vial. I'd kept it after Tannin had fished it out of Coda's pocket, more out of spite than usefulness, though I'd told myself a hundred times it might help to understand what I'd been given.

I picked it up and studied it in my hand. "Esme should see this."

Tannin followed my gaze. "The vial?"

"She knows traders," I said. "Coda didn't brew this himself, which means someone gave it to him."

Tannin's jaw tightened, and he nodded. "Come on. She's in the east tower."

I tucked the vial into my pocket and followed him into the hall. Tabitha hopped to the floor and trotted ahead of us as if she'd appointed herself our escort.

We crossed the ballroom, the afternoon sun laying long stripes across the marble. At the stairwell, Esme's new authority already hung in the air like a clean scent—voices obeyed more quickly, steps moved more decisively.

It struck me that Jax's choice to promote her had been more than strategy, it had been a signal. *Trust this wolf. She is mine, and therefore yours.*

The east tower armory smelled of oil and cordite. Sunlight slanted through narrow arrow slits, turning dust into drifting silver. Racks of bows lined one wall, bundles of arrows, some fletched, some not, lay in open crates. On the central table, Esme and Amara were assessing halberds, their blades stacked like fallen moons.

Esme looked up first. She'd tied her hair back with a strip of leather, and a smudge of grease streaked one temple like war paint.

"Good afternoon, Princess," she said, clipped but not unkind. "What do you need?"

I pulled the vial from my pocket and extended it to her. "This is what Coda used on me. I was hoping you could tell me where it came from."

Esme didn't answer at once. She turned the glass over in her hands, studying the subtle twist in the neck, the shade of the green glass, the way the tin collar had been crimped and wired, and finally, the wax. She worked at it with a thumbnail until a sliver lifted, revealing the faint impression stamped into its face—three dots forming a triangle under a crescent line.

Her pupils sharpened. "Ahh," she breathed. "The Romari."

I gave her a quizzical look.

"The gypsy outpost west of the old toll bridge," she elaborated. "They use a crescent and three stars as their trader mark." She flipped the tin collar over with a knuckle. "And this knot—see how it's wired, not soldered? They don't waste solder on blockers. They save it for healers' vials and sleep draughts."

My heart kicked hard. "So, Coda bought it from them?"

"Most likely," Esme said. "That would explain his disappearance a few days before the attack."

"How long does it last?" I asked, trying not to sound desperate.

Her lips flattened as sympathy softened her eyes, and she shook her head. "I don't know. I'm afraid only the Romani would know."

I chewed on my lip as I mulled that over. "Well, how far away is the outpost?"

Esme's gaze shifted to Tannin before returning to me. "About a day's journey."

"Absolutely not," Tannin snapped as I turned to him before I could even voice my request.

"The Romani are the only ones who can tell us how long the effects of the tonic last," I argued.

"So what?" he countered. "What does it matter if they tell us it's six days or six weeks?"

My rising desperation was triggering my temper, causing little feet to kick inside my belly. "It matters because then we'll know what we're dealing with. Knowing how long the effects last will tell us what to plan for. And maybe they'll have a solution."

"I'm not gambling your life or the lives of our children on a maybe," he asserted. "I'm not taking you out of the kingdom."

I arched an eyebrow at him. "In case you haven't noticed, I'm just as safe out there as I am in here. We have no ward, no magic, and fewer fighters than we had a week ago."

His jaw clenched, his teeth grinding as he continued to glare at me.

"Besides, I'm going whether you come with me or not," I added.

He scoffed. "You don't even know the way."

I shrugged. "All the more reason for you to escort me."

He pinched the bridge of his nose and closed his eyes, letting out a long-suffering sigh.

I couldn't just sit in this castle, watching everyone else taking action. My magic was our most powerful weapon against the cusith, and we all needed it back. I didn't care if he locked me up in my room and posted guards outside my door twenty-four-seven, I *was* going to that trading outpost, no matter what I had to do to get there.

"I can take you," Esme volunteered after a beat of tense silence.

Tannin and I both looked at her, him with defeat and me with hope.

"I know the way better than anyone else," she said. "And I've dealt with them several times over the years. They know me."

Tannin folded his arms. "So, your first act as second beta is to put the princess's life at risk in the forest?"

She cut him a confident glare. "No, my first act as a second beta is to ensure she doesn't die trying to wander through it on her own."

He let out a heavy sigh, then shook his head. "Fine. I'm coming too."

Joy burst in my chest, but I kept my expression cool and collected, with only the crack of a smirk in the corners of my lips. "Thank you."

"But if we're doing this, we're doing it on my terms," he said. "We'll leave at first light tomorrow morning. Walking will take far too long, and we can't afford to be out after dark. We'll have to go in our wolf forms to cut as much time as possible."

Esme and I both frowned at him.

"But I'm human," I reminded him.

"Which is why you're going to ride on my back," he said. "I'll have Finnick, the pack leather craftsman, produce a saddle for my wolf to wear. That way you'll be able to ride safely and comfortably."

"Okay," I agreed, appreciating the idea. Then I frowned again, chewing on my lip. "What do we tell Jax?"

Tannin's form stiffened, a shadow falling over his eyes. "Nothing. Jax would never allow us to do something so reckless, and if he hears about this, he'll do everything in his power to stop us."

A knot of guilt twisted in my stomach, my mouth filling with a coppery taste. "Won't he notice us missing?"

Tannin glanced out the window, where Jax was directing several people below. "He's got a lot going on, what with the new pack training he's developing. Hopefully, he'll be too preoccupied."

Esme's expression sharpened, professional now. "I'll cover my absence with Amara and Aldric and put Morain on watch scheduling with Esther. Droger can bark at the kitchens in my stead. Just as long as we get back before nightfall."

Tannin sighed heavily, nodding as he stared down at the floor. "Okay. I guess we have a plan. Esme, meet us outside the garden at dawn. Aliya, let's go find Finnick and hope he can fashion a saddle on such short notice."

He led the way toward the stairs, but I paused, turned back to Esme, and quickly hugged her before following him out. I was so grateful for her help. Jax definitely made the right choice in appointing her as second beta.

I just hoped I was making the right choice in forcing both betas to abandon their posts and join me on this possible fool's errand.

<h1 style="text-align:center">CHAPTER 3
TANNIN</h1>

The early afternoon sun shone brightly in the center of the sky as Aliya and I crept into the garden, ensuring few shadows to betray our trek to Finnick's shop. Voices carried from the courtyard on the other side of the castle, but still, I wanted to be as quiet as possible and stick to the tree line until we could slip into the village.

I kept seeing the same image when I blinked—Aliya perched on my back, her hands tight on leather straps, my paws beating against the ground, and a single bad step turning speed into devastation. It wasn't the fall I feared, it was the jolt. Two tiny lives inside her being shaken like dice.

"This is foolish," I muttered to myself, to Fate, to the itch under my skin that wouldn't stop until we had a plan that felt like more than hope.

Aliya's hand slipped into mine. "It's necessary," she assured me.

I wanted to disagree, but I couldn't deny the truth of her earlier argument. We needed her magic back if we had any hope of defending against the cusith. Jax's plan of training everyone was a last-ditch effort, one that might end with the entire pack perishing. This kingdom had already seen one population go extinct, and the thought of a second made my insides hollow out.

"Come on," I said, squeezing her hand, then towing her behind me to follow the tree line.

Thankfully, we made it into the village without being seen and headed straight for our destination.

Finnick had set up his workshop in the southern center of the western quadrant. He'd claimed the space three days after we arrived and turned it into a shrine to practical miracles. Leather looped from ceiling pegs like drying meat. Strips of rawhide hung in tidy rows. There were awls in cups, stamps in trays, and thread in cakes of wax. The place smelled of oil and hide and something like pepper.

Finnick looked up from his workbench when we stepped inside, his hands already black with polish and a strip of dark leather across his lap. Finnick was a few years older than me, late twenties maybe, but a hunch to his posture and the rust-colored scruff that framing his face made him look middle-aged.

"Beta," he said with a nod for me. He stood and inclined his head deeper for Aliya. "Princess."

"Hey, Finn," I said. "I'm just gonna cut to the chase. We need something unusual."

His mouth tilted at one corner. "Those are my favorite problems."

I shut the door and slid the drop bar into place, not because I feared thieves but because I needed fewer eyes. "This stays between us," I prefaced. "No one else."

Finnick's gaze flicked between my face and the locked door. He nodded once. "Understood."

Aliya stepped forward with that queenly grace she carried without trying. "I need to ride Tannin in his wolf form safely. We were hoping you could craft a saddle for me to sit on."

His eyes lit with intrigue as he studied both of us. "When do you need it?"

"Tomorrow morning, but hopefully as early as possible," I said.

"Hmm." He rubbed his scarred thumb along the grain of the leather in his hands, thinking. "Wolves aren't built like horses. We don't have withers to hold a pommel, and our spines flex more, our backs drop when we run. If I strap something too rigid to you, you'll both hate me by the first hill."

"I already hate you a little," I said dryly.

His smirk widened, and he held out his hands in a beckoning gesture. "Let me have a look at you."

I glanced at the shuttered windows, at the slit of light at the bottom of the door. The workshop was secluded enough, but I couldn't help but be wary.

After a beat, I stripped down, gathering my clothes and setting them on top of the workbench. The change came like a crack of heat along my bones, easy and practiced as breathing. Fur sprouted, limbs lengthening, teeth and claws sharpened. The floor rose toward me and I lowered toward it, then I was on four paws, the leather and oil smell suddenly as potent as a miasma.

Finnick circled me, hands behind his back as he examined me like a lab rat. I'd been naked in public thousands of times—it was the way of our kind—but being so closely scrutinized had my insides clenching nervously.

"You're bigger than I remember," he teased lightly.

I chose to take that as a compliment.

He leaned over my side and pressed two fingers to the ridge where my shoulders rolled. "The saddle can't sit here. It needs to float. If it pinches this, you'll lose your stride."

He turned and looked at Aliya. "Where's your center of gravity?"

"Nonexistent," I replied for her, my playful sentiment dulled by the growl of my voice.

Aliya laughed anyway and laid her hand on my head, her thumb smoothing between my ears in that way that made my hackles forget they existed.

"I'm fairly balanced," she said to Finnick. "Though it has gotten much harder as quickly as my belly is growing. I'll definitely need something to hold onto."

"And something to keep you from sliding with the babies," he said, already moving.

He hauled down a roll of thick, supple leather from a shelf and set it on the table. "We'll do a low pommel and a raised cantle, forming a sort of cup for your seat so you don't fight momentum. I'll add a breast collar to keep the saddle from sliding back and a crupper to keep it from sliding forward."

Aliya blinked. "A what?"

"A strap under the tail," Finnick said. "He'll hate it."

I bared my teeth in a very human expression, which he pretended not to notice.

"And we'll pad the belly cinch wide," he continued. "Wider than a horse's, to spread the pressure so it doesn't bite. Two cinches, actually. One belly, one farther back. Both with quick releases. Princess, if anything goes wrong, you pull left, then pull right, and you fall free. Understood?"

"Yes," she said, though her eyes flashed when he said *fall*.

"No metal rings," I said. "If we run, they'll jangle."

Finnick nodded. "I'll stitch leather loops with waxed thread for tie-down points." He looked at Aliya's middle, then back at her face, respectfully blunt.

"We'll add a sling. Not for the babies," he added before I could bite him. "For your hips. Think of it like a belt that cradles from both sides and takes the bounce off your back. The weight will be in the fabric, not in you."

Aliya touched her belly as if it had ears. "That sounds...better."

He reached for a scrap of chalk. "Let me sketch it, and you tell me what scares you."

He chalked fast, the design of a saddle quickly coming together on the top of the work bench with impressive artistic skill. He added two short, stout handholds stitched to the pommel, then he drew something that looked like a folded strap against the saddle's left side, with a looped tail.

"What's that?" Aliya asked.

"A drop step," he said. "When you mount, you won't jump from the ground every time. Wolves are tall. You'll flip this down with your hand, step up, swing over, and it flips back with your heel. It's quiet and eliminates the needs for metal hinges." He glanced at me. "You'll stand still for her."

"I'll be a statue," I promised.

"Statues don't breathe," Aliya said softly, looking at me in that way that made everything inside me turn warm. "Do that, at least."

Finnick rummaged in a crate and produced a bundle of sheepskin too clean to have lived in the forest.

"Padding," he said, rubbing it between his fingers and thumb.

"You'll thank me for this when he's running at top speed." He weighed the sheepskin in his hand again, as if calculating how many layers it would take to tell the ground to be kind.

Then he clapped once, focus sharpening his eyes. "Alright, I can build a first pass in two hours using a wagon tree as the base. Not perfect, but good enough to test fit. If it works, I'll refine through the night."

"Two hours?" Aliya's eyes widened. "How—"

"Because I'm brilliant," he said without heat. "And because I've made harnesses for crates on wolf backs before. Not for riding, but the tree is the same."

"You've done this?" I asked, startled.

"Carried loads," he corrected. "Meat for winter, supplies over ice, things like that. Wolves don't like it, but sometimes we need legs more trustworthy than wheels. There was a year the river didn't freeze right and we had to—" He cut himself off with a shrug. "Stories for another time."

I nodded and exhaled a preparatory breath. "Okay, let's do it."

He nodded and set to work, first taking measurements of a dozen different angles of my body, then getting to cutting. I shifted back to my human form to be useful, fetching supplies as soon as he asked, then working with Aliya to sand edges and rub them with tallow till they gleamed.

The sound of it all—the pulling of thread, the soft *thunk* of a punch through hide, the rhythm of Finnick's breath—smoothed my anxiety into something that felt like purpose. Something about using my hands toward a goal always seemed to narrow my focus away from any inner turmoil, and right now, I was grateful for it.

When the rough prototype lay on the table, Finnick wiped his hands and looked at me. "Go ahead and shift. Let's try it on you."

I did, positioning myself like a model on display. I braced for discomfort as they lifted the saddle tree together, but when they set it on my back behind the roll of my shoulders, discomfort didn't come. The weight spread wide, not deep. It was more like a heavy coat in winter.

Finnick's hands moved quickly around my ribs as he ran the first cinch under my belly. He eased the strap snug, not tight, then added the second cinch farther back. He fitted the breast collar next, adjusting until the Y sat equal over my chest without choking. Last came the crupper, slid under my tail with the sort of apology only a craftsman can give without words.

"Alright," he said, stepping back to look at me the way painters look at their murals. "Princess?"

Aliya moved as if every motion had been rehearsed with the moon watching. She flipped down the leather step with her toe, placed one foot, and rose smoothly. She swung her leg over and settled into the shallow seat, her breath catching a few times until it found the rhythm of mine.

The room went so quiet, I could hear my own heartbeat in my ears. She was lighter than I anticipated. The sling hugged her hips the way Finnick promised, absorbing the bounce I'd been bracing to protect her from, and her knees sat where my ribcage wouldn't mind them.

"Are you alright up there?" I asked.

"I'm alright," she whispered, and I felt the truth of it through the line of her body.

Finnick adjusted the cantle a finger's breadth, tightened the second cinch a hair, then loosened it back half that because he listened to instinct better than rulers. He guided Aliya's foot to the drop step folded back under the leather, showing her how to nudge it down without looking. He tapped the quick-release tails lightly, so she'd know how they felt under her fingers instead of by sight.

"Walk," he instructed me.

There wasn't much space in this shop to move around, but I took several slow, cautious steps. The saddle didn't slide. The weight didn't pinch. Aliya swayed with me as if we'd done this a hundred times in dreams.

"Turn," Finnick said.

I did, careful not to disturb the shelves. The breast collar took the pressure and kept the tree straight. Aliya's left hand tightened and then loosened. She learned the arc of my shoulder quickly, the way to lean into it without fighting my balance.

"Okay, I think we have enough here for me to create the finished product," Finnick said. "It would be better if I could see how it works with you at speed, but under the circumstances, we'll have to manage without that."

He helped Aliya down, then began to unfasten the straps as Aliya watched carefully. I was relieved when the saddle was removed, and I shifted back with a new respect for horses.

"Come back this evening," Finnick said as he set the saddle on the workbench. "I should have it ready after dinner... sooner if I didn't have to go to that training thing Jax is doing."

I stepped into my pants and pulled them. "I'll tell him you're working on armor, which actually isn't a bad idea now that I think about it."

His brows perked, and he nodded in agreement. "I'll get right on that—after this is finished, of course."

"Thanks, Finnick. We'll return tonight."

He nodded and went right back to work before we even headed toward the door. The sun hung lower in the sky, telling me I'd soon be needed at the courtyard to help with training. We had to get back before we were missed.

Though, as much as I believed in this plan, I couldn't deny that part of me hoped Jax would catch us. Aliya's safety would be completely in my hands during this stealth mission, and I was terrified of what would happen to her and our babies if I failed.

JAX

The massive black wolf snarled at me, spittle stringing from his canines, and I snarled right back.

Tannin's wolf lurched, his shoulder slamming into my ribs. I slid under, lowered my weight, and let his force travel past, my jaws ghosting the hinge of his foreleg without closing. He twisted swiftly and tried to hook my hock with his forepaw to topple me. I popped my hips, planted myself, and drove my chest into his to steal his base, snapping at his muzzle just enough to mark the angle that would break a bite if either of us meant it.

Around us the courtyard ringed tight with wolves, their ears pricked and their claws ticking on the flagstones as they watched us. The only humans standing were the archers Esme had already pulled into a neat line at the far wall. Everything else that could bite stood on four legs.

Tannin feinted high, his mouth open for my throat.

I showed him my throat and didn't give it, dropping low at the last heartbeat and ramming his shoulder with mine. He went light for a blink, stunned, then rolled and came up on my flank to test my hocks. I slashed a paw across his nose in a warning that would've blinded a fool, but he was no fool. He gave me a wolfy grin and came back harder.

We weren't performing, we were teaching. Every move was a lesson.

This is where you put your weight, this is where you don't. If your teeth can't reach, your body still can.

I let him crowd me toward the balance plank because I wanted the watchers to see that losing ground wasn't losing the fight. He pressed relentlessly, and I gave patiently.

When his hind paw crossed itself for an instant in eagerness, I flowed to the outside and checked his ribs with mine to turn him sideways. My jaws caught the soft hollow underneath his jaw with just enough pressure, and he stilled.

I eased off, letting him right himself.

Across the square, the archers' strings gave a soft collective twang as Esme ran them through a dry warm-up.

"Relax that elbow. Don't lean into your shot. Breathe out," she instructed.

Tannin's ear flicked toward the sound. He surged again, low and fast, and we clashed once more. He bumped my knee the way we'd practiced a thousand times, and I let it buckle, using the fall to hook his foreleg and throw him over my hip. He fell and slid backward, laughing in that short wolf way, then charged.

We tangled until the ring around us leaned in so hard I could feel their breath on my back. Then I broke clean and shook dust from my coat, turning to face our audience.

"You saw two truths," I said, my chest heaving but steady. "One—hips win. If your hips are wrong, your teeth don't matter. Two—throats are traps. Hocks and shoulders are where survival lies. You want a creature to stop moving? Take its movement."

The wolves hung on my words like ropes in a turbulent tide. Now it was time to test how well they listened.

"We're going to start by splitting everyone into groups," I announced. "Amara and Elvira will take the women. Tannin, Hayden and Asher will take the men. And the children will be with me. Go."

The sea of fur shuffled and separated in the directions their leaders led, and I guided my group of young, high-energy pups to the far eastern corner of the courtyard.

They bounded after me, twenty small and medium-sized wolves, their ears too big for their faces, their curiosity bigger than the yard. Twila led like she'd been born with rank in her bones, her coat a dark, unruly river and chalk still smeared on her nose from some earlier crime.

"Split up into teams of three," I rumbled. "As pups, your strength is not in mass or muscle, but in numbers. Your team must learn to move like one body. If you're not big enough to bite deep, you need to be fast enough to make a bite possible. That's your job. You harry, you trip, you blind, and then you get out of the way so the big mouths can finish."

The pups broke off into groups of three, a bit more playfully and less disciplined than I would have liked. But I had to remind myself that children learned through play, and if they could find enjoyment in this exercise, I needed to let them have it.

Twila's tail whipped as she pushed to the front of her team. A small gray nudged her shoulder in challenge, and she nudged back, asserting her dominance. I had to admire her budding Alpha energy.

I paired each team against another, having them fight while I critiqued their movements and offered guidance. With their energy and determination to win, it was easier than I expected to teach them. Perhaps it was because the primal nature was more potent in pups. They hadn't had a lifetime of humanity to dull their instincts.

A tiny cinnamon wolf on Twila's team missed a feint and tumbled. Twila shoulder-checked the threat for her and shoved her friend back into the line with a growl I'd be proud to hear at twice her size. The cinnamon pup shook herself, planted, and did not fall again.

"Again," I said, and their little bodies swarmed again.

After perhaps an hour of training, my charges were doing better than the groups of adults I stole glances at. They had learned to slide under lunges, to put as much priority on hocks as they did on throats, and to use the momentum of being thrown to their advantage.

We worked until tongues lolled and the sun hung just above the western mountains. The pups were barely panting, but everyone else was visibly spent, and we couldn't afford to push this session into nightfall.

"Enough," I barked, and the courtyard exhaled.

The elders ushered everyone into the castle for food and water, and the courtyard slowly emptied. Esme unstrung bows and sent archers by threes to oil and rack them while Amara stacked straw dummies against the wall.

Twila launched herself at me and then remembered herself mid-air, landing with both front paws just on my toes. She wagged, the entire back end of her body trying to detach with enthusiasm.

I lowered my head and bumped her forehead with mine in a silent gesture of praise.

She went still all over, pride making her eyes bright. Then she trotted off with her triad like a general who'd just won a small war and didn't want anyone making a fuss about it.

I shifted at the fountain base and climbed back into my clothes as the last of the pack disappeared for the evening. The village was still and quiet, the only sound that of voices carrying from the castle doors.

The first hints of navy lined the eastern horizon like a warning, and I wondered how many eyes watched me from the slowly growing shadows.

Today was only the beginning. We'd continue training every day, and eventually we'd be an army worth contending with. All we needed was time.

I just hoped the cusith—and Fate—would give us enough days for that to happen.

CHAPTER 5

ALIYA

I was awake well before the first glow of morning drifted through the curtains, though honestly, I wasn't sure I slept at all. My mind wouldn't stop playing scenarios of all the things that could go wrong on this journey, but it had to be done. Varynia needed my magic back.

I needed my magic back.

Jax had worked himself so hard yesterday that he'd slept like a log, which meant he didn't stir at all when Tannin and I crept out of bed.

Guilt was like poison in my veins as I gingerly put on comfortable clothes in the corner of the room with my back to him, trying not to glance at his sleeping form. I hated keeping secrets from him, and he would be furious when he discovered us gone, but as long as this trip resulted in getting my magic back, it would be worth facing his wrath when we returned.

Finally, I was fully dressed in smart riding clothes—a loose long-sleeved shirt, thick trousers, and sturdy boots. I wrapped a strip of gauze tightly around my belly for added support. Not that I didn't trust Finnick's craftsmanship, I just wanted to take every precaution to keep my babies safe.

I slid my palm over the curve of my belly, relieved to find that the twins were just as listless and peaceful as Jax, unburdened by my own feelings of unease and anxiety. I hoped they stayed that way until the day was done.

A hand gently landed on my shoulder, and I jumped, letting a gasp slip through my tight lips.

Tannin loomed around me, pressing a finger to his pursed lips, then mouthing the word *Sorry*.

I let out a shaky breath, willing myself to calm down, to focus. If I was this jittery now, I'd be completely useless on the road when it counted.

"You ready?" he whispered so softly that I relied on the movement of his lips to understand.

I nodded.

With a simple nod of his head, he led me to the door. I was beyond grateful when the slab of wood gave without creaking, and we floated into the hall like a pair of ghosts. Tannin closed the door so slowly, so gently, taking great care to turn the knob back to its resting position without making a sound.

A false sense of relief came over me before I schooled it. We might have gotten past Jax, but we still had to sneak down three flights of stairs, across the ground floor, and out of the garden entrance without anyone seeing us. Not to mention we had to get past the sight of the deltas on watch duty.

We softly padded down the hall, keeping our feet on the long, narrow rug in hopes of muffling our steps. Many of the elders resided on this floor, and several of them were at the age that turned them into early risers.

I reminded myself that they'd have no reason to question me moving about. I was pregnant. I was the princess. I could give them any excuse, and they'd buy it.

Still, I knew that the fewer eyes fell on us, the better.

The stairs weren't as forgiving as the bedroom door. At least half of them creaked as we descended, locking my shoulders in a constant cringe, and my face in a grimace until we'd finally landed on the ground floor.

We turned along the shadowed wall that ran between the den and the ballroom, heading toward the kitchen.

A figure stepped out of the kitchen, and the silence tightened in my ears until I could hear the pounding of my own pulse. Esther stopped in the archway and regarded us with that keen, flinty gaze of hers.

"Why are you creeping around like thieves?" she asked, her tone both suspicious and playful.

I opened my mouth and then shut it again, because anything I offered would either be too much truth or not enough of it.

Esther's eyes moved from my face to Tannin's. She took in my attire and the early hour, and something in her expression shifted by a degree that only people who had lived with her would recognize.

"If you insist on using the kitchen entrance, be sure to close it firmly," she said, as if this were an ordinary household instruction. "I've seen mouse tracks on the counters, and I'd prefer to limit their access to our food."

I nodded, too surprised by her strange reaction to come up with a response.

She reached out and straightened the collar of my shirt with a maternal gentleness. "Am I to assume you'll be home in time for dinner, or should I save some for you?"

"We'll be here for dinner," Tannin said, his words both a reassurance and a promise.

She nodded, then patted Tannin's shoulder and said, "Good luck," before she shuffled past us into the den.

We quickly breezed through the kitchen and out into the garden. I did make sure to close the door firmly as Esther had requested. Esme stood on the other side of the wooden fence, her posture stiff and possibly impatient. The saddle hung at her side in her right hand.

Without a word, she turned and strode quickly into the trees, and we wasted no time in following her. The morning was crisp and chilly, the fog from our breath hinting at the coming autumn. Dew silvered the leaves, the moisture softening the brush underfoot so it didn't crunch at our steps.

Once we were far enough into the forest canopy for the castle not to be visible, Esme stopped, set the saddle on the ground, and began to disrobe. Tannin followed suit.

As many times as I'd seen grown men and women strip in front of me in the past weeks, you'd think I'd be used to it by now, but my cheeks still burned, and I felt the need to avert my gaze in an offer of privacy. I heard Esme chuckle, which only made me feel more foolish and naïve.

Tannin handed me his and Esme's clothes, which I stuffed into my satchel, and shifted. Watching them transform never failed to amaze me, and without an imminent threat to prompt his transition, he did so elegantly.

The sight was both terrifying and beautiful.

He stood square and calm while Esme lifted the saddle, and I steadied it onto his back. We worked together to fasten the straps under his belly and around his neck. The sharp sound of the crupper tightening made Tannin snarl and jerk his head angrily at Esme, who tossed him a smirk and wink.

I flipped down the leather step with my toe and placed my left foot where Finnick had taught me to put it. I rose without jerking and swung my right leg over. The sling gathered the bounce and spread it across my hips rather than my belly.

I set my hands on the low grips that sat in place of a horn, finding the under-cantle strap with my left fingers and letting them rest there lightly so my hand would know the shape without looking.

Esme stepped back and studied our faces. "I will lead ten paces ahead and angle back if I want you to slow. If I lower my tail, drop low. If I raise it, hold still. Otherwise, do not stop."

Tannin lowered his head for a breath, and I could practically feel his doubt and agitation seeping into me from beneath the saddle.

I leaned forward enough that my forehead touched the warm place between his ears. "If I feel even a whisper of wrong, I will ask you to stop. I won't try to prove anything to anyone. I will only try to be as safe as we need to be."

He exhaled, and the air moved along my knees in a rush that sounded like agreement.

Esme shifted, dropping onto her paws. She glanced back at us, gave us a single nod, and then bolted into the forest.

"Hold on," Tannin's wolf grumbled.

I tightened my grip so hard my knuckles turned white, lowering myself into a rider's position.

Tannin leapt, the sudden speed whipping my hair behind me as I held on for dear life. My heart lurched into my throat, but where I should've felt fear, I felt only exhilaration. I was riding on the back of a massive wolf, who was sprinting as fast as he possibly could through a forest. Had a more magical experience ever been had?

The sling held me steady, and the under-cantle strap gave my hand something stable to hold. Just as with horseback riding, I adjusted to the rhythm of Tannin's movements, and the saddle absorbed as much of the bounce as Finnick promised.

The air lifted tears from the corners of my eyes that had nothing to do with grief. I pressed closer over his shoulders, letting my weight become part of his balance, and held on while Varynia disappeared behind us.

CHAPTER 6
ALIYA

B y the time Esme raised her tail for the last slow-down, the sun stood high, and my legs were beginning to tremble from holding my position in the saddle. The sling had done its job, but my inner thighs ached, my hips felt overused, and a line of strain pulled across my lower back. But the twins stayed quiet, which mattered more than anything else.

When Tannin lowered to let me down, the ground felt unsteady for a few breaths, as if I'd spent days at sea and not hours on a wolf's back.

The two shifted back to human form, and I handed them their clothes from my satchel.

Once fully dressed, Esme pointed through a screen of birch and hawthorn trees. A loose ring of wagons sat in a shallow clearing, canvas faded in some places, bright in others. The lane between them was narrow and swept clean. No one stood in the open with a spear.

"We will walk the last stretch," Esme said. "Stay close behind me."

I adjusted the satchel so it would not bump my hip, smoothed my shirt, and let Esme set the pace. We entered the lane with our hands visible.

A woman stepped out from between two wagons before we had to decide where to look next. Her colorful garments of red and gold were like something out of an Arabian fairytale. She wore a top that only covered her shoulders and chest, loose fitting pants that swayed in the gentle breeze, and a scarf around her neck that covered the bottom half of her face.

"Casmi," Esme said, tipping her head. "We need your judgment on a particular vial."

She didn't seem to be wearing any weapons, and if she was, she didn't reach for one. She studied us, then shifted her attention to me.

"Tell me what you want," she said in a sharp, almost musical accent.

"My name is Aliya," I said. "I am Princess of Varynia. I wanted to ask you about a vial we believe came from this outpost."

I removed the vial from my satchel and held it out in my palm. The green glass caught the noon light, and the black wax still pressed to the lip carried the faint crescent and three stars signature.

Casmi took the vial and turned it with a slow, practiced hand. "This is ours," she said. "It's a magic blocker. A man who smelled of wolf bought it a few days ago."

Her confirmation strung a chord that resonated a deep note in my chest.

"Coda," I said. "He served among us and betrayed us. He slipped this into my drink a few nights ago."

Her eyebrows ticked upward. "You can wield?"

"Not anymore," I lamented, casting my gaze to the ground for a moment. "Like I said, I was dosed with this just before a horde of cusith attacked my kingdom. I couldn't use my magic. People died because I couldn't do my part."

Casmi's mouth thinned. "I'm sorry. The cusith have been hunting along our routes as well. We have few wielders, and most of them work with pots and bottles, not sigils. We can mend bodies and brew protections, but we can't use magic offensively. We only have spears for that."

She pointed to a wagon in the center of the camp, where the tipped heads of a dozen or so spears poked out between burgundy curtains.

"How long does this blocker last?" I asked.

"A few weeks, if the dose was heavy, and your body did not fight it," she said. "This batch is strong."

The chord in my chest went flat, releasing acid into my gut.

"Weeks," I breathed in a higher pitch than I intended, looking frantically between Tannin and Esme. "We can't afford to wait that long. Is there anything I can do to make it disperse faster?"

She folded her arms over her midriff and pursed her lips, giving me an appraising gaze. "Well…we do have a reversal tonic. The taste is unpleasant, but the results are immediate."

Hope nearly burst a hole through my sternum as it leapt inside me.

"We'll take it!" I gushed desperately. "Please. Name your price."

Casmi did not answer immediately. She weighed us the way a buyer weighs a cart—not only what sits on it now but what it could carry later.

"How much, Casmi?" Esme prompted, all business and no bullshit.

"What I want from you is something no amount of coin can buy," she said.

"Which is?" Esme asked.

"As I have said, the cusith have been a problem for us as well. With no walls to shelter us, we're sitting ducks out here, prime for slaughter. We need a permanent home."

Tannin, Esme and I exchanged glances.

"You want to come to Varynia?" I asked to clarify.

She nodded. "In exchange for the reversal tonic, you will welcome Romari caravans into your kingdom and offer us homes of brick and mortar rather than wood and canvas. We've been wanderers for far too long."

The expressions on Esme's and Tannin's faces darkened as they nodded, echoes of a lifestyle they knew all too well.

"Okay," I agreed. "Once I have my magic back, I'll be able to finish securing a ward around the kingdom that will give us all protection from those monsters."

Casmi lifted her chin with a pleased yet calculated expression, then turned toward the cart from which she'd emerged, returning shortly with a similar vial in one hand.

In my desperation, I reached for it before she offered it, but she withdrew her hand, holding the vial behind her back.

"More than that, you will open a door for our wielders to study whatever magic you know," she said. "Our wielders only know what has been handed down to them over the generations, but we have no books to study. We have people who can learn sigils and casting if someone shows them. If you intend to build a kingdom that survives the next season, you will need more hands like that. I want the agreement from you now."

I didn't need to look at Esme or Tannin to make my decision. We had lost almost a third of our people the night of the attack. I was the only wielder, and it had only taken one small potion to render my magic useless. Besides, Varynia was always meant to be a kingdom where both wolves and wielders lived in harmony.

Agreeing to this wasn't a sacrifice, it was providence.

"We have a deal," I said, extending my hand for a shake to seal it. "We will welcome all of you into the kingdom, and I will give your wielders access to every book on the subject I have. I've only been practicing myself for a few weeks, but I'd be happy to teach you all I know."

Casmi's gaze held mine a moment longer, and then she gripped my hand and shook it. She pulled her other hand from behind her back and set the vial into my palm. The liquid inside was clear with a faint yellow tint.

"You will do exactly as I say," she said. "Drink two swallows. Wait for the first burn to pass, then drink two more. Stop there. Do not empty the bottle in a single try. If you do, your body may panic and reject the draught."

I nodded, prying off the cork and holding it up at my eye level. "How long before it starts to work?"

"It should work within a few minutes," she said. "Do not pull at your magic while the knot is loosening. Let it come to you. If you force it, you may tear the place where the binder sat."

I glanced down at my belly as the flutter of little kicking feet tickled the inside of my skin. "Will it hurt my babies?"

She shook her head. "Neither this potion nor the first will affect them at all. The magic of placenta."

I nodded, took a deep, calming breath, then lifted the vial to my lips. Tannin's hands were on my shoulders, steadying me as I drank the way Casmi had instructed. Two swallows, then pause for the burn to fade, then two more, until the vial was empty. The taste was sharply bitter, but any nasty flavor was worth my magic.

Warmth spread outward in small pulses. I felt it under my ribs, along my spine, and then behind my eyes. It wasn't pleasant, but it did not feel wrong. Then it dissipated, leaving my torso and limbs feeling cold in its wake.

With a shaking hand, I lowered the vial, uncertain whether I felt a difference or not. I stood in place, waiting as all three pairs of eyes watched me keenly.

What if this was some kind of trap? What if this gypsy had been somehow in league with Coda, and the potion she gave me would kill me? What if—

Like the first breath of life, that familiar electrifying sensation bloomed in my core, and suddenly every color seemed more vibrant, every sound more musical, and every scent more fragrant.

"It worked," I breathed.

"Are you sure?" Tannin asked, his hands gripping my shoulders more tightly.

I lifted my hand, and without even having to speak the incantation I'd memorized, my magic responded. Flames ignited in my palm in whoosh of air. I fluttered my fingers through it for a moment, letting the fiery tendrils lick harmlessly at skin, before closing my fist to snuff them out.

Casmi's eyes were wide when I looked at her again.

"You are a powerful wielder," she said, a note of respect in her voice.

"So I've been told," I said.

"Thank you so much for this, Casmi," Esme said. "In return for what you have you done for our kingdom, I will stay behind and escort you to Varynia myself. You could use a wolf's protection as you make your way through the forest."

Casmi gave Esme the first honest smile I'd seen from her. "That would be much appreciated."

Esme gave her a curt nod, then turned back to us. "As for you two, you should get going if you want to make it back before nightfall."

Tannin rounded me to face me. "Are you okay to ride again?"

A wide smile bunched my cheeks. "I'm better than I've ever been. Let's go."

His shoulders released a tension I hadn't realized they'd been holding, and he pressed a kiss to my forehead before slipping his hand to the small of my back to guide me away.

"Stay safe, Esme," I said as walked back into the foliage. "I'll prepare the way for you and our guests."

We left the lane the way we had come. No one followed or called out. The wagons returned to the quiet work of midday.

Tannin disrobed once more and shifted, and I did the work of fastening the saddle myself like it was second nature to me now, then gathered his discarded clothing.

I climbed onto Tannin's back with confidence. Once I was secure, he gathered himself and broke into a run. I leaned forward, kept my knees soft, and held the strap. The soreness in my hips flared and then settled into a tolerable rhythm.

I felt so much lighter now, so much stronger, and there was a constant dull buzz of energy—of magic—humming through my entire body. I felt indestructible. And with the promise of more wielders joining us soon, I felt hope for the first time in days.

JAX

Aliya and Tannin were nowhere in sight. I hadn't seen either of them all day. When Tannin didn't show up to help me with the training session, that was when worry truly set in. Where were they? What were they doing?

By late afternoon, I had trained the pack hard enough to mute the noise in my head. I drove the spear line through three extra rotations and kept the archers on the cadence until their releases sounded like one breath. Every order was a way to stop myself from picturing a dozen ways Aliya and Tannin could have been harmed.

It worked until the drills ended and the square thinned. When there was no one left to coach, the worry came back sharper.

I checked the den, the library, the kitchen—all of Aliya's favorite haunts—but she wasn't in any of them. Were there still traitors among us? Had one of them finished the job that Coda started? Or worse, had a rogue cusith somehow found her and stolen her from me?

I rounded to the garden, hoping to find Aliya pruning something, rather than evidence that she'd been dragged away.

She wasn't there either.

Panic festered in my chest, seeping white-hot into my veins. The last rays of sun were creeping up the side of the castle, soon to disappear completely. I should have gone off in search of her as soon as I noticed her missing. I shouldn't have shrugged off my unease as paranoia. I should have—

Something moved in the trees of the forest, and I whipped my head in that direction.

At first, I thought it was a stag. Then the shape cleared. I recognized Tannin's wolf immediately, loping to a stop, with none other than *my pregnant mate* riding on his back.

Relief hit so hard that my knees felt unsteady. Fury took its place a breath later.

They'd *left* the kingdom. They'd gone galivanting off to Gods only knew where, and they'd done it without telling me a damned thing.

I stomped into the trees as Aliya slipped off his back, the two of them apparently unaware they'd been caught. I intended to fix that.

"Where the fuck have you two been?" I asked in a dangerously steady voice that promised menace more clearly than any roar ever could.

Aliya froze just beside Tannin, who tucked his ears and lowered his head as he cautiously watched me approach.

She straightened and turned to face me fully, conviction on her face where fear, or at least guilt, should've been.

"We went to the Romari outpost," she said with her chin held high.

"You did *what?*" I seethed, my nails itching to extend into claws.

"Esme recognized the vial of the magic-blocking tonic as being sourced by them," she said, taking a step closer. "We needed to find out how long its effects would last."

I clenched my fists, ignoring the way my sharpening canines scraped against the inside of my lips. "And did you?"

"We did better than that." Tannin shifted to his human form, and I only noticed the strange saddle strapped to his back when it slid off his naked body as he stood. "We bartered for a reversal tonic. Aliya has her magic back. She can finish the ward."

Aliya nodded, as if trying to convince me.

"You took our *pregnant* mate into the cusith-infested forest on a horse's saddle?" I hissed.

"It's not a horse's saddle," Aliya said. "We had Finnick craft it specifically for Tannin."

A humorless laugh choked dryly up my throat, and I looked up at the sky through the leaves and branches as if asking it for patience.

"Not only did you put both of your lives in danger without telling me, but it was also premeditated enough for you to hire a craftsman for the job? You both lied straight to my face."

"We didn't lie to you," Aliya said pleadingly, putting her hands up as if to touch me comfortingly.

I jerked away. "Omission is a lie. Sneaking out of *my* bed in darkness is a lie."

"But it had to be done," Aliya insisted. "Training the pack is only going to get us so far. We *need* my magic. We need that ward finished. And if I had to omit certain things to you for that to happen...I'm sorry, but it was worth it."

"And if you had died out there, would it have been worth it then?" I demanded, fighting the fur that bristled beneath my skin.

Neither of them answered.

Relief and wrath warred inside me, and both needed a release before I shifted and destroyed half the forest.

"Both of you will come with me. Now," I said in a tone that forbade argument.

Aliya stepped toward me with the grace and confidence of her station, but Tannin swallowed hard as he obeyed. He didn't know what was coming, but he knew me well enough to know he wasn't going to like it.

I turned and led them into the castle and through the halls and stairways without a word.

When we got to our room, I held the door open for them to go inside. Aliya entered without blinking, but Tannin eyed me cautiously as he entered. I closed and locked the door, then turned to face my prey with narrowed eyes.

"Jax, look... I'm sorry, but she would've gone anyway," Tannin said. "I was only protect—"

"Sit down," I commanded, pointing to the armchair in the corner.

He did so quickly, his posture rigid and on guard.

"You will sit in that chair until I tell you otherwise," I said. "If you get up, I'll find a more colorful way to punish you."

"Punish?" Aliya asked, her hand blindly reaching out for the bed post to steady her.

"Take your clothes off," I demanded in lieu of an answer.

The heat in my voice reached something inside her, and she began to strip out of her boots, pants and shirt, then finally unraveling the gauze wrapped around her belly. I would take care not to disturb that part of her.

The sight of her naked body in front of me gave my fury somewhere to go, my boiling blood pumping straight down to my hardening cock.

"Bend over on the side of the bed," I said.

A frightened thrill sparked in her eyes, and she moved much more timidly to follow my command. She might be the princess of this kingdom, but I was her Alpha, and I was going to make sure she never forgot that again.

She braced her forearms on the bed as she bent over, her belly hanging low and her taut ass sticking out as if it begged for what I was about to do.

I strode up behind her, admiring the creamy, supple mounds for a moment. With the tip of my foot, I gently nudged at the inside of her ankle, and she understood, spreading her legs out a few inches more.

"What are you going to do?" she asked in a small, breathy voice.

I put my hands on the curve of her ass cheeks, and she jumped. The skin was so warm and soft under my palms and fingertips.

"I'm going to make sure you never keep secrets from me again," I whispered.

I inched my thumb between her cheeks, pressing over the tiny pucker of her anus, and she let out a clipped whimper. Keeping my thumb in place, I angled my hand so my fingers could reach her pussy. It was hot, wet, and ready for me.

Without preamble, I slid my finger inside her, pulsing hard and fast, in and out. She moaned low in her throat, her knees shaking at the sudden, uninvited pleasure. Then just as suddenly, I pulled my finger out and smacked her right ass cheek hard enough for the clap to echo in the room.

She hissed, bending her knees and veering her ass away from my hand. I gripped her hips and moved her behind back to where I wanted it.

"Don't move," I ordered. "Or it will only last longer."

Stealing a peek at me over her shoulder, she nodded, her eyes glistening.

Good.

Again, I fingered her roughly, feeling her get close, and then withdrew and smacked her ass cheek. She flinched, but this time she didn't sway.

Pink handprints were already staining her creamy skin. It wasn't enough for me. I wanted them red.

I got down on my knees, trapped her hips with my hands, and buried my face in her dripping pussy. I fingered her asshole while I devoured her clit, raking my tongue against her sensitive flesh as I shoved up inside her again and again.

I smacked her ass over and over as I feasted on her pussy, her cries getting louder and sharper with each new torment I introduced. Her lips tightened and her thighs clenched as she screamed at what would be the first of many orgasms, and her sweet juices filled my mouth and dripped down my chin.

I got to my feet once more. I shoved my pants down without fussing with the zipper, fisted my cock, then pushed it into her soaking heat. Fuck, she felt so good, so tight, and so deliciously wet.

I thrust into her more ferociously than I ever had before, slamming my pelvis against her ass relentlessly and making her reddening cheeks jiggle. I slapped her ass every few thrusts in between gripping it hard enough to bruise.

I fucked her until she came a second time, then withdrew from her pussy and slid my cock into her tight little asshole instead. I had to go slow at first, her muscles fighting my entrance, but when they finally gave, I slammed into her with restless abandon.

Her screams filled the room, and I didn't give a fuck who heard them beyond these walls. I intended to continue as long as my body could stand this indescribable pleasure.

I glanced up at Tannin through heavy eyelids. He was watching us with the kind of agonizing hunger that would drive any man mad. His hand was over his pants, pressing over his own erection.

"Don't fucking touch yourself, or I'll rip your dick right off," I barked, making him immediately snatch his hand away. "You don't get to come tonight. You will watch."

Again and again, I switched between her pussy and her asshole, never slowing down, pushing her through one orgasm after another. Her ass cheeks were striped with pink and red marks, and every inch of her backside was covered in her own juices.

My anger bled out of me through my aggression and sweat, leaving only sinful bliss behind. She felt so good. I wanted to come, but I didn't want to stop.

I had to think of the babies. I could harm them if I pushed her too far. Her face was streaked with tears, and her screams quaked with sobs.

I slowed down, caressing her abused ass with softer, more loving hands. Letting my restraint go, I thrust into her more carefully, longer, and my pleasure built to unthinkable heights.

Finally, I came, settling as deep inside her pussy as I could reach. My hot seed spilled into her, and I lowered myself onto her back without letting my weight push on her.

I kissed her shoulders and back as I scooped my arms around her.

"Please, never scare me like that again," I murmured, pleading now.

"I won't," she whimpered. "I promise. I promise. I promise."

My dick was still twitching when I pulled out of her, pleasure still pulsating through me, but I climbed onto the bed and pulled her into my arms. She curled up into my embrace, burying her face into my chest as she shed quiet tears.

I loved her so much. She was everything in the world to me. I'd deal with the impending guilt over my treatment of her tomorrow. For now, I was so just so grateful that she was here with me, and that she was safe. And hopefully, the lesson I'd just dealt would stick.

CHAPTER 8
ALIYA

A light yet uncomfortable pressure against my kidney had me rolling onto my back in bed as I tried to savor my first restful sleep in days, but the rustling of fabric against my sore bottom made that impossible. No more sleep for me, and probably no more sitting for a while.

I shifted onto my other side, gazing at the soft morning light caught in the window's curtains as my eyes tried to adjust from the rude awakening.

I had known Jax would be angry with me, but I never imagined he would punish me for my transgression, and certainly not in such an... intimate way.

I couldn't say I'd hated it. Though my insides heated at the memory, my aching ass and chafed entrances refused to thank him for the treatment.

Aside from those things, I felt incredible, powerful. The heaviness that had pressed at the edges of my thoughts since the attack had lifted, and the familiar hum of power lay where it should, quiet but present.

The twins answered before I could form a word. A flutter of little feet kicked beneath my resting palm. They would be here soon, and I still had so much work to do before they came.

Jax stirred beside me. He watched my face the way he watched the tree line—alert and careful, without crowding.

"How are you?" he asked softly, like he was afraid I might break.

"Fine," I said. "Better than fine. I felt almost blind without my magic. Now I can see more clearly than ever."

He nodded, though there was a shadow on his face, a slight downward tilt to his lips. I suspected he felt badly about how he'd behaved last night. *Good.*

His eyes moved down to my belly. "And the babies? Are they okay?"

Another stronger kick beneath my hand, as if he or she recognized the voice of her father.

I smiled. "They're fine, too. In fact, they're both kicking like they're doing a log dance. Here."

I took his hand and set it where mine had been, waiting for the next small kick. When it came, his mouth eased.

"Wow," he said, his eyes glistening with some gentle emotion. Then he leaned his face close to my belly and placed a tender kiss there. "I can't wait to meet you."

I kissed his forehead, then shimmied down the center of the mattress, ignoring the smarting of my ass cheeks. "I just hope they give me enough time to finish the ward before they come."

"You're getting out of bed?" Jax asked, propping himself up to watch me. "I thought you'd need to rest, after yesterday."

"I didn't fight to get my magic back just so I could sit uselessly in bed," I said. "We need the ward, and I intend to finish as much of it as I can today."

He pursed his lips like he wanted argue, then let it go. "Okay. I'll make sure you are guarded at all times."

"Thank you."

Tannin roused as I got dressed, and then the two of them followed suit. I wasn't the only one with important things to do today. Tannin explained about the deal we'd made with the Romari as we went down the stairs, so they needed to make sure there were enough empty houses ready for when they arrived with Esme.

I went to the kitchen and quickly devoured a fresh apple, grabbing several more to nourish me throughout the day so I wouldn't have to stop.

Outside, the air held that clean edge that follows a cool night. The square was already busy. Bows lay unstrung on tables for oiling. Spear shafts leaned in neat bundles against a low wall.

Esther sat at the elders' bench with Wilda and Morain, watching the flow as if she were weighing it for the day's use. When she saw me, she gave me a knowing smile that hinted at pride, and then a nod. I'd never understand how she knew the things she did. I might have magic, but she had a precognition that I envied. Then again, maybe it was better not to know.

Hayden shadowed me as I returned to the spot along the perimeter where I had left off. There were no visible signs to suggest the exact location, but I could feel the magic's hum as clearly as I could see, so it wasn't difficult to find.

Foot by slow foot, I worked my way along the kingdom's edge, waving my smoking sage brush and repeating the incantation so often that the words started to lose meaning—or they would have if I knew what they actually meant.

I took breaks every time the use of my magic started to drain me. As eager as I was to finish the ward, I couldn't afford to push my body too hard at the risk of hurting the little angels growing inside me.

I realized halfway through the day that I had forgotten to pack a water bottle, but Hayden offered me his without me having to ask. He might be young, but he was also sweet, and I hoped the coming battle wouldn't steal that from him.

By the time the sun had nearly finished its arc across the sky, I'd only covered another fifth of the distance I needed. I wasn't even halfway done, but I tried to view it as a glass half full situation... without much success, however.

I could only do as much as I could. I had to remember that. And for today, I couldn't do anymore, not with the sun about to set.

More exhausted than I realized, I turned back toward the castle. In the courtyard, the afternoon drills were ending. Amara unstrung the last bows and set them to one side for oiling. The spear line leaned their poles in the rack Finnick had built from scrap and patience.

Twila stood near the elders' bench, posture very straight. She looked at me like a child trying to judge whether it was safe to smile. I nodded, and she allowed herself a small one.

Esther rose as we crossed the square. She looked me over as if confirming that all the parts that should be attached still were, then turned to business.

"When you have washed your hands, come to the kitchen," she said. "I have a request from the elders, and I want your help."

"What kind of request?" I asked.

"Essentially, time and strength in a bottle," she said. "I have watched the sessions. Some of the elders feel they should carry a share, as do I. But we can't do it in our current states. We need something that will let us move fast for a short time without physically harming ourselves."

I paused as the weight of her request settled on me. "You want me to brew a vitality potion."

"I do," she confirmed with a nod. "And I've already found the perfect one. I've gathered the necessary ingredients but need your magic to give it the finishing touch."

I held back an indulgent laugh. I really loved Esther. "Okay. Let's do it."

I changed to a clean apron in the kitchen and tied my hair back. Esther had already set a pot to boil and laid out what she had gathered —nettle for iron and stamina, elderflower for breath and calm, ginger for warmth, willow bark for pain, hawthorn for heart, and a jar of honey.

We worked methodically. I bruised the ginger and set it to simmer with the nettle, while Esther measured the elderflower and hawthorn and added them once the boil decreased to a steam. We let the willow bark steep off the flame to keep the bitterness from drowning the rest.

When the scent turned round and warm instead of sharp, we strained it through clean cloth and stirred in honey until the bite softened. Then I spoke the necessary incantation to imbue the magic it needed.

While it cooled, I wrote instructions on small tags. "One spoonful, warm, before work. Not more than once per day. Not after dusk. Not for those with fluttering heart or fever. Drink water after. Eat something with salt."

"We should also make a joint salve," Esther said. "Some will think they need the draught when they only need their knees to stop grinding."

"Agreed," I said. "Tallow, comfrey, beeswax, and rosemary. I can have a batch done by nightfall."

She bottled the vitality potion for the morning while I got to work on the joint salve. Hell, *I* would need some of that when the night was done. A delightful ache covered my entire body, the kind that meant I had been productive and effective.

Now, the elders would be able to fight, and soon, the Romari would come, and we'd have double the fighters and so many more wielders. Hope was on the horizon, and I clung to it with every ounce of strength I had. I prayed it would all be enough when the cusith returned.

CHAPTER 9
TANNIN

As I stood in the courtyard with every pair of elder eyes on me, I wasn't yet sure if the task Jax had assigned me for the day was an added punishment for sneaking Aliya out of the kingdom. The elders had been out of commission for years—decades for many of them. And I already had little patience for the old dogs.

The elders stood in a loose arc across the courtyard in front of me, sleeves rolled, eyes clear in a way I had not seen in years. Aliya's tonic had gone down like a good broth, and for the next hour, it would make their old joints behave. It didn't turn anyone twenty again, but it made them willing and able to try, which was the point.

"We will keep this simple," I said. "Small steps. Short drills. If anything hurts in a way that feels sharp, you stop and tell me. Pride does not win fights. Habits do."

Wilda lifted a practice spear, lighter than the standard shaft.

"I want the habits back," she said. Her hands looked steadier than yesterday.

"Feet first," I said, tapping the chalk line. "Set your stance, with your knees unlocked and your hips under you. Stick and step. Stick and step."

They matched me in halting unison. Esther kept her chin level and her elbows in, remembering faster than most. Borik planted too wide and let the spear drag his shoulders forward.

"Shorten your base," I told him, and moved his back foot a palm's width. "Be a hinge rather than a fence."

He tried again and didn't fight the correction.

I broke the spear group into pairs with padded shafts. "You're not trying to win," I said. "You're trying to not be where the hit is going to land. Deflect, step, recover."

We moved through the first exchanges. They were out of practice and honest about it. That honesty made them easier to teach. Morain's shoulders loosened by the third pass. Wilda grinned when her hands began to answer without thinking. Droger was quicker and more forceful than I anticipated, and I wasn't sure if his use of force was out of focus or spite.

After a few drills, he grunted and planted the butt of his spear on the flagstones. "This is pointless. We're not going to learn anything with these baby steps. I'm the most agile I've been in thirty years. I want to *use* it."

The majority of the group rolled their eyes and offered a chorus of long-suffering sighs.

"Oh, come off it, you old sod," Wilda mumbled.

"Some of us appreciate these 'baby steps', as you call them," Esther chided.

"Well, I don't," Droger complained. "I want a real fight. Who wants to have at it?"

He cast a gaze of challenge around the group, though I couldn't say it was very intimidating.

I arched a brow and approached him. "You think you're ready for an actual fight?"

"Absolutely," he declared, puffing out his chest and holding his chin up high as he tightened his grip on his padded spear.

I smirked. This might be fun, after all.

"Okay, then fight me," I said, grabbing my own padded spear from the stack.

The set of his spine changed by a degree. He rolled his neck and sniffed as I turned to face him.

"The rules are simple," I said. "First clean touch to shoulder or hip wins."

"You call that winning," he said. "I call that a warm-up."

"Then you should be able to do it twice."

The other elders formed a wide ring around us as we faced off, a mixture of disdain, amusement, and intrigue on their wrinkled faces.

Droger held up his spear in striking position with both hands. I widened my stance enough to make sure he saw it and waited.

"Feet," I reminded him. "If you forget them, the rest of you forgets everything."

Without preamble, he charged at me. I let the first jab slide past and tapped his shoulder with the butt of mine on the turn. He grunted, corrected, and came again. The second pass he tried to crowd me. I stepped aside and clipped his hip, not hard but clear. The ring made a sound that was not quite laughter and not quite shock.

"One more," he demanded, determined to save face.

"Sure," I shrugged. "Take a breath before we run it again." I didn't want to break the old fool, rather merely put him in his place for once.

He shook his arms out and nodded, taking only a few seconds before he came at me again.

The third exchange lasted longer. He remembered to keep his hips under him and to stop bracing like a wall. I still took his shoulder, but he made me earn it.

When we broke, I touched my spear to his as a sign of respect.

"You move better than you swear," I teased.

"I do everything better than I swear," he said, and the corner of his mouth tried to smile before he strangled it.

Either way, he seemed content to go back to the "baby step" training regimen I had established, as he fell back into his previous formation.

We went back to work. I broke the elders into triads for a short shield drill—no shields yet, only poles held across their bodies to learn spacing.

"Talk to each other," I said. "Short words. Left. Right. Hold. You will think it makes you slow, but what it actually makes you is clean."

They muttered through it in low voices, then began to say the right things at the right times. Morain surprised herself by calling *Hold* exactly when she should have. Wilda caught Borik before he stepped into a gap. The tonic kept their breath easy and their hands from shaking. The rest was repetition.

After forty minutes, I called a halt.

"We're going to take a break," I said. "No arguments. Get some water and take a seat."

To my surprise, no one argued, not even Droger. Perhaps his little stunt showed them that the vitality potion hadn't made them invincible. Or perhaps they held caution closer to their hearts than they let on. None of them wanted to take this burst of energy and strength for granted.

When everyone had drunk, we picked up the second block—light footwork, short feints, and a simple fall that wouldn't twist knees.

By the time the hour ended, the potion had clearly begun to fade, which was our cue to stop. I made them place the poles into the rack and sit, while I spoke to them like any other unit.

"You all did well," I said. "Even with a potion, I hope I can move half as well as you when I'm old and gray."

Raspy snickers followed by a few coughing fits skittered through the group.

"We will continue to train like this as long as you all want to, but not a single one of you is forced to train," I clarified. "I sincerely hope it never comes to it that we need you in battle."

They broke up in good order, their forms sagging with exhaustion, but their expressions alight with pride.

I felt a similar warmth in my chest, and I was glad that Jax had assigned me this task, regardless of his intentions.

I'd never much liked the elders, especially after they had so easily discarded us over our mating to Aliya. But this afternoon, I got to see their true spirits. They really did care about the fate of the pack, enough to risk their brittle bodies in combat training, with the possibility of battle itself.

As the elders filed inside, the sound of distant, approaching voices and the turning of wheels over cobblestones had me looking toward the main road.

The Romari had arrived, their caravan bright as a parade but quiet as a trickling river.

Esme appeared first, walking at the head of a queue that stretched back along the road. Casmi came beside her, shawl tied close, her eyes noting everything without making a show of it.

Behind them rolled three wagons with mismatched wheels and

canvas stamped with a crescent and three stars. Families followed on foot with bundles and folded tents. No one pushed. No one lagged. They were tired but orderly.

Jax paused his training session at the sight of them, instructing the children to go into the castle for food while he handled our newcomers. Aliya suddenly appeared in the courtyard from the west. She must have seen or heard them approach from the perimeter where she was still working on closing the ward.

The three of us gathered and strode down the promenade to greet them.

"Hello, Romari," Jax said to all of them. "I am Jax Gray, Alpha of the Black Wolf pack. I would like to formally thank you for freeing up my mate's magic so that she can secure the kingdom for everyone who needs its protection. Welcome to Varynia."

I held my breath on a snort. Two nights ago, he was punishing us for seeking their aid, now he was orating like a gracious host. But that was his part to play.

"Casmi." Aliya stepped forward and gave her a sweet smile. "You will find hot water and empty beds in the houses on Meadow Lane and Aria Row. They are yours for the taking. Let us know what else you need."

Casmi gave a short bow that was not subservient, only acknowledgment of the gesture.

"Thank you," she said. "It will be nice to sleep *inside* for a change."

"This way." Aliya gestured for them to follow her into the inner cloister of the village.

She had already marked door lintels with chalk so no one would need to waste time looking. She moved among the wagons without raising her voice, pairing families with houses, pointing out water barrels and wood stacks.

Jax and I helped lift trunks through narrow doorways and carried heavy chests up stairs. A boy with quick hands and a cautious father held a chair while I turned it sideways to fit the stair corner. The ordinary work of arriving filled the next hour. Mattresses unrolled, kettles set on stoves, windows cracked to let out the stale air.

Twila appointed herself guard of hinges and followed me from door to door to test whether any needed oiling. She took her job seriously and wrote down the squeaky ones on a scrap of paper as if she were commanding a regiment.

"Put one drop, not three," I told her. "You don't need to drown a hinge."

She repeated the instructions back to me and then to anyone who would listen.

As dusk fell, the lamps along the inner streets came on. Aliya stood at the north end of Meadow Lane with a folded slate and a piece of chalk. A small group of Romari stood with her—three young women with ink on their fingers, an older man with careful hands, and a young teenage girl who watched everything and said nothing.

"I will hold lessons at the library starting tomorrow afternoon," Aliya said. "Two hours each day to begin. We will start with basic elemental spells. I have found fire and air to be very useful, not only in both offense and defense, but also with everyday tasks. Bring a note-book and a willingness to learn."

Meanwhile, Jax was talking with Casmi just outside the house she'd chosen for herself. I knew I wouldn't be of much help with Aliya, so I moved over to Jax.

"We've recently started mandatory combat training sessions for the entire pack," Jax was saying. "We'd be happy to include whoever of your tribe wants to join. We start at three in the afternoon."

"Done," Casmi said with a crisp nod. "My people know how to follow a schedule when the person setting it respects their time."

She looked at me as I approached. "You help with drills?" she asked.

"I do," I said. "Your people who prefer blades or poles can work with me, and Esme teaches archery and spears. We keep sessions short and clear. No injuries if I can help it."

"Good," she said, satisfied.

We finished by carrying in a last stack of blankets and pushing a table back against a wall so a family could sleep on the floor without stumbling in the night. The sounds of a new camp inside old walls settled—a kettle whistle, a low song to a child, the clean scrape of a chair across stone.

Back in the courtyard, Jax stood with Esther and watched the line of lamps. He looked tired and solid. Aliya came to my side and let her shoulder touch mine for a moment.

"How did the elders do this morning?" she asked.

"Surprisingly well," I said honestly. "The potion you brewed works the way you said it would. They felt strong for an hour and they learned, mostly without complaint. Though I might have had to teach Droger a lesson in humility and patience."

She giggled. "And here I was thinking that old dog was past learning new tricks."

I snickered. "Come on, let's go inside. I think we've all earned an early night."

We walked back toward the castle doors. The castle didn't feel quiet, exactly. It felt balanced. We had new people inside our walls and elders who could hold a spear for an hour. For the first time in weeks, the weight of our fate felt shared by more shoulders than ours, and that was its own kind of victory.

Something felt different this morning as I made my way to the section along the perimeter where I'd left off with the ward. I had so much energy, you'd think I'd taken some of the vitality potion I brewed for the elders.

Maybe it was just knowing how close I was to finishing the ward. With only about a quarter of the distance left to cover, I was determined to complete it before the day's end.

I couldn't have asked for more beautiful weather to do so. Despite the chill in the air and the damp in the ground, the sky was the clearest blue, and the birds chirped as they flitted about with energy to match mine.

Yes, I was going to finish the ward today, and then we'd all *finally* be safe.

Casting the ward had turned into a routine that I could perform without thinking. Ignite the sage until it smoked, wave it in front of the length of my body as I recited the incantation, then step to the left and do it all over again. It was slow and monotonous work, but it would pay off with the ultimate reward.

"Well, that's all you've got left," I said to the tiny end of the sage brush that remained. Why hadn't I remembered to make another one before I came out here? Stupid pregnancy brain.

I wobbled my way to the garden and knelt down beside the sage patch to pick a fresh bundle. Warmth suddenly ran down my legs in a rush, soaking my pants and filling my shoes.

I looked down, startled and then embarrassed. Had I really just soiled myself? I'd had little leaks in the past week, but nothing so dramatic—and mortifying—as this.

"Wonderful," I muttered as I slowly rose to stand. "Now I need to wash up and change. What a perfect waste of time."

With my head tucked down, I swept into the kitchen, hoping to evade notice so I wouldn't have to explain about my ridiculous accident.

Because I wasn't watching where I was going, I bumped right into Raya's back as she crossed from the fridge to the counter.

"Sorry," I muttered, trying to swerve past her.

But she stopped in front of me and turned to face me, blocking my path out. "Oh, sweetie, are you—"

She sniffed the air, and I slid my gaze up to her face. The scrunch of her nose made me cringe and sent heat rushing up my neck. *Oh, Gods, she can smell it!*

Then her eyes widened, and she looked down at my waist. "Did you—"

"I just had a little accident," I interrupted. "It's nothing."

She gripped my upper arms, her face becoming more animated. "No, it's everything."

I cocked my head, confused.

"Twila!" she called out loudly over her shoulder.

"No, no, please—" Why was she calling more attention to this?

But it was too late. Twila came skipping into the kitchen, an eagerness to help brightening her youthful face.

"Fetch your brother and Jax," Raya instructed her. "Tell them it's time."

Her little brow furrowed. "Time for what?"

Raya scoffed. "Just tell them. They'll know what it means. Go."

Twila shrugged and scurried back out the way she'd come.

"What do you mean, it's time?" I asked.

Her expression softened as she held me in her maternal gaze. "Dear, you're going into labor."

"What? No, I think I just—"

A cramp tightened low and hard in my abdomen, unlike any I had felt before. I gripped the edge of the counter and breathed through it.

"Oookay, I think you might be right," I hissed through my tight throat and clenched teeth.

"Come on, let's get you to a bed," Raya said as she steered me out of the kitchen. Then she called out, "Labor! The princess is in labor!" so loudly that her voice echoed off the castle walls and marble floors.

Esther and Wilda rushed into view faster than I thought their old legs could carry them, each taking one of my hands or arms to help me shuffle toward the stairs.

"I can't," I breathed, shaking my head at the staircase. "Let's just do it here, in the den."

"Labor can be a very long process, and not a pretty one," Esther said with a calm I envied. "Trust me, you're going to want your privacy."

"But I can hardly walk," I pleaded as another wave of pain crippled my torso.

Suddenly, a strong and warm pair of arms scooped me up from behind, and in the next blink, I was looking up at Tannin's gorgeous face from the safety of his embrace.

"I've got you, love," he said, steady as the tide.

"Where's Jax?" I panted through the pain.

"He's coming," he reassured me.

I was so desperate for a bed beneath me, for an end to this pain, that I just nodded.

He carried me swiftly up the stairs and into my old room on the third floor, with his mother, Esther, and Wilda keeping a close tail on us.

They got me onto the bed and propped me with pillows behind my back and at my side. Someone tucked a rolled blanket under my knees to ease the pull on my lower back.

Another cramp hit, longer again, and I swore at myself for not brewing anything for this day. I had made tonics for elders and salves for knees, but I hadn't set aside a single draught for my own labor.

"You can be angry at yourself later," Esther said, blunt and kind in the same breath. "Right now, you just need to breathe and push when I tell you. This will take as long as it takes."

"Of course, it will," I said between my teeth. The next wave took away my words again.

The hours settled into a rhythm that didn't care about time. Jax stayed on my right with a cool cloth and a steady voice. Tannin took the left and braced me when I needed to change position. Raya came and went with water, towels, and small useful things I wouldn't remember later. Wilda adjusted pillows and my hair, and Esther kept everyone in line with her sage commands.

When the cramps were still far apart, I walked the room between them, leaning on a shoulder when I needed it.

When they came closer, I knelt with my arms over the footboard and breathed with my head down.

When they were close enough to steal the gaps, I lay on my side and let Esther direct my breath by count and hand. I cursed once in a way that made Raya grin, then swallowed the next one and saved my breath.

"You're doing so good," Jax said quietly every time a wave let me hear him. "You're so strong. We're with you."

"You can squeeze as hard as you like," Tannin said, offering his hand. "You won't break me."

I eagerly took his hand, and despite his declaration, I caught him wincing a few times when pain tightened my grip to iron.

Sweat ran into my eyes. The room smelled like hot water and clean linen. Between contractions, I was sore and irritated at the small indignities of my body. During them, I was a narrow line of work and breath, nothing more.

At some point, the pressure changed. It shifted lower and became an urge that had nothing to do with choice.

Esther met my eyes and nodded once. "It's time. When the next one comes, you bear down. Short pushes at first, then longer when I tell you. Keep your jaw loose. Don't waste your breath on words."

The next contraction rose. I gripped the back of my knee with one hand and Jax's forearm with the other and bore down. The pressure eased and then returned stronger. I bore down again.

Esther counted in a calm tone that never wavered. Tannin braced his hand against my back, so I had something to push into. I felt the stretch, both hating and welcoming it because it meant my hard efforts were paying off.

"You are close," Esther said. "Again."

I pushed until my vision sparkled and then breathed because Esther tapped my shoulder to remind me to do it. I pushed again.

The first baby crowned and slid free in a rush that made me gasp. There was a beat of silence and then a firm, strong cry.

Raya laughed once, a quick bright sound.

"A girl," Esther said, her voice gentle and warm. "She's beautiful."

I tried to look at the bundle in Raya's arms, but my vision was too streaked with sweat and tears.

"Tannin, cut the cord there," Esther told him. "Jax, put your hand on Aliya's shoulder. Good. One more to go."

They set the baby on my chest for a moment. The dark-haired baby was warm and slippery and heavier than I had expected. Her mouth worked until she found my skin. Then the next contraction took me, and they lifted her to Raya to clean and wrap while I bore down again.

The second baby came quicker. My body had learned the path. Two pushes did most of the work. The third finished it. The baby came out with a shorter cry that turned into a steady complaint.

"A boy," Esther said. "From the looks of it, he's just as strong and stubborn as his fathers."

They set him on my chest next to where the girl had been. He was as warm and solid as his sister. He blinked and then shut his eyes like the light was too much trouble.

I cried then, not dramatic, just a simple release of pressure and fear. I'd survived. I'd made it. My babies were here and they were safe. Jax bent and kissed my damp forehead. Tannin rested his head against my shoulder and let out a breath that trembled at the end.

I let my body relax, and everything in me seemed to melt into the sheets beneath me. The chaotic static electricity that had seemed to sizzle the air throughout this long process slowly settled, like the calm after a storm. All was quiet, save for the little squeaks coming from the two tiny creatures to whom I'd just given life.

Once the babes were wiped clean, Jax and Tannin came to sit on the bed on either side of me with one of them cradled in either of their arms. Then they set both little ones into my eager embrace.

"Have you decided on names for them?" Esther asked, her voice soft as if afraid a higher volume would spook the babies.

Jax and Tannin exchanged a curious glance, then both looked at me.

"Luna," I said, looking at our daughter. She was named for the moon and my wolves. "And Damon, after my father."

"Luna and Damon," Jax repeated, as if sealing their names by speaking them aloud. "Welcome home."

Luna rooted until she found skin and quieted. Damon rested a hand against my collarbone as if testing whether I was real. Jax's hand covered both without pressing. Tannin's fingers traced the edge of Luna's blanket and then stilled.

I was exhausted and sore and very aware of how little I had prepared for my own body to be pushed to its limits. But I was also calm in a way I'd never felt before.

The ward still needed to be finished. The training would begin again tomorrow. There was so much work to be done. The world wasn't suddenly simple. But for now, I intended to savor this glorious, precious moment.

War was just on the horizon, and I had no way of knowing how much time we had left.

CHAPTER 11
JAX

I was a father. I'd known this was coming, and I'd expected it to feel like a heightened version being an Alpha. Now, looking down at the little angel in my arms, I realized I was so very wrong.

Being an Alpha compelled me to put the safety of the many over the needs of the few. But being a father... I knew I would sacrifice everyone else to protect my daughter and son.

I just hoped it would never come to that.

The room was quiet as dusk fell. Tannin and I took the chairs by the bed and split the watch without saying we were doing it. He had Luna, small and fierce, even asleep, bundled against his chest. Damon was in my arms with one fist tucked under his chin like he had a decision to make.

Aliya was out cold, needing the sleep. The color had come back to her mouth, and the tight lines around her eyes had smoothed. Every so often one of the babies made a small sound, and she shifted, but she went under again before worry could fully rouse her.

"We should make this room the nursery," I said in a low register so as not to disturb her rest. "It's right across from ours, so we'll hear them when they need us—hopefully before anyone else does."

Tannin smiled without looking away from Luna. "I like it. It's the room Aliya grew up in. I think the overwhelming scent of her will comfort them."

I inhaled more deeply, realizing he was right. This room was more filled with her scent than any other in the castle, even the room the three of us now shared.

"I can have Finnick build cradles to fit the wall under the window," he went on. "And we should put a rocking chair where you are sitting. I think Aliya would appreciate that."

"Probably two of them," I said. "I have a feeling more than one baby will cry at a time, and we can't expect any one person to tend to them both."

He nodded. "Good point."

"We'll also need shelves for linens, hooks for the slings, and a bolt on the door high up so the older children cannot wander in when everyone is asleep."

"Yes. I suspect Twila will want to check on them often, but she's too young to be with them unsupervised."

We fell quiet again. I studied the boy in my arms and tried to decide which of us he resembled. His brow looked similar to mine. His mouth was definitely Aliya's. The peach fuzz of his little head was too short and thin to distinguish color yet.

"Let me hold Luna," I said, rising to trade off our bundles. "I'd like to get a good look at her features."

He chortled as we exchanged the babes. "Why?"

"I'm trying to figure out which of them I fathered," I replied lightly. Though it didn't really matter—the love I felt for both of them was instinctual and equally immeasurable.

"Hmm," Tannin hummed pensively as he inspected the fidgeting Damon in his arms. "He seems restless and very stubborn. Clearly *your* traits."

I snickered and scanned Luna's face as if committing every line and curve to memory. Unlike Damon, Luna had quite a bit of hair, all of which was dark brown—a trait that neither Aliya nor Tannin possessed...

Aside from that, she was a miniature version of her mother—same heart-shaped face, same button nose and full lips. She was going to be heartbreaker when she grew up, which meant Tannin and I probably had a few bodies to bury in the distant future.

"Whatever their paternity, I hope they both get the best of the three of us," I said. "Your perseverance and ingenuity, my leadership and strength, and Aliya's intuition and kind heart."

Aliya's breath deepened. Her hand moved to where the babies had been lying earlier, and when they found only the quilt, alarm woke her fully.

"It's alright," I soothed. "We have them."

Her gaze flicked to both of us on either side of her bed, and her body visibly relaxed.

"How are they?" she asked, her voice rough with sleep.

I smiled wide. "They're perfect."

She pushed herself up against the pillows. "Bring them here," she said, all business. "They will be hungry."

We passed the babies to her one at a time and adjusted the blanket so she could nurse without a draft. Luna latched and settled. Damon took a little longer, then found his way and relaxed against her. Tannin sat on the edge of the bed and smoothed Aliya's hair back while I poured a glass of water for her.

"How do you feel?" I asked.

She struggled to rub her left eye without moving Damon. "Sore and tired, like I could sleep for days, and it still wouldn't be enough."

"We'll try to let you sleep as much as you need to." I took Luna from her and handed her the glass of water.

She took it, but only looked at it for a moment, her eyes distant.

I knew that look. I sat down and waited for her to voice wherever her thoughts had gone.

She opened her mouth, paused, then finally asked, "Does anyone know where the cusith come from?"

That certainly wasn't what I'd been expecting.

I glanced at Tannin. He shook his head, the furrow to his brow matching my frown.

"I honestly don't know," I said thoughtfully. "I'm not sure if anyone knows. I never thought to ask that question."

"I don't believe they've always existed," she said. "Not like all other animals and creatures. If they had, there'd be a lot more stories about them. And probably less of us alive today."

I considered that. She made a good argument. I couldn't imagine early man would've survived those vile, clever beasts. And they weren't wild. Their recent coordinated attack proved that.

"Why do you ask?" Tannin asked.

"Well, I was just thinking, maybe if we knew where they came from, we'd be able to find some clues about how to defeat them."

The door pushed open without a knock. Esther never knocked when her hands were full. She came in with a bowl of broth, a folded cloth, and that look she got when she intended to do ten things in five minutes and make you thank her for seven of them.

"Good," she said, taking us all in with one sweep. "Your color is decent. Your pupils are even. And no one looks faint. Have you eaten?"

Aliya nodded. "Some. I can eat more."

"Please do," Esther said, and set the bowl on the bedside table. "I can see about having one of the Romari brew you a potion for the pain, perhaps something to help you heal faster."

"That would be fantastic." Aliya shifted Damon to her shoulder and rubbed his back. "Esther, where did the cusith come from?"

For a moment, the room held its breath, as if it, too, was waiting for her answer.

Esther's mouth tightened, and she shook her head. "I don't know. No one living inside these walls has heard such a tale, or even asked for one, strangely enough. My guess is that if such a tale exists, it would be in a book somewhere in this castle."

Aliya's eyes widened with the spark of determination I knew all too well.

I leaned forward and put an assertive hand on her knee. "You can scour the library after you've rested. For tonight, you just need to lay in bed, care for our babies, and let *us* care for *you*."

Aliya frowned and huffed out a breath through her nose. She knew I was right.

Esther checked the bandages under the sheets, adjusted a pillow, and moved the water jug to the bedside table as well.

"Call if anything feels wrong," she said. "If her sleep becomes too still, if her color or temperature changes. Even if you think it's nothing, it's better to be certain."

I nodded. "We will."

Esther left as quietly as she had come.

The room settled again. Aliya switched Damon to the other side and watched his face with a softness I had seen only in her. Luna had drifted into a satisfied doze in my arms and made small, contented sounds that squeezed my heart.

All the people I loved most in this world were in this room with me. I wished I could shut out the rest of the world and keep them in here with me forever. I wished I could forget about wards and cusith and training, shrug off the weight of saving everyone from the doom that loomed over the horizon.

Just for tonight, I would. I hoped Fate would allow me that much.

CHAPTER 12
ALIYA

My sleep had been restless. When it wasn't broken by tiny, hungry cries, it was tainted by nightmares of foul-breathed fangs and rotting gray fur. So, when the first rays of light crept through the curtains, I was eager to get out of bed and make myself useful.

I wasn't quite up for continuing the ward around the kingdom just yet. Every time I thought about it, my body screamed at me for more rest. If I couldn't do that, I would do the next most important thing—ensure that no matter what, at least my babies would be safe.

Jax and Tannin were still dozing in the chairs from last night when I slipped out from under the blankets. Luna and Damon breathed in small, even breaths, bundled in a cradle Finnick had produced from nowhere before midnight, with promises of a second one to arrive today. The man was a marvel.

I kissed each tiny forehead before slipping quietly out of the room.

At this time of morning, the castle was silent and still. I made it down to the ground floor and out into the garden without passing a single soul, for which I was grateful, because the last thing I wanted was a lecture from Esther or Raya about resting.

The sage in the garden was still glistening with dew, making the ground too lazy to hold on when I pulled out a bundle. I took it to the kitchen, dried it off with a cloth, and then braided it into a short shaft. It should be plenty enough for me to cast the ward inside the nursery and finish the ward outside.

I returned up the stairs with as much swiftness as my aching body would allow and crept back into the nursery. My mates and babies were still asleep, and I hoped the smell of the smoke wouldn't interfere with that.

I lit the end of the sage braid with my magic and started the ward at the door, waving the smoking side up and down and whispering the incantation as I slowly circled around the room.

When I finished, the walls, floor, and ceiling hummed with protective magic. Sweet-smelling smoke hung in the air like a fine mist. I whispered the babies' names to the door, not because the ward needed it, but because I did.

Then I turned to the crib and picked up Luna with hands so gentle, they could have caught an egg without it cracking. She stirred slightly but didn't wake. Tucking her into one arm, I scooped up Damon with the other.

It wasn't until I got to the door that I realized my predicament—with both my hands preoccupied, I had no way of opening the door.

Wait. Yes there is.

I drew on the well of power in my core, and without having to call it by name, the air around me shifted, funneling to the doorknob and turning it for me.

"I love magic," I whispered with a smirk.

I willed the air to push the door open, and it creaked as it swung outward.

With a sharp, nasal inhale, Jax woke behind me, and I froze.

"Where are you going?" he asked through a yawn.

I turned to face him. "I'm going to the library. I don't know how long I'll be there, so I'm taking Luna and Damon with me so I can feed and change them when they need it."

He pushed his fingers along his scalp and shook out his thick black hair as if that would rid him of his drowsiness. "Okay. Just, please, don't push yourself too hard today. And call us if you need anything. I can have Esme take over my training sessions if necessary."

I nodded. "I'll be fine." I hadn't felt this light and energized in a very long time.

He rose from the chair, stiffness from sleeping evident in his movements as he came up and placed a kiss on each of my and the kids' foreheads.

"I love you," he whispered.

My whole body warmed. "I love you too."

Though the door was already open, he moved past me and held it open anyway, ever the gentleman.

By the time I got down the stairs and into the library, my arms ached at the weight they were carrying. The twins couldn't have weighed more than eight pounds each, but apparently that was enough for my under-utilized muscles. I hoped carrying them would get easier.

I carefully set them both on the floor, relieved when neither of them roused. I hoped their sleep would last long enough for me to find what I was looking for.

I should have gone straight out to the western stones. The ward around the kingdom was three-quarters done, and my plan for the day was inked in clear lines.

Turning to face the tall shelves, I closed my eyes, cleared my mind, and felt for the tug of intuition that had never failed me before. I let it guide my feet until I was standing in front of the farthest right edge of the shelves. I ran my fingertips along the spines without reading titles, following the intangible tether, and felt its end where the wall met the floor.

A row of herbal compendia sat too neatly above a warped baseboard. I lifted three, then the fourth, and found the shelf back cracked along one edge.

Behind it, wrapped in cloth that had once been red, lay a book the size of my forearm. The leather was dry and scalloped at the edges. Someone had sealed the strap with wax and then pressed a mark I didn't recognize—a circle split by a line.

I unsealed it with a breath and a thumb. The first page was cramped with a careful hand and dated in a script that belonged to a different era. The title had been written twice, once in the old language and once below it in a later, more familiar hand. The newer line read: "On the First Wolf and the Walking Curse."

The text didn't begin like a ledger. It read like a tale told to children who had already learned that some stories bite.

Long before our grandmothers' grandmothers, when the oak in the north pasture was still a sapling, there was a wolf who gathered the restless and called it justice. He turned hunger into argument and argument into blood. He wanted what he could not hold, and when he could not hold it, he burned it. He and his followers killed hundreds and took the outer farms and the smithy by the river.

The hand shifted here, a different scribe continuing the line.

The uprising broke in a day and a night. The leader fell to a blade that bore three names. The bodies were laid out for the river fire. A wielder stood and said death was not enough. She spoke a curse that tied him to what he had made. "Walk," she said, "until you learn the cost of every step." She wove rot into it so he would never forget.

My throat went dry. The next lines were short and harder to read. Someone had pressed too hard with the pen.

She did not know what she was making. He rose from the pyre as a thing that did not heal and did not stop. The beast killed dozens on its way into the forest. Those it killed did not stay quiet. They woke later and went looking for him. Their teeth carried a poison that threw the same rope over each body it entered after breath had gone. The bitten did not rise at once. But when they did, they remembered his face and followed it.

I turned the page with more care than I meant to. Marginal notes ran along the edges—short, tight comments that sounded like the voice of a keeper of records. *See also: black bite. Do not bury near others.* The story continued, part myth, part record.

The first ones followed him into the bones of the hills. He gathered them and taught them to wait where the guard was thin. They learned to press in packs and to pull back when the light grew. They learned to make more of themselves when famine came. We called them by a new name then, because the old name would not hold them. They were the cusith.

I shut the book long enough to breathe and then opened it again. If magic created them, magic could end them. That wasn't hope, it was logic. A curse is a shape. Shapes can be broken if you understand the angles that hold them.

The rest of the chapter held specifics—fragments of the original curse phrase, a list of places that failed first, a note about iron pins driven into salt at the four corners of a burial ground, a margin line. *Flame does not end it unless you sever the tie before the burning.* The last entry was a warning—*Do not call his true name into a circle. Names tie knots as easily as they untie them.*

I stood very still and let my mind put the pieces where they fit. The leader hadn't simply been punished, he had been bound to an idea—walk until you learned the cost—and rot had been woven into it. The bite carried a weakened echo of the same working, but only if the victim died. The newly made creatures found the first one because the curse gave them a direction to fall.

Which meant there were at least three places to cut—the master's binding, the echo in the bite, and the line that pulled the newly dead toward the source.

A squeaky cry sounded behind me that I instinctively knew was Damon's without having to look. A gut feeling, similar to the pull of intuition, told me he was hungry.

I set the book on the couch and rushed to pick him up before his cries could wake his sister. I failed, and now they were both crying.

This was going to be a long day, but I was determined to find an answer to the cusith problem once and for all. The fate of the kingdom —the world—Damon and Luna—depended on it.

CHAPTER 13
ALIYA

The day had been long and, ultimately, unsuccessful. I had spent most of my time reading through the hidden book, but without the original spell used on the first cusith, I couldn't create a counter-curse.

It didn't exactly help that Luna and Damon needed me so much. I hated thinking about it like that, and guilt had been a constant battle throughout the day. I loved them so much and wanted to do everything I could to protect them. But I also needed to care *for* them, which took so much time and energy. How could I both protect them and tend to them?

Now that night had fallen, I tried to let myself just enjoy holding them.

I rocked the twins and told them a story my mother used to tell me, the one about the miller's clever daughter who outwitted a fox by trading questions for time. I knew every line. After she died, I used to tell it to myself, imagining her voice with each word. It was a way for me to hold onto her, to pretend she was with me.

Luna's eyelids fluttered at the rhythm of my rocking, while Damon's fist rested against his cheek. The small chair creaked in its slow motion, a sound that had already started to mean peace in this room.

The horn shattered it.

Two short, one long—north sighting. A breath later, one short and one long—south. Then three short in quick succession from the west. A breach.

I stood so quickly, the chair bumped the wall. The twins startled and then settled when I caressed their brows.

"Stay asleep," I whispered, as if they would listen.

I laid them in the cradle, felt for the hum of the ward on the door with a palm, and ran.

The corridors were already filling as archers sprinted up the stairs past me, determined to quickly get to their posts on the roof. I crossed the ballroom and burst into the courtyard. Jax was on the fountain steps, calm and loud as he barked orders at our gathering ranks.

"Lines," he called. "Spears front. Archers second. Triads to the alley mouths. Elders to the doors. Hold until I say push."

Esme was everywhere at once, placing bodies where gaps waited and thrusting spears into frantic hands.

Tannin met me halfway across the square, his eyes wide with alarm. "Where are the twins?"

"They're safe in the nursery," I said as I continued toward Jax. "I put a ward all around the room this morning. Even if the worst should happen, they'll be safe."

His face turned stoney at my words, but he nodded.

"How much of the ward is unfinished?" Jax asked as I reached the fountain.

"About a fifth," I said. "I planned to finish it tomorrow."

"You need to finish it now," he said.

"I should stay and—"

"No," he interrupted. He didn't raise his voice, but he didn't have to. "Your only job right now is the ward. Ours is keeping the beasts off your back while you do it. Go."

He was right, and every part of me hated that truth.

"Stay with her," Jax ordered Tannin with a clap on his shoulder. "She's our mate and the mother of our children. Keep her safe at all costs."

Tannin nodded once. "I will."

The first wave flooded up the promenade like a storm. Shapes lunged from the tree line, too fast, too quiet, glowing red eyes low to the ground. Cusith.

All able bodies shifted as one, exploding out of clothes and charging to meet them. Those who'd been trained with spears held a wall around the courtyard, points braced, feet set.

Arrows arced above us from the rooftops and fell like a curtain of deadly rain on our enemies. The creatures recoiled and circled, then pressed again when the first draw of arrows stopped.

"Go!" Jax shouted to us, pushing Tannin's shoulder. "Finish it."

I ran for the perimeter with Tannin at my left, bursting out of his clothes and into his wolf as he raced to keep up with me. We cut through alleys, taking the fastest path to the location where I had left off.

At the first corner, two cusith slunk from behind a broken cart. Tannin surged forward, low and fast, and met them with clean, brutal efficiency born of a thousand drills.

I didn't stop to watch the rest. I couldn't afford to. I kept sprinting until I reached the open field.

With shaking hands, I jerked the sage braid from my dress pocket and got to work. My magic was quick to respond, but in my panic, the fire I called was an explosion that roared on the end of the braid, nearly burning my fingertips.

I hastily waved it to snuff it out, but the action only gave it fuel.

"Dammit," I cursed.

I needed to find my calm. If I kept operating with high stress, I was going to hurt myself before the cusith got the chance.

I forced myself to be still and take a long, deep breath. When my heartrate slowed and my breathing softened, I willed the flame to dissipate. It vanished immediately, leaving a smoking—if not ashy—end on the braid. Only half of it remained. I hoped that would be enough.

As quickly I could, I went through the motions of waving the smoke along the perimeter and reciting the incantation. I said the words so fast that they began to slur together as I sidestepped over and over again. But I could feel the magic waiting in the air, begging to be completed so that the ward could give it use.

"Left!" Tannin roared from behind me. In the next instant, he leapt over my shoulder and caught a cusith mid-leap, tackling it to the ground.

As much as I wanted to see that he was okay, I couldn't pause to watch the encounter. Staying focused and continuing my work was the goal.

In minutes, I had covered several dozen yards. If I had moved at this pace all along, I would have finished days ago. But I couldn't think about that now. Thoughts of my people, my mates, my babies up in the nursery invaded into my mind, but I pushed them all out, determined to keep my focus as I pressed faster and faster.

Behind me, the horns kept blowing. Two short, one long—north sighting again—then quieter calls as reinforcements shifted the pack. The ward line flickered in my head like a sketched map. It wanted closure. I could feel the whole network aching to lock.

So close. I was so very close! Only a few more yards to go!

"Aliya," a voice said behind me.

Every hair on my arms lifted. The voice was familiar in a way that my soul knew to be a threat, but wrong in a way that multiplied that threat tenfold.

The sage braid slipped from my hands and landed on the ground. Slowly, I turned around, my blood roaring in my ears.

The creature prowled twenty paces away, body distorted and fur rotting, but the eyes still held a hint of their original dark brown beneath the red that nearly engulfed them. His mouth split too wide over teeth like broken knives, and he laughed, the sound a mockery of what it used to be.

"Coda," I breathed.

The creature stalked toward me, slowly and taunting, like a predator playing with its trapped prey.

I shook my head, the only part of my body that apparently was frozen with shock and fear. "But how? You weren't killed by one of them."

"A gift," he said, his voice rattling in an eerie way that chilled my quaking bones. "An old friend found me dead and discarded at the forest's edge where your filthy mates left me to rot. He spilled his venom into me and brought me back, giving me new life as something powerful enough to finish what I started."

His words were distorted and barely comprehensible, but my soul somehow derived meaning from the sounds my ears could not, and my mind reeled with their implication.

That was why his body disappeared. You don't have to die by a cusith's venom to turn into one. That must be why the wolves burned their dead, an old tradition formed out necessity that the pack forgot. By denying Coda the right of a funeral pyre, they practically handed him the curse.

"Your death is going to taste so sweet," he rattle-snarled. "I'm going to savor every last drop of your suffering. And then, when your heart finally stops beating, you will be mine forever."

He lunged toward me, and my magic instinctively flared in my core, urging me to employ it.

Suddenly, a massive black wolf rammed into him mid-arc before my mind could catch up with my magic.

Jax.

I hadn't even seen where he'd come from. One heartbeat, I was alone with a monster, and the next, my Alpha mate had intercepted him.

They collided like a pair of lightning bolts, crashing hard to the ground as they clawed and chomped for blood. It was so dark, and they moved so fast, I couldn't distinguish one from the other. All I could see was a blur of fur and flashes of claws and fangs.

I had to do something. Coda could not win. But what could I do? I couldn't see clearly. What if I hurt Jax instead?

So I closed my eyes and let my intuition be my sight. It had never failed me before, and I prayed to every star in the sky that it wouldn't fail me now.

I lifted both hands and called heat. It responded immediately, the fire's glow illuminating through my eyelids as the powerful warmth engulfed my palms. I held them out and surrendered myself to my intuition as I sent the ball of flames shooting forward and opened my eyes.

The spinning sphere of orange light struck the back of the monster Coda had become, its glow illuminating his fetid gray fur as it caught fire like dry grass.

The blast stopped the fight instantly as Coda let out a high-pitched shriek of pain. Jax leapt away as Coda's rotting form became a blazing inferno. Coda didn't even have time to roll or try to escape the heat. It swallowed him with a voracious hunger, growing brighter and angrier until he melted and dissolved into embers and ash before our wide eyes.

Silence fell in a ring around us, and Jax collapsed onto his side as his form shrunk and his fur rescinded. For a beat, I thought he was just exhausted from the fight, but I soon realized something was very wrong.

I rushed forward and dropped to my knees at his side. His hand came away from his side wet and dark, and my eyes flitted to the spot to find deep gashes in his abdomen beneath his ribs. They were too deep, and blood was pouring out of him too quickly.

"Jax," I said, my voice breaking on his name.

"Finish it," he panted. He put one hand on the ground and pushed, trying to get up. "Aliya. Finish. The ward."

His hand slipped out from under him, and he smacked back down onto the bloodied grass, his eyelids fluttering as his body slackened.

My world narrowed to one horrible truth—Jax was dying.

CHAPTER 14
TANNIN

I spat the foul taste of cusith blood onto the stones beside the slain beast, which was a lot harder to do in wolf form. Ultimately, I knew I'd be unable to rid my mouth of it until the battle was over —if I even survived.

I had more important things to worry about than the bittersweet rot on my tongue, so I swallowed hard and raced back to the spot I had last seen Aliya along the perimeter.

I froze.

Aliya was gone. In her place was a pile of ashes from which smoke still wafted upward. And there was blood everywhere.

I drew cautiously nearer, inhaling deep through my nose as I lowered my snout to the ground, terrified of the verification that would shatter me entirely.

But the blood wasn't hers. Neither were the ashes.

Oh, thank the Gods!

The relief that flooded through my system stopped just as suddenly and as powerfully as it rose.

The scent wasn't hers—it was Jax's. Not the ashes, those smelled like burnt cusith. But the blood... Jax had been wounded, and judging by the amount of his blood soaking into the dirt and grass, he'd been injured very badly.

Had Aliya taken him somewhere to heal him? *Please, please, let her be alright.* I had to find them. I had to help any way I could.

Locking my senses on the scent of Jax's blood, I followed it like a trail of breadcrumbs, slinking through the shadows in the alleys back toward the castle as fast as I could move without calling attention to myself.

Howls and shrieks surrounded me in stereo, but I couldn't stop to investigate or intervene, not until I knew my best friend and mate were alive.

"Still choosing the back ways like a coward," a voice said.

I froze. Not at the sound—cusith snarl and shriek—but at the words. They were ruined and thick, rattling like a pebble in a tin can, but I heard them nonetheless.

A beast came out of the shadow between a leaning fence and a broken millstone, careless in the way of something that believes the ground belongs to it. One eye was filmed with white. The other looked at me like it recognized me.

And somehow, I recognized it too, though my mind refused to accept the truth my soul knew.

"Tannin," he rattle-purred, drawing out my name as if savoring the sound on his tongue. "You always were a spineless little bastard."

I didn't dare move, just stared at him in a state of disbelief.

It couldn't be. He'd been dead for seven years. I'd killed him myself and tossed his body into the strong current of the river. He couldn't be... this.

His muzzle pulled into a horrific smile that was never kind when it was human and was worse now.

He took a step forward and sniffed. "Do you remember the old tent, boy? The one you burned to the ground because you tipped the oil lamp with your little stumbling feet?"

I didn't move. He knew he had found a vein.

"Do you remember how your mother begged until her voice broke while I whipped you for it?" he asked. "I did so much to mold you into a real man, but you'll always be that same sniveling little pup."

"This... This can't be real," I said, the rumble gone from my wolf's voice. "I...killed you. You're dead."

His mangy tale flicked behind him. "Yes, but unfortunately for you, I didn't stay dead. Maybe death will finally forge you into a being worth existence."

What the hell did that mean? How could he be here right now, and as a cusith? Was I losing my mind?

"Tannin?" called a familiar female wolf as paws stomped toward me from behind.

The cusith's head turned toward the sound and his wicked smile widened. "Ah, and there's the bitch now. How I have missed her..."

My mother ran up to my side, but I moved one step sideways to block her from his view. "Stay back, Mom."

"What are you doing? Kill it," she barked at me.

"Didn't you know?" the cusith snarled. "He already did."

My mother stopped moving behind me, pushing her body into me as if for protection from what she'd just heard.

"Did—Did it just speak?" she yipped in alarm.

He began to circle us, testing for a gap, though for me or my mother, I wasn't sure.

"You should have stayed dead," I growled.

"You should have burned my body like you did the tent," he countered sharply. "Nice little knife, right under the ribs. Didn't even have to look me in the eye when you killed me. Dragged me down the ravine like a sack and washed your hands of me."

His gaze flicked over my hackles to my mother. "Did you tell her? Does she know her quiet boy isn't quiet at all?"

Behind me, Mom's breath hitched, and I cringed at the damning sound of her recognition and understanding. *There's no more hiding this secret from her now.*

The creature that used to be my stepfather dropped his head and charged for us. I lunged as soon as I saw movement, determined to keep him from getting to my mother.

I met him low and took the foreleg at the elbow joint, then released before his counter bite could close on my muzzle. He slashed for my neck. I shoved my shoulder into his chest to steal his reach and felt his claws rake high along my back, too shallow to end the fight, but deep enough to draw blood and wrench a whine from my throat.

"I always said you were soft," he grunted. "Soft like your mother. A pet dog, not a wolf."

I circled him to the right, where the fence board leaned. He turned to keep me in front. I feinted for the left hock, but he committed his hips to that defense. I pivoted tightly and drove for the right instead. My teeth met tendon. He shrieked and snapped his jaws. I released and danced back, tail low, hackles up, breath steady.

He charged. I let him clip my shoulder and spun with the impact to stay on my feet. He bit air. I bit flank. He slammed me into the fence. It broke and showered us with splinters. I felt one stab into the bruised muscle along my ribs and rode the pain back into movement.

The wound I had dealt his hind leg made him slower. That knowledge made him angry, which made him wasteful.

I drove him down the lane where the cobbles were uneven and the gutter dipped. He planted and lunged for my belly. I leapt, went up and over, and raked his spine on the way past. He howled and bucked, caught my flank with a blind swipe, and opened skin.

We traded blood. I put pressure on the bad leg again. He snarled and committed both forelegs to the strike, which was a mistake if you were fighting something who knows how to take a joint away.

I took his wrist, twisted with my chest and the full turn of my body, and felt the joint go. He hit the ground hard, rolling in an attempt to recover. I stayed on him, forepaws high to pin his shoulders, and pressed all my weight onto him. In his jerking, he exposed his throat, and I didn't waste the opportunity, sinking my teeth into the tender flesh of his neck.

He bucked and tried to rake my belly again, but I ignored the pain, clenching my jaws tighter and tighter until—*snap!*

He stopped moving.

I didn't let go right away, waiting until the beating beneath my teeth faded entirely, as that foul-tasting blood filled my mouth once more. This time, I was going to make absolutely sure he was dead.

Finally, I released, climbed off him, and stepped back, chest heaving and ears scanning. Mom moved forward, slowly and certainly, stopping beside me. Her head nuzzled into the side of mine, a gesture of love and reassurance.

"Is it true?" she asked, her wolf's voice soft. "You killed him?"

For an instant, the sounds of battle and bloodshed dissolved around us so that only our voices could be heard.

"Yes," I confessed, and a weight I'd been carrying for so long shifted on shoulders, not disappearing, just changing form.

"Why didn't you tell me?" she asked. "Why would you carry it alone?"

"Because you had carried enough," I said. "Because I love you. Because I will always do what is necessary to protect you and Twila."

She closed her eyes, breathed once, and opened them again. "It's a mother's job to protect her children, not the other way around. I'm so sorry I failed you."

I nudged her with my hip. "You failed at nothing."

She huffed, unconvinced.

"Doesn't matter now," I said. "He's dead for good this time. He'll never hurt any of us again."

She nuzzled me once more, then began to lick the slashes on my shoulders.

As much as I appreciated the attempt to clean my wounds, I pushed away from her, still needing to find my family. My injuries could wait.

"Jax and Aliya are missing," I said. "I think Jax is badly hurt. I have to find them."

She nodded and stepped sideways, away from me.

"Will you be alright?" I asked.

She looked down at the mangled, bloodied body of her mutated ex-husband. "I'm not the same woman he knew back then. I can take care of myself." She tipped her snout upward. "Go. Find them. I'll be fine."

After one long, uncertain look at my mother's beautiful wolf, I turned and sprinted toward the castle.

Please, please, let Jax and Aliya be in one piece.

CHAPTER 15

JAX

P ain trimmed the world into steps and breath. Aliya took most of my weight, her shoulder locked under my arm, and refused to slow. The world blurred as she towed me through one alley after another, and the searing heat scorching through my veins blinded me to most of my surroundings no matter how hard I tried to hold on.

"You should finish the ward," I said, the words scraping on the way out. "Save them. Forget about me."

"I am not leaving you in the dark to die," she said with a finality against which there was no arguing—I was too weak for that anyway.

"W-where are we going?" I mumbled as my feet began to drag behind one another.

"The safest place for me to heal you is behind the nursery ward. Just hold on."

I was only aware we were inside the castle when the bright lights of the ballroom had my eyelids squinting. I tried to hold some of my own weight as we began to ascend the stairs, but I felt too heavy and too light at the same time.

Somehow, we made it up. She shouldered the last door and brought me into the nursery. We passed through the ward like surfacing still water, and quiet fell like cool cloth. Two tiny breaths rose and fell under the blankets. That sound reached parts of me the pain couldn't touch.

She guided me to the bed and slid a folded blanket under my shoulders to keep the wound from pulling.

"Stay here," she said. "I need to get the spell book."

"Aliya—"

"I heard you," she said, sharper now. "And I am still staying."

She leaned down to kiss my forehead, the sensation like a balm on my burning flesh, then turned and slipped out.

The ceiling lowered and rose with each breath. I fixed my attention on the twins' breathing to anchor me. My fingers tightened around the sheets as the room wavered and settled. The pain became a weight I could balance for a few heartbeats at a time.

Then something colder crept in under it.

It began like a string stretched across bone, not sound, but pressure shaped like a command. It offered a simple bargain. *Stop holding. Stop fearing. Walk. Run. Kill.*

The thoughts became images of blood and death that brought dark urges. A need to cause pain, a hatred so potent it deafened everything else.

"No," I said, or thought I did. My mouth might not have cooperated.

The latch whispered, and Aliya returned with an old book clutched against her bosom. Her eyes met mine, and though I could see her concern, her love, I couldn't feel it.

"Talk to me," she said. "Where are you?"

"Here," I said. The word felt borrowed. "Something...calling."

Her eyebrows twitched with some unknown emotion, but the fear that sparked in her eyes was indescribably captivating. When her gaze flitted away, anger flared in my chest. I wanted more...more fear.

The edges of the room dulled as if the curtains had been closed. The door felt a pace farther away than it had a breath ago. The not-voice found a hinge inside me I didn't know I carried and pressed. It didn't use words, but the meaning was clear. *Let go. Kill. Walk. Be free.*

"Stay with me," Aliya pleaded. She came closer, palm firm over the wound, eyes locked on mine. "Your name is Jax. You are my mate, my Alpha. I need you. Stay."

The room began to look foreign and somehow detestable. Angry heat ran up my side and across my chest in a slow line. The call slid along it like water finding a cut in stone.

My mind split into two worlds.

In one were the things I knew—the shape of Aliya's hands, the exact pitch of a twin's sleepy sigh, the training phrases I had hammered into the pack until even the stubborn ones could say them half-asleep. *Center. Stack. Breathe. Count the shoulders, not the mouths.*

In the other, something else laid out its own simple order. *Open, bite, tear, run.* It showed me how easy the world could be if I stopped naming each part. It offered the black-and-white of hunger and motion. It promised that the ache in my ribs would vanish when everything was teeth and distance.

Aliya pressed harder. Pain burned white and dragged a sound out of me. The burn helped for a beat. It was a truth I could hold onto.

Her face slowly swam back into place.

"Come back," she said. Her voice cracked and she flattened it again. "Jax. Come back."

The call didn't argue. It surged.

It poured images that were not mine into my mind. The safety of shadows in the forest. Mutilated and dismembered bodies littering the ground as far as the eye could see. A face like a hole in the air that wanted all other faces to turn toward it.

Every time I reached for a name—Aliya, Luna, Damon—the images put teeth on it and pulled. I shoved them back and they returned, patient and stronger.

I reached for older anchors. The way Aliya tasted when I kissed her for the first time. The look on Tannin's boyish face when I saved him from the pack bullies. The day I found out I was to be the Alpha because my father had died.

The call began to learn those shapes too and mock them. It offered its own allure, the kind you feel in your teeth when a blade hits bone. It set its rhythm under my ribs and invited my heart to match. It whispered—not in words, but in dark, voiceless promises—*If you stop resisting, you will not need to remember anything.*

You will never forget me. Follow. Walk.

I dragged breath in on a count and out on double and tried to put the pain in a box. The box broke. I built another. The call stepped through both.

A thought flickered—*if I die, I will walk*—and it wasn't fear that followed it but a cold, flat acceptance. The call liked that shape. It pressed harder.

Aliya's mouth moved, but it took an extra heartbeat for sound to arrive. "I need you to be stubborn, Jax. Be the man who stood up to the elders for our mate bond. Be the man who braved an unknown world for the hope of a new kingdom."

I wanted to answer that I was trying. The call translated "trying" as "tiring" and offered an end to both.

The name I had carried since I could speak felt too small. Something inside stood up and tried a new one that had no form and too many teeth. My body moved because it had decided to obey the simpler command.

I was on my feet before I knew I had chosen to stand. The floor shortened to a strike's length. Space lost detail and turned into lines of approach—throat-height, window latch, cradle rail, movement, heat, pulse.

The part of me that still had a name shouted through cotton. The rest tracked the warmest thing in the room and aligned hand and forearm the way I had trained them a thousand times—only this time, the target was wrong.

I crossed the space in two strides and caught Aliya by the throat. The wall met her shoulders with a dull thud. The fear that now lived in her eyes was food to my soul, and I wanted to feast. I felt her pulse under my fingers, and nothing about it felt like home. It read to the wrong part of me as a simple answer to a simple need.

Bite. Tear. Walk.

Aliya didn't claw. She set her hands on my wrist to keep air moving and made me look at her so I would see exactly who I was about to kill.

CHAPTER 16
ALIYA

For several long, choked breaths, my mind refused what my eyes were telling me. Jax's pupils had gone wide and flat. His grip on my throat was wrong—too strong, too sure—and the smell of his hot breath carried the sour edge of rot.

He was still breathing. His heart was still beating under my palm. But the call riding Coda's poison had already dug hooks in him and was tugging.

"How?" I rasped. "You're still alive."

His mouth moved, and the voice that came out was his laid over something older, something darker. "He's close," he snarled, the words rattling and scraping. "Master is close."

The words chilled me more than the pressure on my windpipe. That was the missing piece. The poison wasn't only killing him, it was a tether. If the master drew near enough, the amount of venom in Jax's blood gave him purchase before death finished the work.

"No," I said. I wrapped both hands around his wrist, not to pry—he was too strong for that—but to make him feel me as something other than a target. "Stay with me. Fight it. Let me heal you."

He pulled me forward and slammed me back against the wall. The room jumped in my vision as pain screamed in my skull, my shoulders, my back.

The cradle rattled. Both babies startled, but the ward held the cradle steady against the sill.

I dragged air through a narrow passage and tried again. "Jax, look at me. I'm Aliya. Your mate. Your children are here. Your hand is on my throat because something is lying to you. Let go."

For half a breath, the pressure eased, the faintest hint of light returning to his eyes. But then blackness swallowed his eyes, and the pressure increased tenfold.

Faster than I could think, he pulled me off the wall and threw me to the side. My world spun as I sailed across the room, then came to a sudden halt as my side struck a hard, unforgiving surface.

Something popped. Pain flared sharp and clean, and spots danced in my vision as I struggled and failed to pull a full breath.

He stepped toward me with the wrong stillness, a predator measuring distance. My magic surged to my hands on reflex, but my mind, my heart, my soul, refused to use it.

"Jax," I said, my voice broken and clipped. "Please."

He knelt in front of me, and suddenly, his hand was an iron grip in my hair, dragging me against the floor and hurling me across the room again. My scalp screamed with pain even after he released me, and the cries that wanted to break free were strangled by my broken rib.

Gasping and croaking, I slapped my palm onto the floor and pushed myself up, my head wobbling on my neck as I tried to meet his gaze.

"Please...don't...make me...do this," I panted in staggered breaths.

But the blackness in him didn't give. The cruelty on his face didn't soften. And a horrible certainty settled into my chest.

He was going to kill me. And the only way to stop him was for *me* to kill *him*.

I couldn't do that. It was an impossible choice. The man I loved with every fiber of my being was still in there. How could I end his life? How could I go on knowing I'd killed the mate Fate had chosen for me? And how could I ever look Tannin in the eye again knowing I'd killed his best friend?

He bumped the cradle as he came for me again, the rude movement making both babies let out sharp cries.

The sound made him stop, and he glanced toward the source. There was no love in his expression as he regarded them, only an irritation at their wailing, like they were nothing more than pests needing to be squashed.

A potent, irrefutable force exploded inside me, something older than magic and more powerful than any pain he could inflict on me—the love a mother has for her children.

With unfamiliar strength and speed that I didn't have time or care to question, I shot to my feet and brought both hands up, gathering fire. Tears streamed down my face at what I was about to do, what I was being forced to do, but I would do anything to protect my children— even kill one of two people I loved most.

"Stop!" I screamed. "If you touch a single hair on their heads, I *will* incinerate you."

He didn't look away from the crying twins, like he couldn't hear me at all. He set his hand on the cradle rail.

"I said stop!" I shouted.

He turned to face them fully and reached his hands toward them.

A fissure tore through my heart. "Forgive me," I whispered, readying myself to release my flames.

Two pairs of tiny hands reached up toward his descending hands in the same breath.

Suddenly, light hit Jax like a hammer.

It didn't explode or roar. It traveled from two small palms to his chest in clean lines, white and gold both at once, as if the air had found a new way to be bright. It struck him square and lifted him off his feet. He hit the floor hard and rolled until he smacked into the wall, where he lay still on his back, eyes open and empty.

Shock had me frozen for a blink that felt like an eternity. What the hell just happened? Did...Did the twins just...

The world snapped back into focus, and I snuffed out my hand flames, stumbling to him and dropping hard to my knees. Pain from the broken rib flared, but I didn't care. I pressed my hands to his chest, then to the wound at his side.

The gashes were gone.

Not scabbed. Not scarred. Gone. New skin lay where torn flesh had been moments ago, flush with heat and smooth as alabaster. Under my palm, his heart thumped with the thick, honest beat of a man who had almost been lost but was not.

"Jax," I said, because I couldn't say anything else yet. "Jax?"

His eyes moved like someone surfacing from a dream. He blinked, focused, and found my face. His eyes were his again, his pupils rescinded back to flaunt his beautiful blue irises. Confusion collected itself into recognition. His hand lifted half an inch and then found my wrist, gripping it with just the right mixture of softness and force.

"What...happened?" he asked, his voice raw. "I—Aliya, are you hurt?"

I laughed once, a small, cracked sound, and then started crying because my body had to do something with the fear that had nowhere to go.

"Just a little banged up," I said. "But it's over now. You're alive."

He tried to sit, but I pressed him back gently.

"Don't move," I said. "Just breathe."

He did. He let me control the pace. It was enough to keep the room from sliding again.

"What happened," he repeated, slower now. "The pull... He was in my head—"

"The original cusith is close," I said. "The venom from Coda gave him some kind of hold over you. He started to ride you before your body was finished dying, and I couldn't stop it." I swallowed hard against the ache in my side. "The twins did."

He frowned. "What?"

I looked over my shoulder at the cradle. Their crying had stopped, as if they somehow knew the danger had passed.

"They reached for you," I explained. "Together. It wasn't fire. It wasn't any training I have given. It looked like the ward feels when it locks. It hit you and it...healed you, of both your wound and the venom's control."

I still couldn't believe what I'd witnessed. Where did that power come from? How did they know to use it?

He stared at the ceiling for three long breaths. Then he looked back at me, and the fear in his eyes turned to something else—cautious, humbled awe.

"They healed me," he said.

I nodded, and the tears came in another brief, undignified rush. "I was... I thought I was going to have to choose, Jax. Between you and our children. I was ready to kill you to keep them safe." Saying it hurt worse than the rib, but the truth needed air anyway. "I would have done it."

His hand tightened on my wrist, not in anger, only in understanding. "Killing me would have been the right thing to do, my love. You should protect our babies before anyone else. I'm so sorry I put you through that. So, so sorry." He angled his head toward my wrist and brought it up to his mouth to cover it in a dozen gentle, desperate kisses.

"It wasn't your fault," I said. "I'm just glad it's over."

As soon as I said the words, I knew they were false. This wasn't over yet. It wouldn't be over until we vanquished the cusith completely. There was still a battle raging beyond these walls, and the pack needed us now more than ever.

"Are you okay to stand?" I asked him.

He nodded and got to his feet, then, without being asked, helped me to mine. He guided me toward the bed, where the spell book lay waiting for me.

I'd never performed a healing spell on myself before. The only time I ever had was the first time I met Jax. There was irony here somewhere, but I didn't have the time to find or appreciate it.

"Tell me what you need," he said as he lowered me to sit on the mattress.

"I just need to focus," I said, then added, "and maybe a hand to hold."

He happily slipped his hand into mine and squeezed it, sending warmth I desperately needed up my arm and into my core.

I put my free hand over my throbbing, sensitive rib as I read over the healing spell. Then I closed my eyes, focused all my intention on healing myself, and spoke the words that somehow brought me full circle.

Magic swirled from my belly, through my arm, and back into my side. It was warm and tingly, soothing in the way that lowering into a hot bath was. My rib slowly slid back into place, the sensation the strangest I'd ever felt—not painful, but almost ticklish. And just like that, the pain vanished.

With my hand still pressed to my side, I ventured a full breath, relieved to find that my lungs could expand without hindrance. I took several more, my eyelids fluttering with the relief they brought.

Then I closed the book and stood with Jax's hand still in mine.

"It's time to end this," I declared. "One way or another, this war ends tonight."

JAX

We left the nursery at a run. My fatherly instinct had me reluctant to leave the twins alone in that room, but after experiencing their powerful magic first-hand, a deeper part of me knew they'd be fine. Besides, they had their own private ward to protect them. The rest of the kingdom didn't.

The corridor smelled like smoke and iron. Howls and shrieks echoed outside as horns called along the wall in a steady cadence—hold, shift, clear. The pack hadn't folded. That was all I needed to hear.

We hit the stairs, crossed the ballroom, and came out into a court-yard that looked like an echo of the morning's work. Arrows bristled from hay bales and door posts. Water buckets stood in lines. Blood ran in thin threads toward the drain by the fountain.

Tannin tore past us in his wolf form, muzzle dark, hackles high, eyes sharp. He scanned us in one glance, checked that we were both standing tall, then cut down the north alley to intercept a pair of shapes testing a gap.

"It's time to finish the ward," I said as I shifted and landed on my forepaws. "I'll keep them off you."

A sound rolled over the square that was not a horn or a howl. It was low and broad, like a door being dragged across stone, and so eerie that it shook my very bones.

Shapes moved at the tree line. For a heartbeat, I thought the shadows themselves had shifted. Then something emerged onto the path.

This beast wasn't like the others.

It filled the lane between the buildings with a body too big for the space. Its hide sloughed where rot had worked under the skin. Ribs showed through flesh that tried and failed to knit. When it breathed, the air came out in shards. Its eyes were wrong, too aware, too direct, and the kind of glowing red reminiscent of the fires of Hell. And the stench!

The battle came to a ceasefire around us as all paused to pay this thing reverence, either out of obedience or sheer horror. Other cusith drew back to give it room, while our people stepped closer to each other as if grouping could save them. But this beast didn't seem to care about them. Its nightmare-personified glare was fixed on us across the promenade.

Tannin came to heel at my left, his shoulder brushing my thigh. Aliya stood at my right, her hand finding my back for reassurance. I stood my ground, waiting for some signal that would decide our next move.

The half of its mouth that had flesh covering its teeth curled in a wicked sneer. When it spoke, the sound found every surface and set it humming.

"Long time," it said, the words a series of clicks and deep rattles that somehow formed coherent thoughts. "Long walk."

Aliya's chin lifted. "Who are you?"

"The first," it said, as if pleased to be asked. "I had a name once…a sound I no longer recall. They thought they cursed me, but instead, they turned me into a god. A god that would one day destroy and rule them."

Its head tilted, speaking as if the courtyard were a hearth, and we had all taken chairs. "I learned to talk again while my tongue rotted. I learned to count while I lost fingers. I learned patience as my bones broke and healed crooked. I walked out and found that every person I touched remembered me when their breath stopped. They rose and looked for me. I taught them to wait and bite and bring me more."

Tannin shifted against me, a subtle nudge to strike, but I tilted my hips toward him in a silent negation. This thing wanted to talk, to gloat, and I was going to let it buy us time.

"Your wolves learned to ruin the meat," it went on, a little amused. "They burned their dead. They put iron through hearts. They buried far from other bodies. I stopped making armies and started making households. Smaller bites. Villages first, then scattered families. Picked them off like ticks. But I kept the plan."

It sniffed the air. Its lip curled, showing yellowed and blackened teeth filed down and regrown wrong.

"When I heard the plague had stolen my victory from me, it saddened me," it said, almost tender. "But then the wolves returned, forming a new, fragile kingdom of their own with the last princess. The sorcerers that cursed me and the wolves that betrayed me, all in a single mouthful."

Aliya stepped forward, and the cusith's eyes narrowed on her. "We are not the same kingdom that cursed you. Your quarrel isn't with us. The people who turned on you are long dead."

It laughed, the sound reminiscent of an avalanche echoing through trees. "I know. Some of them walk with me now. They are mine, and soon, you will be too."

She put her hand over her chest, her eyes shimmering with a kind of remorse this thing didn't deserve. "I'm so deeply sorry for the wrongs committed against you by my predecessors. Let us help you. I can find a counter-curse. I can set you free. I can give you peace."

Its forepaw rose and slammed on the cobblestones, shaking the ground with its fury. "I *am* free. And I will only know peace when the entire world bows at my feet."

"It doesn't have to be this way," she insisted with a sweetness that intended to grip his heart.

It was evident to me this thing had no heart. It had rotted away long ago with the rest of its organs, flesh and fur.

"I wonder... Is your blood as sugary as your voice? I can't wait to taste it." It dropped the pretense of conversation and moved for her in a blur that seemed impossible for its size.

Instinct shot Tannin and me forward. We met it halfway.

It swung with a forelimb that had once been an arm and now ended in a rake of claws, but I dodged it, leaping for its neck, my claws slicing through flesh that was thick and dry as rawhide. The cuts didn't last. Just as soon as the flesh tore, it knitted back together like a netting of slimy, sentient spiderwebs.

The stench coming off its hide hit like smoke too close to the lungs, closing my throat and blurring my vision with stinging tears.

Tannin hit its flank at the same moment and turned teeth toward tendon, not belly. He knew how to ruin movement first.

The thing shifted weight and flung him into a barrel hard enough to burst the bands. Staves clattered. Tannin rolled and was up before the next breath.

Aliya's hands lit with contained fire. She threw a tight jet at the joint where the neck met the shoulder. The blast blackened meat and burned away rot, but the creature only staggered for a blink before burn festered over.

The field widened as our pack found the rhythm around us. Wolves took the edges, forcing smaller cusith to turn and show flanks. Arrows rained down from the castle roof, and spear carriers finished what the arrows started. Esme called lines from the roof without raising her voice. Esther moved through fallen bodies and pulled the living back into shape with hands that never shook.

"Close the ward!" I barked to Aliya without letting go of the monster.

"Not yet," she said as she hurled another fireball.

The thing heard and smiled. "Finish your circle. It will be nice to have new walls to decorate."

It swiped at me, but I quickly scaled around its neck, setting my sights on the newly festering flesh where Aliya had burned him. If I could expose the bone before the flesh "healed," I might be able to sever the tendons and cripple it.

Tannin hit its bad leg again, the one we had already burned, and dragged. The limb gave a little. It adapted, shifting to three points and a tail like a club that cracked stone.

Aliya flared heat in a sheet, not a ball—she had learned—and cut off its line of sight. I used the smoke and closed to strike at its eyes. It turned its skull at the last instant, and I ruined a cheek instead. It didn't bleed right. What ran down my hand felt more like the river mud that had stuck to my boots after a flood.

It spoke again, its breath smelling like wet wood that would never be dry. "I wore men like shirts until they fell apart. I learned every lesson your grandfathers forgot. You gave me time. The person who cursed me gave me eternity."

"Eternity ends," Aliya said, and sent a line of fire straight through the mouth. It burned. It screamed. The sound rattled windows.

But it didn't stop.

The pack pressed the other cusith back toward the trees. Our people weren't breaking. That mattered.

The master saw it too and changed tactics. It feinted toward me, dropped its center, then whipped around and went for Aliya again, fast enough to make the cobbles blur.

I moved to intercept and wouldn't have made it if Tannin hadn't cut across and taken the hit with his full weight. The impact knocked him sideways and slid the creature off its angle.

Aliya pivoted and threw heat point-blank into the eye. That one burst. It howled and snapped blindly, catching my forepaw with a rake that opened skin beneath fur. I kept the arm and gave up the flesh. Better that than a throat.

A horn call rose from the west—two short, one long, then a long— our signal that the lane by the kilns was open and clear. We had room if we could take it.

"Now!" I called.

Aliya didn't argue. She broke right and ran for the last stretch of the perimeter, smoke and heat rolling off her like a cloak. Amara and Hayden turned their lines to cut lanes in front of her.

I took the monster's attention the simplest way I knew—by stepping into its reach and making sure it couldn't ignore me.

It obliged.

We traded space and pain. It may have been bigger and stronger, but I was faster. It had reach, but I had angles. I gave up ground slowly, step by step, keeping its skull pointed away from Aliya's path. Tannin harried the leg we had ruined and shot in to tear and get out before its tail could break ribs.

We learned its timing. It learned ours. It feinted a stagger, waited for me to commit, then tried to crush me between body and ground. I put a forearm up, braced my legs, and let the bulk take the stone instead of my spine. The impact made my teeth ring. I slipped out and swiped my claws deep along the base of its jaw, severing a chunk of putrid flesh clean off.

It laughed, a dry, broken sound. "You think this is the worst shape I have worn. I learned to crawl without legs. I learned to bite without a tongue. I learned to wait."

"Learn to die!" Tannin barked.

Aliya reached the line, and I felt the air change. The thing felt it too. It tried to break off and go for her.

I hopped onto its neck, digging in all four paws and sliding down the length of it to tear as much flesh as possible. Tannin took the opening and went for the hamstrings with a savage, practiced bite.

The leg broke. The monster stumbled and caught itself with the tail like a third arm. I put my body between it and Aliya again and set my feet.

It gathered to leap. I stepped inside the coil and hammered its ear with my paw. Bone cracked, and pain arced up my arm to my shoulder and raked across my chest, but I didn't give it the noise it wanted.

With a mighty swipe, it flung me, and I hit the ground on my back, rolling until my other three paws could catch me.

It turned its head toward the sound of Aliya's breath. The ground under us changed tone. The ward caught.

The master felt it. The wrong eye went wide. It looked up and around like a man who had arrived early for a meeting and finally noticed the walls.

"Now," I said to Tannin, and we went for its throat together, careful and brutal at once.

It wouldn't die easy. It hadn't for centuries. But for the first time since it stepped into our street, it couldn't step out.

The pack tightened the line around the smaller cusith and drove them against a wall they couldn't see. Esme put an arrow through the monster's remaining eye. Aliya emerged from the alley with sage ash on her fingers, and the whole weight of the kingdom came back to stand behind us.

The fight of our lives had started and for the first time, it felt like we might actually finish this thing.

CHAPTER 18
ALIYA

The ward held. I could feel it in the way sounds separated—arrows, horns, footfalls—each distinct, not the single, constant smear of noise we had endured all night. Inside that circle, the fight narrowed to two fronts—the pack and Romari sweeping the streets to break the smaller cusith, and the three of us facing the master where the courtyard opened to the promenade.

Jax and Tannin fought in their wolf forms, one dark as storm steel, the other black as wet oak. They worked as one body without speaking. Jax went high to shred flesh, while Tannin drove low to break legs or force weight onto bad ones.

The master adjusted as if he had rehearsed us for years. Rot hung from him in ropes, and still he moved with speed that didn't match his size. When my fire seared him, the wound boiled and then closed over with more of that half-dead flesh. When I blasted heat into the joint at his shoulder, the limb sagged for three breaths, then found its line again. He learned our timing and made his own.

Around us, Esme's archers picked lanes and pinned smaller cusith for spear teams to finish. Romari poles cracked bone at doorways. Elders guarded thresholds with padded shafts and stubborn feet.

I threw a tight thread of flame through the master's remaining eye. It burst in an explosion of thick, yellow goop. He turned his head as if annoyed and swung his tail like a club, cracking the corner of the nearest wall.

Jax slid under the sweep, went for the throat, and barely escaped the rake of claws that would've opened him from neck to pelvis. Tannin took the hamstring he'd been working at, buying me seconds. The creature dropped to three points and used the tail for a fourth.

"Again," I told myself, and forced my breath steady.

I sent a line of flame straight into the roaring mouth once more. The sound he made rattled the shutters. Black fluid hissed, and the stink of rot hit the back of my throat. He shook once and kept coming.

The burns I'd inflicted had been a mistak3.. I could see it now that fear had stopped shouting in my head. Every wound seemed to feed the curse. The body didn't heal, but instead, the rot multiplied and filled the space. It was not recovery, it was reclamation. How do you kill something that thrives on its own destruction?

Jax crashed into the shoulder and drove in with everything the wolf could give. The master took the hit, flexed, and rolled him. Tannin hit the opposite hip and knocked the creature off balance by a hand's width, enough to keep Jax from being crushed flat.

I flung heat again, this time at the base of the skull. The air sizzled. The flesh charred. The stink worsened. And the monster laughed.

The giant beast leapt. Jax slipped to the side, and the forepaw struck cobble where his spine had been, cracking the stones and upending their outer edges.

Tannin darted in and bit deep into the bad leg, snarling with effort as he tore it backward. The master dragged him two body lengths before Tannin let go to avoid the smashing of the tail. Jax hurled his full weight into the ribs and took the recoil that threw him clear across the lane.

None of it was enough.

"Every wound only makes him stronger," I muttered to myself.

I reached for more fire and stopped, useless heat pooling in my palms. The idea arrived as if I had pulled it on a rope from the nursery. Not heat. Not harm.

Healing.

The twins' light had struck Jax before death finished its work and had closed the door in the master's face. Healing magic is what saved him.

If this thing was a walking curse, then "heal" would not mean repair. Healing would mean forcing the body to choose purity where rot had been the answer. Healing would demand a pattern the curse couldn't satisfy. The contradiction would tear.

The beast reared to crush both wolves at once. They braced to take the hit together.

Altering the intention of the magic ready in my palms, I raised both hands toward the monster, spoke the spell I'd just performed on myself in the nursery, and released.

A beam of soft but brilliant light funneled from my hands and into the creature's chest, hitting him like cold water flung on a kiln.

He let out a shriek the likes of which I'd never heard before, a high, tearing sound that made the hair on my arms stand and my teeth ache. He folded around his own chest, as if the very air had turned into knives. The rot on his hide writhed, his matted fur extending straight out as if charged with static electricity.

Where the magic touched, the meat didn't char or boil. It whitened, then fissured like old plaster under a hot sun. He tried to swipe at Jax and Tannin, but the paw stuttered and collapsed under its own weight.

I held the light and widened it, but it cost me. Healing at that scale was work that drained energy in large quantities. But I kept breathing. The pack felt the change and pressed the small fight outward.

"Again," I said, and laid the spell deeper, not on the skin, but into the rules the curse had written.

Live, I told it. *Live clean.*

His body had nowhere to put that order. Rot couldn't obey a demand for health. The contradiction climbed through him like frost.

He stumbled and clawed at the cobbles. Black fluid spilled from his festered gashes, his pores, running clear halfway down before going dull as sand. He tried to laugh and produced a ragged cough. He tried to stand, and the tail that had braced him a moment ago turned to ash at the tip and drifted off like dandelion fluff in a breath of wind.

"Hold him," I said, and Jax and Tannin did, wolves braced, teeth ready, not striking now, only keeping him in the center of the street while the spell did the work.

He looked at me with the one ruined eye that still had any meaning left in it. There was understanding there, not of mercy, but of the fact that the game he had played for centuries finally had a victor, and it wasn't him.

"Witch," he rattled, and the word was almost grateful in its fury.

"Mother," I corrected.

He crumpled. Not like a man. Not like the others. He sagged as if strings had been cut, and the form that had been held together by stubbornness, hatred, and a curse, began to loosen into the air.

Flesh dried and scaled and became dust. Bone cracked and flaked. The hollows in his skull collapsed inward. He fell into himself and then into the cobbles, and soon all that remained where he had been was only a dark stain that the next breeze lifted and carried away.

Across the village, the smaller cusith dropped as if a net had been cut.

The ones at the spear line fell to their knees and then to brittle pieces. The pair at the bakery door sagged, mouths open, and then blew away like ash shaken from a hearth. On the roof, Esme lowered her bow by inches as the target under her sight turned to dust mid-breath. In the alley, Morain leaned against a post and watched the creature she had been holding at bay with a padded pole collapse into nothing.

A chain reaction raced through the streets, along the lanes, up the stairs, over the walls, and then there was only wind and grit and the ordinary weight of an autumn night.

Silence came in two beats. First the fighting stopped, then everyone realized it had.

I stood very still because the price of the spell had arrived. My hands shook, and I couldn't feel my knees.

Jax reached me first, already shifting and catching my elbow to keep me upright. Tannin arrived a heartbeat later and braced me on the other side, fur giving way to warm, blood-caked skin. For a moment, the three of us stood in a triangle, holding and being held, the world settling around us in a new shape.

"Is it over?" Amara called from a nearby roof, her voice careful, as if she might break the spell if she said the wrong thing.

Esme answered without flourish. "Yes."

No one cheered at first. Relief was a slow, quiet tide that washed over the living. Then someone laughed—a short, disbelieving sound—

and someone else sobbed. Horns sounded once, not an alarm, but the agreed upon signal for clear.

People stepped back from doors and lowered spears. Esther sat down on a stoop and put her head in her hands for exactly three breaths before she stood and started counting and commanding again.

I let go of Jax only long enough to look him over. He was whole. The line across his chest bled shallowly and then stopped. Tannin's flank was a map of cuts that would eventually heal. Both had eyes I knew, ice-blue and forest-green. They looked at me as if I'd done something impossible. I shook my head because I hadn't, not by myself.

"It was healing," I said. "Healing is the opposite of rot, compassion the opposite of cruelty. That was the answer all along."

Jax's face melted into an expression of loving awe. "Only you could kill someone with kindness. Your sweetness saved us."

"*We* saved us," I said, and looked toward the north wing where the nursery window sat quiet under its veil. "All of us."

I looked at my hands, ashen and steady, and then at the faces of the people who had chosen to stand with us. The battle was over. The kingdom remained standing. And we would never have to worry about the cusith again.

CHAPTER 19

TANNIN

It had been a solid month since the battle, and the castle finally felt like home.

We had filled the empty rooms with people instead of echoes. Survivors who had walked out of broken hamlets, Romari caravans who decided to stay, families who had heard there was a kingdom with a ward meant to protect and not exclude.

The carpenters taught the newcomers how to build. The mill turned steadily. The schoolhouse was full and stayed loud on purpose. In the mornings, Amara's archers held a lane for drills. By afternoon, the same lane hosted a market, and I couldn't walk its length without someone trying to give me honeyed nuts or a skewer of roasted apples as thanks for something I barely remembered doing.

Today we moved benches, lit lamps, and stacked the courtyard with chairs. We braided willow through the rail along the second-floor gallery and tied streamers that the younger deltas had dyed with beetroot and onion skin. Finnick polished the brass bell until it remembered it was made to shine. Esther laid out a table with a book that had once recorded tallies of oats and now held new names and dates that mattered more.

We were going to be married—properly, openly, in the light—Aliya,

Jax, and me. After all, a kingdom needed a queen, and a queen needed her kings.

I dressed with hands that didn't always feel like mine anymore, because life had shifted so hard, my body sometimes needed time to catch up. The shirt was white and plain. Jax wore his with the sleeves rolled to show the scars he no longer bothered to hide.

Aliya's dress had been made in three long evenings by a group of Romari women who didn't ask permission to help—soft cream, wide sleeves, a braided belt with copper worked into the strands. She looked like herself and also like a future we hadn't dared to picture two months ago.

Twila burst into our room without knocking, because titles never slowed her down. She wore a crown of dogwood and wild thyme and a dress two sizes too big that Esther had taken in. She clutched a basket of petals whose origins I chose not to ask about.

"You're late," she announced, even though we weren't.

"We're waiting for your procession," Jax said with a straight face.

"Good," she said, then turned to me. "Will you throw flowers if I get distracted?"

"I will," I said. "I will even put them in the right place."

She squinted at me, considering whether I was teasing. "You better," she said, and ran off again.

Mom arrived a moment later with Luna and Damon. The twins had grown into their mouths a little and looked less surprised by their own hands. Mom glowed with a pride that made my chest ache. She handed Luna to Aliya and shifted Damon against her shoulder.

"You can breathe," she said. "All the people who have something to say will say it after you've said your vows, not before."

Aliya laughed and kissed Luna's forehead. "Will you stand with them?"

"I will," Raya said. "Twila will stand with them too when she remembers she is supposed to."

"She'll remember when the basket is empty," Jax interjected.

"Then I will refill it," Esme said from the doorway. She had cleaned her boots and braided her hair, which was as close to formal as she got.

"Are we ready?" Aliya asked.

"We are," Esther said behind Esme. She always had a way of arriving when a question needed an answer. "And so is everyone else."

We stepped into the hall and followed the sound of the bell to the courtyard. Faces filled the space—pack, Romari, survivors we had taken in, elders standing shoulder to shoulder. Casmi stood near the front with her people behind her, skirts neat, hands clean. I caught her eye, and she tipped her head, a small salute that meant more than any speech.

The aisle ran from the castle door to the fountain, which we had draped in willow and copper ribbons. Esther stood on the step with the ledger. Amara held Twila just before the turn and whispered something that made her very solemn for three whole seconds.

The bell rang once more, and the square grew quiet. Twila marched. The first handful of petals landed in a tight, perfect line. The second scattered like confetti. By the third, she was conducting her own choreography, but the aisle stayed bright with color, and that was enough.

She reached the last step, realized her basket was empty, and looked wildly around. Esme—who had prepared for this moment—held up a second basket. Twila accepted it as if she had just been handed command of a battalion and began again with renewed dedication.

Aliya, Jax and I walked the petals together, Aliya in the center, me on her left, and Jax on her right, the way we always fit.

People didn't cheer. They made room and looked at us with the kind of attention you give to something you want to remember exactly as it was. We climbed the fountain steps and turned to face them. Raya stood to one side with the twins, who took in the light and the sound without fussing, which felt like its own blessing.

Esther opened the ledger and set a ribbon over today's page. "We are gathered to do what should have been done long before now," she said. "Not because paper makes love truer, but because a promise shared with the pack makes the pack stronger."

No one spoke. Even the babies stayed quiet.

"In our tradition," Esther went on, "vows are simple and specific. We ask three things. Will you protect each other, even from your worst ideas? Will you share the work, even when you are tired? Will you tell the truth, even when it will cost you? If you mean yes, you say it with your whole mouth."

She looked at Jax first.

"I will," he said, not loud, but with a weight that carried to the edges.

She turned to me.

"I will," I said, and felt the words land in my bones like a key finding its lock.

Then she turned to Aliya.

"I will," Aliya said, steady as a tightened string.

"Good," Esther said. "Then the pack has heard." She nodded to Casmi.

Casmi stepped forward with three narrow bands she had commissioned in the market and finished last night in the warmth of our kitchen. Thin copper hammered with a Romari star pattern, with iron worked underneath so they would keep their shape.

"From our hands to yours," she said. "Copper to carry warmth, iron to carry intent."

We took the bands and slid them onto each other's ring fingers.

Then it was the Romari's turn. Aliya had spent afternoons in the library with them for weeks, teaching them various spells from her litany of magic books, and today they arrived with a plan.

Four wielders raised their palms and opened delicate shapes that balanced between light and craft. Threads of pale fire unwound from their fingers and climbed the air like vines, weaving above our heads into a canopy that flickered and then held. Elderflower-colored lanterns bloomed in the weave.

A line of small fountains rose around the square and fell again without spilling—a trick Casmi's niece had learned three days ago and perfected this morning. The light bent in careful ways, turning the marks on the walls into a fresco of the last month—houses being rebuilt and filled with new families, the market growing longer and longer each afternoon, and the ward shimmering over Varynia every time someone new entered with invitation.

It was not overwhelming, it was precise and kind. People started to breathe again, shoulders dropped, and someone near the back began to hum an old wedding song that hadn't been sung in too many years.

Esther nodded to me. "Your words," she said.

I had written speeches and then torn them up. I didn't trust myself with long sentences. I spoke the way I fought. Direct and true.

"Aliya," I said, locking eyes on her beautiful face that stole my breath for two heartbeats. "You found a way for us to live when I had stopped assuming we would. You carried the line for all of us and taught us how to carry it with you. You take my breath away multiple times a day, and I promise to set my body between you and whatever tries to take yours. I promise to listen when you say stop. I promise to be honest when I'm afraid and to be stubborn when we need stubbornness more than comfort."

"Jax," I said, turning to him. "You have kept me upright since I was a boy pretending I didn't need help. You taught me to move with a pack and to stand when standing was all there was. I promise to take the hit when it saves you an inch. I promise to tell you when my temper is a problem. I promise to follow your plan until it stops working and then help you make a better one."

I could feel the square listening. All I cared about was the way they looked back at me.

Jax went next. "Aliya," he said, and if his voice wavered once, no one minded. "You walked into my stubbornness and made something useful out of it. I promise to ease your burdens without taking your agency. I promise to set you in front of gates and make sure you have everything you need to open them. I promise to ask before I try to protect you from something you don't want to be protected from."

"Tannin," he said. "You've saved me more times than I can count and never once asked for applause. I promise to keep your secrets when they're yours and tell you hard truths when you would rather not hear them. I promise to remember that your silence is work, not absence. I promise to stand at your shoulder as long as I breathe."

Aliya spoke last, taking Jax's hand first. "Jax. You are the ground under my feet. I promise to make home a place you can stand without bracing. I promise to stop you when you try to carry the whole world alone. I promise to keep the ward humming and your heart steady."

Then she took my hand, and her smile broke open a little. "Tannin. You are the hand that steadies my heart. I promise to let you be gentle when the world is not and fierce when I forget how. I promise to listen for the things you don't say and to ask for help when I need it, because you taught me that asking isn't failing."

Our hands intertwined, he turned to face Esther.

Esther closed the ledger and set her hand over it. "Then it is seen. You are a family under this roof and under this sky. If anyone has a practical objection, speak now or carry it to your grave."

No one spoke. Jax huffed a quiet laugh. Twila, who had forgotten her basket and was staring up at the canopy of lights with her mouth open, remembered her job and threw one last handful of petals directly at our feet.

"Good," Esther said, satisfied. "Kiss your spouses, then eat."

We did as we were told. It wasn't a staged kiss, it was a set of relieved, grateful touches that had nothing to prove.

The square exhaled. Music started somewhere near the bakery—someone with a fiddle and someone else with a drum made out of a grain bin—and people drifted toward the long tables we had set with bread, meat, and pieces of fruit that had somehow survived the battle.

The Romari lowered the canopy to float just above head height and shifted it as the sun moved, keeping the courtyard in a constant soft light. The younger wielders traded tricks, making flowers open and close on command.

When Luna fussed, a boy no older than twelve coaxed a tiny ribbon of cool air to brush her cheek, and she settled, making him stand taller by a handspan. Mom watched all of it with a look that made me hope the old bruises inside her were finally choosing to fade.

Twila took her role as flower girl to its logical conclusion and recruited two younger children to "inspect the petals for distribution quality," which meant throwing them into the air and measuring how they fell. When they landed on my boots, she pretended she had planned it. I bowed gravely and asked whether my shoes had passed inspection. She informed me that they had exceeded it.

As the long afternoon rolled into evening, people told stories and corrected each other's memories in ways that made both versions truer. Casmi stood and thanked the pack for teaching her people and for taking their caravans in as more than commerce. Morain and Wilda raised cups to the elders, who had discovered that a body can learn new tricks after sixty. Esme was at first quiet and then said one short sentence about the number of names in the ledger before and the number now, and the square fell silent for that heartbeat and honored both counts.

When the lamps were lit and the first stars found the gaps in the canopy, Jax tugged me by the wrist toward the fountain where the steps had been cleared. Aliya took my other hand. We stood there for a breath and watched our people dancing and eating and arguing about whether the meat needed more salt.

"Better than we dreamed?" Aliya asked.

"So much better," Jax said. He looked at me. "You still want the quiet home we talked about?"

"I want this," I said, and I meant the whole thing—the ward humming, the Romari's careful light, the sound of small breaths in the nursery, the promise under my skin and on my finger. "And the quiet home."

"We can have it all," Aliya said. "We will build it all."

Mom crossed to us with the twins—Luna blinking at the lights, and Damon asleep and heavy. Twila trailed after her with a serious expression and a piece of bread she had clearly stolen and justified. Raya placed Luna in my arms and Damon in Jax's, then adjusted Aliya's belt because it was riding high and she couldn't help being useful.

"Guard of tiny toes reporting," Twila said, planting her fists on her hips.

"You are promoted," I said. "Chief of Petal Distribution and Tiny Toe Protection."

She accepted the title with a small nod that somehow contained an entire career.

Aliya leaned her shoulder against mine. Jax rested his forehead briefly against my temple. We stood for a while and watched our people be exactly what we had hoped they could be. The Romari's canopy shifted as a breeze found its seams and made the lanterns sway. The ward hummed. The bell shone.

We had the wedding we deserved, without traitors in our midst or monsters bursting down our doors. The kingdom around us was larger than our original plans and kinder than my worst days had allowed me to expect.

Tomorrow, there would be roofs to mend and crops to tend and lessons to teach.

Tonight, there were vows on our fingers, babies in our arms, and the kind of love I would gladly kill for over and over—and finally, the hope that I never would have to again.

EPILOGUE

ALIYA

Five Years Later

I hadn't exactly been prepared for motherhood when it found me, but no amount of magic in the world could prepare anyone to mother a pair of twin wielder wolves.

I walked into the nursery to find the toys were stacked into a perfect tower without hands, a ribbon of light drifting lazily around the cradle that had become a bookshelf, and a loaf of rye levitating on a whisper of air with two small wolves stalking beneath it like hunters following a particularly confident bird.

"Down," I said to the bread.

It obeyed, if only because Damon lost focus and sneezed, which sent the loaf wobbling into my arms.

Luna looked up at me with her tongue out and no shame at all. I tried to hold my face stern and lasted three seconds. They bolted for the hall before I could decide whether to scold them or laugh.

Jax leaned in the doorway, his shirt open just enough to tease, and eyes bright. "Your children are monsters."

"*Your* children are monsters," I agreed, and handed him the loaf. "Where is their co-conspirator?"

"Under the table in the library," he said. "Twila taught them how to make the little lights dance when Esther is trying to read. Esther pretends not to notice and then assigns Twila three extra chores."

"Good," I said. "It's a complete system, then."

We followed them down the stairs, hoping to intervene in whatever mayhem they were about to instigate next. A trail of muddy paw prints led us to the kitchen.

Tannin came from the garden with a basket of apples. He set the basket on the table and crouched just in time to catch Damon when he slithered under the bench and tried to make a break for the ballroom. He scooped the pup up without comment, pressed his nose to Damon's ear until the pup huffed a laugh, and set him back on his feet facing the other way. Luna attempted the same trick and got the same result. They resigned themselves to shifting back and being children long enough to accept oatmeal with honey and slices of apple.

Outside, Mill Lane filled the way it always did on market mornings. Romari wagons set their poles. Trappers from the north hills stacked cured skins under shade. A woman from the lake kingdom unrolled lengths of dyed linen we could never have made ourselves and argued prices like sport.

The ward had held through five winters and four storms that tried to tear roofs from rafters. I'd extended it a mile beyond the old boundaries last spring to cover the new cottages on the river lane. Two other settlements had grown up down the road—one a cluster of houses around the mill we'd rebuilt, the other, a garden hamlet close to the willow grove. People who had once called themselves nomads sometimes found they preferred a place that welcomed them.

We never turned away a caravan. We made room, and in return, we found that we had more hands and better songs, sharper tools and tastier recipes.

Trade routes found us once we put a bell back in our tower and a promise on our gate. Word of a ward you could trust traveled faster than carts. We built a river quay from old stone and new patience and now barges came up with copper and salt and down with timber and flour.

The lake kingdom sent bridge plans and a stubborn engineer who taught our children why arches don't fall. We sent back a team who taught theirs why wards don't either. Letters arrived and were answered. Once a month, a royal courier in a red coat stopped to share news and take ours farther inland.

The twins knew all this the way children learn a house—by living in it. When we walked the market, they padded at our heels or sprinted ahead as pups, ears too big, tails up. Every stall had something for them to sniff or steal. When they knocked over a basket of pears, they bolted, then turned back and levitated the fruit—not very high, and not very steadily—into the bucket while apologizing at volume, which made the vendor laugh and charge me half price.

"Your pups are getting stronger," Casmi said, falling in beside me with her own basket of late raspberries. "My niece says Luna can strike a match with her fingernail, and Damon can pull a breeze through a closed room."

"I know," I said, and tried very hard to sound like a mother with control of her household. "We are teaching them focus. And not to practice on the elders."

Casmi grinned. "Wilda enjoys it. She pretended to scold and then showed them how to make steam curl into shapes without setting the kettle on fire." She paused, then added in her practical tone, "Five new wagons came in at dawn—two from the south road, three from the old stone path. They think they will stay. I have them on Coppersmith Row for now. Amara says that lane needs another watch post."

"We will move one," I said. "Esme won't argue if it means fewer corners for children to make trouble."

"Which children?" Casmi asked, her eyes on my twins, who were trying to convince Twila that flower petals should count as currency.

"All of them," I said.

By midmorning, the courtyard had turned into an accidental festival. A Romari quartet drew music out of a fiddle, a pipe, a drum, and a pot that had no business sounding good. The schoolroom emptied in a trail of chalk dust and enthusiasm, and the children flowed into the square to chase our pups and be chased in return.

We held council at a corner table because formality had died early here, and none of us missed it. Jax and I sat with Esme, Casmi, and Hayden to plan the next caravan's departure and the following week's training slate. We had nothing to say about cusith, and no one needed us to.

Wolves being wolves, there was always a fence to mend, a stolen chicken to adjudicate, a question about whether an alley should be widened to let carts through or narrowed to slow children down. We liked those problems. They were honest.

"Three more from the east," Esme said, sliding a short list across the table. "A father, a daughter, and an uncle. The father can mend shoes. The daughter can't stop reading. The uncle is loud and seems useful."

"Put them near Finnick's, then," I said. "And give the girl to Raya for the afternoon. She will find her the right books and tell her when to put them down and eat."

Esme nodded. "Done."

Tannin returned from the river with his hair wet and a knot of boys on his heels. He had become the person parents sent their problem sons to when the boys got too fast for their mothers and too proud for themselves. He taught them to move their feet and not their mouths. He set them to work hauling stone and left them too tired to set anything on fire. I loved him for it every day.

"Two boats in," he said, dropping onto the bench beside me. "One with iron nails, one with oranges."

"Oranges?" Twila materialized, as if the word was a spell. "Real ones?"

"Real ones," Tannin said, and produced one as if by magic.

She grabbed it and began peeling the skin off like she hadn't eaten in days. Though she was a young woman now, she still reminded me so much the young pup I had played dolls with all those years ago. In a few more years, it would be time to find her a suitable husband. I wasn't exactly looking forward to that.

By late afternoon, the light slanted gold across the square. The twins had given up mischief for a time and napped in a heap on a blanket in their wolf skins, paws twitching as if chasing something in their dreams.

Raya sat in the shade and mended a shirt with stitches so small you had to lean in to see them. When Luna startled awake, Raya was there before the hiccup became a cry. She touched the pup's forehead, and the child settled, safe in a home that finally felt like one to her too.

We'd held lessons for the Romari wielders at the same time each day, and now they held their own. I watched from the door as Casmi's niece led the class through a set of breathing patterns I had taught her and then added a trick of her own that kept a roomful of power from humming too high.

She caught my eye and grinned. It reminded me of the first day she had made a fountain rise in a circle without spilling. We never stopped learning, and she taught me just as much as I taught her.

Near sunset, I took the twins for a run. Jax and Tannin shifted the instant we cleared the castle. I climbed onto Tannin's back, and the three of us loped toward the ridge under a sky that promised a clear night. Riding him had become a favorite pastime of mine, and I'd long ago abandoned the need for the saddle.

We turned circles around the pups and let them sprint hard and then fall back in laughing tumbles. They teased us with bad ambushes and were ambushed in return. We guided them to the stone at the western bend where the ward's line shone for those who could feel it, and they pressed their paws there as if greeting an old friend.

Finally, we paused at the ridge to watch the sun set beneath the mountains. Luna and Damon sat with their flanks pressed to my sides, warm and breathing fast, their ears twitching as the night rose. I put my nose into their fur, breathed them in, and felt something inside me that had clenched for years finally settle once and for all.

We ran back as the first star showed. The gate watch waved us through without ceremony or worry. Inside, music made from three instruments and ten hands braided the square into something soft. The Romari had hung glass lanterns under the gallery, and the light swung in a slow arc that felt like a promise kept. Twila demonstrated a complicated game that involved jumping in time over chalk lines. She lost, cackled, and declared the rules had changed.

Jax bumped my shoulder with his, wordless and sure. Tannin set a piece of bread in my hand, and kissed Luna's nose when she tried to steal it.

The twins shifted back and forth between skin and fur, too excited to choose. Damon blinked solemnly at the music, then laughed at something no one else could hear. Luna summoned a tiny ribbon of light and sent it drifting toward the fountain. I caught it in my palm and let it go.

"Are you happy, my love?" Jax asked as he came up behind me and wrapped his arms around my waist.

"Yes," I said. "Completely."

It wasn't that everything was perfect. Roofs still leaked. Knees still ached. Children still disobeyed. We still argued about where to put the next watch post and how to price winter apples when the crop came in lean.

But when I lay my hand on the lintel each night, the ward answered with a calm that felt like a heart at rest. When I woke, the air held the good kind of noise—pans and voices and small howls accompanied by laughter. People came through the gate because they heard a rumor that we would make room and keep promises.

The twins fell asleep in a tangle at our feet, half wolf, half child, fully ours.

Happily ever after wasn't a spell. It was a collection of small choices made every day and a stubborn refusal to stop making them. We made ours, and Fate answered. And when the lanterns finally guttered and we climbed the stairs to bed, I knew the shape of tomorrow and was glad for it.

THE END